# Gwendolyn Zepeda

### GRAND CENTRAL
#### PUBLISHING

NEW YORK    BOSTON

Copyright © 2009 by Gwendolyn Zepeda

All rights reserved. Except as permitted under the U.S. Copyright Act of 1976, no part of this publication may be reproduced, distributed, or transmitted in any form or by any means, or stored in a database or retrieval system, without the prior written permission of the publisher.

Grand Central Publishing
Hachette Book Group
237 Park Avenue
New York, NY 10017

Visit our Web site at www.HachetteBookGroup.com.

First Edition: January 2009
10   9   8   7   6   5   4   3   2   1

Grand Central Publishing is a division of Hachette Book Group, Inc. The Grand Central Publishing name and logo is a trademark of Hachette Book Group, Inc.

Library of Congress Cataloging-in-Publication Data

Zepeda, Gwendolyn.
    Houston, we have a problema / Gwendolyn Zepeda. — 1st ed.
        p. cm.
    Summary: "A plastic Virgin Mary and a fortune teller are a girl's best friends in this laugh-out-loud novel about a superstitious young woman who doubts herself when it comes to finding love and living her life" — Provided by publisher
    ISBN-13: 978-0-446-69852-8

    1. Single women — Conduct of life — Fiction.   2. Man-woman relationships — Fiction.   I. Title.
    PS3626.E46H68 2008
    813'.6—dc22

                                                                    2008007889

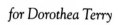

*for Dorothea Terry*

*Houston, we have a problema*

1

Dreaming of snakes means someone will die.

Dreaming of death means someone will get married.

Jessica Luna was dreaming of a wedding when the ringing phone woke her up.

"Hello?"

"Hey, chiquitita."

She had snatched her cell from the nightstand automatically. Now she rolled and squinted at her glowing alarm clock: 1:17 a.m.

"Guillermo? What happened?" she whispered.

"Nothing, chiquitita."

Was it still Wednesday? Jessica rolled onto her pillow. Through the window, between the gauzy lavender curtains that looked gray in the dark, the full moon peeked down at her. Her eyes adjusted to the moonlight and ran over the familiar objects in her bedroom—her tall white dresser; the ironing board stacked with clean laundry; the pictures on the wall; her walnut vanity covered with bottles and boxes and lucky cat figurines. She sighed.

She hated when Guillermo called in the middle of a weeknight. She should hang up on him. She *would* hang up. "Why are you calling so late?" she said instead.

"I wanted to hear your voice, corazón."

"Okay, well, you're hearing it. What do you want?" He had never called her *corazón* before.

"Are you mad at me, chiquitita? Don't be. I can't help the crazy things I do. I'm just a crazy mojado, right? Is that what you think of me?" As always, he sounded completely unhurried. And his accent—that slow, relaxed drawl—wasn't the nasal singsong of the construction workers that yelled silly things at her on downtown streets. No, Guillermo's voice came from someplace deeper, down around the mountains and plains west of Monterrey, where he'd been born. He sounded like a stream over smooth rocks. Like syrup on hot pancakes. Like warm fingers down her back.

"No, I don't think you're a crazy mojado." She laid her head back on the pillow, untangling the phone from her hair and cradling it to her ear. Through the open bedroom door, she heard the refrigerator compressor start its soothing murmur. She felt her heart ease from middle-of-the-night panic down to listening-to-Guillermo calm.

"Soy loco, chiquitita. Loco para ti. Listen. I've been thinking. You and me, chiquitita . . . we should run away to Washington."

"To Washington?" she said, like a kindergartner repeating after her teacher.

"Yes. Have you ever seen Washington in the summer, corazón? It's beautiful. We should go there to pick cherries. You and me. Leave all those men who are too stupid to appreciate you and go away with me."

"Mm . . . I don't—"

"We'll live in a cabin and have all the cherries we can eat. I'll paint the cherry trees. You can bake a hundred pies. We'll make love."

She let herself imagine it for a moment.

"We'll make love and you'll have my babies. Strong sons to help with the work. Beautiful daughters to help cook the food. They'll be strong, like you, with big feet."

"Hey—"

"Big, beautiful feet. We'll name them Jennifer, Heather, Amber, Taylor...Madison, Dylan, South Dakota..."

She knew he was just being silly. But it was a nice kind of silly, coming from him. "Have you painted a portrait of me yet?" she asked suddenly, remembering the last conversation they'd had the week before.

"Yes," he murmured. "I'm working on it now. It's a painting of a bottle that is shaped just like you are, on the hips."

Before she could protest, he went on. "Something else made me think of you today, chiquitita. A surprise I think you will like. Hunter had kittens."

"What? I thought Hunter was a boy."

"Yes. You and I both thought the same thing. But Hunter had a secret. Era una mujer," he said.

"So are you going to change her name now? To South Dakota, maybe?" she murmured drowsily.

"No, chiquitita. I could change her name, but it wouldn't matter. She's still a Hunter, and she probably has a secret name that we'll never know."

No matter how outrageous his words were, his voice always made her feel the same. She could probably keep warm on the cherry farm with his voice alone. "How many kittens did she have?"

"Just enough, chiquitita, to eat me out of my house and my home. Come to see them."

Sometimes she suspected Guillermo was just pretending that he couldn't speak or understand English so well. She couldn't help but think that this was a little game he played so that he'd have one more excuse for not doing what she expected him to do. For instance, he could pretend not to understand when she said, "Call me tomorrow," or hinted that she would love to go out to a new restaurant for dinner instead of eating tacos at his place, as good as his tacos were. And she was convinced that he didn't call regularly because he wasn't ever clear on if and when he should. He simply said, "We'll talk soon, chiquitita." She could have made a list of things he said or didn't say, and what he had "misunderstood," but then she'd be denying that his accent turned her on.

She sighed. "Okay. I'll visit you and the kittens. When?"

"Right now," he said.

"Guillermo, you know I can't come right now. I have to work tomorrow."

"Come tomorrow, then."

Jessica concentrated. The next day was Friday, she figured out.

The thing was, Guillermo lived out in the boondocks, and there was no such thing as just dropping by for a visit. Once she was there, the minutes would time-warp into hours, and the next thing she knew, she'd be forced to spend the night. Plus, the weekend before, she'd *wanted* to come over, but he'd been unavailable. His phone had been turned off—whether because he was ignoring her or because he'd forgotten to pay the bill again, she'd never found out. "I don't know, Guillermo. I'm really busy." If he really wanted her to come over, she decided, he'd have to try harder.

"Please, chiquitita. I miss seeing your beautiful face. I'll cook for you. Stop being mad at me and come over. I promise to make you happy again."

Jessica sighed. It was frustrating, the way he expected her to just forgive and forget, over and over again. This time she was mad at him because two weeks before, she'd invited him to accompany her to her friend Marisol's birthday party. He'd promised to meet her there. Then, as so often happened, he'd failed to show up. A week after that, he'd left her an airy voice-mail apology, with some lame excuse about his truck breaking down. It wasn't the first time he'd done this sort of thing, either. It was just the last in a long series that she'd put up with it.

She knew what he had in mind as far as making her happy, if she were to go over to his place. And it wasn't cherries or kittens.

"Okay...," she told him, feeling equal parts resignation, shame, and wicked excitement. "Maybe."

**2**

"Hello, Jessica? Are you awake, girl?"

"What? I'm sorry, Rochelle. What did you say?" Jessica dropped the pencil she'd been idly twisting through the ends of her hair. It fell onto a pile of papers and big blue files on her desk. She'd spaced out and wasn't sure if it was a result of a restless night after Guillermo's call or because her insurance job was far from stimulating. She turned in her rickety orange tweed office chair to give her co-worker full attention.

"I said it's almost lunchtime. Are you going out or staying in?" At a faux wood desk exactly matching Jessica's, Rochelle stretched her purple-polyester-clad legs and idly looked over the instant soup packets in her desk drawer.

Jessica glanced to the corner of their little room, at Mr. Cochran's dusty grandfather clock. It had finally hobbled around to noon. "I'm going out. Will y'all be okay without me?"

"Sure we will, honey."

Jessica balanced the last file of the morning on her out-box, then picked up her ancient, blocky phone and dialed the company's most popular three-digit extension.

"Tech Support," said the man at the other end.

"Hey, sexy," she whispered. "We still on for lunch?"

"Of course."

"Meet me at the elevator in two minutes."

She hung up and reshouldered her bag and violet mock-croc laptop case, leaving her monitor to lapse into its Hello Kitty screen saver. "I'm going to lunch, you guys. See you in an hour."

Across the room, Olga looked up from her game of online bingo, a half-eaten SpeedSlim bar at her lips. "Already? Gosh. The morning went by so *fast*. Who are you going to lunch with today, Jessica?"

"See y'all! Have fun!" Jessica was out the door.

At the elevators, Xavier Flores stood waiting in his uniform of blue button-down, slightly clashing striped tie, and black Dockers and wearing his unstylish wire-framed glasses. He stood out among the executives littering the hall, given that he was one of the few men at McCormick who didn't have gray hair. He was also among the *very* few people in the company who were under thirty. He would have been really cute if he ever took Jessica's advice on his clothing, which she offered him all the time for the sake of their friendship. But, as he'd explained more than once, his job wasn't worth being fashionable for. So she settled for teasing him instead.

"Nice outfit," she whispered to her friend. "You look like my old chemistry teacher."

"And you," he whispered back, "look like you busted out of Catholic school."

She looked down at her sedate skirt and pastel twin set and laughed. He was wrong, of course. Catholic school students didn't wear awesome ankle-strap heels like hers.

The elevator bell rang and they stepped into the tiny mirrored chamber, where one of the younger partner-wannabes was already waiting.

"Hey, X-Man," he said. Xavier nodded in return. Jessica saw the freckle-faced broker's reflection as he looked her up and down from behind and then gave Xavier a sly thumbs-up. Xavier ignored him.

"We can't take too long this time," he told Jessica quietly. "I told Dunson I'd have the new network up and running today."

"Don't worry. We'll eat fast."

Once they were safe in Xavier's Subaru, Jessica brought up the subject that had been on her mind for two days. "Guess who wants to see me tonight."

"The salesmen at Macy's?" he guessed, eyes on the road.

"No. Well, yeah, probably, but guess who else."

"Hopefully not What's-his-name. The guy you're supposed to be finished with. What'd he do, show up with a dozen roses?"

"Well...," Jessica said. "Not *exactly*." Not unless you could count the handful of wildflowers he'd left at her apartment door the week before, while she'd been at work. Sometimes she regretted ever having told Xavier about Guillermo. It was hard to explain her attraction to Guillermo without going into cheesy — or X-rated — details.

Xavier made a gesture that invited her to come out with the rest of the story.

"Look, it doesn't matter *how* it happened. The point is, he called to ask me out, and I can tell that he's learned his lesson."

"Oh yeah? What lesson is that?" His expression was teasingly skeptical.

"That I'm the most awesome woman he's ever met, and that he'd be stupid to let me go."

Xavier shrugged. "Oh, okay. Well, there you go, then."

Jessica had expected a little more resistance. She'd already had her argument prepared, in fact. No use wasting it.

"Like you can talk, Xavier. You've been trying to get back with Cynthia this whole time."

"What are you talking about?"

"Don't even. I saw you at her desk last week."

Cynthia was Xavier's ex-girlfriend, who worked on the forty-fourth floor, where they kept the prettiest, most useless assistants for the biggest big shots at McCormick. Jessica had gone upstairs to pick up a file and seen Xavier hovering over her desk like a fly. Although he'd dated her for only two months and had been broken up with her for three, Jessica could tell by Xavier's perplexed face right now that her suspicions were correct. He wasn't over Cynthia yet.

Instead of replying, he got out of his car and walked around to her side to open her door. They were at Taqueria Aztlán, a hole-in-the-wall where they could talk as loud as they wanted about their corporate colleagues and everything else.

They sat at their usual table and ordered their usual chicken quesadillas. A handful of chips with salsa later, Jessica was ready to pick up where they'd left off. "So tell me. Did you beg Cynthia to take you back?"

Xavier sighed, but patiently. "Jess, I was at her desk giving her *tech support*. You know—that thing they pay me to do here?"

"Is that what the kids are calling it these days? Did you install some *hard*ware?"

"No. I was checking her system for a virus."

"Can't you do that from downstairs?" Jessica asked, breaking a chip neatly in two.

"Normally, yes. But she said she had a problem that I had to come see."

"I bet she did. And did you see it?"

"It was nothing. She'd unplugged her monitor by accident."

Jessica raised her eyebrow. "Xavier, nobody unplugs their monitor by *accident*. She just wanted you to go up there. What did she say? Do you think *she's* trying to get *you* back?"

He shook his head as he finished off the last of the red salsa. "Seriously? I think she really is that technologically challenged."

Like a genie, the waitress showed up with their chicken quesadillas. Like a devil, Jessica found herself wanting to press further into Xavier's personal business. She peered at his face over her iced-tea glass. "If Cynthia *did* want to get back together, would you?"

"No. I've learned my lesson. No more pathetic office romance for me."

Jessica remembered when he'd first broken up with Cynthia and spent weeks avoiding her floor altogether. That was when he and Jessica had first started going to lunch on a regular basis, instead of just striking up conversations about coding whenever they met in the break room.

Jessica knew better than anybody how reluctant Xavier would be to hook up with Cynthia again, or with anyone else at McCormick. However, Cynthia was one of those evil little doll women, with long, long hair and flowery size four dresses. The kind who *seemed* stupid but were extremely clever when it came to wrapping men around their petite little fingers. Jessica worried about Xavier, because even though he was smart, he was also too nice for his own good. He was always opening doors for women, even if they didn't appreciate it. He was always incredibly polite and charming with all the secretaries at McCormick, even when they drove him crazy with their ridiculous tech support demands. He was the kind of guy who obviously loved his mother, and therefore he always treated women like gold—even when they didn't necessarily deserve it. Jessica had the feeling that if Cynthia wanted him back, Xavier might have a hard time saying no.

Not like she could call his kettle black, though. Not with everything she'd been putting up with from Guillermo. All the times he'd completely flaked on their dates… All the times he'd promised to take her somewhere exciting but then failed to follow through.

Suddenly, as she sat there looking at her sad friend Xavier, the sun streamed through the window and hit her in the head, making her think clearly.

She wasn't going to see Guillermo tonight. Deep in her heart, she knew it'd just be more of the same. He'd act as though he cared about her. They'd have sex. She'd go home and he wouldn't call. Or he'd flake on their next date and give her some lame excuse. It was time to move on. It was time to change the subject, too, Jessica decided.

"So, what's been going on with you outside McCormick and Cynthia?" she asked.

"Same old nothing. I got a new contract, setting up a system for a drywall company. I'll probably do the whole thing over the weekend."

Being burned by workplace love wasn't the only thing Jessica and Xavier had in common, it turned out. They both did freelance computer work on the side, too.

"Oh, well, that's good. Finish it early so you can party with the hotties, right?"

He ignored her obvious baiting. "Yeah, right. More like go to my parents' and help my dad clean his gutters."

Jessica loved to tease Xavier about the fact that he almost never went out. Secretly, she admired the way that he *wasn't* interested in the bar and meat market scenes. Although her clubbing definitely made for some fun and wild moments, Jessica had to admit that it got old after a while. Clearly, Xavier was secure enough to do his own thing. She wished she could be more like him sometimes and be happy with quiet weekends.

When they'd finished eating, Jessica cleared a space near the quesadillas. "Here. Let me show you what I've been working on." As she pushed her own plate over, a hidden jalapeño fell off of it. "Oh, there was one more. Did you want it?"

"Now that it fell on the table? No thanks," he said, polite as ever.

Jessica picked up the pepper before any germs could stick and handed it across the table to him. "No, it's still good. Here. Eat it."

"Jess, I don't want it."

"You must have, or it wouldn't have fallen off the plate. C'mon. You have to eat it now, or you'll get a fever blister."

Xavier laughed as he took the jalapeño from her hand and dropped it onto his napkin. "Where do you come up with these crazy superstitions?"

"What? Didn't your mom ever tell you that? About the food cravings and the fever blisters?"

"No. She was more into spilled salt and holy water. Come on. Show me what you wanted to show me."

"All right. Here it is."

Jessica reached under the table and unzipped her laptop case to show him her latest web site.

Later that afternoon, back down the beige halls at her beige desk, Jessica meditated on her theory that four to five p.m. was the longest hour of the day. Especially on a Friday. The longest of her life, it felt like, today. She'd done all the work she could stand and was now checking the clock every five minutes.

Although it wasn't as though she had a reason to be in a hurry. She wasn't going anywhere. Was she?

If she saw Guillermo again, it was true that they'd repeat their same old pattern. But now she had to wonder, what was so bad about that? Whether he called her afterward or not, she'd still be doing the same things in the meantime: Working. Shopping. Going out dancing with Toby. Working some more. Why not switch things up a bit and have a little fun, even if the price was a little drama?

Her body sank lower in the antique office chair, trying to find some comfort. Her head, however, floated thirty miles away. Far, far away from McCormick, to a little house in a field on the edge of town where everything still grew wild. And to the person who lived in that house, waiting in its bedroom, lying across the bed.

Naked.

She shook her head and forced herself to focus on the wind damage spreadsheet on her desk. She *had* to stop thinking about Guillermo. She had already decided, once and for all, that she wasn't going to see him again.

Hadn't she?

Toni Braxton sang mournfully from Rochelle's radio, as if in empathy.

Why had Guillermo called? Why did he always have to call just when she was almost totally ready to give him up?

Unfortunately, Madame Hortensia hadn't been there during his phone call to help her decide what to do. Jessica always sought her advice because Madame Hortensia took the ways of the universe into consideration and made Jessica aware of signs she was sure she'd miss otherwise. But now Jessica had to decide on her own.

She sighed and stared at the Hello Kitty on her screen saver.

*Give me a sign. Should I go to Guillermo's tonight, or should I forget about him and move on?*

Hello Kitty's cherry print outfit morphed into Gothic black as Jessica waited, eyes closed. Behind her, the radio spat out a burst of static.

"Jessica," called Fred from his office, "if a gentleman calls, tell him you won't be going ... that is, tell him that *I* won't be going to the GlobeCo happy hour this evening, would you, please?"

Jessica closed her eyes and concentrated. *Give me a sign. Should I go to Guillermo's or stay home and work?*

"Did you ladies read the news?" Rochelle said. "Another girl turned up missing the other night. Police said she was on the way to see her boyfriend. She should have been going to church instead."

*Just one sign!* thought Jessica as loudly as she could. *Please!*

"Yes!" squealed Olga.

Jessica opened her eyes. "What happened?"

"Oh, nothing. I just won this solitaire game, finally. It took me forever to figure it out."

Jessica exhaled the breath she'd been holding into the last sigh of the day. She couldn't deny it, could she? The answer was clear.

**3**

She hadn't always been so superstitious. No, back when she was young, Jessica had no use for the superstitions people would share with her. When her mother had offered to light candles for her college finals, Jessica had waved her away. When her friend Toby's mother had warned her against wearing so much unlucky black, Jessica had scoffed. When her friend Marisol's parents told her about the chupacabra footprints they found at their ranch back in Durango, Jessica had laughed.

Not anymore. Now she knew better. There were things in this world that went unseen. Things that couldn't be explained. She knew now that it was safest to protect herself, with traditional knowledge and sometimes a little salt over the shoulder. And a Virgin Mary overlooking it all.

Three years ago, Jessica had learned this the hard way.

It was about a year after she'd graduated from the University of Houston with her BA in art history. She'd gotten a job in a run-down neighborhood just east of downtown, at the Centro de Artes Culturales (formerly the Centro de Arte Cultural de Aztlán, until Jessica had pointed out that the acronym, CACA, didn't spell what they wanted to represent). As curator for the Centro's new gallery, it was her job to discover and coordinate exhibitions for local Latino artists. The pay wasn't much—barely more than minimum wage, actually—but Jessica had felt incredibly lucky to land such an opportunity at her age.

As it turned out, her job description had included a little more than enjoying art. She was also expected to serve as accountant, receptionist, and personal chauffeur to artists-in-residence while she planned, organized, publicized, and cleaned up after all the exhibits, all on her own. The hours were insane, and on top of it all, no one gave her credit for the work she did.

At first, she didn't mind. She was servicing her community, wasn't she? Also, she was dating Robert Fernandez, one of the Centro's most successful artists. No matter how much work they gave her, she always managed to find time to steal away with him in one of the supply closets or under the fire escape stairs. She knew it was wrong, but she couldn't help herself. There was something about Robert that made her want to throw caution to the wind. He'd been her first. In retrospect, she now realized that he hadn't been all that. He hadn't even been a very good artist. But still... To this day, the smell of turpentine turned her on.

One morning, after she'd been at the Centro for a year and sleeping with Robert for about six months, Jessica had gotten annoyed with the little plastic Virgin Mary hanging from her rearview mirror. It had been a gift from one of her aunts, and it kept swinging back and forth, hitting her windshield as she drove over potholes on the way to work. Fed up, she pulled over and took it down, feeling a little guilty but putting it away in the glove compartment all the same.

That turned out to be the mistake that led to the worst day

of her life. With one careless action, she ended up bringing bad luck into every aspect of her life. First, at work, Jessica's boss dropped a bomb on her.

"Jessica, I can't afford to keep you here anymore. Not unless you can work on these grant numbers and make a way for us to get more money." She was shocked. The timing of his news couldn't have been worse.

Jessica was preparing for the unveiling of Robert's newest mural that evening. On top of getting everything organized for the big night, she now had to think of ways to raise extra money, not just for her own salary, but for her community. For Latino art.

But all these concerns were shoved to the back burner when Robert's *other* girlfriend—the one carrying his baby—showed up at the unveiling that night. Jessica was floored. She had never seen any hints of him leading a second life. Suddenly, she was one of those women on daytime TV that she criticized for being so oblivious. But there hadn't been any clues, ever. She wanted to figure out how she could have been so blind and what the hell he'd been thinking. But she didn't even get to hear his excuse, because his babymomma dragged him away by the hair before he could explain.

"Is this the skank you've been two-timing me with?" she'd screamed. "Oh, *hell*, no!"

As Jessica had stood there with tears oozing down her face, her boss had walked up and ordered her to clean up the vomit of a drunken gallery patron. When it rains, it pours. And Jessica was stuck without an umbrella. And soon to be without a job. She'd decided to take matters into her own hands.

She'd quit her job on the spot, then gone out with her friend Toby and gotten drunk.

"What in the world am I going to do?" she'd asked him and the club. "My life is ruined. I can't believe I was so stupid about Robert. I've been humiliated in front of the art community, and now I don't have a job. What am I supposed to do now?"

"I have an idea," Toby had said, "but you have to promise not to laugh."

"Do I look like I feel like laughing? Tell me."

"You need to visit Madame Hortensia."

Before that night, Jessica had believed that fortune-tellers were just con women who told sad housewives what they wanted to hear. After an hour with Madame Hortensia, though, Jessica had become a believer.

"Hello, m'ija," she remembered the old woman saying the first time they'd met. "You look sad."

Madame Hortensia had known things about Jessica that a stranger had no logical way of knowing: that she was tired of living with her parents; that she used to be Catholic but had stopped going to church soon after her quinceañera; that she had been unlucky with her career and in love.

That night, Madame Hortensia had made three eerily correct predictions.

One: "A life-changing opportunity will come to you from an unexpected source."

Two: "Someone important to you will help you get over a bad relationship."

Three: "Another tall, dark artist or musician will have an impact on your future."

The first thing Jessica did after leaving Madame Hortensia's was to dig the Virgin Mary out of her glove compartment and hang it back on the mirror, where it belonged.

Within a week, her sister, Sabrina, had nagged Jessica into temping for a friend on maternity leave at McCormick. Even though Jessica knew nothing about insurance and hated to be bossed around by her sister, she took the job so she could get away from the Centro. When Sabrina's friend gave birth, Jessica still hadn't found any jobs related to art history. But then Sabrina's friend had decided not to come back to work, and McCormick offered Jessica the job permanently. It paid fifteen thousand a year more than her curator job had, so Jessica couldn't refuse. And so, without meaning to, her sister gave her the means to finally move out of their parents' house — a life-changing opportunity if there ever was one. So that was Madame Hortensia's first prophecy fulfilled.

While all that was going on, Jessica's idol, Amber Chavez, was going through a very similar situation to Jessica's romance-wise. Amber Chavez, the dancer who'd started out singing cumbias in Mexico and gone on to become a hip-hop sensation in the United States. Amber Chavez, the beautiful sex symbol who'd made big butts like Jessica's trendy. Amber Chavez was the woman who had everything, and she'd gotten her heart broken by DJ Beat-a-Lot, the producer of her smash hit CD.

Jessica followed the story in every tabloid, admiring Amber's grace under pressure. Throughout every trial and tribulation, Amber remained classy and well dressed. Instead of throwing Beat-a-Lot's engagement ring back in his face, Amber sold it on eBay and converted the proceeds to scholarships for poor Latinos.

It couldn't have been a coincidence that on the day Jessica got her first big paycheck from McCormick, Amber Chavez appeared on the cover of *People*, completely transformed. She'd gone from a sultry, raven-haired pop star to an angelic, blond-streaked starlet announcing her first movie role. As soon as Jessica saw that, she understood exactly what Madame Hortensia had foreseen. Jessica carried the magazine to her stylist and said, "Make me look like this." One hour and ninety-five dollars later, she strutted out of the salon with a new lease on life and Robert totally forgotten.

And now, three years later, here she was, just as Madame Hortensia had predicted. Hair still awesome, wearing nice shoes, carrying a new purse every week. Checking her e-mail in an office on the fortieth floor, under a framed poster of the word SUCCESS. Jessica realized that luck had finally found her, and she didn't intend to mess things up again. From now on, she was keeping an eye out for signs from above.

And all those signs were pointing at Guillermo.

It had been almost six months since she'd met him. Obviously, he was the other tall, dark artist mentioned in Madame Hortensia's third prediction.

As Jessica sped down the highway, through the fields and pine trees that led to his house, she pondered the mystery that was Guillermo.

For some reason, no matter how many times she promised herself otherwise, she hadn't been able to get over her fascination with him. He was an artist—a painter—which of course made him a little flaky to begin with. Jessica knew from experience how forgetful and unrealistic painters could be when they got involved with their work.

But she'd expected more from Guillermo. They'd been seeing each other for five months now, and with anyone else, she would have demanded some kind of commitment by that point. Not that Guillermo was seeing other people—not that she knew of—but he hadn't given her anything so far. No promises, no settled dating routine... He didn't even tell her that he loved her. Not in so many words, at least. He was like a stray cat who kept coming back for more food and petting but never wanted to live inside her house. He was basically nothing more than a long, long fling.

Yet every time she felt she'd had enough and was about to give him up for good, he would do something maddeningly lovable and rope her back in. He had a way, through his calm voice and demeanor, of making her feel that she'd been angry over nothing. Making her feel she was just being silly for not enjoying what they already had, indefinitely, forever.

Here she was now, for example, driving to his house to see kittens. She should be using this time in her car, she knew, to plan out the lecture she'd give him over not returning her last few calls. But she also knew, already, that that lecture would never be delivered. He'd charm her out of it, the way he always did.

Sometimes she suspected that she kept hanging on to Guillermo for just that reason. He was so outside normal conventions and concerns, he made her forget everything that was boring and stressful in her life. For an hour or two, at least.

She drove through his gate slowly, trying to protect her Accord's paint job from his overgrown trees and shrubs. They seemed to have doubled in size since the last time she'd been here, out in this heated sundown. Two strange pit bulls rushed out to meet her car and scare her to death. Their barking drowned out the music from her CD player, and saliva dripped from their jagged teeth. They were like hounds of hell.

It must have been an omen. I knew I shouldn't have come, she thought.

All the windows in Guillermo's little pink house were dark, so she stayed in her car with the engine running. His truck wasn't there, unless it was parked in the scraggly grass behind the garage or hidden behind the overgrown garden. She dug through her white patent-leather purse for her phone.

Just as she found it, the glass-paned door opened and Guillermo appeared in the doorway, wearing bleach-spotted jeans and nothing else. He stretched his arms above his head, then strode over to her car. The dogs turned and gave him all their attention.

Jessica turned off her engine and cautiously opened the door.

"They're beautiful, aren't they?" he said.

"Who?" She looked around for something beautiful on the premises.

"My new perritos. Napo and Josefina."

"Sure. Just gorgeous." Jessica was out of her car now, but carefully keeping Guillermo between her and the pit bulls.

"You look beautiful, too." He leaned down and cupped her chin with his hand. Somehow, his hand against her skin felt rough and soft at the same time. Like always. He turned back to the dogs and spoke to them at some length in Spanish, gesturing at Jessica while he did so. They stood silently, panting and smiling, as if they could understand him. Then, one by one, they slunk up to her and licked her hands. All traces of the savage animals she'd first seen were gone now. Guillermo waved them away and they scampered off, mild as sheep.

"There. Did you miss me?" he murmured before kissing her lips. Then he took her hand and led her across the gravel drive to the garage.

Jessica heard the pitiful mewing before she saw what was making it, and immediately forgot all about the dogs. She stepped over boxes and paint cans to get to the far corner of the garage. In a nest of faded towels, four kittens tumbled over one another and into their mother, who lay there looking tired and proud.

"Aw!" Jessica's heart completely melted. Guillermo smiled at her as if he'd made the kittens himself, for her.

"Let me go get her more food," he said.

Jessica noticed empty sardine and tuna cans all over the floor. That was so like Guillermo, to feed them better than he fed himself. He came back with another sardine tin and knelt beside the cats. They played with the kittens while their mother ate. Jessica fell in love with them all, but the black one was already her favorite, because of the brave way he looked up into her eyes.

"I knew you would like them," Guillermo said. "Now, every time you visit, they will know you. When you're not here, they will cry in my window and ask me why."

Jessica had to smile at his assumption that she'd continue to visit regularly.

When Hunter was ready to nurse her babies again, Guillermo led Jessica inside.

In the living room, she saw that he'd pushed the gold cam-elback sofa and matching Queen Anne chair to the wall. The rest of the room was filled with easels and canvasses in all stages of completion.

Jessica knew the house belonged to his grandmother. The year before, she'd become ill and had moved into Guiller-mo's parents' house in Monterrey. It had been decided that Guillermo would move out of his efficiency apartment in the Houston area and into the house, to take care of it until she returned — if she returned.

"Are you getting ready for a show?" she asked.

"Maybe. If the people call me again, now that my phone is fixed."

She assumed he meant the Houston Council on Latino Arts, whose number she'd given him weeks before. But she knew better than to push for details. Like her, he was super-stitious and hated to jinx opportunities by talking about them before they panned out.

On the nearest canvas, he'd penciled a light sketch. It looked as if it were going to be a person reclining, but she couldn't tell any more than that. Next to that was an easel covered with cloth. Jessica reached to uncover it, but Guillermo shook his head. "Don't look at that one. It's not ready yet. Here, look at this. I've been wanting your opinion of this one."

He led her across the room to yet another easel. This one held a still life she hadn't seen before. He'd painted a bottle, a mango, half a lime, and a bulb of garlic.

"What do you think?" he said.

Jessica studied it carefully. "Are you done with it yet?"

"I don't know," he said, staring at the painting critically

himself. "I thought I was, but now I think maybe it needs something else."

Jessica looked again. "Maybe . . . maybe another lime, right here." She pointed to a blank spot on the painting. "A quarter lime, facing this way."

Guillermo looked as if he could imagine exactly what she did. "That's a perfect idea. You're good," he said. "You have good eyes. You should be painting here with me instead of typing papers for old men all the time."

Jessica smiled. It was nice to be appreciated, she thought, for something she was really good at. Especially by an artist as talented as Guillermo.

"Come on," he said. "Later you can tell me what you think about all the other ones. But right now let's relax."

He led her into the kitchen, saying, "Please don't notice this mess," waving his hand around to encompass everything.

His kitchen, as usual, was a disaster area. The knotty pine cabinets were all ajar, and the counter was covered with paintbrushes, discarded palettes, jars of colored water, and lime wedges. However, he'd obviously cleared enough space to cook. And he'd cleaned the tiny table in the corner and set two places.

"Here. Sit down," he said, leading her to one of the folding chairs in his makeshift dining nook. "Let me bring you a plate. No, wait. I have a present for you." He disappeared into another part of the house. Jessica could hardly contain her curiosity.

He came back carrying a small wooden box and put it into her hands. On closer inspection, she saw that the lid was intricately carved with flowers and tiny birds. "Guillermo, this is beautiful. Where did you get it?"

"I made it." At Jessica's look of surprise, he explained, "I had the box already, but I cut the flowers and finished painting it yesterday."

Jessica ran her fingers over the carvings, which he'd obviously sanded smooth.

"I put the flowers you like — the ones that were in my garden in spring — and I painted it your favorite colors."

They were her favorites — all of them. "But I never told you my favorite colors," she said.

"You always wear them," he explained. "I know which ones you like best because you smile more when you wear them."

Jessica couldn't help but smile now.

He went back to the stove to make her plate. Jessica sat back and watched him wait on her. She knew he was doing it only to get her in a good mood and to avoid the lecture he knew she would give him sooner or later. Still, it was nice to relax and watch him worry about her for a change. She wished he could be like this all the time, but without her having to get mad first. And without his shirt, the way he was right now. His lean muscles flexed and unflexed as he worked and definitely put her in a good mood.

She watched him pile their two plates with rice and something that looked like thick, dark gravy. It was mole, she realized, smelling the slightly spicy, slightly peanut-y aroma. With turkey. She hadn't had mole since she was a child.

Guillermo brought the plates to the table, then went to the refrigerator for drinks. "There's beer," he said, "and tequila."

Jessica raised her eyebrow. "Didn't I leave some diet soda last time I was here?"

"I poured it in the sink. I keep telling you, chiquitita, you shouldn't put unnatural things in your body. I'll make you some tea, with hierba buena."

"No, that's okay. I'll take a beer," she said. Suddenly, she couldn't wait to taste the food. She didn't want to wait for him to make tea.

Finally, with two bottles of Negra Modelo in tow, he sat down. Even though she was eager to taste his creation, Jessica had to take a moment to look at his face first.

She could look at that face all night. The high cheekbones, the perfect nose, the delicate but still masculine chin. That mouth... He looked like an Aztec warrior. Or a brilliant art student, plus a few extra years. Actually, he looked a lot like Leo Fiorenzo from *Young Lives to Live*. But unlike the actor, Guillermo had proven that he was definitely straight. He was the hottest guy she'd ever dated. Not that the others had been dogs... and not that she was bad-looking, herself... But she'd never imagined she would score a man as good-looking as Guillermo, especially as hot as he looked right now.

He was waiting. Jessica took the first bite. Guillermo watched and waited for her response.

"Mm," she said, looking for a napkin and immediately wishing she hadn't put so much into her mouth.

He looked around for a napkin as well, then handed her a paint rag from the counter. "What's wrong? Not spicy enough?"

"No, it's spicy enough," she said. It reminded her of the curry at her favorite Thai restaurant—except hotter. She'd already swallowed the mouthful and now fanned at her lips. "How much chile did you use?"

He held her beer bottle to her lips with one hand, then reached over to the counter with the other, this time for a lime.

"Here. I'm sorry, chiquitita." He spilled a little beer out of the bottle so that it ran down the side of her mouth. He put down the beer and quickly wiped her face with his fingers, then licked them. Although her lips were burning, she had to laugh. He smiled sheepishly and handed her the lime. "I tried to make everything romantic for you, and now I'm messing it up."

She laughed again. She couldn't help it. He looked so silly and helpless, trying to be macho and sweet at the same time, hands full, with no shirt on. He even had a little patch of blue paint glistening in his black hair, she noticed now. "Stop," she said, taking his hands before he could dab at her face with the rag, which smelled a little like turpentine. "Stop, Guillermo. I don't need you to make everything romantic."

"Okay," he said. He seemed relieved. He sat back down, visibly relaxed, leaning into his chair and taking a swig of his own beer. "I'm glad you came over. It feels like I haven't seen you in weeks."

"You haven't," she said. She wanted it to come out bitterly, but it was a little too late for that.

"I'm sorry," he said. "I've been working so much. I forget the time. And you're always so patient with me. I don't deserve a woman like you." He reached around the table and stroked her hand.

"No, you don't," she said—again, not as harshly as she could have. "Guillermo, if you miss me so much all the time, why don't you call me more often?"

Very briefly, she saw a look cross his face. Not of annoyance, exactly, but more like the look of a hunted animal. Of a man who didn't want to be tied down. But maybe she imagined it, Jessica thought, because just as quickly, he smiled and looked penitent instead.

"Didn't I tell you, chiquitita? My phone was broken because I forgot to pay the bill. But I did call you, when I could, last night."

Jessica sighed. She *could* have argued with him. But suddenly she wasn't in the mood. Like he said, he had called her when he could. And here she was now, in his house. What was the use of lecturing him now? She might as well just relax and enjoy herself. Guillermo may not have been very reliable, but he was at least good at getting her to relax.

He stood and picked up both their drinks with his left hand. Then, with his right, he helped her up and pulled her toward the bedroom. She went along without protest.

His bedroom was the one part of his home that was neat. He always said it was because he liked having a peaceful place to rest. The house's single air-conditioning unit hummed softly in the window near the headboard of the full-size bed, which was covered with the soft, worn quilt his mother had made.

On the tall pine dresser, against silver-framed photographs of his family, he'd propped up snapshots he'd taken in the countryside outside Monterrey—his pets, a waterfall, the mountains under which he'd grown up. Jessica's only experience of Mexico was a few trips over the border to party with Toby and one visit to Marisol's parents' ranch a long time ago. But ever since meeting Guillermo here in Houston, she'd wanted him to take her back with him to Mexico. He made it sound beautiful—full of peaceful people who did what they wanted to with their lives, instead of skyscrapers and corporations full of unhappy robots. But when she asked him about a trip, he always said it was too depressing and he didn't want her to be sad. She knew that he hadn't been back since he'd traded in his green card for U.S. citizenship several years before.

A faded border of wallpaper roses held up the tiny patch of ceiling above their heads. It was such a charming, homey little room, she almost felt guilty about what they always ended up doing in it.

He set the beers on his nightstand, then lay across the bed, propped up on the headboard, and reached out for her to join him. The light of the lamp played across his chest, and Jessica stopped feeling guilty. She slipped off her sandals, then sat on the edge of the bed and swiveled to face him.

"How was work today?" she asked.

He finished his beer in one long swig and carefully set the empty bottle on the floor. "I didn't go to work."

"What? Why not? I thought you said you were supposed to finish that house by the end of the month."

"I was," he said. "But then the man's wife was talking to me, and now I'm painting her picture instead."

Jessica raised her eyebrow. "Does her husband know that?"

"If she told him, he does. I didn't ask. She's paying me a lot of money. Let's not talk about that anymore. No more worrying, okay?"

Before Jessica could say anything else, he reached over and put his arms around her waist, tugging her down onto the bed. She ended up lying next to him, facing him, with her head on his arm. He traced the line of her jaw with his fingertip.

"So, corazón. When are you going to quit your job so you can stop looking so sad?"

"I don't know. I guess when you get rich and pay my rent." She managed to look at him defiantly, even while his touch was already forcing the tension of the afternoon out of her body.

"I'll pay your rent if you come live here and cook for me."

She knew he was kidding, as usual. He knew she couldn't cook. "How about I order us pizzas, and you paint my picture instead?"

He took his hand from her face and placed it on her hip, where the hem of her skirt was riding up of its own volition. Then he leaned down to kiss her neck.

That familiar feeling started up. A slow, simmering sensation radiating through her body.

"If you want," he murmured against her ear, "I'll paint your picture right now."

She pressed herself against him, then turned her face to his so she could lick his lower lip.

"No, that's okay," she whispered. "Later...."

# 4

Jessica liked that she could walk through Guillermo's house totally naked, with no curtains on his windows, and not worry about being seen. The nearest house was four acres away. It was as if he lived outside the normal rules. Also, she liked that she could walk through his house naked and not worry about being seen by *him*.

Once, at the dentist's, she'd read a magazine article called "Under the Covers and Beyond: How to Hide Your Figure Flaws the Morning After." It had advised her to say, with a sexy shiver, "Ooh, it's getting chilly in here," and then wrap her boyfriend's blanket around her body like a toga while getting out of bed.

With Guillermo, she didn't need to hide anything. Her friend Toby had told her once that her butt was like J. Lo's, but with a Quarter Pounder and fries. Guillermo didn't seem to mind her extra curves, though. He told her that her body was beautiful. And he was an artist, Jessica reasoned, so he should know.

Back in the living room, she examined his latest work again. The still life was done in acrylic. Next to that, there were mountains under a red sun, done in oil. His style called to mind Rivera and Kahlo. Jessica loved that his work reflected Mexican influences but never resorted to the clichéd skeletons and roosters that so many Latino artists—like Robert, her ex-boyfriend—were painting today. Guillermo was really good. She wished she could paint half as well as he could. But she definitely couldn't. She'd found that out a long time ago.

"What happened to the mermaid?" she asked as he emerged from the bedroom to get another beer.

"I sold it."

Despite the fact that he didn't lift a finger to promote himself, Guillermo had a small group of loyal patrons—mostly rich people whose portraits he'd painted after painting their homes. The mermaid had been Jessica's favorite, and she wistfully imagined it in some rich old guy's house. "Who'd you sell it to?"

"Carlos."

"Not Carlos who does the flooring?"

He nodded. "He gave me fifty dollars."

"Fifty dollars?" Jessica was instantly annoyed. This wasn't the first time he'd practically given away one of his paintings. "Guillermo, you could have gotten *five hundred* dollars for that painting. Or even way more than that. Why did you sell it to *him?*"

He shrugged. "He wanted it for his daughter. His wife is making her a room full of the Little Mermaids, he said. He only had fifty, so I took it."

Jessica folded her arms and said nothing.

"And also," he added as if he'd just remembered, "I needed money to pay the electricity bill."

"Guillermo..."

There was no use launching into a lecture about the proper

way for him to manage his artistic career. She'd helped him as much as she could, trying to hook him up with the few art connections she knew from her days at the Centro, but he was too proud to accept more than that. She had offered to make him a web site, to help him set up shows, even to be his manager. He always refused. On the one hand, she had to admire him for wanting to succeed on his own. On the other hand, though, it annoyed her that he was too stubborn to see how much he needed her.

She turned to tell him this in a non-nagging way and then noticed, again, the easel that was covered with cloth. She walked over to it.

"Chiquitita...," said Guillermo. She looked over at him, but he didn't say anything else. The look on his face was hesitant. All of a sudden, Jessica realized what this painting must be. She reached out and, unable to help herself, pulled up the cloth.

It was exactly what she thought: Finally, he had done a portrait of her. Guillermo had painted her nude, leaning back on the camelback sofa, in sunlight. From memory, obviously. She smiled.

She leaned close to get a better look. He hadn't done the face yet. Or the hair. So far, there was only the body, and now that she saw it up close... Jessica took a step back now. It *wasn't* her. She looked harder. It was someone thinner. Someone *else*.

Suddenly, the room was too cool. She took a striped wool blanket from his couch and wrapped herself up in it.

"Who's this?" she asked. "Someone from a magazine?"

His face was cool, nonchalant. "No. She's one of my

patrones... my client. The one I was telling you about, whose husband hired me to paint their house."

Without vain women wanting their portraits done, Guillermo wouldn't have been able to afford art supplies. Jessica knew this. But this was the first time he'd painted another woman in the nude. Since Jessica had been dating him, that was. That she *knew* of, that was.

"Are you sleeping with her?" she heard herself ask. Loudly.

"No. I'm painting her. Because she's paying me a lot of money."

Jessica took a deep breath. Okay. Well, that wasn't such a surprise.

Guillermo went on, clarifying his explanation. "She did *ask* me to sleep with her..."

Jessica's deep breath left her all at once.

"...but I said no. Because if I did, she'd want the painting for free."

Drawing the blanket tightly around herself, Jessica shoved past him, into his bedroom, to get her things. He followed her, with no attempt to cover his own vulnerably naked self.

"Why are you upset, chiquitita?" he asked, as if genuinely puzzled. Within moments, she had on her skirt, backward, and her blouse, inside out. He watched, amused, as she gathered her purse, sandals, and underwear from the floor.

It was a good question. Why *was* she so upset? She'd come here to have sex with him, and she'd had it, and it'd been good. Who cared what he did when she wasn't around?

"You shouldn't be so jealous over me," he said.

His words made Jessica pause. Was that it? Was she jealous?

He jumped back to avoid the sharp kitten heels dangling from her fist as she shoved past him again, this time to the front door, which she managed to slam behind her. He followed and continued making his case, calling out to her as she hopped across the rocky drive.

"Even after she pays me, I'm going to tell her no. Chiquitita, come on. You know that I don't like skinny women! I like them round and big... like you!"

The last thing she saw as she peeled out on the gravel was Guillermo standing naked in the moonlight, with his fellow dogs running in stupid circles behind him.

As she sped down the empty highway back toward the city lights, her Virgin Mary rocked back and forth. It seemed to be saying, *No, no, no.*

"Oh, hush," Jessica said. "I know. I *know.*"

**5**

A much bigger plastic Virgin Mary stared at Jessica from her mother's porch on that humid Saturday morning. An orange cat rubbed against it and then threaded through the aloe veras, meowing lazily as Jessica opened the screen door.

"Mami! It's me!"

"M'ija." Her mother met her at the door, kissed her cheek, and led her into the rosy velour living room. "There's barbacoa on the stove. Make you a plate."

Her mother walked to one end of the couch, where she was in the process of folding socks and boxer shorts and piling them into little pyramids. Her father sat on the other end, with a plate of tacos on his lap and an open can of Tecate on the coffee table. Jessica couldn't help but notice the beer and the fact that it was barely eleven a.m. At least he was wearing socks this time, and his undershirt. Half the times she visited, he'd be sitting there in his pajama pants and nothing else.

"Jessi!" He raised an arm for her hug.

"Papi!" Jessica kissed her father's cheek.

Jessica went and made herself a plate of barbacoa, beans, and tortillas, then added a pineapple empanada for good measure. She joined her parents in the living room, where *Sábado Gigante* played on the gigantic TV with the sound down low.

"How've you guys been? How's work, Mami?" Her mother was the longtime secretary of Jessica's alma mater, Hawthorne Elementary.

Her mother didn't look up from the laundry. "Oh, you know. All the kids are going crazy, ready to be out for the summer. Then my boss is after me to finish up some free lunch report he should have done back in January."

"Those people wouldn't know how to run that school without your mother there to do everything for them," her father explained. Jessica knew this well. She herself had been there, done that, and bought the T-shirt. Papi turned to Mami and said, "You should do what I do, vieja. Tell them to go to hell."

"Sure. Then they'd fire me and we wouldn't have money for those beers you like to drink."

Jessica turned to her father. "How about you, Papi? What's up at the plant?"

Her father shook his head with the mock angry face that always reminded Jessica of the matador in the velvet painting they used to have. "Those lazy burros never want to fill the bottles fast enough, and then the bolillos upstairs give me lip, so I tell them all to kiss my ass." He meant the guys who worked under his supervision, who all happened to be Latino, and his managers upstairs, who all happened to be white. "Listen to this... The other day, one of the district managers came to inspect the plant. He comes up to where I'm working, all dressed in his fancy suit, and says, 'Hey, you — you speak English?'"

"What'd you tell him?" said Jessica.

"I said, 'Sí, señor. I es-speak inglés...I speak enough

English to understand that you don't know worn-out couplings from a hole in your ass!'"

Jessica laughed. Papi raised his beer to emphasize his point, and she quickly bent to slide one of her mother's crocheted coasters under the can. She knew her father was exaggerating. He actually got along with his bosses very well, or else he wouldn't be a supervisor at all, considering that he had no degree and hadn't even been a citizen when he'd first started at the plant so many years before.

But he still liked to tell his stories, in which he was the beleaguered brown man standing up to the Anglo-Saxon masses threatening his dignity. And, in a way, Jessica couldn't blame him. She remembered more than one incident from her youth where white people *had* assumed that her father didn't speak English—that, and worse. It didn't happen anymore, but she saw how things like that could make a man bitter.

Her father had been through a lot of drama since coming to America. Jessica knew, for instance, that watching his oldest daughter marry a white man had almost been too much for Papi. He'd complained for months, asking why a Mexican man wasn't good enough for Sabrina. Jessica felt sorry for him, knowing that he took the whole thing very personally. But, eventually, Papi had realized that David made Sabrina happy, and he got over it.

But that had been two years ago, and Papi never said a word about it now. In fact, he got along with his son-in-law, David, very well. So as far as Jessica was concerned, he deserved to talk a little trash in the privacy of his own home. It wasn't as though he were actually *racist*. He was just blowing off a little steam.

"I'm glad you're just making up stories, viejo," said Mami. "Because if you really did smart-talk your bosses like that, you'd lose your job."

Papi rolled his eyes and waved dismissively, then looked over at Jessica. "Stand up, m'ijita. Turn around. Let me see how pretty you look."

Jessica gave him an exasperated smile but did what her father said. She got up and did a quick turn. She'd recently been to her stylist's, so her dark brown hair gleamed with fresh caramel highlights. Although she was wearing only a T-shirt and jeans, she'd chosen the jeans carefully, along with high-heeled sandals, to make the most of her healthy figure. Her stomach was still relatively flat, but her butt was what kept her from buying pants in single-digit sizes.

"You look good," Papi said. "You look like a movie star."

"Jessica, are you gaining weight?" her mother said, squinting at Jessica's hips. Unfortunately, Jessica had always been a little more full-figured than her mother.

"Mami—"

"No, vieja. She looks fine. She looks perfect," said her father.

Grateful for her father's defense, Jessica pushed a cat off the upholstered side chair and sat back down. Her father continued, "Don't let your butt get *too* much bigger, though, m'ijita. You don't want all the men at your job chasing you around."

"Papi!"

"Be quiet, viejo," said her mother. "She doesn't work with a bunch of dirty old men like you."

"Hmph." Papi took another sip of beer. "I wouldn't *have* to chase anybody if I had a woman who wanted to look pretty for me at home."

Jessica knew her father was just teasing, like always. Her mother did still look good for her age. She stood there at the couch in a cute pink tracksuit, not at all fat after having two kids. Her face was still pretty, even if it showed a few wrinkles from frowning right at the moment. Was it just Jessica's imagination, though, or did Mami's bun of long brown hair suddenly have more gray streaks than before? Still, she looked good for her age. Papi just liked to tease her.

"You've got a hardworking woman at home," Mami told him. "That's more than you deserve."

Papi's eyes flashed. He turned and appealed to Jessica with his next shot. "I bought your mother a pair of high heels. Beautiful red ones. But does she ever wear them? No."

"Where am I going to wear them to? The laundry room?" Mami said.

"Why do I have to *take* you somewhere? Why can't you just wear them for me here, at home?"

Her mother just shook her head and kept folding, folding, not even bothering to reply.

"Maybe you *have* been wearing my high heels," Papi said. "To work, to look sexy for your boss."

At that, Jessica's mother finally looked up and threw a pair of his underwear at him. "Viejo!"

Jessica sighed. Her parents never seemed to get tired of their mock arguments, but she and her sister, Sabrina, did. Time to remind them that she was still there. "So what have y'all been doing?" she asked.

They both considered the question. Then they both

shrugged. "Working," said her mother. Jessica wasn't sure what she'd expected them to say. Maybe that they were planning a whirlwind vacation? Or that they'd actually left the house over the weekend?

Papi took another sip from his beer. "What about you, m'ija? How's your work? Are they still paying you good?"

"Good enough, I guess." That reminded her — she would give them a little money before she left.

"Have you called your sister?" asked her mother.

"No. Why?"

"You need to call her. She wants to know when you're giving the web site to David. I told her you would probably take it to the barbecue today. It's finished, isn't it? Sabrina says David's paying you a lot of money."

Jessica rolled her eyes, but not so her mother could see her. "Mami, I uploaded it and e-mailed him the link this morning." It bothered her, the way her mother and sister would discuss what Jessica needed to do, as though she were six years old and not twenty-six.

"Oh. Well, you're still going to her barbecue, right?"

"I guess."

"There'll probably be a lot of David's friends there," her mother said, faux casually. Jessica knew that they conveniently took her age into consideration when it mattered to them. That was, it mattered to them that she was in her late twenties and still single. All she said was, "I bet."

"Be sure to wear something nice."

There was no use arguing, so Jessica said nothing. Ever since Sabrina's wedding two years ago, she and Mami had been annoyingly enthusiastic about Sabrina's plans to marry

Jessica off to one of David's friends. Jessica wasn't ready to get married—especially not to some golf-shirt-wearing business major.

"And?" her mother asked. "Anything else?"

"What do you mean?" Jessica knew what her mother meant, though.

"Don't what-do-you-mean me. Have you been seeing anybody?"

"Ma..."

"Well? Come on, m'ijita. You're twenty-six years old. What are you waiting for?"

"I'm not waiting for anything. I'm just living my life."

"Jessica..." Her mother took a freshly folded washcloth and wiped at a water ring on the table. Now Jessica wished that she hadn't interrupted her parents' mock arguing. Mami scrubbed hard and said, "What was the point of going to college and moving away if you weren't going to meet a good man and get married?"

"I don't know. So I could get a job and not live off my parents for the rest of my life?" Jessica's voice was as sarcastic as she could get away with.

"M'ija, we just worry about you," said her mother. "What are you going to do for the rest of your life? Work every day until you die? Waste your time dancing and getting drunk with loquitos every weekend until you get old and end up alone?"

Jessica sighed. Mami was referring to her gay-bar outings with Toby. She'd obviously been talking to Mrs. Jimenez, Toby's mother, who lived next door. Between Toby's big mouth and Mrs. Jimenez's, Jessica could barely have a social life without everyone in the world knowing about it. At least, thank God, Mrs. Jimenez didn't know about Guillermo. Otherwise, Jessica would undoubtedly be hearing about it right now.

"Mami, Mrs. Jimenez just exaggerates. We don't get drunk every weekend." It was more like they got tipsy, and only every *other* week.

"Baby, it's not about you going out," Papi cut in. "Shoot, if I could, I'd be going out with you. It's that we worry about you living all by yourself. It's not safe. Plus, you're not getting any younger."

Jessica gasped. *Not Papi, too.*

"That's right, m'ija," said her mother. "You're not. And we only tell you because we care about you."

"Y'all—"

Before Jessica could protest any further, Mami turned to Papi. "And what do you mean, you'd go out with her if you could? You don't take me out, so you don't need to go anywhere."

Jessica forgot about her own victimization, surprised at the vehemence in her mother's voice all of a sudden.

"What?" said Papi. "I *would* take you out. You never want to go!"

"What are you talking about? You never offer to take me out. And don't say for Mother's Day—that didn't count. I didn't want to go to that beer joint with your stupid friends."

"Oh, so now they're stupid, huh? Am I stupid, too? Maybe I should go there now, so you don't have to look at the stupid man you married anymore."

What was going on here? Jessica wondered. This was

beyond the normal teasing she was used to hearing from her parents. This sounded like out-and-out fighting.

"How about you go to the garage instead," said her mother, "and fix the lawn mower? That way I won't be the only person doing something useful all weekend."

"Fine," said her father, slamming his beer on the table. He got up and started for the door, then turned and went to the kitchen. He emerged with a fresh beer and gave Mami one defiant look before going outside and slamming the door behind him.

Her mother made a hand gesture of dismissal at Papi, muttering, "Good. Stay out there and drink all damn day."

Before Jessica could say anything, Mami gathered a pile of socks and hauled them to the bedroom. Then she swept back through the room and into the kitchen without stopping to note Jessica's reaction. "Here, m'ija," she called. "Let me make you a plate. Eat at your sister's tonight, and then you'll have this barbacoa for tomorrow morning."

Jessica followed her mother into the kitchen, knowing better than to ask questions. You didn't mess with Mami when she was in plate-making mode. Jessica was reminded, suddenly, of Sabrina's wedding, when Papi'd had a little too much tequila and started spinning David's mother around all over the dance floor. Mami had gritted her teeth and packed up the entire wedding cake in neat, aluminum foil saucers that she'd pressed on everyone in range. Then, calmly as a robot, she'd crossed to the edge of the dance floor and stood, arms folded, just looking at Papi. When she'd caught his eye, he'd returned his comadre to her husband and, without another word, followed Mami out of the hall.

Now, in the same meek way, Jessica mumbled thanks for her shiny package and made excuses to leave. Mami's crossed arms prevented Jessica from handing her a twenty, so she left the money on the coffee table and got the heck out of there. She shot a sympathetic glance at the garage as she got into her car. She didn't know what all that had been about, but she wanted out.

# 6

Jessica was so shaken by her parents' arguing that she almost ran over a squirrel as she backed out of their driveway.

"Be careful!" she yelled at it out the window. It wasn't a black squirrel, luckily. She was pretty sure the superstition about black cats extended to black squirrels. This one was brown, but still—killing a squirrel probably *wasn't* good luck. Jessica put on DJ Kabuki-Oh's latest to calm her nerves.

"Get your ass on the dance floor!" yelled Kabuki-Oh from the stereo speakers.

Yeah, she wished. Jessica wanted to fast-forward to ten o'clock that night, when she'd be getting ready to party with Toby and forget all the stress and drama of this week. That was what Guillermo was supposed to do for her last night—help her relax—and look how that had turned out.

Instead of taking the right on White Oak toward her own apartment, Jessica found herself heading left. Slowly her maroon Accord crept against the bayou, to the side of the Heights where the houses still had chipped paint. Unable to shake her feeling of restlessness, she let the car lead her. Really, though, she knew exactly where she would end up. She was going to get professional help.

A little purple house with white shutters and black curtains stood where she finally pulled against the curb. In the window nearest the door was a flashing neon sign, a red hand inscribed with a white circle and star. The sign above the door, hand-painted in Gothic letters, read, MADAME HORTENSIA, PSYCHIC AND NOTARY PUBLIC.

Jessica parked and walked up the porch steps. The door was ajar, so she went right in.

Velvet-draped chairs and a card table waited in the center of the living room. Maroon chiffon scarves covered both lamps in the room, giving it a lighting scheme similar to the nocturnal rooms at the zoo.

In contrast with this mysterious atmosphere was the bright kitchen, visible through the doorway. It held a small, wiry-haired old woman in a flowered T-shirt and polyester slacks, peeling a potato at the sink. She wiped her hands on a little towel before hobbling out to greet Jessica. "How are you, m'ijita? I haven't seen you in a while."

"Fine. Madame Hortensia, do you have time to do a reading?"

"Yes, yes, claro que sí. Let me just..." The woman drifted slowly through the bead curtain that led to rooms Jessica had never seen.

Jessica took a seat at the black velvet table with her gold vinyl purse on her knees, because it was bad luck to put it on the floor. Madame Hortensia returned achingly slowly, bringing a mahogany box, then arranging it and herself at the table. In the reddish light, she transformed from a regular neighborhood grandma to the all-knowing figure Jessica needed to see.

"Piensa en que quieres saber. Do you have questions, m'ija, or do you just want a general reading?" The old woman laid out the cards in precise patterns as she spoke.

"I have questions, yes. And I want to know what's going to happen in the future, too."

"Of course. Think of your questions, then. Say them in your mind."

What were her questions this time?

How about: What the hell was Guillermo's deal? Did he want to have a real relationship with her or not? Or was he seeing other women, giving them the runaround like he gave her?

Should she give him up once and for all, before she ended up going crazy and killing him?

Or could she make him change?

If she did give him up, what would happen next? Would she ever meet anyone else?

"Ready?" the old woman asked. Jessica nodded, and up flipped the first cards.

The Sun, the World, and three of those circles with stars in them, like the one on the neon sign. Jessica didn't bother to study the details. She could never make heads or tails of all the stars and sticks and cups and people on the cards, and that was why she paid someone else to do it.

"O, sí. Ah, yes...," Madame Hortensia said to the cards. Then, to Jessica: "Now, remind me, m'ija, what we said the last time you were here."

It had been two months ago. Jessica remembered it well. Things had been going well with Guillermo then, so they'd talked mostly about money. "We said that I had improved my finances, and that this would enhance my life."

"Mm-hmm. And did these things come to pass?"

Jessica thought back to the end of March. She'd just gotten

paid for Toby's friend's web site. She'd put some of the money in savings and bought a new comforter set and USB drive with the rest. Also, she'd finally switched from generic cereal to name brand. "Yes, things happened. Money did enhance my life."

Madame Hortensia nodded. "And did the cards say something else?"

"That I would help to enrich the lives of others."

"And did you?"

Well, sure she had, Jessica thought. She'd given her parents money every pay period, and she and Sabrina had gone in together on steam-cleaning Mami's carpets. Also, she'd done volunteer work for ALMA, the nonprofit organization where her friend Marisol worked. She tried to think of something else.

She'd been there for Toby when he'd needed a shoulder to cry on, hadn't she? And at work, she'd done all the things her bosses didn't know how to do for themselves. But that one didn't really count, since she was getting paid for it. However, at least she could say that she'd livened up the place for Olga and Rochelle, who'd be bored without her. And for Xavier, who would probably work himself to death if she didn't make him go out for lunch once a week.

"Yes, you were right," Jessica concluded. "I did enrich the lives of others."

"Okay. And what did we say about romance?" Madame Hortensia asked.

Jessica felt herself blush. "That my romantic life seemed confused, and that I had to be careful not to go down the wrong path with any tall, dark strangers."

"And how has that been going?"

Now Jessica knew for sure that she was blushing—she felt it up to her ears. Why couldn't they do this with a curtain between them, she thought wistfully, like at confession?

"Well, let's just say there hasn't really been any good, clear path to go on. So far." There. That was all Jessica was going to say.

Luckily, Madame Hortensia was done asking questions. She tapped each of the three overturned cards with her thick, chipped fingernail. "These represent your recent past. You were a good daughter, making your way in the world, being successful for yourself and for loved ones. You may have made some mistakes, but nothing too bad."

Jessica nodded, resisting the urge to bite her thumbnail.

"And now you want to know what comes next, verdad? Maybe what comes for you in love? Or money?"

"Yes. In both, please."

Hortensia flipped over the next three cards. They were another jumble of symbols, with a knight and a woman on a throne. "Hmm. Very interesting."

"What is it? What do you see?"

"I see...opportunity."

Jessica leaned forward.

"Opportunity for money, *and* in love."

The old woman glanced up to check Jessica's reaction to this. Jessica smiled and nodded so that she would continue.

"You will meet a new man."

"Really?"

"Yes. A rich, handsome man. Possibly a new love interest."

"Huh."

Madame Hortensia waited.

"So, I'm not supposed to keep seeing the guy I'm with right now?" Jessica asked.

"I didn't say that, m'ija. What you do or don't do with the current man is up to you. I'm just telling you what I see."

A new, rich, and handsome guy? Jessica wondered where she'd meet him. It couldn't be at work. A lot of the guys there were rich, but almost none of them were handsome. Unless they were planning to hire someone new.... But even if they did, it'd probably be the same kind of guy as all the others — old, white, bad hair, boring.

Maybe Sabrina was planning to set her up with someone again. But Jessica didn't have high hopes for that, either. Her sister really had no concept of Jessica's type. Sabrina always picked out clones of her own husband. David was nice enough, Jessica had to admit, but he simply wasn't her type.

"Where am I supposed to meet this new man?" Jessica asked.

"Uh...let me see." Madame Hortensia flipped up another card. It had a big shining cup and nothing else. "The cards don't say."

"*When* am I supposed to meet him?" asked Jessica.

"It didn't say that, either."

Jessica pointed. "Well, what does that cup mean, then?" Obviously it meant something.

"That he will be a very good man. Handsome. Successful. Nice."

Jessica tried to imagine it.

"Doesn't leave his dirty clothes on the floor," Madame Hortensia added.

"What about the man I'm already seeing, though? What's going to happen with him?"

The old woman turned the next card. It showed a dark-haired man hanging upside down from a tree. She smiled her grim little smile, the one that made Jessica think that her dentures didn't fit right.

"Well, if you want to stay with this man, then he doesn't have anything to worry about, does he?"

Best to come right out and ask, Jessica realized. "Okay, but... Is he cheating on me? Is he seeing someone else?"

Madame Hortensia stared at the hanging man for a while, finger pressed to her temple. "How long have you been seeing this man again, m'ija?"

It had been since Christmas, so... "Five months."

"Has he given you a ring?"

"A *wedding* ring? No."

"No, I meant a promise ring."

"What? No," said Jessica. Madame Hortensia must have meant like in the olden days, when boys gave girls their class rings to wear on chains around their necks. Jessica wasn't sure they even had class rings in Mexico, but Guillermo had never given her jewelry in any case, so the answer was no.

"So..." Madame Hortensia seemed to be searching for a clearer vision of the future. She rubbed her temple and closed her eyes. "So, let me be sure... Is this man your novio, or more like a... como se llama... a friend with benefits?"

Jessica raised her eyebrows at this terminology. It sounded as though Madame Hortensia had been watching *Sex and the City*. "Well, I guess he is kind of a friend with benefits. I mean, it is mostly about the benefits."

"I see."

Now that she was saying it out loud to an unbiased party, though, Jessica realized that wasn't exactly the case. "But it's turning to more than that, kind of," she clarified. "At first it was just physical, but now we talk about things."

"Like?"

"Like art. And our dreams. And...he likes to talk about me running away with him."

"To Mexico?"

"No. To Washington. Or California." Or, once, even to Canada. But Jessica kept that one to herself, since it was so extreme. She knew people who'd been there, and they'd told her it didn't even have Mexican restaurants.

"This is the other painter, no?" asked Madame Hortensia. "M'ija, does this man have his green card yet?"

"What? Yes. It's not like that. He's not looking for that." Was he? Jessica wondered. No, he couldn't be. He was here legally. She knew that. Madame Hortensia still looked skeptical. Without meaning to, Jessica blurted out, "He used to call me chiquitita, but now he calls me corazón." As soon as the words came out of her mouth, she felt like a complete dummy. What did it matter whether he called her one name or the other? She sounded like one of those pathetic women on *Oprah,* making excuses for staying in a dead-end relationship.

However, Madame Hortensia smiled at this. Her first real smile of the reading.

"I'm beginning to understand. You're like me, m'ija. We love our Latinos, don't we? Even when they drive us crazy."

Jessica blushed again.

"Well, okay," the old woman continued. "Still, there is a man coming up in the future. Rich, handsome, and nice."

Jessica furrowed her brow. Who the heck could it be?

Madame Hortensia went on, "And even if you don't end up with this man, this will be an opportunity. Friends with benefits means you're free to make friends with someone else, verdad? If your painter has other friends, why shouldn't you? See what happens, then. Take a few chances, and see if he notices."

Ooh. That sounded...wicked. Even a little *slutty*. Jessica was surprised at the old fortune-teller.

Madame Hortensia saw her quizzical look and winked. "You're young, m'ijita. You should be having fun. If a man wants to keep you to himself, he can try a little harder and let you know."

"But what if he doesn't? What if I go out with someone else, and Guillermo gets hurt and *doesn't* try harder?"

"Well, then you know. He's not the one for you."

Jessica was so consumed with this train of thought, she didn't even notice the old woman flipping up the next cards.

"As for your job, I see it getting better for you, but only if you keep your eyes open for opportunity."

"Really? You mean I'm going to quit working in insurance?"

"Possibly."

"What will I be doing instead?" Jessica asked. Was there a card that represented web design? The next one had two sticks with leaves, which could mean anything.

"Maybe if you marry the new, rich man, you'll be able to quit your job," Madame Hortensia suggested.

Jessica frowned. Her job was boring, but she liked working. She wasn't ready to become a housewife.

Seeing her face, the old woman added, "Or maybe you will find a better job."

Jessica realized then that Madame Hortensia knew a lot about cards and omens, but probably not too much about modern career options for women. But just because she couldn't come right out and say "freelance web design" didn't mean the cards hadn't foretold it. Jessica would just have to keep her eyes open for the big web site contract that would help her make the switch from administrative assistant to entrepreneur.

"So, when is this job opportunity going to happen?" she asked, just in case the cards would give a time frame.

Madame Hortensia flipped up more sticks, more stars, and another woman on a throne.

"Soon," she said. "Very soon."

Jessica nodded. It was twenty dollars well spent.

"In the meantime," continued the old woman, "I have something you might be interested in." She got up and went through the beaded curtain, to the room Jessica had never seen.

She came back with . . . a box of soap.

"Here you go. This will help you."

The box was crudely decorated with a drawing of a man on his knees. Above him, a woman in a tight dress pointed at his head.

"What's this?" Jessica's voice was skeptical yet still betrayed her interest.

"It's a special soap, from my new line of products. It's meant to put a man under your spell, so that he does what you want him to do in love."

"Wow." Jessica had seen Mexican soaps like these before, of course, but she never knew they were supposed to be magic. "So, this will make Guillermo act like a real boyfriend?"

"If that's what you want it to do," Madame Hortensia said. "Just concentrate on what you want while you bathe with this soap."

"Wait. If I'm supposed to use it on myself, then how does it work on someone else?"

"Just bathe with it and concentrate on the results you want. It will give you the aura you need to accomplish your heart's desire."

"Wow," said Jessica again. This was *hard-core*. Why hadn't the old woman given her this to begin with? "Thank you, Madame Hortensia. I really appreciate it."

"Ah, m'ija..."

"Yes?"

"The soap is seven dollars."

"Oh. Sorry. Here you go." Jessica took out her wallet and paid up.

7

Jessica passed through her apartment's vine-covered gate with her head full of Madame Hortensia's words. She was waiting for two opportunities now. A man and a job. Really, it made perfect sense. Going out with a new guy *would* force Guillermo to commit to her, wouldn't it? Now that she thought about it, he was probably trying to do the same thing to her. That thing about painting the skinny old rich woman? He just wanted Jessica to get jealous and chase him that much harder. It was so obvious.

Even as she told herself this, she recognized her thoughts for what they were: a lame attempt to make excuses for Guillermo's behavior. Not to mention the fact that she kept putting up with it.

She sighed as she circled the courtyard pool, which was fuzzy green. This May hadn't yet been hot enough for anyone to skim off the algae and dead frogs for a swim. It was kind of gross, really, but Jessica wouldn't complain. This apartment was a total steal for being so close to downtown, and her neighbors were nice. Her landlady, out tending tomato plants in her housedress, waved as Jessica climbed the rickety metal stairs to her door with the rusted gold number 16.

Jessica waved back, but her thoughts were elsewhere. She was mentally time-traveling back to December, to the fateful day when she'd gone to pick up Toby for a little outlet mall shopping. Mrs. Jimenez, Toby's mom, had been having their house painted that day. She'd introduced Jessica to the painter, saying he was her cousin's son. And that was when she'd seen Guillermo for the first time. Shirtless. Muscles glinting with perspiration as he'd pushed a long brown roller against the wall.

Jessica had written down his number in order to get an estimate. And when he'd shown up at her place a week later, she'd gotten way more than that. Even though sleeping with strangers was totally out of character for her, it was as though she'd been possessed. There was chemistry between them such as she'd never felt before. And besides, he wasn't *really* a stranger if he was Toby's second or third cousin. So it wasn't as if she'd been in any danger. . . .

Unless you counted the danger that was developing feelings for someone you'd meant to be only a one-night stand.

Looking back now, she saw that she'd gone about things all wrong. Guillermo was a classic mexicano. That meant no matter how modern she herself was, she should've gone old-school on him and played hard to get. That was the only way to have a relationship with a Latino — she'd have to use *Rules* girl mind games.

Really, though, she was being too hard on herself. If she was honest, she had to admit that she hadn't *wanted* a relationship with him back then. Had she? No, she'd wanted to use him just as much as he hadn't minded using her.

As the using went on, though, he'd become a bad habit she just couldn't break. And it wasn't just the sex, either, although that was a big part of it. There was just something about him. His art, his lifestyle, the way he didn't care what anybody thought. The way he made her laugh. His crazy impulsiveness.

Inside her apartment, as she searched for the stopper for her old-fashioned enamel tub, Jessica remembered the day back in March when Guillermo had called her early in the morning and asked her to go to the beach with him. It was a Tuesday, but he'd convinced her to call in sick, put on a swimsuit, and go. They'd driven south in his old truck, down to Galveston, and found that it was still too cold to swim. The beach was almost deserted. But they'd stayed for hours anyway, splashing and laughing in the shallowest waves and then sitting on the sand and holding each other in order to keep warm. After drying off, they'd had burgers and beers on the boardwalk and talked about nothing much at all. Then Guillermo had driven her around parts of the town she'd never seen, telling her the history of various crumbling churches and statues. He said he'd read about them in a book and had wanted to see them ever since.

After that, they'd gone back to the ocean and stayed until dark, then driven back to her place and made love until late into the night. It had been the best mental health day of her life—a memory that kept coming back and making her return to him again and again.

Guillermo could totally piss her off sometimes, when he canceled their plans or didn't call her for a week. But at the same time, she had to admit that he was the only thing that got her blood racing.

The magic soap tingled.

Then it itched.

Then it made her skin turn red.

Crap! thought Jessica as she poured water and then astringent over her legs.

She hopped out of the tub with a towel wrapped around her waist and ran to her laptop. After it booted up all the way, she got online and did a search for "Houston fortune-tellers." A list of names and addresses came up. She searched until she found Madame Hortensia's phone number.

"Bueno?"

"Madame Hortensia!" Jessica was relieved to have caught her at home.

"Yes?"

"This is Jessica Luna. I just left your place? With the soap?"

"Okay." She sounded distracted. Jessica could hear dishes rattling in the background.

"Madame Hortensia, I used the soap, and it made me break out in a rash!"

"Oh no. I'm sorry to hear that," she clucked sympathetically. "Rinse it off and be sure not to use it again."

"Okay, but what does this mean?" Jessica's voice rose to a more panicked pitch. "That Guillermo won't ever do what I want? Or that I need to be stronger? Or—"

Madame Hortensia stayed calm. "It means you have sensitive skin, m'ija, and you have to be careful not to use soaps with too many scents or artificial colors."

"Oh." Jessica had already known that, actually. Everything she applied to her body was hypoallergenic. In her eagerness to make Guillermo into the kind of boyfriend she wanted, she'd used Madame Hortensia's soap without even reading its label.

"Ándale, m'ija. I'll give you a discount on your next reading, okay? I have to go now—I have other clients."

Jessica hung up with a sigh. Her legs were still red, but at least they weren't itching anymore. Her cell phone rang. It was Sabrina. Jessica had forgotten to call her earlier and make up an excuse not to go to the barbecue.

"Hello?"

"Where are you? Are you coming to my barbecue or not?" her sister demanded.

Making her voice very serious and hardworking, Jessica said, "I can't. I'm busy."

"Doing what?" Sabrina asked suspiciously. Jessica hesitated too long, and Sabrina caught her. "You're not busy. Just come over."

"Sabrina, come on. You know I'm not into the suburban social thing. I barely know your friends."

"I know. That's why you'll come over, so you can meet them. It'll be *fun!*"

"Sabrina—"

"Come on, Jessi. You promised *last* time that you'd come *this* time. Come *on!*" This time it was less of a coax and more of a threat that her sister would throw a tantrum. She wouldn't stop until she'd gotten her way. Jessica knew this from experience. Also, she realized that she could eat a good meal at Sabrina's for free.

"Okay, fine. Fine. I'll go."

At least now David could hand her a check for the work she'd done on his site, instead of mailing it to her or having Sabrina give it to Mami. After hanging up on her sister, Jessica turned to her laptop and checked her handiwork one last time. The web site that would educate the world about her brother-in-law's restored 1957 Ford Fairlane was now perfect. Every byte of it, from the photo gallery, to the slide show with classic rock sound track, to the forum where David's fellow car freaks could share their own obsessions. It was a totally silly website, but he was paying her well.

If she played her cards right, she could probably get him to show the site to his friends while she was there, at the barbecue. And then, who knew? Maybe she'd get some more business.

In fact, she realized all of a sudden, maybe this barbecue would end up being the job opportunity Madame Hortensia had foreseen. Maybe one of his friends would want to build a site about his golf scores. Or maybe David had an HTML-illiterate boss who was dying to start a blog and spew his political views all over the Internet. Although in that case, it'd probably be some hard-core right-wing thing, and Jessica didn't know if she'd want to be responsible for putting that on the web. But still. She would go to the barbecue and keep her eyes open for opportunity, just as Madame Hortensia had said.

# 8

As usual, there was traffic all the way to Sugarland. Or Yuppieville, as Jessica called it when describing it to Marisol. For the millionth time since her sister had become Mrs. Sabrina Luna Hoffman, Jessica wondered why David had bought them a house so far away. What was the use, she wondered, of having a big, fancy two-story if it was twenty miles from downtown and anything interesting? Sugarland was nothing but strip malls and chain restaurants. Jessica shook her head at the third Chili's she'd passed on the way. Then she turned up her CD player and inched her way along behind the SUVs.

She hadn't stressed over what to wear. It seemed as though none of her sister's friends ever did—they showed up for everything in uniforms of cropped pants and golf shirts. So Jessica was wearing jeans and one of her favorite T-shirts. It was red with a glittery black cat silhouette, and it said BAD KITTY across the chest.

The only parking she could find was a block from her sister's house. She wedged in between a Yukon and a Lexus and then stepped out of her car and started her walk of shame. She was embarrassed to be spending weekend time outside the Loop. The suburbs totally weren't her scene. It must have been the subdivision's designated barbecue day, because everyone had smoke and top 40 light rising from their back-yards. Jessica peered at each house as she walked past to make sure she got the right one. They all looked the same — two stories in taupe or beige, with carefully boring landscaping. She recognized Sabrina's by her butterfly wind chimes and then by her skinny husband and his light brown hair. He was standing in the garage with two of his friends, showing them the Fairlane. Seeing Jessica, he immediately called out her name with an expression that showed he was genuinely glad she'd come. She had to smile back and remind herself that for a goofy white guy, David wasn't so bad. Even if he had exiled her sister to this suburban wasteland.

She walked over and let him introduce her to the other men in the garage.

"This is my sister-in-law, Jessica. She's the one who made my baby's web site." He patted his baby's hood. "Jessica, the site looks awesome. I already showed it to the guys. Oh — meet Lloyd and Todd." All three look-alikes smiled at her.

"Hi. Actually, I think we've met already," she said to Todd. "On New Year's Eve." This was the last guy Sabrina had tried to set her up with. His lame sense of humor and color-blind taste in clothing had turned her off completely. Not to mention that he had the modified anchorman hairdo — all molded down except for a gel-hardened curl on the forehead.

Todd reached for her hand. "Good to see you again."

"Hello, Jessica. That's a pretty fancy web page you made for a junk heap like this," said the older guy, indicating the Fairlane and smiling at his own joke.

Jessica smiled back. "Thanks. I'm glad you liked it. You know, I can make sites for cars that aren't junk heaps, too. Or for anything you want. And I'm cheap — just ask David."

The old guy chuckled pretty loudly at that. "Well, I wish I did have a reason for you to make me a web site. But I don't really get on the computer much outside of work. Hell, I can barely work my e-mail when I'm at the office."

Jessica could totally imagine him bothering some poor admin, needing help with his e-mail, just as Mr. Cochran always bothered her. There was no use pushing it with this guy. He'd probably be too high-maintenance as a client.

After taking leave of her brother-in-law and the others, Jessica took the walkway into the backyard. There, on the patio set, Sabrina sat entertaining her husband's friends like the belle of a really boring ball. Jessica noticed that she'd cut her hair even shorter. Now it was a chin-length bob. As usual, her sister wore her little gold quinceañera earrings, her wedding rings, and no other jewelry. And almost no makeup. And boring khaki capri pants with a plain white tank top. Jessica remembered how, when they were young, people had always thought they were twins. Not anymore. For a split second, Jessica almost felt bad about what she had on. Were her jeans too tight? Was she wearing too much eyeliner? Were her own earrings too big? Jessica had to be honest: Sometimes, for a split second, being around Sabrina's friends made her feel out of place. Maybe even a little trashy.

No, she told herself firmly. I look good. Sabrina's the one who's underdressed.

Jessica received her sister's hug and got introduced to three women who looked like mannequins in the windows at the Gap. One turned out to be Todd's fiancée, one was the e-mail-disabled guy's wife, and the other was married to the guy in the blue polo who was hovering near the women. Jessica learned their names and then, once she found out that none of them needed web sites, forgot their names and took a diet soda from the cooler.

These people, she reflected for the millionth time as she perched on a flowery lawn chair, were all the same. They were bland beige clones who stood around laughing fake laughs at unfunny jokes and complaining about golf clubs and swimming pools and other things that Jessica couldn't afford and wasn't interested in.

Not her brother-in-law so much. David was nice — very down-to-earth, once you got to know him. Even if he *had* been the one to move her sister out here, where she'd morphed into a Pod Person wannabe. Sure, he was obsessed with his car, but not because it was worth a lot of money. He did make a lot of money, but he didn't brag about it. In fact, Jessica had the impression that if Sabrina hadn't bossed David into buying her a house, he would have been happy in someone's garage apartment, as long as he had his Fairlane and a few video games.

All his friends, though, were boring. Jessica had always imagined that getting married meant having someone to spice up your life. Not so in Sabrina's case. It was as though her sister had OD'ed on dried flowers and *Martha Stewart Living*.

"David will have the burgers ready in just a few minutes," Sabrina announced, "and then we'll dig in."

"What, no brisket? No chicken and sausage, beans or rice?" Jessica said, but so that only Sabrina could hear. "Why'd you call this a barbecue if you aren't serving real food?"

"Hush, mensa. I didn't have time for all that." Sabrina didn't even seem ashamed.

"You didn't have time? It's not like you have a job," said Jessica. Sabrina had quit her receptionist gig at Halronburco a year ago. "Shoot, Mami works hard all day, then throws a big barbecue and sends everybody home with leftovers. What's your excuse?" Even though they were adults now, the sisters still pushed each other's buttons as they had when they were children.

Sabrina remained unperturbed. "I don't know how to mess with that stuff. If you wanted beans and rice, you should've cooked them yourself."

Touché.... Jessica had never learned to cook their mother's beans and rice, either.

She sipped her soda and listened to the others talk about property taxes for a good fifteen minutes. Then one of the women looked out at the huge empty yard and asked Sabrina if she was still planning to put in a pool.

"We haven't decided yet."

"Well, you guys have waited so long, you might as well just put in a playscape instead!" said Todd's fiancée.

In response, Sabrina blushed and gave a quick little smile. Jessica raised an eyebrow. Was this how she was supposed to hear that her sister was considering starting a family?

Jessica reflected on how much Sabrina had changed since she'd married. Sure, they could still relate to each other, but just barely. Back when they were kids, Sabrina had been her idol. And sure, they'd had their arguments, as all sisters do. But for the most part, everything Sabrina did, Jessica had wanted to do, too. Sabrina got a perm, and Jessica wanted a perm. Sabrina said she wanted to be a glamorous executive assistant when she grew up. Jessica didn't know exactly what that meant at the time, but she wanted to be one, too. Sabrina would lie on her bed flipping through *Brides* magazine, and Jessica would be right there with her, helping to pick out dresses.

"When I get married, you'll be my maid of honor," Sabrina had explained. "Then, two years later, you'll get married and I'll be your matron of honor."

And now here they were, two years after the first wedding, and Sabrina had left her behind. Jessica wanted to be more than a secretary now. And Sabrina, meanwhile, didn't have to work at all. And with no work at all, Sabrina had more money than anyone in their family.

But that wasn't what bothered Jessica, not really. It was that now that Sabrina was married, she had stopped confiding in Jessica—she'd traded her in for David's friends' wives. Who knew, though? Maybe Sabrina needed new people whose lives she could plan, now that Jessica had messed up the original plan by failing to get married.

Sometimes Jessica wondered if her sister had outgrown her. Maybe Sabrina thought David's friends, with all their money and middle-class American manners, were more sophisticated than Jessica. Maybe, Jessica thought, I don't meet her standards. Maybe that was why Sabrina was always trying to set Jessica up with one of David's friends—so that he would make her change. Jessica wondered, now, if Sabrina saw her own sister as a sad, poor Latina from the ghetto.

That actually was how Jessica felt around these people. She couldn't help but feel different and less than. It was something that she had never really admitted out loud. And it was a complex she was sure she'd inherited from Papi. She wasn't an idiot. All her life she'd heard her father talk about us versus them, meaning Latinos versus white people, and she'd always disagreed with him. But then she'd started working at McCormick and experiencing some of the same things Papi had talked about.

"Sabrina," exclaimed one of the Pod People, "when are you and David going to come out and play golf with us?"

Jessica wrinkled her nose and stopped listening. At first she'd been bored, and now she was starting to get annoyed. Not only were there no business prospects here, but the food was pathetic. Although she'd dreaded Sabrina's trying to set her up with someone, Jessica was so bored now that she was beginning to wish Sabrina *had* thrown her at some bachelor in a golf shirt. Otherwise, what was the point of being here? She might as well have stayed home, eating cereal and conserving gasoline.

Or she could've stayed home and worked on a mock-up web site. Then maybe Guillermo would have come over to apologize. Then she would have accepted his apology, and then they could have spent the whole evening... Her mind wandered into her bedroom and under Guillermo's shirt.

No. No more of that. Not until he'd learned his lesson, at least.

Then again, Jessica reconsidered, there wasn't any harm in thinking about what would happen *after* he changed his ways. She stared into the spinning blades of the portable fan as they pushed the humidity around, blowing her hair into the sticky trap of her lip gloss. Vividly, she felt Guillermo's hands on her naked hips, pulling her down closer to him. He would run his hands over them, in complete appreciation of every curve. Through half-closed eyes, she envisioned the way he would stuff a pillow between her head and the headboard with one hand, so considerately, without missing a beat.... *God, yes.*

She jumped up out of her chair. That was enough thinking. Luckily, none of her sisters' guests had seemed to notice her mental vacation. She had to distract herself—get her mind off that man. But she couldn't sit here and listen to the Pod People conversation anymore, either. They had moved on to insurance, and Jessica made it a point never to discuss that crap on weekends.

She decided that if she could just find something decent to eat, her afternoon at Sabrina's wouldn't be a total waste.

After excusing herself with a mumble, Jessica made her way through the back door, into the frigid quiet of her sister's kitchen. There, she foraged for materials. Hidden in the very back of the refrigerator, Sabrina had corn tortillas. Further inspection yielded a little pot of beans a la charra and some Cotija cheese. There was also a gourmet-looking jar of what turned out to be green salsa. "Heck, yeah," she whispered. Her sister wasn't a *total* sellout after all. Jessica found half a deli rotisserie chicken that would do for the meat.

She set to work on the marble counter, making herself a plate. She concentrated on the assembly of her food, *not* on any painters or their soft, strong hands. By the time she'd tapped out her calculations on the microwave, she was cool and collected again. While she waited, she twitched her hips in a dance of anticipation, humming a song from DJ Jump-Up's latest CD. The microwave pinged and she sang quietly to the plate as she took it out. "Do it for me one time, baby..."

"Make my body move," sang a voice behind her, completing the line.

Jessica whipped around with a gasp, almost dropping her plate in the process.

A tall, blond man stood there. Apparently, he'd been watching her for a while. His green eyes looked at her, then down at her plate full of tacos. He smiled appreciatively. "Wow. Looks like this is where the real action is."

9

Hi. I'm Jonathan," he said, offering his hand.

She should have felt embarrassed, probably, but instead Jessica was intrigued. With a somewhat sly smile, she shook his hand. "I'm Jessica. How do you know that song?"

"DJ Jump-Up? Who doesn't know the undisputed master of Latin house music?" He said it with mock surprise and sobriety, as if they were discussing classic literature.

Jessica laughed. "Besides every other person at this party, you mean?"

"Well now," he said, still pretending to be serious. "We can't fault them for being ignorant, you know. Not everyone is lucky enough to be exposed to good music."

"No, you're right. That's true." Setting down her plate, she surreptitiously studied this Jonathan guy, wondering where in the world he had come from. Instead of a pastel golf shirt, he wore jeans and one of those retro Cuban resort shirts that were becoming so trendy now. His hair, dark ash blond, was a little longer than what would be considered strictly professional. He was tall and sort of gangly, but not in a bad way—not at all. He looked as though he could be a regular at any of the coffee shops or clubs in her neighborhood. But he definitely wasn't the kind of guy she'd expect to find at one of Sabrina's get-togethers.

As if he'd read her mind, he said, "I work with David at Halronburco."

Jessica imagined him in the mailroom or maybe working on someone's computer.

"Hey...Jessica. I remember now," he went on. "You're the one who did the fan site for David's Fairlane, right?"

"Yeah, that was me. But that wasn't my idea. That's not the kind of thing I normally—"

"No, it was good. Cutting-edge. It's not your fault your brother-in-law's a total geek." His smile was warm. His eyes really were very green, she noticed. "I especially liked the way you Photoshopped your sister's picture into the rearview mirror."

"You saw that?" Jessica couldn't suppress a wicked smile. She loved adding extra little touches like that to her sites, and most people never noticed.

"I did. It was great. So, is that what you do? Web development?"

"Yes. Well, on the side. When I'm not at my day job, in insurance."

"Oh yeah? Which company?" he asked, seemingly with great interest.

"McCormick. It's a brokerage." She didn't want to talk about her job. Who cared? She'd rather go back to talking about music or anything else.

"I have a friend who used to work at McCormick, way back," he said. "Are they still using the Dictaphones and the mimeograph machines?"

"Dictaphones yes, mimeographs no. But I heard they have an abacus in Accounting." She kept her face mock serious, as he had done earlier. "Why, do you have an interest in antique business machinery? Maybe I could take you on a tour sometime." This guy wasn't exactly her type, but Jessica was never one to shy away from harmless flirting, especially in an otherwise boring situation.

"That sounds good," he said. "But I'd be more interested in taking you out sometime. Are you going to see the Bombay Crew at Sun Bar this weekend?"

An electric thrill went through Jessica before she had time to formulate a response. This cute, funny guy had just asked her out, right in the middle of her sister's kitchen. And then she realized that this, right here, was what Madame Hortensia had predicted — a man who would make Guillermo jealous! And he was cute, too. Not *exactly* her type, but she wasn't planning to marry this guy. She needed him only long enough to get Guillermo's attention.

"Do you have a card?" he asked, snapping her back to the present.

"Um...no." She looked around for something more sophisticated than a paper towel that she could write her number on.

"Well, here. Take mine, then." He took one out of his wallet. She glanced at it and saw that his last name was Randall. Under his name, it said, "Vice President, Consulting."

What the heck? she thought. He was a vice president at Halronburco? Jessica immediately felt awkward, almost tricked. If he was a corporate big shot, why was he standing here dressed like a normal guy, talking about Latin house and Indian hip-hop? She didn't know what to think.

Meanwhile, he was saying, "I came by to drop off some

files for David, but I can't stay. If I'd known there'd be someone interesting at this barbecue, I wouldn't have made other plans—"

Just then, Sabrina burst in through the back door. "There you are!" She looked from Jessica to Jonathan to the plate of makeshift tacos on her counter. "What are you guys doing?"

"I just met your sister," Jonathan said. "Where've you been hiding her, Sabrina?"

She laughed and punched him playfully on the arm. "Nowhere. I've been trying to get her to come out and visit for months. But she's always running around downtown, just like you." She flashed him her most charming smile, then turned back to her sister's dinner. "Jessica, I would've let you have another burger. You should've just asked."

Despite all her phony middle-class manners, Sabrina could be pretty blunt. And clueless sometimes. And *embarrassing*. Jessica opened her mouth, hoping something polite yet withering would come out of it. Instead, Jonathan spoke.

"Sabrina, don't let me interrupt your time with your sister. I'm taking off now."

"Oh, wait!" she protested. "Don't go! You haven't eaten!"

"I'm sorry. I wish I could stay, but I really have to go. I'll catch you guys on the next one. Let's have dinner. I'll e-mail David." He turned to Jessica. "It was really nice meeting you." She smiled politely, and then he was gone.

Sabrina picked up one of Jessica's tacos and took a bite. "Mm. Good. Okay, so what did y'all talk about?"

Jessica snatched the taco from Sabrina's hand. "Nothing."

"Really? Dang."

"Dang what?" Already, Jessica was suspicious.

"I sent him in here so he would see you and maybe ask you out." Sabrina was completely off the cuff, as if it were normal to constantly pimp out one's sister to strangers. Jessica frowned.

"Why are you making that face?" her sister asked. "Didn't you think he was cute?"

Jessica made her face neutral. No use giving Sabrina's nosiness any ammunition. "Sure. If you like that type."

"I thought he *was* your type. With the teenage clothes and the no-name coffee shops and all that. He's just like you. Except that he lives in a nice town house and drives an *Audi*." Her voice trilled on the last word as if she were announcing that he was Bill Gates.

Jessica knew, then, that the whole thing had been too good to be true. This Jonathan guy hadn't been what he seemed at all. It was unfortunate, too, because he really had been cute. Not that she'd actually been interested. But still. She rolled her eyes in annoyance at her sister's predictability. "God, Sabrina. You're such a…"

"What? A nice sister?"

"No. You're such a *coconut*. Why do you keep trying to set me up with David's stuck-up corporate friends? Are you hoping I'll turn white, too?" Jessica kept her tone light, but she really wanted to hear what her sister would say to this.

"Whatever," said Sabrina. "If marrying a nice guy and living in a nice house makes me white, then say hello to your bolilla sister."

Jessica shook her head. Her sister had no shame.

Sabrina went on with her mission. "But did you like him or not? You want me to tell David to tell him—"

"Sabrina, I don't even *know* this guy."

"So ask him out for coffee and get to know him."

"I told you, he's not my type."

"Because he's white, right? You're so racist, Jessica. Just like Papi."

Jessica gasped. If there weren't half a taco still left on her plate, she would have walked out the door right then.

## 10

And then she says, 'You're racist, just like our dad!' And I was like, 'Oh, my God, I can't believe you just said that.' Can you believe she said that?" Jessica hit the accelerator hard and wedged her way between two SUVs that didn't want to let her merge onto the freeway. She'd decided to call her friend Marisol so she'd have company for the long drive home from Sugarland.

"Not that you were *racist*, no."

"I know, right? Wait, why are you saying it like that?" Jessica demanded. Marisol hadn't sounded completely convinced.

She didn't answer right off the bat. She was at work, as usual, and Jessica could imagine her sitting there in her tiny office. She would be dressed in jeans and some kind of peasant blouse, with two or three wood bead necklaces and her long black hair pinned up because it was always too hot at her work.

"I'm not sure I'm seeing the issue," Marisol finally said. "You said he was cute, he made you laugh, and he likes the same crazy music you like. So what's the problem? That this Jonathan guy's a vice president at his job? I don't get it."

Jessica thought it over for a moment. A BMW swept by, preventing her from entering the fast lane. "Well, first of all, Mari, remember that I'm not seriously considering dating anyone else. I'm only supposed to find someone who will make Guillermo jealous."

Marisol sighed into Jessica's earbud. "Because the old lady with the neon hand sign said so, you mean?"

Jessica was indignant. "I told you—Madame Hortensia knows things that normal strangers wouldn't know. She really is psychic. But, okay, aside from that... Marisol, this Jonathan guy is a vice president at Halronburco. That means he has to be one of those big corporate types, like all the annoying ones at my work. Like my dad's bosses who are always putting him down."

"Sure. Some corporate guys are jerks. But you said this one seemed nice."

"Come on, Mari. You know what I mean. I'm not going to mess with somebody who expects me to just drop my culture and...my family...and run out to the suburbs just because he has an expensive car or a big 401(k) or whatever."

"I thought you said he liked the same music as you, and he hung out at the clubs you hang out at. Did he tell you he wanted to marry you and force you to drop your culture?" Marisol said in her counselor-reasoning-with-hormonal-youth voice.

"Of course not. But—"

"But that's what Sabrina did with David, and you don't want to be the same way? Listen, no one's asking you to settle down in the suburbs and start shopping at Pottery Barn. One date with a guy doesn't mean that you're going to marry him and conform to some weird societal norm."

"Well..." Jessica cut off the BMW this time, then gave the rich white-guy driver a sarcastic wave of thanks in her rear-view mirror. "You know what? Really, now that I think about it, he probably didn't even really want to go out with me. Maybe he was just being polite, or networking or whatever. Why would someone like that want to mess with someone like me? Unless he has some Latina fetish or something."

"Are you serious? Come on, Jessi. Stop it. Why wouldn't he want to go out with you? He *could* be someone that actually sees you for who you are and doesn't care about race or money."

"Sure," Jessica said, sarcastic and doubtful.

"Listen, Jessi. I'm not going to tell you to go out with a guy you don't like, just to prove something or to make your sister happy."

"Thank you."

"But at the same time," Marisol continued, "I don't think you should jump to conclusions or write someone off just because he looks like your brother-in-law or because he has a nice car or whatever. If you do that, you're no better than the kind of person you've been describing."

"Wait—"

Marisol went on, undeterred. "You said at the beginning that he was interesting, that you made each other laugh, and that he noticed how good you were at web design."

"Well—"

"Why can't you just believe that he can be a good person, especially when he recognizes how pretty, smart, funny, and talented you are? You know, I almost have to wonder... Okay, listen. Don't get mad, but I'm starting to wonder if, with your whole bad-boy fetish thing—"

Jessica decided to stop this line of thought before it went too far. "Marisol, if this is about Guillermo or Robert—"

"It's not. I'm not saying it's been any one guy."

Jessica sighed. "I'm just trying to keep it real, okay? Just because neither of them had a lot of money —"

"Chica, I'm not saying anything about their money, and I'm not telling you *not* to keep it real." Marisol's voice had become gentle, even a little sad, like a doctor's when he's about to announce that someone has cancer.

"Well, what are you saying, then?" Jessica had the feeling it wasn't something she wanted to hear.

"That you're so used to players now, you might not know how to act when a guy treats you right."

Jessica almost ran into a broken crate that had fallen into her lane. She swerved to miss it. Under her rearview mirror, the Virgin swung in circles, as if she couldn't make up her mind.

"Marisol, that's pretty cold-blooded."

"I'm just saying, Jessi. You know I wouldn't tell you if I didn't care."

"No, I know. But Guillermo's not a player," she explained. "Just because he's a little flaky sometimes, that doesn't mean he's trying to take advantage of me."

Marisol didn't say anything to that.

Jessica went on. "I know sometimes it seems like he gets on my nerves, and that we have a lot of drama. But that's just the way it is. You know — that's how it is when you date Latinos. Dramatic. Spicy. Exciting." As soon as the words were out of her mouth, though, she realized that Marisol never dated people like that.

Ever since they'd met back in kindergarten, Jessica had been the one with man trouble. She'd been the one to get tangled up with the bad boys, right from the start. Marisol, on the other hand, always dated perfectly nice, respectable men. Boring men, Jessica thought secretly. She sometimes wished she could be more like her best friend when it came to avoiding drama. But then, Jessica couldn't help wondering if Marisol ever got to have really good sex — the kind of sex you'd call in sick for.

"I'm sorry," said Marisol, breaking into her reverie. "I'm not trying to tell you how to run your life."

Jessica sighed. "I know you aren't."

"If you don't want to go out with this guy, you shouldn't. But at the same time, if he's nice and funny, why not give him a chance? You know?"

Jessica signaled for her exit. "Yeah, maybe you're right. You know, Madame Hortensia did tell me there was a chance that I'd actually end up with the new guy. But then again, maybe she didn't mean *this* guy," she countered, not wanting to jinx things either way.

She heard Marisol sigh through the phone. "You know, you *could* always just decide on your own, without asking a fortune-teller's advice."

Jessica shuddered. "Yeah, but then who would I blame if things went wrong?"

Marisol laughed. "I don't know, chica. But I'll be here for you if they do."

They hung up and Jessica drove the rest of the way home.

Despite their conversation, she still had her reservations. She couldn't deny that she'd found Jonathan attractive, before she'd found out what he did for a living.

On the other hand, it didn't matter anyway, because he

didn't have her number. She still had his card, but she wasn't going to be the one to call him and then find out that he hadn't wanted to go out after all. And he didn't have her number, so he couldn't call her.

So it was settled. Madame Hortensia had meant someone else. There was no use worrying about it anymore.

## 11

He did call, though. She'd been sitting at her desk on Monday when the phone rang.

"Jessica?" he'd said. "It's Jonathan. Jonathan Randall, from Sabrina and David's barbecue? Sabrina gave me your number. I hope you don't mind."

No, she hadn't minded. Although she'd blown the whole thing out of proportion in her mind the day of the barbecue, hearing his voice again made her realize that her first instinct had been correct. He was a nice guy. So, after getting a positive sign from her screen saver in the form of a Hello Kitty in a teahouse, she'd agreed to meet Mr. Jonathan Randall for coffee.

Now, Wednesday after work, Jessica stood at the counter of Argentine, the Montrose coffee shop with the vine-covered patio, waiting for Jonathan to meet her. Although a tiny part of her felt slightly guilty—what if Guillermo found out and was more than just jealous? what if he was completely devastated?—the rest of her was excited and only a little nervous.

There was nothing to feel guilty about, she reminded herself. She and Guillermo were not in a committed relationship. And besides, she hadn't even done anything yet. She was only having coffee with a guy.

Maybe they'd have fun, though, and Jonathan would turn out to be someone she really clicked with. Although she wouldn't count on that happening.

On the other hand, maybe they wouldn't click, but Guillermo would find out that she'd seen someone else. What if he walked in on them right here, at Argentine? she suddenly thought. What if he then swept Jessica into his arms and confessed his love for her?

Back and forth her mind went, with one possibility and then another. She was making herself dizzy and she hadn't even had any caffeine yet.

"Are you ready to order?" asked the clerk. Her mellow smile indicated that she was very patient, or else a little stoned. Jessica wondered if Jonathan was going to stand her up, then she checked her phone and saw that it was only two minutes past six.

She was trying to decide between the Happy Hazelnut Latte and the Cosmic Cinnamon Chai when he called her name. She turned and saw him framed in the doorway with the sun shining down on his hair. He wore an expensive gray suit and looked totally different. He looked good, actually—but not at all like the guy she'd spoken to so freely at her sister's.

All of a sudden, anxiety rose up inside her like acid reflux. Why, she suddenly wondered, had she agreed to go out with someone she didn't even know?

All she had on this guy was Sabrina's word that he was nice. That could mean anything. Sabrina would think Hitler was nice if he complimented her home decor. What if this Jonathan Randall was one of those white-collar criminals who did insider trading to pay for call girls and cocaine? Again, what if he was one of those guys with a fetish for "exotic" women? Worse — what if he was a Mormon or some weird religion that wasn't into drinking and dancing?

Then again, Jessica mused, Mormons probably didn't frequent trendy Montrose coffee shops.

"Hey. Sorry I'm late," he told her. "You look great."

She looked down at herself, in her now wrinkled sweater and skirt. "Thanks. Actually, you look great. I feel kind of underdressed."

He looked down at his own suit, then waved it away. "What, you mean my work drag? I'm only wearing this because they make me."

Jessica couldn't help chuckling at that.

"So, what'll you have?" he asked.

"The Magical Mocha, I think."

"And I'll have a green tea. Thanks." Jonathan smiled at the cashier and handed her his credit card before Jessica could even think to pull her own wallet out of her bag. "Do you want to sit on the patio or stay in the A/C?"

"No, the patio's good," she said.

She followed him to the patio's far corner table, where a giant mesh of vines shaded them from the hot street. Up and down Westheimer, people were meeting up at other coffee shops and restaurants. College-age kids in vintage dresses, combat boots, and facial piercings walked in and out of the thrift shops and tattoo parlors. Socialites browsed the boutiques, and homeless people browsed trash bins. An almost cool breeze wove its way through the potted trees and into Jessica's hair as a three-piece jazz ensemble tuned up on the opposite corner of the patio. Despite herself, she began to relax. This was her neighborhood. Everything was okay.

Jonathan immediately removed his jacket. Then he sat and loosened his tie. "Sorry about that," he said. "I should've left this stuff in the car. But I was running late and didn't want to make you wait."

"Don't worry about it," Jessica said. He was the only guy in the place wearing a tie, she noticed. But obviously he'd been here before. Again she found herself intrigued. For a supposed VP, he was pretty hip.

"So, how was your day?" he asked.

She didn't know him well enough to launch into a complaint about how nosy or demanding her co-workers could be. So instead, she said, "It was good. How was yours?"

"Insane. I spent all day running from one presentation to another. I'm glad it's over and I'm here now with you."

She took a sip of her drink so she wouldn't have to reply. Normally she was pretty good at small talk, but all of a sudden, she felt shy. His tie was throwing her off her game, she decided. He looked as if he were going to interview her for a job. Or for the position of girlfriend, maybe. She smiled at the thought.

He smiled back. "So, tell me about yourself, Jessica. I know you're Sabrina's sister, that you make great-looking web sites, and that your job at McCormick must be really boring. What else?"

Again, Jessica had to laugh. "That's already way more than I know about you."

"You're right. What do you want to know? I'll tell you anything."

She looked into his sincere, very green eyes and considered the question. What did she want to know about him, then? A lot of things, suddenly. But it wouldn't do to get too personal — yet. She went with a cliché. "Where'd you go to school?"

"Here at U of H."

"Really? U of H Downtown?"

"No, Clear Lake."

Of course. It figured — he'd probably lived in a dorm and everything. "What was your major?" she asked.

"I got a BS in chemistry, then changed my mind and got my MBA at UT."

"Wow." She couldn't help adding in a semiteasing tone, "So, instead of working for a big energy company, you *could* have been a chemist, discovering a new element or something by now."

"Sure." He smiled. "Or, you know — just teaching high school chemistry."

She asked enough questions to figure out that he was in his early thirties and that being a consultant for Halronburco just meant that he found ways to do little extras for their clients and then bill them lots of extra money. He'd grown up in one of Houston's most expensive suburbs. After getting his MBA in Austin and working there for a while, he'd come back home.

"Austin was nice," he said. "Really laid-back. But almost too laid-back, you know? Like they're trying too hard to be Berkeley."

Jessica had been to Austin only a few times, once to help Toby reinstate his license at the state DMV and once to check out the South by Southwest music festival. She'd never been to Berkeley at all. But somehow, she knew what he meant.

"Yeah, I'm not too down with their whole co-op, save-endangered-insects, hipster vibe," she mused. "I guess I'm too much of a city girl. Plus, everybody who leaves Houston ends up coming back, right? It's like a guy whipping his dog, and the dog just keeps coming back for more."

He laughed. "Yeah, that about sums it up. In fact, that's the best description of Houston I ever heard."

By that point, Jessica was much more comfortable. Talking to Jonathan was easier than she'd imagined it would be. She told him her own meager history: born in Houston, went to school in Houston, working here in Houston. He listened attentively, as if she were describing someone much more exciting.

Suddenly, she heard herself say, "Do you like to dance?" Then she immediately wondered what had possessed her to ask.

He went right with the flow, though. "Sure. I love to dance."

"Really?" Now that she'd mentioned it, it *was* an important question. She loved dancing, so it made sense to find out if a guy she was potentially dating liked it, too.

"What kind of dancing are we talking about here?" he said. "Club dancing, or something more formal?"

Really, Jessica's absolute favorite was Latin dancing—especially salsa and merengue. Or cumbias. Or even the polka-sounding rancheras, if she was at a wedding and there was nothing else to do. But she figured he wouldn't know what that meant. "Have you ever danced to Spanish music?" she asked instead.

"Yes," he said. "I can do—okay, don't laugh at my pronunciation—I can do cumbias and rancheras. And a little salsa."

Jessica did laugh.

"Aw...I knew I'd say it wrong." He laughed self-deprecatingly.

"No, it's not that. I only laughed because I was surprised. Because I was just thinking that you probably didn't know what those were."

"See. There's your lesson, then," he said teasingly. "Never assume. So you like rancheras, too?"

"Sure," she said. "Really, though, I'll dance to anything. I'll two-step, if there's nothing else. Shoot, I'll even do the chicken dance if I get desperate."

They both laughed a lot after that. Jessica didn't remember, afterward, anything particularly funny that they'd said. But she was having a good time.

They talked about where they lived. He'd just moved into a town house in midtown, a few miles from Jessica's apartment in the Montrose, because the neighborhood was so "full of character."

"By character, do you mean the crack houses?" she was unable to resist asking. She still remembered when midtown was Fourth Ward—the 'hood. That was before people who looked like Jonathan started taking over.

This launched him into a big speech about the history of Fourth Ward and his involvement with the Neighborhood Preservation Alliance. Obviously, he knew way more about the changes in Houston's inner-city neighborhoods than she did, and he was actually trying to do something positive. She couldn't help but be impressed.

She told him about the neighborhood she'd grown up in before her parents had saved up the money to move to the Heights. He seemed so interested, she ended up telling him about ALMA, where her friend Marisol worked, and their mission to save poor kids through the arts.

"Wow. That sounds great. I've never even heard of ALMA."

"Well, that'll change if I get the contract to do their web site. I'm going to promote those people into the twenty-first century," Jessica told him.

"I bet you will. I can't wait to see the site when you're done. And I'd love to visit ALMA, too. Maybe you could take me there sometime."

It would have sounded like a cheesy come-on if it weren't for the fact that she could tell he really meant it. This was one serious do-gooder kind of guy, she realized. If she took him to ALMA, he'd probably join the board and then actually do some work on it. Maybe she *would* take him.

In the background, the band picked up a little. They started talking about their jobs again, and Jessica found herself admitting the ugly truth about what she did.

"...so, basically, I'm a 'junior broker' when they need someone to mess with the less profitable files, but just a secretary when it comes to everything else."

"Well, there'd be nothing to feel bad about if you *were* just a secretary," Jonathan replied earnestly. "I know if it weren't for my assistant, I'd probably be out of a job by the end of the week."

"You have your own assistant?"

"Well, no. I have to share her with four other guys."

Jessica raised an eyebrow at him. "But I bet you have your own office, huh?"

"Yes." He smiled self-deprecatingly. "I do have that. You'll have an office, too, pretty soon. I can tell. You're too smart to stay an assistant for much longer."

She looked out at the street for a moment, trying to imagine it. "We'll see."

"Hey," he said suddenly. "How about a piece of that carrot cake?"

"Oh, no thanks."

"Come on. I saw you looking at it when we were at the counter."

Jessica felt immediate embarrassment. She hoped she hadn't drooled.

"Come on. We'll share a piece."

They did share a piece. By then, the conversation was flowing easily. They talked about their favorite restaurants, homeless people who'd become local celebrities, and upcoming movies they wanted to see. Jessica eventually glanced at his watch and saw that it was already seven-thirty. They'd packed a lot of conversation into an hour and a half—she felt as if she'd known him for a whole week now.

When the cake was done and the jazz trio got too loud to talk over, they left the coffee shop and walked down the block to her car. Jessica noticed that his shirtsleeve brushed her arm once or twice.

At her car, he turned to face her. "It's still pretty early and I hate to end this now. What do you say we catch a movie? They're playing *Labor Union of Love* at River Oaks."

Jessica considered it. It *was* still early—not even eight o'clock. And she'd been wanting to see *Labor Union of Love* ever since it'd come out.

However...

This was going too fast, she realized suddenly. This was supposed to be only coffee, not a real date. Also, she told herself, this coffee date was more than enough to make Guillermo jealous all by itself. And she hadn't yet decided what to do about him.

Why, then, was she so tempted to accept Jonathan's offer?

She forced herself to say, "I can't. I made other plans. With...my friends." She smiled apologetically.

"Oh, okay. Some other time, then?" Not troubled or embarrassed at all, he turned and continued walking her to her car.

"Sure."

"All right. Then I'll give you a call?"

"Okay. Sounds good."

He leaned in toward her face. Was he going to kiss her right there on the sidewalk? she wondered, feeling her heart speed up a little. No. Instead, he did the half-hug thing, with his cheek almost touching hers.

As Jessica put on her sunglasses and started her engine, she saw him walk across the street and unlock a sleek silver A4. She adjusted her radio and peeked at him in the rearview mirror until he was gone.

Then, after a few deep breaths, she pulled away from the curb and headed toward home. She glanced at her Virgin Mary and couldn't resist giving her a smile.

# 12

The next night, Thursday, Jessica drove herself and Toby down Fairview, threading her car through drag queens as if they were traffic cones. Welcome to the Montrose, where the weekend starts early, she thought as they circled the blocks in search of legal parking. In her passenger seat, Toby fidgeted and whined.

"Oh, my God, we're never going to find a space. Come on, Jessi — just park right there at those town houses. They'll never know we don't live there."

"Forget you, boy. I'm not getting towed just so you can get there a few minutes earlier."

As they walked the three blocks to the club, Jessica waved to people they knew, and Toby waved to people he'd like to get to know.

"So what's been going on with you, Miss Thing?" asked Toby. "Are you still seeing your hot Picasso?"

"Yes." Jessica sighed. "You know — on and off. But then..."

Toby shook his head. "Oh yes. I know the old on and off. Looks like you were the last stop on the Booty Call Express." He threw his arms up in the air and snapped his fingers, calling, "Woo, woo!" like a train.

"Hey! Come on!" Jessica protested, reaching up and pushing Toby's arms back down.

He put his arm around her shoulders as they walked. "Don't feel bad. We all have to visit Dysfunction Junction at one time or another."

"What is it with you and the train talk tonight?" Jessica asked. They'd reached the door of the club. Luckily, there wasn't a line yet. The shirtless doorman held out his hand for their IDs.

"And anyway," Jessica continued, "forget about Guillermo for a sec. I have to tell you something."

"What's that?" Toby asked absentmindedly. He didn't even look at Jessica, as he was busy batting his lashes at the doorman.

"I met someone new."

"What?" Toby swung around in midflutter. But Jessica had already gone through the door.

Inside the auditorium-size club, their conversation was ended by the noise and their struggle through the throng of bodies to make it to the bar. They ordered vodka cocktails from the bartender who always let Toby drink free, then stood and surveyed the scene.

It was the same as every Thursday night at Galaxy. The sunken dance floor throbbed with the shirtless DJ's heartshaking bass. Giant videoscreens on the walls blazed an ever shifting panorama of colors. Although the crowd was dotted here and there with lesbian couples or chubby fag hags, as the gay-friendly straight women were called, it was mostly men. Hot and cold running men, in all shapes, sizes, and colors. And not one of them was interested in Jessica. It was nice sometimes not to have to worry about what men thought about her and the way she looked. The music pumped, making her hips move, and she felt all her cares melt away. She downed the last of her drink and slammed the fruit-garnished glass on the bar. "Let's go."

"Hold on, hold on. One more," said Toby.

As they ordered their second round, the action began. An older man with a graying handlebar mustache zoomed in on Toby. "Hi there," he murmured.

"Whatever," Toby said dismissively, turning his back. The man's mustache drooped sadly as he walked back the way he'd come.

A short bodybuilder with a black tank top and studded leather collar approached.

"Uh-uh, baby." Toby shook his head. "Don't come over here in those acid-washed jeans."

"Hello," said a handsome, shaved-bald man in overalls and nothing else.

Toby held up his palm to the man's face. "Talk to the white girl," he said, then flipped his hand to show the other side. "Because the black girl's not listening."

Jessica shook her head. Some of those guys had looked perfectly nice to her. But she had given up trying to figure out her friend's mating rituals a long time ago.

Out on the dance floor, they whooped and threw their hands in the air. Toby bumped and ground against Jessica like a rap star, then did the same thing with the other men on the floor.

After an hour and a half of grinding under the lights, Jessica became dehydrated. Toby motioned for them to retire to the karaoke room. The crowd there, seated at tiny tables and bar stools, was helping the man on the stage sing "Killing

Me Softly" while the drag-queen KJ conducted with graceful waves of her long-nailed hands. After getting another drink for Toby and a water bottle for Jessica, they collapsed at the first table they found.

Toby brought the conversation back to the subject that wasn't far from Jessica's mind. "Okay — tell me now. You said you met someone new. Who?"

"One of my brother-in-law's friends."

"What? One of the Pod People, you mean?" Toby had heard plenty from Jessica about Sabrina's friends.

"Yeah. Well, no. This one was different," she said. Toby gestured impatiently, so she continued. "He works at Halronburco with my brother-in-law, but he dresses better. And he likes DJ Jump-Up. We had coffee yesterday, at Argentine."

"What?" Toby exclaimed in his customarily melodramatic style. "Why didn't you tell me? What does he look like? Cute?"

Jessica felt her face flush for some reason. "Sort of, yeah. He's blond. Tall."

"Oh hell, yes, girl!" Toby's voice was fervent. "But hold on. Hold on a *minute*. When's the last time you saw Don't Call-O Montalban?"

"Guillermo, you mean? Friday night."

"Oh, my gosh! You hooker! And how was it? Did he service your muffler right?" Toby bit into his cherry seductively.

Jessica was so used to his off-color commentary, she barely noticed it anymore. "Yes. But then he ended up pissing me off, like always. Actually, I don't think I'm going to see him for a while."

"What? Why?" said Toby. "Did my mom tell your mom you were seeing him, and your mom got mad?"

"No. Wait—you didn't tell your mom I was seeing him, did you?" Jessica narrowed her eyes at him suspiciously. Toby had the bad habit of sharing secrets with his mother, and Mrs. Jimenez was notorious for turning around and telling those secrets to Jessica's mother.

"What? No! Of course not," Toby protested. "I'm just saying—why would you stop seeing Guillermo when he's so freaking hot? You're just starting out with this new guy. Jessica, you didn't sleep with him last night, did you?" His voice was more hopeful than shocked.

"No. Not even. We haven't even kissed."

Toby made a dismissive gesture then, as if that fact negated the whole date.

Jessica paused to take a long drink from her water bottle and collect her thoughts. "It's just that I'm tired of Guillermo's attitude, you know? It's been almost a week since I got mad and ran out of his house, and the jerk hasn't even called to see how I'm doing." She felt her face heat as she warmed to her subject. "All he's doing is skipping work, feeding stray animals, and painting portraits of skanky old women. He only calls me when I'm mad at him, and then he makes lame excuses. And I fall for it, so we can have make-up sex, even though we haven't technically made up. Then he goes back about his business and forgets about me. Over and over again."

"I thought you liked that stuff," Toby said. "Didn't you say he caused drama, but it keeps you from being bored? Plus, I thought you liked how he's all impulsive and into his art and doesn't care about money and all that material stuff."

Jessica snorted. "I do. I did, I mean. But that was before I realized that it's been too long since I've been on an actual date with someone who wants to get to know me and not just my body. This new guy, Jonathan, took me on a normal date. And he doesn't play games. He called me two days after we met. And then asked me out on a second date at the end of the first one. Why can't Guillermo be impulsive and artistic, but still call me up and take me out for coffee, like a normal boyfriend? Now I'm wondering what else I've been missing by dating flaky artists." She looked at the drag queen onstage, then remembered to tell Toby the part he'd be most interested in. "And anyway, Madame Hortensia predicted I was going to meet Jonathan."

"Ooh. She did? Cards or palm?" asked Toby, leaning forward to catch every detail. He was an occasional client of the fortune-teller himself.

"Cards," said Jessica. "She said I'd meet a handsome, rich man and I could either go with him or else choose to stay with Guillermo."

"But why can't you do them *both*?" said Toby. "Did she say? Because I know Guillermo doesn't have a dime to his name, but that man is *fine*. Girl, if he wasn't my mother's cousin's son..."

"Then nothing would happen, because—hello—he's straight," said Jessica. For some reason, the thought of Guillermo dating Toby, although ridiculous, made her a little jealous. Then, for the tenth time since Wednesday night, she felt guilty for having gone on the date. Then, for the *hundredth* time, she reminded herself that Guillermo hadn't called in nearly a week, so she shouldn't worry about cheating on their nonrelationship.

Toby, obviously noting the tangled emotions playing across her face, said, "Jessi, if you want Guillermo to act right, you have to play hard to get. Quit going over to his house whenever he calls you. Quit being home when he shows up. Leave your phone off once in a while. Make him chase you. Latinos are into that stuff."

Jessica shook her head. A year ago, she might have eaten up his advice. "No. I'm tired of that *Rules* mess. Why does it have to be that way? Why can't he just be honest and admit he wants to be with me? *If* he does." She stared into the water bottle she was swirling. That was a sobering thought. Did he really want to be with her? Sometimes she thought he did. Then again, maybe she didn't want to find out Guillermo's honest answer to that question after all.

Toby sighed. "Girl, who knows? If I could figure out men and their ways, I'd be on TV."

Another man on the stage sang another sad song. Jessica heaved a sigh of her own. Why couldn't love ever be easy?

Through the floor, up the legs of her stool, and into the bottoms of her feet, she felt the familiar bass line of her favorite club song, Sir Beat-a-Lot's "Come Again," pounding in the other room. She reminded herself that she'd paid cover to be here, and she wasn't going to waste it worrying about Guillermo. She could always do that later, when she was home alone.

"Come on. We're here to dance," she said, and led her friend back to the floor.

**13**

Friday morning, at work, Jessica's cell rang. It was Sabrina.

Jessica rolled her eyes but quickly answered before any of the guys noticed the ringing. "Hello?"

"Hey. Did Jonathan call you on Monday? He said he was going to. What'd he want?"

"Sabrina, I can't talk right now. Let me call you later."

She ignored Jessica's dismissal. "Did he ask you out? What'd you tell him?"

"Who said he called?" Jessica wasn't about to tell her business to Sabrina—that woman was nosy enough as it was. Suddenly, though, Jessica changed tactics, realizing this was her chance to question her sister about Jonathan. "Sabrina, how well do you know this guy? He's not secretly an ax murderer or anything, is he?"

"What? Girl, no! He's *super* nice. David's been friends with him for a long time. You know, now that I think about it..." Jessica heard her sister go into matchmaker mode. "I should've set you up with Jonathan a long time ago. Except I thought he was already seeing somebody. So he asked you out and you told him yes? Where are y'all going to go?"

Jessica spoke aloud to the air. "Yes, Mr. Cochran. I'll get that to you right away." Across the room, Olga looked up from her solitaire game in confusion. "I've got to go, Sabrina. I'll call you later."

"Jessica! Babosa—"

Jessica hung up, then switched her cell to vibrate just as her work phone rang.

"Jessica Luna."

"Jessica. Hi. It's Jonathan. Do you have a minute?"

She looked around the room. Olga and Rochelle seemed busy, but she leaned as close to her phone as she could to keep them from overhearing. "Yes," she said. "How's it going?"

"It's going good," he said. "I wanted to tell you, I had a great time Wednesday."

She smiled. "I had fun, too."

"Good. So...I was wondering if you have any time to hang out this weekend. I know it's late notice, but I was thinking, if you wanted to see that movie with me..."

Jessica repressed a giggle. Once again, she felt a rush of excitement at being pursued by someone like Jonathan. So far he hadn't turned out to be an annoying corporate clone. And, she told herself, he had good taste in women.

And he knew how to treat a woman, obviously. Unlike Guillermo. Again, Jessica felt a flash of annoyance at the difference in the two men's behavior. Jonathan barely knew her, but he wanted to get to know her. Guillermo had known her for half a year already, and he wasn't even making an effort. Well, she thought, at least Guillermo made something easy for her—the decision to tell Jonathan yes.

"I'd love to go to the movies," she told Jonathan. "Do you still want to see *Labor Union of Love?*"

"Yes. Unless you want to see something else."

"No, let's see that one. I love Amber Chavez," Jessica said. They made plans for a late afternoon show the next day and said good-bye.

Jessica got up and went down the hall.

In the ladies' room, she examined her reflection in the mirror. She'd done this a hundred times before, of course. But this time she was trying to see what Jonathan saw when he looked at her.

Toby always joked about her curves, and she always joked right back, saying she was hot enough to get any construction worker she wanted. Her curves had certainly gotten Guillermo's attention. But what about Jonathan? Would a guy like that appreciate a woman like her? she had to wonder. She reasoned that he was interested in her looks enough to pursue her this far, but what if she was just more round than what he'd been able to see in the coffee shop or in her sister's orange Tuscan kitchen?

And then she turned and looked over her shoulder at the rear view. What would he think when he saw—*really* saw—her? She tried to remember if he'd seen her from this angle yet. The first time, she'd been standing by Sabrina's kitchen island, so no.... At Argentine, they'd mostly been sitting down.... What about when she'd walked out to the patio? she suddenly remembered. How had she looked? She wiggled her ample hips at her reflection, trying to simulate walking, and watched to see if anything jiggled.

"Girl, what in the world are you doing?" Rochelle stood in the doorway of the restroom, watching Jessica with great interest.

Jessica spun to face her. "Nothing. Just...nothing."

Rochelle chuckled and said, "You look fine. And your phone's been ringing off the hook."

Back at her desk, Jessica picked up a message from Marisol and immediately called her back.

"So how'd it go? Tell me everything, quick," Marisol said right off the bat.

"It went good. But I can't talk about it here," said Jessica.

"Darn. Okay, well, that's not the only reason I called." Marisol sounded rushed, as she always did at work. "Remember how I told you we were trying to get a grant to do the web site?"

"Yeah?"

"Well, we got it. And I told Esmeralda that you were perfect for the job, since you used to be an ALMA student and all. But she says you still have to go through the formal bid process with the board. So, how fast can you come up with a presentation?"

"Oh, my God. I don't know. How much time do I have?"

"Well, Web D Lux is presenting next week," said Marisol.

"What? Web D Lux sucks!" Jessica wrinkled her nose in distaste. "They use templates!"

"I know. They're coming in Wednesday, though."

"Okay. I'll be there Wednesday evening, then," Jessica said resolutely. She would just have to work on her demo all weekend, she told herself. When she wasn't out with Jonathan, that was.

"All right," said Marisol. "I'll tell Esmeralda. I gotta go, chica. It's crazy busy over here."

"Okay. Marisol — thank you so much."

"Of course. What are best friends for?"

Xavier was too busy to meet for their usual Friday lunch, so Jessica had planned to eat at her desk and surf the web. But now she decided to go eat on the patio and make notes for her ALMA presentation instead. It helped that she knew

ALMA so well. She and Marisol had attended art classes there when they were kids. And she'd done volunteer graphic work for them before.

As she took the elevator downstairs to the deli, Jessica realized that this was another one of Madame Hortensia's predictions coming true.

## 14

Jessica had gone home Friday and worked on the ALMA site, then woken up Saturday morning and worked on it some more. Then it was break time, so she decided to get some lunch and do a little shopping.

At the mall, while she searched through sale racks for a top that might look cute on a date to the movies, Jessica's cell rang. She hung up all the clothes hangers she'd been carrying and dug the phone out of her purse.

It was Guillermo calling. Jessica was so surprised, she dropped her phone. By the time she picked it up, it'd stopped ringing. She watched the screen hesitantly, wondering if the voice-mail icon would pop up.

After several moments, it did. She immediately listened to the message.

"Chiquitita. Hi. You said I don't call you enough, so I'm calling you now. Where are you? Having a good time, I hope. Okay, well...I hope you aren't still mad about what happened. I don't care about that woman, chiquitita. I thought you knew that I was kidding and I only care about you. Well, okay...call me back. I still needed you to look at the rest of the paintings. I'll cook for you again. If you're hungry."

Jessica hung up and felt a wave of guilt wash over her. Guillermo had called to apologize and profess his feelings for her, and here she was shopping for an outfit to wear with another man.

*No,* she told herself then. *Don't go down that road.* He hadn't even actually apologized, she realized. Really, he hadn't even sounded as if he felt that bad about what he'd done. How many times, she reminded herself, had they been through stuff like this? How many times had he said insensitive things, or neglected to call her, and then played it off with a few sweet words? And she'd let him get away with it. And now, she forced herself to realize, he was calling her because he needed her help, and not even for a real date.

"Not this time," she told her phone, before dropping it back into her bag. "Too little, too late."

Later, back at her apartment, she tried on all the new tops again before deciding on the best one. She'd decided to wear jeans, since it would be cool in the theater. She checked her reflection in the mirror. Yes, her butt was big, she told herself, but there was no use trying to hide that fact. Jonathan would either like it or lump it, she decided.

It was obvious, when he showed up at her front door, that he liked it.

"You look great," he said, looking her up and down, but not in a lecherous way.

"Thanks," she said. "You do, too." And he did. He didn't wear his jeans tight, like Guillermo, but he still looked good in them. His T-shirt and tennis shoes, she noticed, looked as though they each cost more than her entire outfit.

"I like your place," he said.

"Do you?" she said, wondering if he was being polite. She

liked her apartment but couldn't imagine him feeling comfortable in a dump like this if he owned a town house in midtown. "I would give you a tour, but this is pretty much all there is to see." She indicated the living room/office and the kitchen with a sweep of her hand. The doorways leading to the bed and bath were visible from where they stood.

"It's awesome," he said, smiling. "We need to head out if we're going to make the five o'clock show."

She followed him down the stairs and out to the street, where he'd parked his Audi. He held the door for her, and she climbed into the leather interior. After making sure she was comfortable, he drove them to the theater.

Jessica's phone rang again. She glanced down and, seeing Guillermo's name, frowned and turned it off.

"Did you need to take that call?" Jonathan asked, all solicitous smiles from the driver's seat. "Go ahead. I don't mind."

"Oh, don't worry," said Jessica, smiling back. "It was no one."

It was too bad, Jessica thought, that after such a good beginning to their evening, the movie had been terrible. As they emerged from the theater, she decided that Amber Chavez had totally sold out.

"That Amber Chavez—she's really beautiful," said Jonathan. "You kind of resemble her, actually. I bet people tell you that all the time."

Jessica said, "No, you're the first." It was funny—she *wished* people told her that all the time. But they didn't, because no matter how many highlights she got, Jessica really looked nothing like the actress. Did Jonathan just think all Latinas looked the same?

She was wondering how worked up she should let herself get over that when he asked, "So what'd you think of the movie?"

"I don't know...." She didn't want to hurt his feelings, since he seemed to have liked it. And since he'd paid for the tickets. But at the same time, what was the point of going to a movie with someone if you weren't going to share your opinions of it afterward? "I'm just getting tired of these movies where a bunch of minority people need a white guy to save the world for them," she started up. "Like Kevin Costner in *Dances with Wolves*. Or Tom Cruise in *The Last Samurai*, or that blond guy in *Lambada: The Forbidden Dance*. Why is it that only white guys can be heroes? No offense...."

"None taken." He seemed genuinely interested in her opinion, so she went on.

"Plus, Troy Grodin wasn't a convincing hero anyway. He couldn't even read his lines, much less start a union and save all those people from the INS. *Plus*, he and Amber Chavez had no chemistry at *all*."

Jonathan laughed. "Yeah, you're right. Plus, there's no way he could have driven a Mustang over a river like that. I know—I've tried."

Jessica laughed, not even knowing whether or not to believe him.

"All right. So that one was no good," he said. "I'll have to take you to a better movie, to make it up to you." By then, they were in the parking lot. "In the meantime, what do you say we grab something to eat?"

He'd said the magic words. She was starving.

"Anywhere you want to go," he said.

It was refreshing, Jessica thought, to be with a man who was so considerate and accommodating. "How about Moonlight Diner?" she suggested.

"Good choice," he said.

At the diner, they took a corner booth. At Jonathan's urging, Jessica ordered a strawberry milk shake along with her burger and fries.

"I'll probably gain five pounds by tomorrow," she said ruefully.

He pretended to look her over, then said, "You have a long way to go before you need to worry about that."

Jessica demurred modestly but was secretly pleased and relieved to find that he didn't think she was too fat. Not that *she* thought of herself as fat—she didn't. It was just good to know that her self-confidence held up in a multicultural setting.

While they ate, Jessica and Jonathan chatted about other movies they'd hated and movies they'd liked. He was into action and she was into romance, but they both agreed on comedy and indie films. They traded funny stories about their work. Jonathan's was about a demanding client, Jessica's about her demanding bosses. Then the talk turned to music.

"Seriously—I'd really like to take you to a show next Friday, if you're free," he said. "Do you like Junior Ruiz?"

Jessica had only just heard of Junior Ruiz, the reggaeton DJ, and was surprised by Jonathan's in-depth knowledge of the latest trends. She agreed to go to the show with him, and Jonathan was flatteringly pleased.

"We can go to dinner first," he suggested. "Do you like sushi?"

"I love it," Jessica said.

"Have you been to Ahi?"

Again, Jonathan impressed her. Ahi was the trendiest sushi bar in midtown, and it required reservations at least a week in advance. "I haven't been yet," she admitted. "To be honest, I'd be scared to go and have the valets laugh at my car."

Jonathan laughed himself. "It's not one of those kinds of places. You'll see — it's fun."

As usual, he paid the check while she was still fumbling with her wallet, waving away her offer to go halves. As they walked out to the car, Jessica felt dizzy. Whether it was from the sugar rush or the fact that she'd just accepted date number three with a Halronburco vice president, she wasn't sure.

The ride back to her place passed quickly in a blur of streetlights. As he walked her up to her door, Jessica couldn't help but feel some butterflies. It was their second date — if you counted the coffee as the first. Was he going to kiss her? Should she invite him in? She tried to remember the last time she'd gone on a typical second date, instead of seducing or being seduced by someone in an entirely inappropriate way.

At the top of the stairs, she remembered that she didn't have anything to offer him anyway, except for diet soda. If she was going to date this guy on a regular basis, she told herself, she'd have to buy a couple of bottles of wine. Classy wine. And a corkscrew.... *Stop it*, she told herself. *You're mentally babbling.*

When they reached the door, though, she managed to turn to him with perfect poise and a smile. "I had a good time."

"I did, too."

She took her keys from her purse and held them tight as

she unlocked the door, so he wouldn't see her fingers tremble and know how nervous she was. Finally, the door open, she turned to him again, her mind racing over multiple options of what to say.

"I can't wait to see you next week," he said, leaning forward. "I'll call you, okay?"

"Okay," she said, looking up at him. As he leaned closer, her eyelids seemed to know just when to close. Very lightly, his lips brushed hers, his hands holding her shoulders gently.

Then he pulled away, and her eyes opened to his smile.

"Okay. Bye!" Before she had time to say anything else, he turned and left.

She stood on her balcony and watched him drive away, then thought, Well, that wasn't bad at all.

Inside her apartment, she kicked off her shoes and threw her purse on the table, then remembered her phone. It was still off.

There'd been two missed calls, one with a message. From Guillermo.

"Chiquitita...are you still mad? I told you I was sorry. I'm sorry, okay? Call me back."

Shaking her head, Jessica hung up the phone and left it on the table for the rest of the night.

# 15

Monday morning at work, after murmuring all the necessary greetings and taking care of the guys' biggest "emergencies"—Fred couldn't find a file, and Ted needed help opening a client's e-mail attachment that turned out to be a video of a donkey knocking down a farmer—Jessica checked her horoscope online:

"An unexpected phone call leads to exciting new possibilities. Your lucky number is 17."

She thought over all the work she'd done on the ALMA web site the day before, trying to remember something that had involved the number 17. Just in case, she tapped her pencil on her desk seventeen times.

The tapping apparently caught Olga's attention, because she looked up and started in with her usual questions. "So, did you go on any dates this weekend, Jessica?" she called across the room.

"Olga, go on and leave that girl alone," said Rochelle. "All your busybodying's going to get you in trouble one of these days."

"What?" Olga said innocently. "Jessica's young and pretty, and *single*. She should be out with men. *Rich* men. Oh, that reminds me...come here, you two."

Jessica and Rochelle went over to Olga's desk and formed a gossip huddle.

"You want to know what I heard?" Olga whispered loudly. "Mr. Cochran's thinking about hiring another broker for our department."

"Really?" Jessica's eyes widened at the prospect of something interesting happening at their office.

"Mm-hmm. He says we've been getting so much big business, we need someone to do the smaller files so the guys can have more time."

Jessica frowned. "Well, they could just give those to us."

"Not me," said Olga, shaking her head. "I don't want to be a broker. I have enough to do taking care of Mr. Cochran."

"Well, me and Rochelle, then," said Jessica.

"Who'd do our work, then?" said Rochelle.

"They could hire another assistant to help out. That'd be cheaper than hiring another broker," Jessica said. "Plus, they wouldn't have to train us. We already know what to do."

"I don't know about that. I don't know that I'd be wanting to do all that extra work," said Rochelle.

"Mr. Cochran could give us both a raise. A new title. Business cards. We'd be real brokers, full-time." Jessica was getting excited just thinking about it. It'd be nice to have her own cards. She'd have to buy some suits, too.

"Well, I don't know about all that," said Rochelle. "Something tells me Mr. Cochran isn't going to see it that way."

"Then we'll just have to make him see it that way," Jessica said. "Come on, Rochelle. This is a good opportunity for us. You don't want to keep doing the same thing forever, do you?"

Before she could reply, Mr. Cochran opened his door and cleared his throat. "Olga, I need you. If you ladies aren't too busy."

Olga jumped up to help him. Jessica and Rochelle went back to their desks.

Jessica wasn't sure if the new broker job was supposed to be confidential information. But if not, she'd tell Mr. Cochran she was interested as soon as possible. It was a really good opportunity — just like Madame Hortensia had told her to watch out for.

She had to wonder, though, if the ALMA web site was already her one big job opportunity, was she supposed to bother with pursuing a promotion at McCormick?

Maybe, to be safe, she should try her best to snag both. At least until she could go back to Madame Hortensia and find out which one was the sure thing.

**16**

The next day at work, Jessica had lunch in the cafeteria with Tiffany Wyman from the forty-second floor, her occasional source of office gossip and hangover commiseration. The minute she got back to her desk, Olga called out her name.

"Jessica, can you come help me real quick? I have to finish this thing for Mr. Cochran and I can't figure out what happened to it."

Jessica went over and looked at Olga's monitor. It displayed one of McCormick's internal job postings.

| | |
|---|---|
| DEPT: | MIDDLE MARKET |
| POSITION: | BROKER |
| SALARY GRADE: | EX-6 |
| REQUIRES: | P&C LICENSE |
| | TEAM PLAYER |
| REPORTS TO: | J. COCHRAN |

"I can't make this last part line up with the rest," Olga said forlornly.

Jessica reached over to fix it for her. "Is this a job description for our department? For the new broker?" She knew it was. It said so right there.

"I guess. I'm just typing what Mr. Cochran told me to."

Olga held up his yellow legal pad. Jessica saw that he'd written, "Give to HR asap."

There was no use freaking out, Jessica decided as she went back to her own desk. Obviously, Mr. Cochran was posting the job companywide because he had to. It was the law or something—you had to post all jobs internally first. McCormick may have been frozen in the 1950s, but they still had to follow the rules, right?

She had to make sure that she applied and got interviewed first. Who else in the company would even want the job? She was the obvious choice. How dumb would Mr. Cochran have to be *not* to promote her?

Right on cue, the man himself strolled in. Jessica gave him a few minutes to settle himself into his office, then hopped up, smoothed her skirt, and marched in after him.

"Mr. Cochran, can I talk to you for a moment?"

He looked up at her curiously. "Jessica. What is it?"

Now that she was standing before him, she, too, was wondering what on earth she was going to say. "Uh...do you mind if I close the door?"

"Be my guest."

She narrowly avoided knocking over the golf clubs he kept in the corner but managed to grab them and stay poised. *Pretend you're presenting a web site,* she told herself. "Mr. Cochran, I wanted to talk to you about my work in this department."

He looked at her and said nothing. Waiting.

"Since coming to McCormick three years ago, I've learned a lot. I've taken on more responsibilities than my predecessor did, and I've been handling a book of forty-five small accounts on my own."

"Okay." Mr. Cochran's nod showed that he was willing to take her word for it, but that he was in a hurry for her to get to the point.

"So, I wanted to let you know that I enjoy the work I've been doing, and I'd like you to consider me for any new opportunities that may come up in the future." She smiled confidently, hoping she wasn't getting Olga in trouble by hinting about the new broker position.

"Okay. Well, thank you for letting me know that, Jessica. I'll certainly keep it in mind." Mr. Cochran turned to the laptop on his antique mahogany desk. Jessica saw that he was looking at a web site for a nearby bed-and-breakfast. She stood there for a second longer, just in case he was about to mention the broker position opening up. He didn't, so she gave up and turned to go.

"Go ahead and close the door behind you," he called over his shoulder.

Jessica gave him one last smile as she closed it. He didn't notice, and it became a frown as she turned and made her way back to her desk.

Well, I tried, she told herself as she opened a spreadsheet and started a new batch of work. It occurred to her that she had never actually come right out and asked for *this* promotion, but surely a businessman like Mr. Cochran would understand her subtlety. In fact, he'd probably even see it as an asset for dealing with clients. After that, he'd be sure to realize that promoting her was a good idea.

Was it a good idea, though? she asked herself. Being a full-fledged broker meant more than just business cards and new suits. She would have a ton more responsibility, plus she'd have to travel. Not exciting travel, but flying out to meet clients and talk to them about their insurance. She stared at her monitor without seeing it, trying to imagine herself in the new role. It wasn't that she couldn't do the work — she knew she could. The question was, did she *want* to?

All of a sudden, her e-mail pinged. The sender's name was unfamiliar to her. The subject line read, "Take your career to the next level."

She opened the e-mail. It was an advertisement for energizing vitamin supplements.

But, no, it was more than that, she realized. It was a sign. She was meant to want this promotion. After all, there was no point to staying in insurance if she never meant to move upward, was there?

Jessica deleted the e-mail and got back to work.

**17**

On the way home, she plugged in the earbud to her cell and turned it on to check messages. She expected that one or both of her parents had probably called, because she hadn't heard from them in a while. She hoped they'd gotten over their argument from the week before.

Neither of her parents had called, it turned out. But Guillermo had.

"Chiquitita, you never called me back. I was thinking we would do something fun, but I guess you were too busy." There was a pause, and she heard him take a deep breath, as if he were about to do something unpleasant. "Listen, Jessica. I know I hurt you the other day, and I wish I hadn't. Like I said, I'm sorry. If you want me... Tell me if you want me to stop painting other women, and I will. That lady paid me a lot, but not enough if it means you're not going to talk to me anymore." Another pause. "Okay. Please call me back, corazón."

Jessica hung up and drove in silence, not sure what to think.

It was true that Guillermo had been a complete jerk—not just that night, but for weeks on end now. Not only did he say inconsiderate things, but he simply took her for granted in general. It was as if he thought she had nothing better to do than hang out with him, spur of the moment, to talk about art and have sex. And, sure, that had been enough for her at first, but he acted as though that were supposed to satisfy her forever, no matter how long their relationship went on.

She was tired of it. He should have stepped up his game a long time ago. She should have made him.

Then again, she couldn't help but dwell on his offer never to paint other women again. It had surprised her to hear him say such a thing—he was normally so keen on retaining his independence. He must have really been scared of losing her, to make a promise like that.

It was too bad that he didn't realize he had already lost her, practically.

Jessica rounded the curve that led to her apartment, driving on autopilot while his words nibbled at her mind. He didn't realize, she thought, then felt the old guilt again. How could he realize, when he didn't even know she was seeing someone else now?

Was she being fair? Here he was, offering to change for her, but she hadn't even given him a chance to change before moving on with someone else. After all, she told herself, it wasn't as if he could read her mind. Sure, she had gotten mad at him numerous times, but he'd never seemed to take that seriously. It was as if he expected women to get mad at men on a regular basis, as if it were part of a normal relationship. Jessica knew from experience that a lot of Latino men were like that.

What if she had sat him down and explained why she was unhappy with him? Told him that she'd wanted more out of their relationship?

Had she even known that was the case, she asked herself, before she'd started dating Jonathan?

These thoughts nagged at her as she climbed the stairs to her apartment. Then a new one flickered into her head: Why didn't Guillermo want to paint *her*?

The moment she got in the door, her phone rang again. It was Marisol.

"Are you off work?" she said.

"Yeah. I just got home."

"Okay, tell me everything now. I have a break between meetings." For once, there was hardly any background noise on Marisol's end.

While removing the least comfortable parts of her work outfit, Jessica told her friend everything that had happened with Jonathan so far. Then she took a diet soda from the refrigerator and went to the couch. She lay down and listened to Marisol's calm, therapistlike voice.

"So he kissed you once and that was it?"

"Uh-huh. Just once, and not even for a long time. Do you think that means he doesn't like me after all?"

"I seriously doubt it," said Marisol. "He's taking you out again, isn't he? Maybe he's just taking it slow, so he won't scare you off."

Jessica considered this. "Yeah, maybe he sensed that I was already a little scared, because of the suit and the VP thing."

"Right," said Marisol. "You should have told him right up front—your bosses at McCorporate have given you post-traumatic stress disorder."

Jessica laughed. "You're right. Every time I see a white guy in a suit, I have panic attacks because I'm worried he's going to try to run my life."

"But you're going out with him again," Marisol pointed out, "so it can't be that bad."

"It isn't," Jessica admitted. "It's not bad at all. Just a little weird sometimes. He always pays for everything, and we're going to Ahi Friday, which is supposed to be superexpensive, and I feel kind of..."

"Guilty for not paying your half?" Marisol supplied.

"Right."

"I wouldn't worry about it. He's been the one doing the inviting, and it's not like he can't afford to pay, right?"

"No, you're right. It's just...weird," Jessica said. "I'm just not used to this sort of thing, you know? I'm kind of worried I'll show up dressed in the wrong clothes, or I'll use the wrong fork or something. You know?"

"Please," said Marisol. "You use chopsticks better than anyone I know. Quit worrying. You're so funny—a lot of women would be complaining if the guy *didn't* have money."

Jessica chuckled. "Yeah, well, if I were that kind of woman, I'd still be a virgin right now."

It wasn't that *every* guy Jessica had ever dated had been poor, or jobless, or some total lowlife, she reflected later that evening, after she'd eaten a Lean Pocket for dinner and was painting her toenails in front of the TV.

Most of her previous boyfriends had grown up pretty much like her—in not-too-fancy houses, in not-too-fancy neighborhoods. Their parents had all worked hard for what they had. Some of them had parents who had never learned English.

She felt most comfortable around people who knew how it felt to go to school in hand-me-downs or to eat tortillas and beans for dinner sometimes. Or even to have the electricity shut off once in a while, which had happened to her family. She'd brought a boy home from school to work on a project, and when they'd gotten there, the lights were off because her parents hadn't been able to pay the bill. The boy's name was Bryan. Jessica had had to explain in great detail—why the lights were off, why they hadn't paid the bill, the fact that her parents, unlike his, didn't have tons of money in savings in case of emergency. It was one of the most embarrassing things that had ever happened to her. Sabrina had managed to avoid the whole situation by staying at a friend's house that weekend, Jessica remembered.

Her family hadn't always been poor. But those memories were a part of her, and they shaped her. She was pretty sure it also influenced whom she decided to befriend and even affected whom she chose to date. She preferred men who'd grown up like her, who'd had to work for what they wanted. And who had dark hair. And dark eyes. Like Guillermo.

Thinking of Guillermo again made her remember the voice mail he'd left.

She put down the nail polish bottle and picked up her phone again. After calling up his number on the screen, she sat and stared at it for a while, wondering what she would say.

*Guillermo, I'm seeing someone else.*

No. Not that.

*Guillermo, I want to keep seeing you, but only if you get a normal day job and start taking me on regular dates.*

She tried to imagine that happening and was completely

unable to. If Guillermo got a normal day job, he wouldn't even be the same person.

Jessica sighed. She didn't know what she wanted him to do. She put the phone back down. Then she realized what she needed: an unbiased, expert opinion.

She decided to visit Madame Hortensia the next day.

# 18

Jessica had just enough time after work to get a reading before her ALMA web site presentation. Luckily, most of the ALMA employees kept irregular hours, making it possible for her to present her concept in the evening and not have to take time off work.

Jessica sped to the little purple house, then hurried up to its front door, wanting to fit as much fortune-telling as possible into her schedule.

"Hola, m'ija. Back so soon?" said Madame Hortensia, setting down a plate of chicharrones and wiping her hands on her kitchen towel.

"I need another reading, please. If you have time."

"We did the cards last week," said Madame Hortensia. "Would you like to try a palm reading this time?"

"Yes. Sure." Jessica sat at the little table and took a deep breath, trying to clear her mind. She didn't want the reading to be influenced by her mood. It was important that she find out exactly what was supposed to happen.

"Okay." Madame Hortensia took Jessica's hand and rubbed the palm with her thumbs a few times, as if cleaning Ash Wednesday ashes off of it. "Let's see..."

She studied each line on Jessica's hand, sometimes tracing them with her fingertip. "Remind me, m'ija, what we said last time."

Jessica sighed. "That I was going to meet a new man, and have a new opportunity in my career."

"And did you?"

"Yes."

Madame Hortensia waited for her to go on.

Jessica wondered how much detail she should go into. Maybe Madame Hortensia, being psychic, already knew what had happened. But she probably wanted to hear Jessica's take on it anyway. "I met the rich, handsome guy and went out with him a couple of times. But now the poor, handsome guy is calling me, wanting to see me again. I don't know what to do. Oh, and there was a new opportunity at my job. And a new job opportunity with another company, too."

The old woman studied her face for a while, then looked back down at her palm.

"Okay. I see in your past a rocky road. You have been through many things, and had to make some tough decisions, no?"

Jessica nodded. It was the truth.

"And now, in the present, I see confusion. You have several choices in front of you, and you don't know which one to take. There are two men. One of them has caused you some pain, no?"

Jessica nodded.

"But now," Madame Hortensia went on, "with this other man entering your life, you are unsure of the future. You're afraid to make the wrong choice, no?"

Jessica nodded again. It was uncanny how you could see so much about a person's life in the palm of a hand.

"Well, you shouldn't be afraid," the fortune-teller said. "In the next few weeks, something will happen. You will receive a sign."

"What kind of sign?"

"It could be anything. You'll have to watch for it. When it happens, you'll know which choice you have to make."

"Okay." Jessica frowned a little. "A choice about what, though? Whether or not I'm supposed to keep going out with the old guy, or whether or not I'm supposed to move forward with the new guy, or what?"

Madame Hortensia let go of her hand and leaned back. "What does he look like, this new man? You say he is handsome, like I predicted?"

"Well, not supermodel handsome," Jessica said. "But pretty cute, yeah. He's tall, too."

"And he's rich?" asked Madame Hortensia.

"Not a millionaire or anything, but he's definitely upper-middle-class. I'm pretty sure he's the guy you predicted would show up," said Jessica.

"Okay." Madame Hortensia nodded sagely, then examined Jessica's palm again. "I see that you're very conflicted, and a single sign might not be enough. There is unfinished business between you and the first man, and you are unwilling to let him go until it's done. At the same time, you are interested in the new man, but something is holding you back, and you need more time before you can make him the priority in your life."

"Yes," said Jessica. "That's exactly how it is!" Now they were getting somewhere. "So . . . what do I do?"

"Go ahead and date the new man," said Madame Hortensia. "But don't go too fast — not unless you see a sign that tells you to move forward. At the same time, try to wrap up loose ends with the first man. Unless, of course, a sign comes that tells you the two of you are meant to be together."

"Okay." Jessica sighed. That was as clear-cut as she could expect to hear it, she supposed.

"Good. Now, on to your career. Why don't you just go ahead and tell me, m'ija, what form your job opportunities have taken? Your palm is a little unclear." The old woman rubbed at it again.

Jessica felt self-conscious and wished she had thought to wash her hands before the reading. "Well, there's a job opening in my department. For a job that's above mine, but it's stuff that I already know how to do." She decided not to get into all the details of marketing and renewing commercial insurance. She didn't want to confuse Madame Hortensia or put her to sleep.

"Is this new job something you want to do?"

Jessica shrugged. "Well, it pays more. And they'd give me my own business cards. And I'd get to buy suits. But I'd have to travel, too. And it'd be kind of boring."

"Have you applied for this job already?"

"Not formally. Not yet," Jessica said. "But I will," she added when the old woman looked up sharply. Sometimes the way Madame Hortensia stared at her during these readings made her feel uncomfortable, like a child stuttering through a spelling bee. Again, she studied Jessica's palm for a verdict.

"Okay. I'm seeing a misty path ahead of you. On the one hand, you have the opportunity for advancement, increased wealth, and respect. But this opportunity is shrouded in mystery. You aren't sure that it's really what you want. On the other hand, you have an opportunity to try something new. But you can't see far up that path, either, and you worry that it may lead to financial instability. Correct?"

"Yes," Jessica said fervently. It was as though Madame Hortensia were seeing her whole life through her palm. "That's exactly what's going on. So what's going to happen? What should I do?"

"You watch for more signs," said Madame Hortensia. "Go ahead and apply for the job, but don't accept any offers until you know for sure that's what you want to do. At the same time, keep working at the other opportunity, and if you get a sign that it's going to work out for you, go ahead and switch jobs."

Jessica sighed. It sounded so easy and clear-cut when Madame Hortensia said it. But she knew that the minute she drove off alone, her life would turn fuzzy and confusing again. It always did.

Madame Hortensia stood up, so Jessica did, too, and fished in her purse for a twenty. Already, she was dreading walking out the door. "Oh, but—Madame Hortensia, what do I do if the other man asks me out for this weekend, too?"

"You mean the painter? The mexicano?"

"Yes."

"Make sure you don't put your date with him on the same night as your date with the bolillo."

"Okay." Jessica felt dumb for having asked. "But...should I call him?"

Madame Hortensia studied her critically and a little impatiently. "If you called him, what would you say?"

Jessica thought this question over. "I don't know," she finally admitted.

"Then don't call him. Unless you get a sign saying you should." Madame Hortensia walked to the door abruptly then, signaling that the reading was over.

Jessica followed, feeling slightly panicked now. "I'm just worried, though. I just don't want to get a sign and then miss it."

"I understand. I might have something that can help you." Madame Hortensia turned and disappeared through the beaded curtain for a while. She came back with a necklace. It was a fake gold chain with a medal that had a pyramid and an eye—not at all the sort of thing Jessica would wear on her own. She held it up for Jessica's inspection.

"What does it do?" Jessica asked dubiously.

"It's for luck, and to help you look out for your signs. So that's eighteen dollars for your discounted reading, plus fourteen for the medal."

Jessica felt silly, but she searched for the extra bills and handed them over. She really did need all the help she could get. "Thank you, Madame Hortensia."

"Ándale. Hurry now, m'ija. My dinner is getting cold."

19

friday, at Taqueria Aztlán, the first thing Jessica did was show Xavier the mock-up of the web site she'd made for her ALMA presentation. "...and so, after I knocked off a few hundred dollars, that's the figure I came up with. Which is still a good hourly wage for me. What do you think? Too much?"

"Not in the real world, no. But you said they don't have a lot of money."

"They don't. But they're not paying for this. They got a grant." They'd skipped lunch for one Friday, Jessica thought, and now it felt as if she were trying to catch him up on two years' worth of events.

Xavier's thoughts on the ALMA site were very encouraging. "Even if Web D Lux's bid is half as much as yours, your site is going to be way better. You were an ALMA student, so you know their organization better than anyone. And your ideas kick ass. Web D Lux is just a cookie-cutter outfit, and you have real artistic talent. Seriously, Jess, I don't know what you're doing working in insurance."

Jessica sighed. "I told you. No one wants a web designer. Everybody wants a web designer, plus programmer, plus tech writer, all for the same salary I get paid as an administrative assistant." She knew this because she checked the job sites religiously, then wished she had gone to technical school instead of college. "Hey, if I need some back-end work on this one, will you subcontract for me? I'll pay you in beans and rice."

"Nah. These jalapeños are good enough." He took hers from her plate.

"So how's life in Tech Support today?" Jessica asked as she spooned the sour cream from Xavier's plate and applied it to her own quesadillas.

"Crazy already. Linda Johnson deleted Special Accounts' shared-drive folder and we had to do a system restore. Then she deleted it again."

Jessica grimaced in empathy. "How do you stand it?"

"By getting out of the building for lunch."

"So what else is going on?"

"Well, Cynthia called to request a new keyboard, because she kept breaking her fingernails in the old one."

"And you were the one to replace it for her?"

"Yep."

"I'm telling you, Xavier, she wants you back."

"No, I don't think so. I'm starting to think that she really does need that much help, whether it's coming from her ex-boyfriend or not. I just didn't notice how high-maintenance she was when we were dating, because I liked going up there all the time."

Jessica snorted. "Uh, hello—how could you *not* notice that she was high-maintenance? No offense, but she had you doing stuff for her all the time."

"No, she didn't. What are you talking about?"

"Come on. You had to drive her somewhere for lunch almost every single day. Then, every weekend you were taking her somewhere crazy and spending tons of money."

"I wasn't spending *tons* of money. It wasn't like she drank or ate a lot," he reflected. "All we did was go to San Antonio once. And then to those cooking classes. And, really, mostly we just went to the zoo."

Jessica shook her head. She wasn't going to say it, because Xavier was her friend, but Cynthia had had him totally whipped. "She didn't deserve all that. I bet you wish now that you'd spent all that time doing something else."

"Why would I wish that? I had fun."

"Right. Then why'd y'all break up?"

"I told you. We realized we didn't have that much in common."

Jessica decided to drop it. She could feel herself getting unreasonably annoyed. For some reason, talking about Cynthia did that to her. Probably because she'd hated seeing Xavier being taken advantage of. She changed the subject. "What are you doing this weekend? Are you going to get fall-down, throw-up drunk tonight?"

"I have to stay late tonight for McCormick's server switch, remember?"

"Oh yeah."

"Then tomorrow's my cousin's wedding."

"Oh yeah. The one who just had the baby, right?" Jessica tried to imagine him at a wedding, there with his glasses and his BlackBerry at the Knights of Columbus hall. "Are you going to dance?"

"Of course. My mom will kill me if I don't go around and ask all my aunts. I won't do the macarena or the Cotton-Eyed Joe, though. That's too much."

Jessica nodded. The Cotton-Eyed Joe *was* too much.

"What about you?" he asked. "Did you and What's-his-name kiss and make up?"

She sighed and picked at her wilted lettuce. "Let's not discuss him, okay?"

"Aw, man. I'm sorry."

Xavier looked so upset on her behalf, she reached out and touched his arm in gratitude. "Don't be. It's no big deal. Besides, you'll never guess what happened."

He pretended to think about it, then said, "You bought another purse and your closet exploded?"

Jessica laughed. "No."

"Tell me."

"Okay. This is totally random, but I met some guy at my sister's barbecue the weekend before last, and he asked me out."

Xavier did look a little surprised at that.

"I know. Weird, huh?" Jessica made a comical face.

He didn't laugh. "What was weird about it?"

"I don't know. He's some vice president at my brother-in-law's work. When he first started talking to me, I thought he was a mailroom guy or something. Then, when he said he wanted to have coffee, I was completely shocked."

"Why? Of course he asked you out. You're pretty." He sounded a little exasperated. Jessica felt herself blush for some reason. She had always assumed Xavier thought of her as just average. Especially since he'd been so in love with Cynthia, the petite princess who made Jessica look like a football player in drag. She stirred some sweetener into her tea.

"So what'd you tell him?" Xavier prompted.

"Well, I went ahead and said yes."

"Hm." He took a bite of his quesadilla. Jessica ate some of hers, too. For some reason, she'd expected him to be more interested in this new development in her life. He took a sip of tea, then finally asked, "So y'all are going out this weekend?"

"Actually, we already went. That Wednesday, then again last Saturday."

Xavier's iced tea went down the wrong way and he coughed a little. "Wow. That was fast."

"I know, right? But the first time was only coffee, and the second time he barely even tried to kiss me." Jessica decided to take the opportunity to ask Xavier's advice. "You're a guy. What does that mean? Maybe he thinks I'm too fat. I told you he's white, right?"

"You're not too fat," Xavier said, still in the exasperated tone. "Did he ask you out again?"

Jessica waited for the waitress to come by and refill their glasses before she answered. "Yes. To dinner and a club, tonight."

"He likes you, then."

Jessica couldn't help questioning his decision. "You think so? I don't know. I mean, he hasn't even *tried* to make a move." She hoped he'd go into more detail about how she looked to other guys.

"Jess, not all guys are like Guillermo, you know." Immediately, Xavier looked embarrassed. "I'm sorry. That was...I'm sorry."

Jessica stirred her pico de gallo and didn't say anything. She couldn't—he was totally right. It was like Marisol had said—she'd become so used to Guillermo's ways, she really didn't know how to act with someone like Jonathan. Someone nice and genuinely interested in her, for more than just sex.

Xavier ate a piece of jalapeño, then asked, "So you think you might get serious with this new guy?"

"Maybe," she said. "I'm not sure yet. I'm still kind of getting over the Guillermo thing. What do you think — should I just move on?"

Jessica liked to get Xavier's perspective on things. He was like a male Madame Hortensia, but not as vague. She trusted his opinion of the web sites she made. And a few months ago, his tactful remarks had totally saved her from going overboard with the fake-flower fashion trend. If anyone's advice was worth taking, it was Xavier's. She looked across the table at him and waited for his verdict.

He shrugged. "He's a nice guy, right?"

"Yes. He's really nice. He treats me like a princess. And he's cute, too."

Xavier shrugged again. "Give him a chance, then, if you want."

She sighed. "Okay. You're probably right. Like always."

"I'm not *always* right." He smiled wryly. "Just most of the time."

Jessica leaned forward for more sweetener, and her pyramid-and-eye medal swung forward from the V neck of her sweater.

"What's that?" said Xavier, noticing it immediately.

"It's...um...a necklace. For luck."

"Oh." He didn't say anything else, but she could tell by his raised eyebrow that he was noticing how funky it looked.

She realized then that it was impossible to feel lucky in cheap, ugly accessories. When they got back into his car, she took off the medal and dropped it into her purse.

That evening, while getting ready for her third date with Jonathan, Jessica spent some time trying to decide what to wear. She didn't want to dress up per se, since they were only going to dinner and a club. But she didn't want to look out of place — or too cheap — at Ahi.

She finally settled on basic black, with a simple halter top and a flounced skirt that managed to be sexy yet flattering at the same time. In fact, it was one of Guillermo's favorites. But she pushed that thought aside, not wanting to think about Guillermo anymore tonight. She dressed up the outfit with silver sandals and a few pieces of jewelry, then checked her hair and makeup one last time. She was a little nervous, as usual, but mostly just excited. She couldn't wait to see Ahi or to hear the new music.

Jonathan knocked at her door right on time. It was immediately obvious from the look on his face that he liked the skirt, too.

"Wow. You look awesome."

"Thank you. Do you want to come in and have a drink before we go?" Jessica was proud of the fact that she'd gone to the grocery store and liquor store after work. She could now offer him red or white wine, a vodka martini, or imported beer.

"We can," he said affably, "but we're getting pretty close to our reservation."

"Oh, okay." Jessica went to get her purse and keys. She

felt—not disappointed, exactly, but a little confused. Jonathan was all about the events, she'd noticed. This was their third date, and he didn't seem interested in taking advantage of her at all. It flashed through her mind, suddenly, that he might be gay. Maybe he was just using her as his beard?

But he dispelled this thought with his next comment. "I wish we did have more time. Actually, I'd like to invite you to my place sometime soon. I just finished doing some renovations, and I'd love to have you over for a drink and show them to you. Maybe tonight, after the..." He gave a self-deprecating laugh then. "Well, I don't want to get too far ahead of myself."

Jessica smiled at him encouragingly as she locked her door and followed him down the metal stairs. "Don't worry. I'd love to see your place."

At the restaurant, which wasn't too far from Jessica's neighborhood, they valeted his Audi and stepped inside to find a crowded waiting area. The hostess informed them that reservations were running behind and they'd have to wait at least forty-five minutes. Jessica tried to hide her disappointment. From the moment she'd walked in and seen the ultratrendy lighting and decor, she'd been dying to try the food. It was too bad she wouldn't be able to now, unless she wanted to stand around for an hour, which she didn't. There wasn't even any seating at the bar.

Jonathan turned to her and started to apologize, but then, suddenly, a man in a suit came out from behind the bar and called his name.

"Do you mind waiting here a second?" Jonathan asked her,

then went to talk to the man. While Jessica watched, they smiled and laughed like old friends. Then Jonathan waved Jessica over to the bar area and introduced them. "Jessica, this is Ron. Ron, this is my friend Jessica."

"How are you?" Ron said to her. Then, to Jonathan, "All right. I hope you guys enjoy dinner. I wish I had more time to talk, but—"

"We understand," said Jonathan. "Do what you have to do."

"Okay. Let's get together for a drink sometime, then. I'll call you."

Ron went over to the hostess then and said something in her ear. Jessica saw that he pointed to them in a subtle way. The hostess nodded, and Ron bustled away.

"Let's just wait here for a few minutes," Jonathan said.

Before Jessica knew it, the hostess was coming to join them. "Your table is ready now, Mr. Randall."

"Was that the owner?" Jessica asked as they followed her to a black-lacquered corner table for two.

"Yes," said Jonathan. "I bring a lot of important clients here for lunch, so he's returning the favor." With a hand on the small of her back, he helped Jessica onto her tall, leather-seated stool.

Their waitress walked up almost immediately, and Jessica saw that she was a beautiful Asian drag queen. Like the other servers, she wore a black suit. The place was trendier than the M·A·C salon in the Galleria. Looking at all the black clothes and hipness dehydrated Jessica, so she ordered plain water.

"Are you sure?" Jonathan asked. "You don't want a drink?"

"Maybe in a little while."

While they waited for her water and his iced tea, Jessica didn't know whether to focus on all the beautiful sushi on the menu or all the beautiful people seated around them. Rich-looking men and model-pretty women were everywhere. Lots of peroxide and implants. And lots of *gorgeous* bags. Jessica spotted the newest Dolce & Gabbana just two tables away.

"The lotus roll is pretty good," said Jonathan. "It's lobster — cooked — and the bigger roe. But they can leave that off if you don't like it."

Jessica glanced over her menu and saw that this lotus roll was twenty-nine dollars. And it didn't even say how many pieces. "I don't mind the eggs," she said. "But I usually just get the tiger-eye."

"Is that all?" Jonathan said. "Come on. Order more than that, please, or I'll look like a pig next to you."

The waitress had glided up and was waiting. Jessica told her, "I'll have the tiger-eye, plus two salmons and one barbe-cued eel."

"There you go," said Jonathan. "And we'll also have a lotus, a dragon, one Cajun hand roll, and the Bayou City roll. And let's try the Go 'Stros roll. And an order of toro, sashimi style. Oh, and another barbecued eel, please."

The waitress glided back to the kitchen. Jessica looked at Jonathan with a raised eyebrow.

"We don't have to eat it all," he said innocently. "I just wanted you to taste all my favorites. This is my treat, by the way."

There was no way Jessica could have afforded the entire meal, but she wanted to at least offer to pay for part of it.

"But you got the movie last time," she protested. "And dinner. And the coffee the time before that."

"Did I?" He smiled. "All right. You treat next time, then."

The sushi was awesome. Jessica ate as much as she could without having to unzip her skirt. The owner had sent over a bottle of sake, and then Jonathan wanted to order another, but she'd had to refuse. She was already getting a buzz.

They talked the whole time, picking up where they'd left off over coffee. This time, Jessica learned about Jonathan's parents, his sister in Oklahoma, more about the volunteer work he did, and a little about his previous girlfriend, who'd moved back to Austin. He gave her so much personal history, it was as if he were trying to hurry and get all the questions out of the way. As if he were interviewing for the position of boyfriend.

In return, Jessica told him a little more about herself. He seemed impressed that she'd been the first person in her family to get a degree. She told him how she'd worked at the Centro de Artes Culturales after graduating from college. She left out the part about her ex, Robert. "And then I went into insurance when Sabrina hooked me up at McCormick."

"Why'd you leave nonprofit?" he asked.

"Because I figured out that I could get paid more as a corporate assistant than I got being the community center's curator, receptionist, chauffeur, and maid. The only way to make any money in nonprofit is to get paid by the hour, as an artist or a teacher. Or as a grant writer who brings in the money for the artists and the teachers."

"That makes sense, I guess," he said, pushing the last of the lobster roll to her side of the table. "It's too bad they didn't see your skills as an artist, though. Your face lights up when you talk about the people you helped."

She nodded thoughtfully, then said, "It's too bad that lit-up faces don't pay the rent."

He laughed. "You're right. They don't."

Maybe it was the sake, or maybe just the fact that it'd been weighing on her mind, but Jessica found herself telling Jonathan all about her department's broker opening and her hopes of getting promoted. He seized on the subject like an underwriter on a new submission.

"Right. Promote from within, then hire someone new to take on the lesser responsibilities. Of course. It's good for company morale. So why hasn't your manager jumped on that chance?"

"I don't know. I'm starting to wonder if he just doesn't think I'm broker material. Which would be ridiculous, because I practically do that job already. I could do it in my sleep." She heard herself say this aloud and thought about the fact that she did feel like sleeping at work half the time. She pushed the thought aside. So it wouldn't be the most exciting job in the world. But she'd already started down the path, so there was nothing to do but move forward.

"Did he tell you flat out that he wouldn't consider you for the position?" Jonathan asked.

"No."

"Good, because that would've been really stupid on his part." Jonathan turned steely-eyed as he bit into his eel and analyzed the situation. "So, basically, he's not treating you like one of the guys. All you need to do is strengthen your pitch. Fine-tune your presentation. Drill down and modify your product to suit your client's needs."

"How do I do that?" If nailing this promotion was as easy as Jonathan was making it sound, then he was her new hero, Jessica thought.

He gave her an appraising look. "Let's see. Do you dress the part? Yes — your business casual looks good. From what I know about your industry, it's pretty old-school. Pretty OBN. But that shouldn't be a problem, either. You're not asking for a management position. . . ."

He mulled it over. He looked at her face, but not with the date smile he'd been using so far. Now he was assessing her like a portfolio.

"What do your boss and the other brokers do?" he asked. "As a work culture, I mean?"

"As a . . . work culture? They sit around reading the paper and letting me do their work, mainly."

"*Wall Street Journal?*"

"Yeah. How'd you know?"

He smiled. "From what you've said, I can imagine their type. What else? I mean, do they do anything after work together? Take martini lunches? Where do they take their clients?"

Jessica knew the answers but never would have thought they'd affect *her* job. "They host happy hours for the clients about once a month. Ted takes martini lunches, but only by himself. Mostly they play golf. Sometimes they take the clients to the Texans' games, but mostly . . . they play golf."

"There it is. Can you play?"

Jessica snorted. "Can you *picture* me playing golf?"

"No. Maybe you could take your clients dancing at clubs instead."

Jessica laughed at the thought. "Okay, so, assuming golf is out, because I'd rather watch paint dry than play golf, what else could I do?"

"Show up at the happy hours and football games. If they don't invite you, find someone else in the company who will."

Jessica ate the last piece of lobster thoughtfully. She figured that it wouldn't be too hard to find a buddy for the happy hours, at least. Tiffany Wyman on forty-two was always trying to get her to go along to those things.

"You just need to get there and be yourself," he continued. "Talk to everyone. Make them laugh, like you do with me. The clients will love you, and your manager will see that. In the meantime, you have to start reading *The Wall Street Journal*, plus any other business publications you can make time for. Find interesting articles that apply to your industry. Then, whenever you can get away with it, mention those articles in front of the boss. If you can hit the fine line — sounding informed as opposed to sounding like you're brownnosing — then he'll be impressed. Those two steps alone will be the most immediate way to change his perception of you. I guarantee it."

Jessica rearranged the ginger on her plate and sighed. This was starting to sound like real work. Spend her free time schmoozing with clients and reading business magazines? That was more than just a slight modification to her "product." It was a complete lifestyle change.

"So, basically," she said, "what you're telling me is, it isn't enough to learn the job and do it well?"

Jonathan's smile became regretful. He shook his head. "Sorry. It doesn't make sense, I know. But they're not looking for someone who can do the job well. They're looking for someone who can represent their brand to the clients. Someone who can take clients golfing and quote Alan Greenspan. The *real* work...that's what they let their assistants do."

Jessica's eyes went wide. No one had ever laid it all out so honestly for her before. The fact that it was an executive type telling her this made it that much more incredible. She felt as though her mind had been blown open—like that day in ninth grade when she'd finally understood quadratic equations. "Jonathan," she said, "you totally rock. Thank you."

"Well, you're welcome. I'm glad to help."

Jessica was glad she'd confided in Jonathan after all. Now she knew she could count on him for good advice.

# 20

After Ahi, they walked a block over to TBar for the Junior Ruiz show. Neither of them had been to that venue in a while, and Jessica saw immediately that it had gone way downhill. The air-conditioning seemed to be broken, and the floor was completely packed with kids in T-shirts and shorts, yelling at the house DJ onstage to play hip-hop.

She could tell by Jonathan's expression that he was willing to make the best of it and wait for Junior Ruiz to come onstage. She wasn't, though.

"Hey," she said over the crowd noise, nudging him on the shoulder. "Want to get out of here?"

"Do you?" he asked, suddenly alert to the possibility of her discomfort. "Okay. Where would you like to go?"

"Let's go back to your place and have that drink."

She could tell by his smile that he was pleasantly surprised. They left TBar as quickly as they'd arrived.

"It's right down the road," Jonathan said as he drove them to his town house.

And it was. He lived in one of the very best-looking town houses in midtown—one of the new red brick ones Jessica often looked at longingly on her way to clubs with Toby.

He parked on the street and led her up to the door. Inside,

the first thing she noticed was the beautiful hardwood floor. Next was the way he'd decorated. There were only a few pieces of furniture, and they were all oversize dark wood. On the bottom floor he had an entertainment center, a roll-top desk, a coffee table, and two espresso-colored leather couches. There was a powder room tucked under the stairs. It was nice, and everything was in good taste, Jessica thought, but it really needed a woman's touch. She mentally put plants in the corners and drapes on the windows.

After they'd gone in a few steps and he'd taken her purse and set it on the desk, she saw that he also had a small piano, near the stainless-steel-filled kitchen, where the dining room would be.

He saw her looking and smiled sheepishly. "My mother made me take lessons. Would you like something to drink?"

She accepted a glass of the same wine he poured for himself. "Show me the rest of your place."

The second floor was his bedroom and master bath. He had a king-size bed, "to fill all the space," he said, with a down comforter covered in gray cotton. There was a dresser and a nightstand and not much else. A sliding glass door led to a small balcony that faced the back of another town house, across a small courtyard.

By then, Jessica couldn't help doing her interior designing aloud. "You could put a painting above the headboard," she said, holding up her hands to show him the dimensions she had in mind. "Something abstract, in blue and black, maybe, with a white mat and teak frame."

He smiled. "I've been thinking that, too—that I need to buy some prints or paintings. Maybe you can come shopping with me and help me pick them out."

Jessica nodded. She would like very much to do that—his place was too beautiful to go without proper decoration.

The third floor was nothing but a small, empty room and a big, empty balcony. At least the view was better there. They could see part of the downtown skyline, between the silhouettes of the other town houses.

Jessica was surprised at the weird use of space. "It kind of tapers as you go up, huh?"

"I know," said Jonathan. "It looks a lot bigger on the outside."

"It's awesome, though," Jessica said. "I would kill to have a place like this." Suddenly it occurred to her that maybe he never wanted to stay at her place for long because it was nowhere near as nice as his. And, really, who could blame him, she thought.

They went back down to the living room, where Jonathan put on some music.

"You don't want to play me something on the piano?" Jessica teased.

He made a face. "No. Sorry. I'm *really* rusty." He sat on the couch next to her, then immediately jumped up again. "Are you hungry? Do you want something else to drink?"

"I'm fine," she said. Now that he was no longer showing her around and there was nothing to do but sit and be alone together, she noticed that he seemed a little nervous. Instead of making her nervous, though, this put her at ease. She hadn't realized before that he might be shy about kissing her. She found it a little flattering.

Looking around the room for something to put him at ease, she noticed a photo album on his half-empty bookshelf. "Show me your pictures," she said.

Relieved, he brought over the album and showed her pictures of his parents, sister, and friends. Jessica couldn't help but smile. They were all good-looking, like him. They looked like people from TV commercials.

"And this is Andy. I've known him since fifth grade." Jonathan indicated a photo of a guy in fishing gear. There were other pictures of Jonathan with this guy and others, in a boat and in front of a tent. "We're going camping again tomorrow. Otherwise I would have asked you to do something else this weekend. Hey, do you like camping?"

Jessica smiled regretfully. "Not really. Camping itself is okay, I guess, but the bugs and the lack of clean showers kind of gross me out."

He laughed. "Well, that's true. I guess I won't invite you to join us tomorrow, then."

Jessica laughed back and took another sip of wine. When, she wondered, was he going to make a move?

He closed the album finally and sat back against the couch. "I had a really good time tonight."

Again, she smiled encouragingly. "I did, too."

"Maybe we can go out again next weekend," he said. "Or have coffee again during the week, if you want. Or dinner."

It was cute, she thought, how he'd suddenly lost his suave powers of conversation. And yet Jessica could tell that he found her attractive. She could almost feel the sexual tension emanating from him as he sat there trying to think of something else to say.

"You look really pretty tonight," he came up with.

"Thank you," she said. Then, she was tired of waiting. It was time to take things to the next level.

She put her hand on his shoulder and leaned forward, eyes half-closed. Quickly, he got the idea and scooted into a better position to kiss her. They kissed. Then they kissed again.

It was nice, Jessica thought. Not exactly fireworks going off, but there were definitely some sparks there. They kissed some more. She slid her hand down onto his chest and felt him start a little before sliding his own hands down to her waist. She leaned back a little and they kissed some more.

There was definitely potential here, she thought. And that was a good thing, because she couldn't have a relationship with no chemistry. She maneuvered herself so that her breasts pressed against him, making him moan very low in the back of his throat. But she could tell he was holding back for some reason. Probably trying to be chivalrous. Or maybe, she thought sympathetically, he had only dated women who didn't like sex very much. There were a lot of women like that, Jessica knew, although she definitely wasn't one of them.

He pulled back for a second to look at her face. His was clouded with passion. "Is this okay with you?" he asked. "What we're doing?"

She suppressed a giggle. "Yes. It's very okay." Pulling him back down to her, she kissed his neck, then took his hand and put it on her breast. He moaned and shifted against her so that she felt, for a split second against her hip, exactly how turned on he was.

Well, she thought, now she knew for sure that he wasn't gay and that he didn't think she was too fat.

Yet he still wasn't going any further than kissing her. If this were Guillermo, she thought suddenly, they'd be naked by now.

And without wanting to, she imagined that it *was* Guillermo here, kissing her on this expensive leather sofa. And *she* moaned aloud.

And then she felt guilty and pulled away. Just a little, but it was enough to scare Jonathan all the way off her. "I'm sorry," he said. "I got carried away. I didn't mean to take it so far."

"No, no...it's totally okay," Jessica said, shaking her head a little to clear the traitorous thoughts. "It's fine. Jonathan, I like you. It's okay."

They smiled sheepishly at each other. His shyness was suddenly contagious, she found.

"Do you want some more wine?" he asked.

"No thanks."

"I'm sorry," he said again. "I feel like such a dork. It's just that...I really like you, Jessica, and I didn't want to rush things and risk scaring you away."

She had to smile at that. How dramatic he was making it sound. But he was just trying to do the right thing, so she reassured him. "I really like you, too, Jonathan. And you haven't scared me away — yet. If anything, I was beginning to wonder if you didn't find me attractive after all."

"Oh no," he said, laughing. "That is *definitely* not the case."

She laughed, too. "Okay. So that's settled, then. What do you say we go ahead and call it a night? We can pick up where we left off next week, if you want." She couldn't say, of course, that the intrusive thoughts of Guillermo had totally ruined the mood for her. Hopefully, though, it was only temporary and she'd have her mojo back the next time they went out.

"Are you free next Friday?" Jonathan asked. "There's a big

show at the House. It should be way better than this TBar thing was."

"Yeah, I'm free," Jessica said. "And I love the House. Let's do it."

They made their plans, then he took her hand and helped her up from the couch.

He drove her home. At her door, they kissed good night. Jessica was glad to see that it was much more comfortable this time, now that they'd broken the ice. She was glad.

Now, she thought as she went into her apartment alone, if only she could stop thinking of Guillermo altogether, then she could move forward with Jonathan. Because finally she was starting to see that that was probably the best course of action.

# 21

At Wong's corner table, Jessica reached out and touched Marisol's sleeve so as not to give her the ojo—the evil eye. Not that Jessica would give her the ojo on purpose, but she couldn't help feeling a little envious. As always, Marisol looked beautiful. She wore jeans and silver sandals, and her long black hair cascaded over the shoulders of her supercute embroidered, obviously vintage blouse.

"Your hair looks good." Marisol reached out to touch it, returning the favor.

After giving the waiter the same order they always did, Jessica gave Marisol the rundown on her date the night before.

"So you just made out a little and then went home?" Marisol asked when she was done.

"Yeah. It was weird. I really thought we were going to go all the way, at first. Then...I don't know. I started thinking about that idiot Guillermo, and it messed everything up." Jessica relived the moment in her mind, then added, "It was almost like he *made* me think of him. I mean, it was almost like it was a sign, you know?"

Marisol raised a quizzical eyebrow, and then the waiter arrived. He put lemongrass chicken in front of Jessica and garlic tofu in front of Marisol. They picked up their forks and dug in.

"I don't know," said Marisol. "Are you sure *you* didn't make yourself think of Guillermo? Maybe because you weren't ready to be with Jonathan yet?"

Jessica laughed. "No. At least, I don't think so. How could I not be ready, when he treats me so well? Anyway, it doesn't matter, because I'm going out with Jonathan again next week, and I'm pretty sure that'll be the night."

"Are you excited?" asked Marisol. "Do you know what you're going to wear?"

"Yes, and not yet. I'm still trying to decide. Maybe something easy to remove," Jessica said with a wicked smile. She didn't want to trip Jonathan up with too many zippers or buttons, if they *did* end up hooking up.

While sipping her iced tea, Marisol glanced surreptitiously at her cell to check the time. Even though it was Saturday, Jessica knew her friend barely had time for this lunch and would be running back to work soon for some counseling session or field trip. She decided to ask about the web site now, before she forgot. "So what'd Esmeralda say about the site? Have they made a decision yet?"

"Yes. They picked you."

"*Really?*" Jessica practically shrieked. "Oh, my gosh. Why didn't you tell me first thing?"

"I'd planned to, but you started talking about your men and I totally forgot."

Jessica's mind was already racing, forging plans. "This is so fabulous. I have to start working on the real site as soon as I get home."

"Okay, but hold on a second. Don't get too excited, because it turns out the grant's not going to be as much as we thought.

It's not even half of what you bid. Esmeralda was going to call you sometime this week and discuss which features of your site we can afford."

Jessica sighed. "Oh, man. It's a sign." Marisol rolled her eyes, but Jessica ignored her. This wasn't her big career opportunity after all. Not that she'd expected the grant money to enable her to quit her day job. But still—she'd wanted to do a big enough site that she could use it to impress other nonprofits and maybe drum up more business.

Now that she thought of it, though, there was no reason she couldn't still do that. "You know what?" she said. "That's fine. I'm going to tell her that I'll still do the whole thing, even for the lower fee."

"No, don't do that. Don't bust your butt for nothing."

"It won't be for nothing," Jessica said. "It'll be a good addition to my portfolio. Plus, I enjoy the work and I like volunteering for you guys. So it's not a big deal."

"Well, I'm sure Esmeralda will love hearing that," Marisol said wryly. She took one last bite of her tofu, then said, "Okay. Sorry to cut it short, but I have to run back to ALMA and be a chaperone for their field trip at two."

"Okay. Well, then call me later. Maybe we can get together again sometime this week." Jessica hated that Marisol was always working so many hours, or else commuting way out to the suburbs, and never had time to hang out. She missed her friend but couldn't complain because Marisol really enjoyed her job.

"Hey, you want to go with me?" Marisol said suddenly. "We could totally use an extra chaperone."

"Um. Right now?" Jessica looked at her cell, as if she had someplace to be.

"Yeah. We're going to the art museums. Come on, it'll be fun. We just did a criminal background check on you a couple of months ago, right? You said you were just going to go home anyway, right?"

Jessica had no reason to say no, really. "Okay, fine. I'll go. But you owe me."


Herding a bunch of little kids around wasn't her usual idea of weekend fun, but it was better than staying home alone, Jessica had to admit. She hadn't been to the museum in forever. Some of the girls she was chaperoning had never been at all. She tried to make it fun and educational for them, pointing out the most famous pieces and her favorites, too. She explained cubism and surrealism and set the example for viewing nude statues in a mature manner.

When they stopped for snacks in the sculpture garden, Jessica helped pass out the juice and fruit cups ALMA got for free from People Helping People with Meals, another Houston nonprofit.

"You're pretty," one of the girls told her.

"Thank you. So are you." With her long ponytail, the little girl reminded Jessica of herself at eight years old.

"Do you have a boyfriend?"

"Uh…"

How was she supposed to answer that? *Did* she? She'd gone on a couple of dates with Jonathan, but he wasn't exactly her boyfriend. As for Guillermo… She might have considered him her boyfriend before, but not now.

The little girl was still waiting for her answer.

"Uh, no. Not really, I don't."

"Why not?" the girl asked. Her eyes were big and innocent and hungry for information that was none of her business. On second thought, Jessica realized, this little girl reminded her more of Sabrina.

"Because I don't need a boyfriend," she replied. "I'm happy by myself. I have a lot of friends and a good job, and that's all I need."

The little girl listened with her mouth open in complete fascination. "Really? What's your job?"

"Uh... I work in insurance. Eat your sandwich now, m'ija, okay?" Jessica was a little annoyed by the girl's ability to make her question all the choices she'd made in life up until now. Jessica almost wished she had just gone home after lunch.

As they cleaned up their tables, one of the little boys ran up to Jessica and yelled, "Miss! Miss! Can we go see the dolly picture again? The one with the melted watches?"

Jessica smiled. She knew he meant the Salvador Dalí piece, and she was proud that he'd remembered the name, almost. She had taught one kid something, at least, and that was a good feeling.

As she herded them through the halls full of paintings and sculptures, Jessica realized that she was someone these kids could learn from and maybe even admire. She'd gone to college. She had a decent job. She had stayed away from drugs. She knew the neighborhoods these kids were from—some of them didn't have too many role models who could say the same. Jessica felt pretty important all of a sudden.

By the time they did the final head counts and boarded the buses outside the sculpture garden, Jessica was completely worn out. She'd probably lost five pounds just walking around. Her throat hurt from calling out to the kids to stay close. But, weirdly, she'd had fun.

Marisol leaned over the seat and whispered in her ear, "After this, we'll go have a drink."

After the last kid's mother had picked him up from ALMA, Jessica and Marisol drove down the street to Agave Rojo.

"Two margaritas, please," Marisol told the bartender the moment they sat at the bar.

Jessica smiled. It was good to see her friend relax for once. While they waited for their drinks, they caught up on all the gossip they hadn't been able to get to during lunch. They traded updates on their families, and Jessica told Marisol about Toby's latest romantic tribulations.

Eventually, Marisol did her duty to ALMA by hitting Jessica up for more volunteer work. "We're going on another one next week, to the butterfly house. Can I sign you up to chaperone again?" she teased, obviously expecting a definite no.

"Maybe," Jessica said. Marisol's look of surprise made her smile. "I had fun today. Seriously. The kids weren't bad at all, and it was nice to put my art history degree to use for once." She took a sip of her drink, then went on. "You're lucky, Marisol. You get to do something useful for a living."

Marisol patted her friend's shoulder. "Aw, come on. Your job is useful, too. What would your corporate clients do without you to handle their insurance for them?"

"They'd get someone else to do it," Jessica snorted. "And that new person would be bored out of their mind, just like I am every day."

Marisol's face was sympathetic.

"Don't get me wrong," Jessica added quickly. "It's not that I don't appreciate my job. They pay me well enough to have an apartment in the Montrose. Even if it's not a new apartment with a working pool.... I just wish I could still work there but do something more creative, you know?"

"Well, maybe you will," said Marisol, "after you get your promotion. Didn't you say the brokers get to do fancy graphic presentations all the time?"

"Yeah," Jessica said somewhat morosely. "If you count navy and white as fancy."

Marisol stirred her drink and mused, "It's too bad you can't play accordion."

Jessica raised her eyebrow at the seemingly random comment. "Why's that?"

"Because we're losing our accordion teacher at ALMA. He just gave notice. He has to go back to Mexico."

Jessica wondered how this could possibly relate to her situation. "Well, that sucks for you guys. Even if I *could* play accordion, though, I would never go back to nonprofit full-time. No offense, but it just doesn't pay enough." She knew that from her experience at the Centro and from the fact that Marisol chose to live in a less expensive suburb in order to stretch her paycheck to the fullest extent.

"It doesn't pay enough if you're on the admin side," Marisol corrected. "But the artists get paid plenty. They're by the hour, but if they teach for us, they wind up getting paid more than me."

"Really?" said Jessica.

"Yeah. Their salaries are totally funded by government

grants. Let me know if you meet any accordion teachers," Marisol added. "If we don't find a replacement, we'll lose part of our funding."

Jessica sighed. Things were tough all over, it seemed. She resolved not to complain about her job anymore. At least she didn't have to rely on grants in order to get paid.

When Jessica finally got home from dinner and drinks with Marisol, it was just getting dark. As she climbed the stairs to her apartment, she heard what sounded like mewing and glanced around. The landlady's cat wasn't there, and he never made noises like that anyway. Had that margarita been stronger than she'd thought? she wondered.

At the top of the stairs, right in front of her door, someone had left a baking sheet full of sand, with a big, hole-filled boot box next to it. She heard the mewing again and quickly bent to pull the lid off the box.

Inside sat a tiny black kitten. Jessica recognized it — it was one of the ones from Hunter's litter, in Guillermo's garage. The kitten had something tied around his neck. It was a torn strip of flowered fabric, tied into a bow. Jessica picked him up and hugged him to her chest, kissing the top of his sweet little head. His mewing instantly subsided.

Also in the box was a can of tuna fish and a postcard. Jessica picked it up. It was from the Centro de Artes Culturales, the nonprofit where she used to work. They were promoting an upcoming art exhibit — a three-man show. The first name listed was Guillermo Villalobos. *Her* Guillermo.

She turned the card over. With a dark, inky pen, he'd written only, "Someone who needs your love."

# 22

After setting up as comfortable a home for the kitten as she could, Jessica played with the energetic little ball of fur late into the night. Then she took him into her bed, where he purred himself to sleep in the crook of her arm. But Jessica stayed awake for quite some time.

Thoughts tumbled chaotically in her head. Why was Guillermo doing a show at the Centro? She'd thought he was getting ready for an exhibit at the Houston Council on Latino Arts instead. She had never even given him the Centro's number.

Of course, she wanted to see his work on exhibit. He hadn't done a show since she'd met him, despite all her nagging. He'd said he didn't like having to pretend that he cared about other people's opinions.

But why, she wondered, had he invited her like this, with a gift left on her doorstep? What did he think—that this would be enough to make her fall right back into a dead-end relationship with him?

"Fat chance," she said to herself. He had another think coming.

She took Guillermo's card from her nightstand and read it again. "Someone who needs your love."

She snorted. He'd deliberately left it open to interpretation whether he meant himself or the kitten. It was sad, the way he couldn't even get a declaration of love right.

A declaration of love... Was Guillermo trying to tell her that he loved her? It had sunk into her brain only at that moment: He was saying that he loved her, wasn't he?

*No*, she told herself. *Don't get your hopes up. He'll never change.*

But then again—hadn't Madame Hortensia told her that the right guy would give her a sign? And wasn't a note at her door quite literally a sign?

These contradictory thoughts chased themselves round and round in her head, like a kitten chasing its own tail, until she fell asleep.


Her phone blasted her awake from a dream about Guillermo planning a wedding for Jessica and the kitten.

"Hello?"

"Are you still sleeping?" bellowed her sister. "I've been calling you all morning!"

Jessica rubbed her eyes and looked at the clock: 10:00 a.m. And it was Sunday. In her dream, Jessica had been wearing an arm cast.

"I'm right here. Quit yelling."

"I'm not yelling," Sabrina yelled. "What are you, hung over?"

Sabrina was probably calling to find out what had happened with Jonathan, and Jessica wasn't in the mood for the Mexican Inquisition.

"Sabrina, I can't talk right now," she said. "I need to...I need to feed my kitten."

She did need to feed her kitten. He was lying next to her, looking at her expectantly. Suddenly, Jessica realized the cause of her dream and the soreness in her body. She'd slept without moving all night long, for fear of rolling over and crushing Guillermo's gift. Apparently, she'd done a good job. Now she needed to get to the store and get some real kitten food, real cat litter, and a real litter box.

Before any of that, though, she had to get her sister off the phone.

"Sabrina, I have to go."

"You need to get up and get dressed. We're having lunch with Mami today."

"What? Why?"

"To make plans for Father's Day, babosa. Get up!"

After hanging up, Jessica rolled out of bed. Why hadn't she remembered that Father's Day was already next weekend? So much had been going on lately. She kissed the kitten good morning and set him on the floor.

She decided to shower, get dressed, then run to the store, come back, and get the kitten situated. She'd have just enough time to meet Sabrina and Mami for lunch.

It was annoying, Jessica thought as she shampooed her hair ten minutes later, the way Sabrina planned things without her and then expected her to show up with no advance notice at all. It was also annoying the way Mami always backed her up. If Jessica had called a family luncheon, she was sure Sabrina and her mother would be too busy to make it.

Was it because Sabrina was married now? Maybe Mami felt they had more in common. They were old married ladies now, while Jessica was a spinster, left out in the cold. Was that it?

Well, whatever. No big deal, Jessica thought as she rinsed the suds from her body. She wasn't going to be a baby about it, she told herself as she got out of the shower and on with her day.

When Jessica arrived at Tía Miquela's, the two of them were already there, talking and laughing over mimosas.

"You should cut it like mine," Sabrina was saying. "And do a rinse over the gray...."

Mami touched the long hair she had tied up in her usual bun. Jessica quickly walked over and took her seat. If their mother was thinking of getting a makeover, Jessica wanted to be there to give input. First, she'd start with *not* cutting Mami's hair like Sabrina's.

"I don't know," Mami said as if she'd read Jessica's mind. "I'm not sure I can cut off that much of my hair."

"Why not?" said Sabrina. "It's so easy to take care of. You'll love it."

"Your father likes my hair long," said their mother, staring down at the table, idly pushing a stray strand behind her ear. Then, suddenly, she looked up and announced, "You know what? I *will* cut it off. It's not like he ever worries about what *I* want."

Jessica was surprised at the vehemence in her mother's voice. Sabrina smiled grimly and patted Mami on the shoulder. Then she turned to Jessica and said, "Okay, now that you're here, let's decide what to do for Father's Day."

Jessica didn't respond to this until after she'd waved over

the waiter and ordered some migas. The waiter was hot. She couldn't help but notice that he looked a little like Guillermo. Not so much in the face, maybe, but in the way he sneaked an appreciative peek at her when he thought she wasn't looking.

Mami and Sabrina noticed the waiter, too. They whispered something to each other that Jessica didn't hear and then giggled. Jessica realized that she hadn't heard her mother giggle in a long time. In fact, she couldn't remember the last time she'd even seen Mami smile.

Sabrina cleared her throat and got back to the business at hand. "I was thinking we could go half on a new lawn mower."

"A lawn mower?" said Jessica. "Papi doesn't even like to mow the lawn."

"Well, maybe if we got him a new mower, he'd start liking it more," said Sabrina.

Mami rolled her eyes. "Sure. In my dreams!"

Sabrina giggled. "I'll send David over to give him lessons."

What was with her sister and the crappy gifts? Jessica wondered. She and her husband had gotten Mami a new washer for Mother's Day. Then again, Mami *had* seemed to like that more than the salon gift certificate Jessica had bought her. But still... It was time to stand up for herself.

"I already had plans for what I was going to buy Papi," she told her sister.

"Oh yeah? What's that?" Sabrina said.

Unfortunately, Jessica didn't actually have any ideas at all. Last year she'd gotten him a bottle of Patrón, and he'd said it was the best gift ever. But she couldn't do that again. Not after the doctor had told him to cut back on the drinking. Jessica thought quick and hard. Maybe a box of cigars?

Sabrina went on, "Come on. Mami and Papi need stuff for the house, and David can get us a good deal on the mower. We'll go ahead and pay for it, and you can reimburse me for your half later. We'll give it to Papi after lunch at Bella Cucina."

"Lunch? I thought we were having a barbecue with Grandpa and Uncle Juanito and everybody."

"That's in the evening," said Sabrina. "David and I can't go to that because we're having dinner with his parents. So we're taking Mami and Papi to lunch first. And you, too."

Their mother nodded. "Jessica, if you can come to the house right after lunch, I need you to help me with the food."

Why couldn't Sabrina help, Jessica wondered, since she was the one making all the plans? While she tried to think of a way to rebel against her sister without going against her mother, the waiter brought her food. Mami and Sabrina changed the subject to new curtains, then to new dish-washers, then to Grandma Petra's health and the latest happenings on *Young Lives to Live*. Then, unfortunately, the topic turned to Jessica.

"So, tell us how your date with Jonathan went," Sabrina commanded.

"Who told you we went on a date?"

"A little bird. Are y'all going out again?" Sabrina prodded while Mami listened like a hawk.

Jessica did *not* want to have this conversation. Especially not in front of their mother, who picked that moment to chime in. She assumed Jonathan had mentioned their plans to David, and David had mentioned them to Sabrina. It wasn't that she wanted to keep her relationship with Jonathan a secret. She just hadn't planned on having to give her family the details on it so soon.

"Is this the one you were telling me about, Sabrina?" asked their mother. "David's friend from work?"

"Uh-huh. The vice president with the blond hair and the Audi."

"Jessica, I hope you aren't going to do anything crazy to scare him away," Mami said in a serious, concerned voice.

"What do you mean?" said Jessica.

"You know. Like talking smart to him. Being unladylike."

"I'm just going to talk how I normally talk. If he doesn't like it, he doesn't have to go out with me."

"See? Like that. Men don't like it when you talk that way," said Mami. Sabrina nodded her head solemnly.

"Mami, you talk smart to Papi all the time," Jessica dared to point out.

Her mother frowned. "Well, that's because your father needs someone to nag at him all the time. We're not talking about him now. We're talking about a good man, who's *worth* marrying."

Jessica was stunned into silence by these words. Sabrina looked down at the table and said nothing.

"M'ijita," their mother continued, "I'm not trying to be mean. I'm telling you not to mess it up with this friend of your sister's, because I want you to be happy."

Sabrina cleared her throat again. "So, did he ask you out again or not?"

Jessica rolled her eyes. "Yes." She decided she might as well admit it, if only to change the subject and keep her mother from bashing Papi anymore.

"Where's he taking you?"

"To a club."

"Ooh. Okay, you'll have to call me and tell me what you're going to wear." Her sister sounded like a publicist. Or a pimp. "You want to be a little sexy, but not *too* sexy. You don't want to scare him away."

"Sabrina, I don't even know how serious things are with this guy yet." Jessica's voice got a little loud. "I don't need you sitting here making up ways for me to trap him."

"Please, m'ija," Mami said. "Your sister's only trying to help. You should listen to her. Look how happy she is with David."

Jessica glared at her sister through the rest of the meal. Why had Sabrina started up all this mess? It was obviously her fault that their mother was complaining about her own marriage so much now — because Sabrina wouldn't stop bragging about hers, making Mami feel bad.

Sabrina didn't notice Jessica's pointed gaze. She was too busy telling Mami about her last Chic Chef party. Sabrina had been married to David for only a few years, and she didn't have any children yet, but she'd already quit her job as Halronburco's receptionist. She'd been "homemaking" ever since, plus selling kitchenware and cosmetics to her friends at those goofy little parties that Jessica never attended.

". . . so it's like I have a part-time job, but I still have time to have a life," Sabrina was saying.

"Some life," Jessica said into her mimosa. "Like I'd want to sit around selling Mary Kay until I popped out a baby."

Sabrina stopped talking and stared at Jessica. So did their mother. There was a long moment where no one said anything at all, and Jessica wondered if maybe she should have kept that last remark to herself.

Then Sabrina replied, "Is that what I'm doing?" Her voice was light, but Jessica saw on her face that she was angry. And, more than that, hurt.

Jessica knew then that, no, she shouldn't have made that remark. Instantly, she felt like a horrible person. Her mother's cool stare didn't help, either.

Back when they were kids, Jessica and Sabrina had been so much closer. Even though Sabrina had been bossy then, too. But there were also the times they'd gone roller-skating or played Barbies together in their room. Or when they'd get hold of the Sears catalog and flip through it for hours, picking out their favorite toys. And wedding rings, and china, and silver, Jessica remembered now. Sabrina had married Tuxedo Groom Ken. That left Jessica engaged to his brother, Earring Magic Ken.

Obviously, Sabrina still wanted that life for herself. And Jessica had just made fun of her for it. They all looked down at their plates in continued, awkward silence as Jessica wished she could reverse time and take back what she'd said.

"Sir," Mami finally said, flagging down the waiter, "can we have our check, please?"

The funny thing was, Jessica thought as they gathered up their purses, she really did love her sister and *was* glad that Sabrina had the life she'd always dreamed of. It wasn't Sabrina's fault that Jessica had changed. The things she'd wanted when she was a child weren't the things she wanted now. Why couldn't Mami and Sabrina see that? And that it was okay? Why couldn't they be satisfied with who she already was?

The most annoying thing was that she couldn't even live her own life in peace. Whether she decided to move forward with Jonathan or not, it almost didn't matter, because her mother and sister would be watching her every move in the background. It was as if they'd already planned her future and weren't going to let her stray from their plan, no matter what she herself wanted.

As they stood to go, Jessica tried to smile at her sister. As upset as she was, she didn't want Sabrina to go away with hurt feelings.

But it was too late. Sabrina turned away and didn't look at her anymore.

23

Monday, after work, Jessica sped home to check on the kitten. Besides the fact that he'd knocked over his water bowl and chewed up the power cord to her laptop, he was fine.

Jessica picked him up and carried him around the apartment, hugging and pretending to scold him. "I should name you Little Brat," she told him lovingly. He mewed as she kissed the top of his head. She wouldn't name him that, she thought, but she did need to name him soon. Because she'd decided to keep him after all. Already she looked forward to seeing him every evening and cuddling with him at night.

The kitten sat on her desk and watched as Jessica made a few last minute changes to ALMA's site for her meeting tonight. Sometimes he reached out a paw and batted at the keyboard with her. They'd been working only a few minutes when Jessica's phone rang. She looked at the screen and saw that it was her mother.

"Hi, Mami."

"Jessica. Have you talked to your sister yet?"

Jessica frowned. She already had a feeling she knew where this conversation was going. "Not since yesterday, at the restaurant. Why?"

"I don't know if you noticed, but the things you said really hurt her feelings."

Jessica decided to play dumb. "What things?"

Her mother gave the short, hard sigh that Jessica had heard so many times during her youth. "Don't 'what things' me. You know — that thing you said about selling Mary Kay and pushing out babies. That was ugly, Jessica. I don't know why you wanted to talk to your sister like that. I think you need to call her and apologize."

Jessica sighed herself, feeling as though she'd been transported back in time. She was fourteen again, getting lectured for ruining something of Sabrina's. As usual, her mother was taking Sabrina's side, and Jessica wouldn't get any sympathy until her father got home. "Mami, I was just kidding when I said that stuff. Sabrina knows that. You know, she's not as sensitive as you think. You should hear some of the things *she* says to *me* when you're not around."

"That doesn't matter," her mother said. Her voice was very stern all of a sudden, as if Jessica had done something way worse than make a few callous remarks. "Your sister has a lot of stress in her life. You need to treat her better. M'ija, please call her and tell her you didn't mean what you said."

"Stress from what? Are she and David breaking up or something?" She'd said that flippantly, but Jessica immediately wished she hadn't and knocked on the wood of her desk.

"No. Knock on wood!" Her mother, Jessica was sure, was rapping on a piece of her own furniture on the other end of the line. "Never mind. It's just...sometimes married women go through problems. You wouldn't understand."

This finally annoyed Jessica to the point of no return. "Well, if I wouldn't understand, then there's no use in trying, so I won't call her. I'm sure she's already gotten over what I said anyway. And if she hasn't, she needs to." She felt a thrill of exhilaration for having said this aloud. When was the last time she'd back-talked her mother and gotten away with it? It'd been a long time. Jessica knew that in the end she would apologize to her mother and then apologize to Sabrina. But not so easily.

Through the receiver, she detected her mother's tongue click of extreme annoyance and braced herself for a scathing reply. Instead, though, all Mami said was, "Ai, Jessica. Sometimes you're so stubborn and inconsiderate. Just like your father!"

And then she hung up, leaving Jessica in complete confusion. What did her father have to do with anything?

Suddenly, her visit to her parents two weeks before flashed through her mind. They'd been arguing. Was Mami still mad at Papi after all this time? Was that what was *really* bothering her?

Glancing down at her computer screen, Jessica noticed the time. She couldn't afford to sit here worrying about this; her ALMA meeting was starting in half an hour. She would have to call her mother back when she was done with that. Now it was time to pack up her laptop and go.

Fifteen minutes later, she drove through the multicolored shotgun shacks that were making way for posh town houses all around the old warehouses ALMA called home. Outside the arts center, kids stood around the lawn and its sculptures, waiting for classes or rides home. The front doors were a riot of flyers and posters for upcoming events. Jessica recognized several she'd made.

Inside, more kids milled throughout the wide lobby and its art exhibits. A teenage girl with a blue tattoo on her bared midriff sang scales in the doorway that led to the auditorium. A younger, plumper girl sat on one of the orange tweed couches and tuned a guitar. Three boys in T-shirts, shorts, and dress boots stomped out ballet folklórico steps that echoed on the industrial tile floor, fifteen feet up to the mobile-strung ceiling.

The receptionist was talking into the phone, writing out a receipt for an anxious-looking mother, and holding up her hand to a small boy who jumped up and down in front of her desk. She glanced over at Jessica and beckoned her in with a movement of her chin. Jessica waved thanks and crossed the lobby to the director's office.

Esmeralda Vargas looked the same as she had since Jessica had been a child, except that now her bushy hair had a little less black and a little more gray. She still wore a long, colorful dress and a handful of silver rings. She, too, was on the phone. Her other hand held an unlit cigarette that she used to wave Jessica into a chair. While Jessica waited, she looked around at the photographs that covered every spare inch of the office and chronicled ALMA's growth from a small neighborhood youth group to the citywide arts organization it was today. Some of these, too, were by Jessica, taken with her digital camera. And, still in its corner behind the door, was the old snapshot of Marisol and herself. Jessica loved that picture. It showed them at nine years old, painting in the same summer art class that ALMA held today.

It was funny...her happy memories of ALMA were what had inspired her to major in art history in the first place. And now here she was, working in insurance. And still doing art for ALMA, although it was a different kind of art altogether.

"Listen, Jessica, I'm not going to be here for your meeting after all." Esmeralda's voice was a smoky rasp. "I have to go and take care of something. But Lupe and Djomme are waiting for you in classroom two. Did Marisol tell you about the grant money, how it's going to be less than we thought?"

"Yes," said Jessica.

"Yes, just one moment, please," Esmeralda said into her phone. Then she covered it with her hand and looked at Jessica. "Then you've been thinking of ways to scale down the site?"

"Actually, Esmeralda, I'm not going to. I'm going to do the same amount of work, for whatever you guys can afford to pay me."

If Jessica had expected Esmeralda to jump for joy at this news, it would be because she didn't know the older woman as well as she thought she did. Esmeralda narrowed her eyes and nodded slowly, holding her cigarette as if she wished it were lit. "All right. Thank you, Jessica. I appreciate it."

She was, now as in Jessica's childhood, a woman of little outward emotion. Which was probably a good thing, Jessica thought as she carried her laptop case and portfolio down the hall to classroom 2, considering all the stress that went into running a nonprofit.

Right outside classroom 2 there was a child's drawing of a big smiling sun. Jessica smiled back at it. It was obviously a good sign.

It had been the most unconstructive meeting of Jessica's life, she reflected as she drove home two and a half hours later. Her mission had been to show the site to ALMA's two art instructors and discuss any changes they wanted made. Lupe and Djomme, it turned out, had completely unrealistic expectations. For instance, they didn't want ALMA's site to be *rectangular*. After talking with them for just a few minutes, Jessica had discovered that neither of them had any experience with web sites or computer applications.

Jessica had been forced to take a step backward and give them a quick lesson in the fundamentals of web design, explaining JPEGs and resolution, format, and fonts.

Then, when she'd explained her vision for ALMA's site, they'd completely ignored the content and, instead, asked tons of questions about the images and colors she'd used. Djomme had wanted to know, in particular, how she'd made one of his murals into a watermark background. So Jessica had spent the last hour of the meeting explaining digital photography and Photoshop.

At least they'd picked it up pretty quickly, she thought as she turned onto her street. It'd been easier than teaching Mr. Cochran to use his e-mail, at any rate. In the end, she'd had to promise to teach them more later in order to get out the door. And still she'd had to schedule another meeting, hopefully for a time when Esmeralda and other business-minded people would be able to attend.

Now, she thought as she climbed the stairs to her apartment door for the last time that day, if only it were that easy to fix things with Sabrina and her parents.

**24**

She really did feel bad about what she'd said to Sabrina. Still, she wished Sabrina hadn't felt the need to bring their mother into it. But then again, she told herself, it was just as likely that Mami had decided to get into it all on her own.

After she'd set down her things and changed out of her work clothes, Jessica carried her phone to the couch and called the kitten to come to her. He was busy playing with one of the toys she'd bought him and ignored her coaxing. Without an excuse to put it off any longer, Jessica called her parents' house. Her father answered the phone.

"Hello."

"Papi? Hi. How are y'all doing?"

"Not good," he said. "Your mother's all pissed off at me for nothing."

"For nothing? What happened, Papi?" Jessica hoped her earlier phone conversation with her mother hadn't started another argument between her parents.

"I don't know," her father said, sounding completely exasperated. "She came home from work and saw that there was a ring on the table, from water or something."

Immediately, an image popped into Jessica's mind. The image was of a Tecate can sitting on the coffee table, without a coaster.

"Then," her father continued, "it was like she turned crazy. She started yelling all this stuff that didn't make any sense."

"Like what?"

"All this stuff about my drinking and how I forgot to mow the lawn, and then something about how I made you be mean to your sister. Seriously, m'ija, I was afraid she was going to have a heart attack. She wasn't making any sense."

Jessica decided it was best not to explain that part about Sabrina. Not right at the moment, anyway. "So what'd you do?"

Her father sighed. When he spoke again, he sounded abashed, like an innocent boy. "Well, I didn't know what to say. She was so upset, I wanted to tell her something to help her and calm her down. So I told her she should just take a day or two off work so she could fix the table ring and mow the lawn herself."

"Papi!" Jessica was surprised. She knew that her father could be a little blunt sometimes, but this was inconsiderate even for *him*.

"I know, I know. I shouldn't have told her to mow the lawn. But I've been so tired lately, you know? And I get tired of her wanting me to do it so fast all the time, before the grass even has a chance to get long."

Jessica made a sympathetic noise. Her mother could be kind of a yard Nazi, she knew. "So then what happened? Where's Mami now?" Suddenly, it occurred to her that her mother might be able to overhear everything Papi was saying.

"Oh, she left. She said something like 'I'm going somewhere where people appreciate me,' and then she ran out the door."

Jessica started in alarm. This was way more serious than she'd thought. Where could her mother have gone? Not back to work, obviously. Maybe to a friend's house?

As if reading her mind, her father said, "Don't worry, m'ija. I'm pretty sure she just went to the grocery store, because I told her when she first got home that we didn't have anything in the house to eat."

For some reason, this whole conversation was giving Jessica a strong sense of déjà vu. Unfortunately, her mother didn't have a cell phone, so Jessica couldn't call and make sure she was okay.

Maybe, she thought, Mami had gone to Sabrina's. Jessica decided she would call her sister as soon as she got off the phone with Papi. But first... "Papi, you need to apologize to Mami as soon as she gets home."

He sighed again. "I know. But I'm getting ready to go out and get something to eat, and I might go to the bar and watch the game, where I can have some peace and quiet. I'll leave her a note."

"No, Papi. Don't go out. Run and get something to eat, then go back home and wait for Mami. When she gets home, tell her you're sorry for everything you said, and for leaving your beer on the table without a coaster."

"No," her father said decisively. "No, it's better for me to do it like I said. When she gets mad like this and leaves, it's always better if I'm not there when she gets home. It gives her a chance to be alone and think things over. I like to wait until she's asleep, so I know she's over it. Then I come home and go to sleep, too, and we both wake up feeling better."

Again, Jessica was surprised. Obviously, then, these arguments were nothing new, and her mother had been angry enough to leave more than once.

How had all this begun to happen without Jessica knowing about it? She visited her parents every two weeks. Or every three weeks, at least.

Sabrina, she said to herself. Her mother had probably been confiding in Sabrina.

"M'ija? Are you still there?"

"Yes. Papi, I really think you need to stay home tonight."

There was a pause. Then he said, "I can't, m'ija. Really, it's better like this. Your mother always feels better in the morning, after she's cooled down for a while."

Jessica didn't know what to say to this. And, again, she had a weird sense of déjà vu.

"You know what?" her father said. "I'll buy her some flowers or something, on my way home tonight. That should work, don't you think?"

"Maybe," Jessica said lamely. Her father was obviously determined to downplay what was going on. There was nothing she could do with him anymore.

So she wished him the best and got off the phone. Immediately after disconnecting, she dialed Sabrina's number.

"Hello?" It was David, Sabrina's husband.

"Hey, David. Is Sabrina there?" Jessica kept her voice light, not wanting to bring him into their family drama.

"Hey, Jessica. No, unfortunately, you just missed her. She left to have dinner with your mom. Why don't you call her on her cell?"

Jessica chewed at her thumbnail. By now, the kitten had finished playing with his toy and had eaten a little kitten chow, and he was trying to jump up onto her lap. "Okay," she said. "Thanks, David. Bye."

But instead of calling her sister's cell, she put the phone on the coffee table. Maybe her father was right, she thought. Maybe it would be best to let Mami cool down for a while. With Sabrina.

# 25

Tuesday, after work, Jessica was agitated. She'd gone shopping for suits downtown during lunch and found a cute pink Chanel knockoff, on clearance, that screamed, "Promote me!"

But now she stood in the building's garage with her trunk open, holding up the suit and wondering if she should go back to the department store right then and exchange it for something else. It was very cute, she thought, but maybe too much for McCormick. None of the female brokers ever wore fabulous pink suits. Then she tried to think of what they did wear and realized there were only one or two female brokers that she knew of. Both were older, and they wore the same thing that most of the assistants did: flowered dresses and khaki suits with elastic-waist pants.

"Well," Jessica told herself, "I'll have to be the one to set the trends." As she put the suit back into its bag and climbed into her front seat, her cell rang.

It was Jonathan, calling to confirm their plans for Friday. Then he said he had to go and the phone call was over. Jessica hung up, bemused, and started her short drive home.

Obviously, Jonathan saw the phone as a tool, not a toy. She could see that there'd be no midnight calls where he told her silly jokes and dreams. And that was a good thing. Wasn't it? He definitely did the dating thing better than Guillermo.

Speaking of Guillermo and the crazy things he did...what was she going to do about his show on Saturday?

And why did it have to be at the Centro? If she went, she was sure to run into all her old co-workers, and they were sure to annoy her. And what if her ex-boyfriend, Robert, showed up? That loser was the last person she wanted to see. Just in case, though, she'd have to wear something nice, so they could all see how much better she was doing since she'd left them.

The problem was, if she *did* go to the show, Guillermo would take it as a sign of forgiveness and then expect her to fall right back into bed with him. And as tempting as that sounded, Jessica was determined not to give in to temptation again.

Plus, what about Jonathan? He wasn't actually her *boyfriend*. It wasn't as though she'd made him any promises or even told him that she wasn't seeing anyone else. But he was taking her out Friday, and she was pretty sure that would be the night they would have sex for the first time.

How cold-blooded would that be, to date Jonathan and let him take her to nice places, to sleep with him and let him think they had something serious going on, and then to go see Guillermo again? Especially if Guillermo was trying to win her back? Jonathan didn't deserve that. If she *was* going to keep seeing Guillermo, she'd have to stop seeing Jonathan altogether, wouldn't she? Without even finding out for sure what would have happened.

She wished she knew which man she was *supposed* to end up with, so she could settle on that man and then move on with her life.

On paper, Jonathan was perfect. He was sweet, successful, attractive. Really, if an objective party compared him with Guillermo, there'd be no contest. But she wasn't an objective party. She knew what Guillermo had that Jonathan lacked: excitement and insane sex appeal. She and Guillermo had chemistry, and that wasn't something you could conjure up at will.

And then there was the culture thing. She wasn't racist, of course, but she had to admit to herself that she had issues about dating a white guy. How well would he be able to integrate into her family, for instance? Would he expect her to do what Sabrina had done and leave her family for the suburbs?

And speaking of her family, what would her father say if she ended up with Jonathan? Yes, he had grown to accept David, but Papi and Sabrina had never been as close as he and Jessica. Would it totally break his heart? Of course, Papi probably wouldn't approve of Guillermo, either. So that point was moot.

Jessica bit her lip as she drove down the street. Madame Hortensia had said there'd be a sign that would tell her what to do. If it had already shown up, then Jessica must have missed it. She made a U-turn right in the middle of Waugh Drive and set off in the direction of the little purple house.

Twenty minutes later, Jessica watched Madame Hortensia take four fake-stone dominoes from a box and lay them on the table. "They're called runes. Want to try them?"

"Are they the same price?"

"I'll give you a discount, since I'm still learning them. Eighteen dollars."

"Okay. Sure, let's try it," said Jessica.

The old woman laid the runes facedown on the table, then shuffled them around before lining them up side by side. "Okay. What did we say last time? Do you remember?"

"That there would be a sign telling me what to do with my love life, and also one telling me what would happen with my job," said Jessica.

"And did that happen?"

"No."

"Nothing? You didn't see or hear anything that made you realize which choice was better? No premonitions or dreams? No feelings guiding you one way or another?"

"Not really. Well..." Jessica reconsidered under Madame Hortensia's intense stare. "There *was* a really good clearance sale on suits at Macy's. But I'm not exactly sure yet that the one I got looks good on me. I guess that doesn't count, then, huh?"

Madame Hortensia stared at her for a moment longer, then said, "Okay. Here we go, then. First, we will ask the Norse spirits about your money."

She turned over the first stone. It was embossed with a symbol that looked like the letter M. Madame Hortensia put her finger to her forehead and stared at it in deep concentration. Then she opened her box of fortune-telling supplies again and pulled out a staple-bound booklet titled *Rune Reading Made Easy*. She flipped through it for a bit, then said, "This one means perseverance."

"What does that mean?" asked Jessica.

"That you won't lose your job anytime soon. Or that if you do, you'll find another one very quickly."

"Well, that's good," said Jessica. "What about the promotion, though? Does it say for sure whether I'm going to get that?"

Madame Hortensia peered at her enigmatically over the rune manual. "Have you applied for the promotion, m'ija?"

"Yes. Well, sort of. I told my boss I wanted him to consider me."

"And what did he say?"

"He said okay. That he would keep it in mind."

"Mm-hmm," said the old woman, nodding her head sagely. "And have you made sure that he does keep it in mind? Have you been showing him how good you would be at this new job, so that he doesn't forget?"

Jessica sighed. She hadn't yet had a chance to get the latest *Wall Street Journal*. She had taken Jonathan's advice and tried to watch golf on TV the other night, but it'd ended up putting her to sleep. She'd been working her butt off on her files, as always, but that wasn't exactly *showing* Mr. Cochran anything, considering he was never around to see it.

"I have been trying, a little," Jessica said. "I'm going to try harder, though."

"Okay," said Madame Hortensia. "Let's go on, then. This next one is for your love."

The second rune showed a slanted X.

"This rune means..." She consulted her booklet again. "Patience. So, something is developing, and you have to wait and see what it is. Have you seen signs of this development yet?"

Jessica thought, then said, "Yes."

"With the blond-headed man? The bolillo?"

"Yes. But also with the other man, too. I've been going

out with the blond man more, and that's going well. But the black-haired man gave me a gift, and he wants me to go to his art exhibit, which could develop into something. Maybe."

"Hmm. Okay," said Madame Hortensia. "Let's move on. This next one is for your health."

Jessica frowned. Why did they have to waste one of the runes on health? she wondered. She didn't feel that they had spent half as much time as they should have on her love life. But the fortune-teller was already flipping up the next rune. It looked like a slanted *F*.

"This means you're healthy," said Madame Hortensia. "But don't forget regular checkups, okay?" Immediately, then, she turned over the fourth rune. It was a line bent into a forty-five-degree angle, like half an arrow. She squinted at the booklet again, then set it down and smiled at Jessica for a little while before speaking.

"This one is very good. It's for your future, and—"

"Oh, wait," Jessica interrupted. "Do you have a rune for family?"

"What's that?" Madame Hortensia's voice was a little terse, as if she hadn't appreciated being interrupted.

"Family. See, I've been having some trouble with my sister and my parents. Well, actually, it's more like my parents have been having trouble, and it's affecting my sister and me." Jessica thought over what she'd just said, then added, "Sort of."

"What sort of trouble are your parents having?" the fortune-teller asked.

"They've been arguing. A lot." As Jessica thought over how to explain it, she felt a weight on her chest. She realized that her parents' issues were something that had been bothering her for a while now, even though she'd been trying to avoid thinking about them. "Madame Hortensia, I'm worried that they might..." She didn't want to say it. She wouldn't say the D-word.

The old woman's face softened, but she shook her head. "M'ija, if your parents are arguing, there might not be anything you can do about it. They are adults, so you have to let them work it out on their own. No one ever knows what's really going on between a husband and wife except for the husband and wife themselves. I suggest you let them do what they have to do."

"Okay." Jessica sighed unhappily. "What about my sister, then? She and I haven't been so close lately, either."

"And why is that?"

"Because..." Jessica tried to come up with a succinct way to explain it. "Well, because she's married, and she and my mother are always trying to make me feel like my life isn't as good as my sister's just because I'm not married, but I don't want to get married, and I told her that, but I guess I said it in kind of a mean way, and now she won't speak to me, and my mother's mad."

Madame Hortensia looked into Jessica's eyes for a moment. Then she said, "Maybe you should call your sister and demand that she apologize for purposely making you feel bad."

Jessica thought this over. "Well... it's not like she *purposely* made me feel bad. Actually..." She gave an embarrassed cough. "Actually, I'm the one that needs to call and apologize to her. Really, she's only been trying to make sure I have a good life. She can't help it if her kind of life is the only good one she knows."

As she said this aloud, Jessica knew it was true. Underneath it all, Sabrina loved her. She never would have hurt Jessica's feelings on purpose.

"So, as I was saying, this rune is for your future, and it means intuition."

Jessica snapped to attention. Intuition for her future — what could that mean? she wondered.

"Listen carefully, m'ija. This means that you have to follow your intuition if you want to be happy."

"Okay. How do I do that? I mean, how do I know what my intuition says, exactly?" Jessica kept talking, wanting to get her fortune straight for once and for all. "I mean, I think a lot of things and have a lot of feelings, but how do I know which one's right?"

"Shh, shh . . ." The old woman thought for a moment, then said, "You have to meditate."

"Meditate?" Jessica immediately imagined a soccer mom sitting in a yoga position with a cup of flavored instant coffee by her side.

"That's right. Not the way you're thinking, m'ija. I mean you have to take some time alone and sit and think about your future. Imagine a future with the blond-haired man, and a future with the black-haired man. Imagine a future with the promotion, and then how your life might be without it. Then you will know what to do."

"Because I'll receive a sign?" Jessica asked hopefully.

"Uh . . . maybe. It *might* come in the form of a sign," said Madame Hortensia. "But most likely, if you take my advice and really think about the paths in front of you, then you'll decide *on your own* which one to take. It might take a while, but soon you will know. And in the meantime, you have to let things develop. Some things you can't control."

Jessica didn't know what she'd expected Madame Hortensia to say, but it wasn't "Meditate and let things develop." It would have been much more helpful to hear, *Yes, Jonathan will be your husband someday*, or, *Go back to Guillermo because he's learned his lesson.*

Or, at least, *Yes, you're getting the promotion, so go ahead and buy more suits.*

Let it develop.... That sounded like it was going to take a lot of time. Like planting seeds for flowers or waiting for a big file to download on a slow connection.

"Madame Hortensia, I need more help than that. I need to know what I'm supposed to *do*. I *need* to know which man is the right one for me." Jessica knew that her voice was getting annoyingly whiny, but she couldn't stop. She really did need help.

"Okay, okay," said the old woman. "Calm down." She got up and went through the beaded curtain. For what? Jessica suddenly remembered the good-luck medal lying at the bottom of her orange Fendi knockoff clutch. That didn't seem to have helped at all. But maybe, she had to admit to herself, it was because that purse had been in her closet all week.

Madame Hortensia came out with a plant this time. "Here, m'ija. This is ruda—a rue plant. It has many luck and healing properties. Do you have a teakettle at home?"

"No."

"Well, that's fine. Just having it in your house is good for you. It's only six dollars, on special today. Do you want it?"

"Sure. Why not?" Jessica gave her the money. "This doesn't answer my question, though."

"Not right now it doesn't, m'ija, but it's good luck, and it'll help you to see the answers. Just keep looking for them. And call your sister. And don't come back unless you have an emergency, okay?"

# 26

The next day, Wednesday, Jessica put on another new suit. As Madame Hortensia had said, it was time to show Mr. Cochran that she was ready to be promoted. She put on the pale blue pants and jacket as though they were a suit of armor and she was ready for battle. Underneath, she wore her chocolate silk camisole with the blue lace. The matching leather mules with the blue satin trim had seemed like a good sign when she'd found them last week at Shoe City. It was time to see what they could do for her now.

She pulled her best bag—the real Gucci she'd found on clearance after Christmas—and her laptop case over her shoulder. One last check in the mirror: She looked damn good if she did think so herself. Seriously—how could Mr. Cochran *not* see that she was the best person for the job?

On her way to work, she hit nothing but green lights. Then, in the garage, she got a space right near the elevators. Then, right outside the elevator, there was a shiny new quarter lying on the freshly vacuumed carpet. She picked it up and dropped it into her bag.

Not just a penny, but a whole quarter—it had to be a sign. She was going to talk to Mr. Cochran today, and the promotion was as good as hers.

An hour later, she was sitting at her desk, working and

looking awesome, when Ted dropped a legal pad on her desk and almost knocked over her latte. "Safety poster," he muttered.

Jessica's flash of annoyance with Ted instantly evaporated. If there was anything about this job she enjoyed, it was designing safety posters. Instead of using the same template over and over, like everyone else, Jessica preferred to customize the posters for each client. Today's was for Brox, an oil rig manufacturer.

The first thing she did was pick out a good background picture of a flaming oil rig from her collection. She was laying out a palette of burnt orange, steel gray, and gas-flame blue when Mr. Cochran strolled in with his morning paper. Jessica followed him to his office in order to take hold of her opportunity.

"Mr. Cochran, do you have a minute?"

He looked up from the papers in his briefcase, then closed it. "Uh...yes, Jessica. What do you need?"

"I was wondering what was going on with the new broker position for our department."

He made a perturbed face. "How did you know about that?"

Jessica frowned right back. Did he not remember their conversation from the week before? "I helped Olga with the posting. Remember, I asked you about it last week?"

"Oh yes. That's right." Mr. Cochran seemed to have lost the conversational thread. He was already unfolding his *Wall Street Journal.*

Jessica persisted. "So, I was wondering when you'll be interviewing for the broker job. Because I'm planning to apply."

Mr. Cochran scratched his ear with his pen and peered at the wall behind her. "Okay. That's great, Jessica. I'll let you know."

Jessica wondered if she should casually mention her subscription to *The Wall Street Journal* now. No, she decided — there was no way to bring it up without sounding fake. "Okay. Well, I can't wait. Thanks, Mr. Cochran."

"Close the door behind you."

That went well, she thought as she went back to her desk. Mr. Cochran didn't seem very enthusiastic, but then he never did. She had let him know in no uncertain terms that she wanted the job. She was being persistent, and he was bound to appreciate that. She practically had the promotion in the bag, Jessica told herself.

Later, at lunch, Marisol hugged her as they took their seats by the aquarium at Mai Lam. "Girl, you look awesome. So what's been going on?"

Over their Thai coffees, Jessica filled Marisol in on all her latest, including her dilemma over Guillermo's art show. It turned out that Marisol had already heard about it through the nonprofit grapevine and had already assumed Jessica would be there.

"I *want* to be there, but I don't know if I should go," said Jessica.

"I don't get what the problem is. If you want to see the show, why don't you just go?" asked Marisol.

"Because..." Jessica sighed. She didn't know why it wasn't obvious to Marisol. "I don't want to end up sleeping with Guillermo again!"

"Then don't sleep with him."

Jessica shook her head and made herself a mental note. As soon as she had more time, she was going to find her friend a hot guy to get it on with. That way, Marisol would understand what she was going through. She tried to explain. "It's not that easy. It's like he has some power over me. I see him, and I can't *help* but sleep with him."

Marisol shook her head. "I can't wait to see this guy for myself. Too bad I can't go to the show."

"Oh, that would be perfect!" Jessica exclaimed. "You could go with me and keep me out of danger."

"No, I *can't* go. We're taking my dad to the ranch for Father's Day, remember? I'm leaving Friday night."

"Oh. That's right." Jessica sighed. She considered telling Marisol about the plant she'd bought from Madame Hortensia and asking what she thought. Marisol had actually been born in Mexico, so maybe she had some insider information on it, like a recipe or something.

But sitting there in a well-lit restaurant in the middle of the day, Jessica suddenly realized how silly she would look, confessing to buying a magic plant. She sighed again. "I don't know what to do."

"Just go, but don't let him see you there," Marisol said with a slight eye roll. "Wear dark glasses or something. Just look, then leave."

"Oh, my gosh. That's a good idea. No wonder you're a social worker."

"Ha, ha. Seriously, Jessica — if it's going to make you this nervous, just don't go. Like you said, things are going well with Jonathan now, right? So forget about Guillermo. Let him find another woman to be his art groupie."

Jessica thought she had been more than just Guillermo's "art groupie," but she decided to let that comment slide for the moment. "Here's the thing, Mari," she said. "I never really told Guillermo I wasn't going to see him anymore. He doesn't even know I'm seeing someone else. As far as he knows, we're just going through one of our regular spats, and I'll forgive him the next time we're together. That's what always happens. He doesn't realize yet that everything's changed."

"So you're going to his big show to tell him about Jonathan?" Marisol asked archly. "Are you going to dump him right in front of everyone?"

"No. Of course not," Jessica said. She stirred her vermicelli, trying to formulate her thoughts. "Actually, I don't know what I'm going to do. Really, I shouldn't tell him anything. Maybe he won't even notice — he hasn't even called me once since leaving the invitation at my door. There'll probably be plenty of women at the show willing to take my place," she mused. It wasn't a happy thought.

"So why go?" Marisol persisted.

"Because . . . I don't know. I just . . . I just can't get him out of my head, you know? I want to move forward with Jonathan, but it's like Guillermo won't let me. I have to go to his show to tell him good-bye — even if I just tell him in my mind. You know? I need some kind of closure here."

Marisol nodded. "Okay, I get you."

Jessica smiled and reached over to pat her friend's hand. It was good to have someone understand her, even if sometimes she could barely understand herself.

**27**

Luckily for Amber Chavez, Jessica had decided to forgive her. The singer, actress, and now model had secretly married her *Labor Union of Love* costar, Troy Grodin, the week before. Jessica had read it on the Internet and then bought *Hola!* magazine for the exclusive pictures of their wedding in Cabo San Lucas. It turned out that Amber Chavez wasn't such a sellout after all. She had a new song out, and the lyrics went like this:

> *I fly around the world*
> *With my diamonds and pearls*
> *But you know I'm still your homegirl!*
> *I love men in every color of the colorwheel,*
> *But you know I'm keeping it real!*

Jessica downloaded the single and couldn't stop playing it. It had a really good beat. Plus, she liked the message. It was true—it didn't matter who you hooked up with. It was possible to stay true to your culture, even if you dated someone from another. Amber Chavez had proved that, and Troy Grodin loved her for it. He may have been a crappy actor, but he was obviously an awesome guy. Just like, obviously, Jonathan was an awesome guy, even if he was different from Jessica.

Also in her issue of *Hola!* magazine was a smoking hot picture of Amber Chavez's ex, Enrique Salvaje, the Colombian ballad singer. After seeing that, Jessica decided to name her kitten after him, because they resembled each other around the eyes. She would call him Ricky for short.

Friday at noon, Amber Chavez's song pulsed from her car speakers as Jessica drove home for lunch to check on Ricky. When she got into her apartment, she was confronted by a horrific scene.

On the living room carpet, in order, was her rue plant, knocked over; a clump of dirt from the plant's pot; a bunch of its leaves, wet and mangled; and a tiny puddle of sticky green liquid. Then, Enrique Salvaje—the kitten, not the singer—fast asleep. At first Jessica thought he was dead. But, no, apparently he was just worn out from destroying and then puking up the rue plant.

He woke up and slowly stretched while Jessica watched anxiously. He seemed fine, but she was still worried. She wanted to call Madame Hortensia but had the feeling the fortune-teller wouldn't appreciate hearing from her without an appointment.

There was one other person she could call—an expert on cats and plants both. Her mother. Jessica picked up her cell and called her mother's work.

"Hawthorne Elementary."

"Mami, it's me."

"Jessica. What's wrong?" Her mother's voice was business-like but concerned.

"Mami, I have this kitten, and I had this plant, and the kitten ate the plant and threw it up." Jessica watched as Ricky tried to climb her leg, then started to sharpen his tiny claws on her hose.

"What? Where'd you get a kitten?"

"I just got him. A friend gave him to me." Jessica bent and gently unhooked Ricky from her stocking. "Is he going to be okay?"

"What kind of plant was it?" her mother asked.

"Rude...ruda?"

"Ruda. A rue plant," her mother supplied. "Did he throw up all the leaves he ate?" Mami's voice was calm now, as if this sort of thing happened all the time.

Jessica checked the carpet again. "Yes, I think they're all out."

"Well, he should be fine, then. Throw the rest of the plant out and get him some catnip instead. Does he look sick still? What color is he?"

"He's black. He looks okay now. He's busy being bad, actually." Jessica was glad they could bond, in a way, over Ricky, but she hoped her mother wouldn't ask her any more. She didn't want to go into details about how she'd gotten him. "So...how've y'all been doing, Mami?"

Her mother lowered her voice. "Fine. I guess Sabrina told you what happened with your father and me. That was nothing. I just felt like going out, and Sabrina met me for dinner. I got home at ten and your father wasn't even there, so I went to sleep. No big deal."

Jessica could tell, though, that her mother had some serious residual anger going on. She didn't correct her mother's assumption that she'd spoken to Sabrina. She wondered if she should take up for her father and relate some of the conversation she'd had with him that night. Then, remembering that Mami was at work, she decided against it. Really, she should just go see them both in person — and she would be seeing them in person, because this Sunday was Father's Day. "So . . . are we still on for Sunday?" she asked tentatively.

"Yes. We'll see you at lunch. You're still coming over to help me with the barbecue, aren't you?"

"Yes." Jessica had almost forgotten about the whole thing. She didn't even want to think about it now. All she could do was hope her parents would be in good moods and everything would come out okay.

Her mother was busy, so they said good-bye and hung up. Jessica hugged Ricky, scolded him, then cleaned up his mess, hoping that his destroying the rue plant wasn't bad luck.

She sped back to work ten minutes late, thinking that it was a good thing she hadn't made plans with Xavier after all. She'd e-mailed him several times, but Tech Support was so busy lately, he barely had time to write her back, much less have lunch. Which was annoying, because she'd been wanting to talk to him in more detail about the ASP coding she needed for the ALMA site. Plus, she hadn't talked to him in forever, and she kind of missed him.

But if they had gone to lunch, Ricky might have eaten more of the plant and been even sicker. So, Jessica told herself as she hurried off the elevator to her department, it was probably all fate.

"Where's Mr. Cochran?" she asked when she got in.

"Oh, you know. Meeting," said Olga.

"And Rochelle?"

"Dentist."

When Mr. Cochran did come in that afternoon, it was with Ted. They stopped in the middle of the room to finish their conversation.

"So HR approved your request for another broker?" asked Ted.

"Yeah. They weren't overjoyed about it, though."

"What's the budget?"

"We have to keep it low. So, someone with less experience, who we can train," said Mr. Cochran.

Jessica focused on her monitor and smiled to herself. Mr. Cochran was obviously easing Ted into the idea of promoting her. Ted probably hadn't even thought about her as a potential candidate. Most of the time he treated her and the other women more like pieces of furniture than people who might have the ability to learn new things.

"Where are we even going to put someone new?" Ted looked around. "In the copy room?"

"We'll probably just clear some space right here." Mr. Cochran waved his hand over Jessica's head. "No use getting bent out of shape about it just yet." He led the way into his office, where he changed the subject to one of Ted's accounts.

Jessica stopped eavesdropping and started filing. She might as well get all of it out of the way now, so her replacement wouldn't have to do so much when Jessica started marketing her new accounts.

That evening, Jessica sped back home to get ready for her date with Jonathan. After checking Ricky's food and water bowls, she sat at her computer and checked e-mail while eating the salad she'd gotten from a fast-food drive-through.

Then it was time to get herself into going-out mode. She turned on some music and went to her bedroom to undress.

The problem, she realized as she stepped under the hot water in her shower, was that the thing with her parents was still bothering her. She had to stop thinking about that — at least until after tonight's date. As Madame Hortensia had said, there was nothing she could do about her parents' arguments. They were adults.

Second, there was Guillermo's stupid art show to worry about. No, she told herself. She *would not* think about that tonight.

Third, Mr. Cochran hadn't said anything directly to her about the promotion yet. If she were a negative sort of person, she'd think that maybe he wasn't really planning to give it to her after all. But that wouldn't make sense. She'd been in middle market for three years now. She could bind coverage with her eyes closed. And unlike everyone else in the department, she had never let a renewal slip.

These thoughts swirled through her brain as she dried herself with a big lavender towel. She had to stop worrying about things. It was stressing her out, and she was supposed to be getting ready to enjoy herself. She felt wound up and out of order, like a yo-yo with a tangled string. If only there was some way she could relax.

Guillermo's face popped into her mind. His face, looking up at her from a pillow. With her hair hanging all around him as she sat on top of his—

Stop thinking about that, she told herself sternly. But she couldn't blame herself, at the same time. How long had it been since she'd last had sex? It felt like forever.

Well, she reminded herself, tonight would cure that problem. Tonight was the night for her and Jonathan. She reached
up and pinned her hair more securely at the top of her head.
The thought of it made her nervous and excited at the same
time.

So far, Jonathan had been the perfect guy. She couldn't
deny it. The only thing missing, though, was that spark. But
she could make that spark happen, she reasoned. She'd never
tried it with a nice guy. Maybe it was high time she did.

Jessica went to her closet to see what was there. Latin
house thumped mutedly from the CD player as she pulled
out the coral dress with the halter neck. She hadn't worn this
one since she'd bought it on clearance at Neiman's Last Call
more than two years ago. But it wasn't wrinkled at all, and
the coral looked good with the color her hair was now. If she
could find the bra that went with it, she'd be good to go.

Luckily, the dress still fit pretty well. She looked at herself
in the mirror. Ricky watched her from the bed.

"What do you think?" she asked him. "Nice, huh?"

Now, which purse went with this dress? And which shoes?
As she thought over her inventory, she suddenly remembered
why she hadn't ever worn it before: She hadn't found shoes to
go with it yet.

An hour later, she emerged from her walk-in closet with
a disaster area behind her. Orange, red, pink, brown, gold,
silver, and bronze shoes lay all over the floor behind her like
soldiers on the battlefield.

On her feet was a pair of black sandals, because she'd
given up. She was already stressed enough without freaking
out over her shoes. The one good thing she'd found was the

ocelot bag she'd bought a few weeks back. Somehow it pulled the dress and the shoes together and made it look as though she'd carefully planned the whole outfit. Could this be her sign? It was, she decided. This date was going to be something exciting.

# 28

Wow. You look amazing," Jonathan said when he came to pick her up.

Jessica felt herself flush with pleasure as he bent to kiss her. "Thanks," she murmured against his ear. She could almost feel him flush in return.

"Are you ready to go?" he asked.

She was. She closed and locked the door before Ricky could run out.

Jonathan took her hand and led her down the metal staircase like a knight leading a princess. Jessica practically felt sparks between their hands.

Jonathan's compliments always sounded so genuine, she mused. *Not* as though he were just BS-ing her so she wouldn't be mad about something he'd done, like someone else she could name.

Jessica shook the thought from her mind. Tonight she was going to give Jonathan her full attention. He was dressed well, as usual, she saw as they walked around the apartment pool and out to his car. Cicadas buzzed in the trees, as if in anticipation. Outside the gate, Jonathan helped Jessica into the Audi, his hands at her waist. She felt a thrill go through her from the touch. Oh yeah, she thought. Tonight is going to be the night.

As they made their way to the club, he concentrated on the road, as always. But she could tell he was excited. She could almost feel it through the air between them.

"I hope you like this place. I think you will," he said. "They're having three DJs tonight, in separate rooms, and one of them is supposed to be really good. I've never heard of him, but I did some research online, and from what you've told me, his style should be something you'll really like."

Jessica smiled. "You're so sweet, Jonathan." When had Guillermo ever gone through so much trouble for her?

Jonathan went on, doing the same kind of random talking he'd done last week at his town house. "But let me know if you don't like it, and we'll go somewhere else. Wherever you want." Jessica realized he was nervous again. Probably thinking all the same thoughts she was, about what would happen after the DJ show. The first thing she'd do when they got to the club, she decided, was get this man a drink. He needed loosening up.

And the second thing she'd do, hopefully, was get him on the floor and dance. When was the last time she'd gone dancing on a date, with an actual straight man? she wondered. It must have been months ago, way back in the winter, with Guillermo.

She and Guillermo had gone to the Acapulco Lounge to dance cumbias. After two clumsy dances, during which he'd led too much and stepped on her toes, he'd parked himself at the bar and started with the tequila. He'd kept promising her another dance, right after the next drink. They hadn't left until last call, when the bartender's shouting startled her out of the half-sleep she'd fallen into on her stool. And because he'd drunk so much, Guillermo had ended up completely useless to her in the bedroom that night.

Comparing that night with right now, she suddenly saw, plainer than ever, what a jerk Guillermo could be. Compared with Guillermo, she thought, Jonathan was Prince Charming.

Why had she put up with Guillermo's behavior for so long? Because he said funny things once in a while? Because he was a good artist? Or was it only because he was handsome? He wasn't *that* good-looking, was he? Okay, he was, actually. The jerk. If Jessica hadn't put up with him, some other woman would have been happy to take her place.

Fine, she thought; let someone *else* learn the hard way for a change.

When they got to midtown and found parking, only a few stars were showing through the cobalt blue haze.

"It's kind of early," Jonathan said as he opened her door. "Do you want to stop at Mode for a drink?"

While they walked the half block to the bar, Jessica people-watched her fellow clubgoers. As always, there were plenty of pretty women on display, their outfits ranging from modest to downright skanky. A blonde with giant implants packed into a yellow tank top tottered by on horrible gold Roman sandals. Jessica looked over to Jonathan to get his reaction. If he'd been Xavier, he would've made a very subtle funny face, like a fake gasp or drool. If he'd been Guillermo, she might have caught him staring right before he regained his composure. Toby would have said something catty. But when she checked, Jonathan was looking down at her and didn't seem to have noticed the blonde, or her packages, at all.

At Mode, they ordered a beer and an apple martini, and as usual, Jonathan handed over his credit card before she had a chance to pull out hers. She decided not to worry about it anymore.

In their corner booth for two, her martini kicked in immediately and she became talkative and jokey. Their conversation was about nothing much at all. She'd planned to ask Jonathan for more advice about her job, but now that she was so far outside McCormick's granite slabs, and starting on her second martini, she had stopped caring. She put her hand on Jonathan's arm and smiled at him conspiratorially. "We're going to have fun tonight." He smiled back and caressed her hand a little before raising his drink in toast.

By the time they made it to the House, things were just starting to happen.

The club really was an actual house, originally. A big one, filling up fast with people who, like her, were ready to dance. Jonathan had been right about the music: It was just the kind of thing she liked. Loud, bass-y house tinged with disco and Latin beats. Everyone was crowded around the stage. Jessica couldn't see the DJ, but she could hear his voice.

"Y'all like that?" he called out. Yes, they did.

"You want something to drink?" Jonathan said. He had to lean close to her ear to keep from shouting it at her.

"Sure." They were standing at the edge of the crowd. Her hips made slow circles of their own volition as the DJ mixed into the next song, warming his way up to a heart-shaking beat. In what seemed like mere moments, Jonathan pressed a martini glass into her hand.

"Thanks!" she mouthed at him. It was already getting warm in the club, and the drink was nice and cold. And not as strong as the one at Mode had been, so she was able to drink it more quickly.

Jonathan said into her ear, "You want to dance, don't you?"

She nodded. He took her glass and left it somewhere, then took her arm and led her away into the crowd.

He wasn't the best dancer in the world, she quickly found. But she didn't mind. Straight guys never were. He worked the classic side-to-side move, and luckily the beer bottle in his hand kept him from clapping. And that was okay. She didn't really *need* a guy to dance well—she just needed one to stand next to her so she didn't have to dance alone.

They went through one song, two songs, three songs, and then she really started getting warmed up. Jonathan stuck with his side-to-side move and kept his eyes on her. Jessica could tell he was enjoying watching her dance. And that was okay, too.

"Girl, I thought that was you out there shaking your ass!" shouted a voice behind her. It was someone she knew—a friend of Toby's everyone called Michelangelo. He was there with a couple of guys and a girl. Jessica knew their faces but not all their names. Jeff and Christine? Casey and Miss Julio? Didn't matter. They were fun.

"Hey, y'all," she said.

"Hi," said Michelangelo to Jonathan, batting his eyes.

Just as they would've done at Galaxy or Tropico or any of the other gay bars in town, Michelangelo and crew positioned themselves around Jessica and their other girlfriend and began dancing as nastily as they could. Jessica thought of it as their gay bang. She laughed and ground her butt against Jeff's pelvis, as if it would do any good. She glanced over to check on Jonathan and saw that he was laughing. She was relieved that he could take a joke. He wasn't possessive or homophobic. In fact, now he was pumping his fist in the air and cheering them on. She found, then, that she liked him more than ever.

Then, suddenly, he was part of the freak nastiness, too, because Michelangelo pushed Jessica against Jonathan and then enclosed them in his arms and tried to hump them both at the same time.

"Woo!" yelled Christine.

"Yeah!" said Jeff. "Ride him like a cowgirl!"

They were all watching and catcalling, so Jessica went ahead and gave them a little show. She shimmied up and down against Jonathan as if he were a stripper pole. The others screamed and clapped.

"Damn, girl!" said Michelangelo. "That almost had me switching teams!"

They all laughed, and then her clubtime friends melted away into the crowd. Jessica turned to Jonathan and smiled apologetically. She could tell by his face that he had been affected by their dancing and was trying to play it cool. She stifled a giggle. It was kind of fun to see the effect she was having on him. She fanned herself, trying to dispel some of the heat that was suddenly coming over her. "Sorry about that. I would have introduced you to those guys, but I can never remember their names."

He looked a little surprised for a split second but then

laughed again. She echoed his side-to-side for a moment while pushing her hair off her face and shoulders. The House didn't have its thermostat set low enough. She was almost perspiring.

"You want to take a break?" Jonathan asked, leaning down close again. She felt his hand on the small of her back. The heat in the room intensified immediately.

"Yeah. Let's get some water," she said.

He led her back toward the bar very chivalrously, then ordered them each another drink and a bottle of water. They leaned against the bar for a while to rest.

"So how do you like it here? Is the DJ good?" he said as loudly as he politely could. She moved closer to him so they wouldn't have to shout.

"It's awesome. I'm glad you brought me."

"I'm glad you like it." He looked down at his beer. It almost looked as though he were blushing. Jessica thought it was cute, the way he'd gotten shy all of a sudden.

"You know...," he said. "I'm glad you're here with me. At first I thought you wouldn't be."

She could barely hear him over the music and the crowd. Cupping her hand over her mouth and pointing it up at his ear, she said, "Why's that?"

"You're probably going to laugh at me, but I was kind of nervous when I called you to have coffee that first time."

"Really? Why?"

"You didn't seem too interested in me when we met at your sister's, I guess. I was worried that you were way out of my league."

"You were?"

He nodded sheepishly. "But I had to try anyway. Even if you shot me down, I didn't want to kick myself later for not taking the chance."

Now it was her turn to look down at her drink and blush. This was a side of him she hadn't expected to see. Here he was, Mr. Smooth Businessman, admitting that *she* had made *him* nervous. When all this time she'd been worried that he was out of her league, because of his job and his money.

Jessica couldn't help feeling flattered. She let that feeling ripple through her for a moment. Then she decided to put his mind at ease. With a smile, she said, "You're so silly. I'm glad you *did* take the chance." And, she realized at that moment, she really was. Jonathan was the best thing that had happened to her in a long time. "Now hurry up and finish your drink. We're letting good music go to waste."

They stayed until the club closed at two. She was still torso dancing, just a little, in the leather passenger seat of his Audi as Jonathan drove her home.

"Now that I know for sure what you like, I'll keep an eye out for more house DJs coming to town." He sounded very serious to Jessica, as though he were making a mental note of something important he had to do. She laughed at that thought.

"They don't have to be house DJs. I'll dance to anything, really. With a good beat, I mean."

He was watching the road so carefully, it seemed to her all of a sudden. Maybe so that he wouldn't look as if he were driving drunk?

Then again, he'd had only beer, so he most likely wasn't driving drunk.

Good thing he was the one driving, then. She'd had all

those crazy apple martinis. And she was little, compared with him, so...It'd be safest if she just stayed in the passenger seat and didn't drive. Instead, she'd just dance, very quietly, on the inside of her body only, so as not to distract him. She tried to do that and then laughed again.

There was no feeling in the world like dancing, she reflected as they climbed the stairs to her apartment. Well, except sex, maybe. Except that dancing lasted longer than sex. Well, *usually* it did. She giggled.

He looked at her suspiciously. "All right. You'd better get inside and get to bed, I think."

"Are you saying that because it looks like I'm drunk?"

"No, not at all...."

"Because I'm not. I'm only a little tipsy." She tried to look at him archly, then had to stifle a hiccup, which made her giggle again.

"Oh, okay. Well, that's good, then. You won't wake up hung over."

That was true, Jessica realized. It *was* good not to be hung over. It was nice of him to think of that, too. He was nice....While she was thinking all this, she'd somehow found her keys at the bottom of her bag and unlocked the door.

"Okay, then," he said. "I'll call you tomorrow, okay? Maybe we can get together for lunch on...Oh, wait, Sunday is Father's Day, isn't it? Well, maybe we can..." His forehead scrunched up a little as he tried to think of what they could do. He looked cute like that. All confused and worried about what he could do to make her happy, because he was glad he'd had the nerve to ask her out and that she'd given him the chance.

"Jonathan," she said.

"Yes?"

"Are you going to come in or what?"

He looked surprised again, but again, only for a moment. Then he was kissing her, and she was kissing him, too.

She didn't know how long it lasted. When they came up for air, their arms were wrapped around each other.

"Come in," she whispered. He did.

They didn't get any farther than the couch. Kissing all the way, they both sank onto it and then kept kissing. Jessica's hand tangled in Jonathan's hair. He was so blond, so cute, she thought as she pulled him against her with the other hand.

This time he really was into it. The way he was kissing her was setting her on fire. Her tongue wound around his as she hurried to unbutton his shirt. His hands searched her body for the zipper to her dress. She led him to it — it was on the side, under her arm — then let him pull the halter strap over her head.

He looked down at her for a moment. Jessica wasn't the most well-endowed woman in the world, but she had enough to keep a guy happy, she knew. Plus, she was glad she'd put on a really cute strapless bra and couldn't wait to see his reaction to it.

The look on his face said volumes. But instead of saying anything himself, he turned his head to the side.

Jessica sat up a little. "What's wrong?"

He inhaled sharply, and she realized he was going to sneeze. Maybe he has asthma, she suddenly thought. Maybe she was putting him under too much stress and he needed an inhaler.

But then, instead, he exhaled slowly. "Sorry about that," he said with a sheepish smile. She smiled back, and then he lunged back at her as if he couldn't wait to be making out with her again. She decided not to worry about whatever it was that had just happened. He didn't seem to be worried now.

"You're so beautiful," he whispered. With her help, he pulled off his shirt. Jessica ran her hands all over his chest and shoulders. His slender muscles turned her on. His chest had a little more hair than she was used to, but it didn't bother her. She trailed her fingers through it. She heard his quiet moan as he nibbled on her ear.

Together, they got her suddenly annoying dress down her torso and off her body, and Jessica kicked it under the coffee table. This is it, she thought as his fingers grasped at her bra hooks. She reached for his belt. We're going to get it on! she thought. The buildup was killing her. She'd never been so ready for anything in her life.

She had undone his buckle and was about to reach back and help him with the bra when he pulled away again.

This time he did sneeze. Not just once, but twice in quick succession. It sounded as though his head might blow off.

From the floor, near her discarded dress, Jessica heard a long hiss. She turned and saw two green sparks, glowing in the dark.

"Ricky!" she cried. She'd totally forgotten about the kitten. It was a good thing he hadn't run out the door when they'd come in.

"You have a cat?" Jonathan stated the obvious. By then, he'd seen Ricky, too. The kitten was standing there with his back arched up as far as it could go, giving Jonathan the most threatening look he could manage. Jessica didn't know whether to laugh or take the kitten in her arms and alleviate his fear.

Jonathan sat up straight. "I'm allergic to cats." Then, as if to prove it, he sneezed again.

"Oh no!" said Jessica. "Are you okay?"

He nodded, then put his hand over his face, obviously trying not to sneeze again. He stood. "I have some stuff in my car that'll keep me from...Oh, wait. No, I don't. I left it at home."

Jessica stood now, too, feeling slightly foolish in her underwear. Ricky took the opportunity to dart into her bedroom. "I'm sorry. I should have told you I had a cat."

"No, it's not your fault," he said. "I should have asked." He sneezed again, three times in a row, unable to help himself anymore. Obviously, Jessica realized with profound disappointment, she had to get him out of her apartment.

She helped him find his shirt, and he put it back on. She offered him water, aspirin, and tissues, but he refused them all, between sneezes. She was annoyed with herself for not having any antihistamines in the apartment.

"I'm really sorry," he said again.

"Don't be," she said. "It's not your fault." She glanced at her dress, wadded up under the table. "Maybe I should...Do you still want to..." She didn't want the evening to end like this. But Jonathan's face and neck were turning red, she saw now. He tried to be unobtrusive about it, but he was scratching his neck now. Maybe he was breaking out in hives, Jessica thought with alarm. "Do you want to go to your place?" she finished weakly, already knowing the answer had to be no.

"No," he said. His voice was as disappointed as she felt. "It's going to take a while for my pills to kick in. And, besides . . . I didn't, um." He coughed uncomfortably, then sneezed. "I don't have anything. I mean, I'm not prepared."

Jessica realized that he meant condoms. He didn't have any. He didn't? she thought, puzzled. Apparently, he hadn't expected them to go all the way, even after last weekend. She had condoms in her bedroom but decided not to tell him that. He was scratching his forearms now and didn't look as if he were in the mood anymore. "Okay. I understand. I guess you'd better go."

"I'm sorry," he said, still scratching as she led him to the door.

"It's not your fault," she said again.

"I'm going to make it up to you next weekend," he said, right before a particularly loud sneeze startled them both.

"Okay." She smiled and kissed him good-bye before he could sneeze again.

After he was gone, she couldn't help throwing a pillow at the couch in frustration. Then she saw Ricky watching her from the bedroom doorway.

"You little brat," she told him as she walked over and lifted him into the air. "Now I know why Guillermo left you here."

But she was just kidding, of course. She stood there in her underwear, petting the kitten. Guillermo didn't even know that she was dating another man, much less that the man was allergic to cats.

Ricky began to purr in her arms. Jessica looked down at the little bundle who'd gone from angry to innocent in a matter of moments. If she hadn't known better, she would have sworn that the kitten was trying to make her feel guilty.

# 29

She woke up a little sore, but not hung over at all.

The only way to keep from being sore next time, she reminded herself, was to go out dancing more often. She went into the kitchen for a glass of water and saw that there was absolutely nothing to eat.

Half an hour later, as she rolled her cart down the grocery store aisle, Jessica let her mind drift back to the night before. It had been great—until Jonathan's allergic reaction had ruined it all.

She thought of the episode on her couch, before the sneezing had begun. She'd been so ready to make love to Jonathan.

And yet he hadn't been planning to make love to her. He hadn't brought any condoms with him, and he didn't even have any at home.

Was it a sign? she wondered. Maybe she wasn't meant to have sex with him.

Without warning, the memory of her first kiss with Guillermo crossed her mind.

And how they hadn't stopped at the first kiss. But not because she'd tried to stop him and failed. No. Obviously, he was used to women throwing themselves at him right away. But for some reason, that hadn't bothered her at the time.

Not enough to keep her from going way further than a first kiss, that was.

The worst part was that it hadn't even been a real date. It was more like a *National Geographic* special on animal mating. Their first "date" hadn't been until a week later, when they'd driven through downtown together to look at architecture, then stopped for burgers before going back to her place.

Her cheeks turned hot at the memory of it all. She pressed her hands to her face and forced herself to think about the little Virgin Mary swinging from her rearview mirror, focusing on it until her head cleared.

There was no use feeling guilty about it now, though, Jessica told herself. All that Guillermo stuff was in the past.

She would go to his show tonight, not because he deserved it, but just to get closure. She would see him one last time in a place where she could have a good last memory. In her mind, she would tell him good-bye. Hopefully, there wouldn't be any stupid nude paintings of other women. But, then again, what did it matter? From now on, as far as she was concerned, he could paint all the desperate old rich ladies he wanted. She wouldn't care anymore.

"After the show tonight, this is it," she thought aloud. She wouldn't waste her time with him anymore. No more shady nonrelationships for her, ever again. She'd learned, from the short time she'd spent with Jonathan so far, that she deserved better.

She pushed her cart slowly through the coffee aisle, smelling the gourmet beans without really seeing them there in their grinders. Then her phone rang, interrupting her empowering reverie. It was Toby.

"Hey, g-friend. Are we on for the Tropico drag show tonight?"

Oh, shoot. She'd forgotten all about that.

"Uh...I don't know yet. What time did you want to get there?"

"Early. Like, at ten. Why? You got a date with your new man?"

Jessica didn't even need to think up a reply, because Toby kept talking. "Two nights in a row, huh? Michelangelo and Jeff told me they saw you humping some white guy at the House. You have to tell me everything, Miss Multicultural Ho."

"It's not like that. I'm not seeing Guillermo anymore."

"Whatever. Tell me all the details later. My mom's waiting to use the phone. Just tell me if you're going tonight or not. And don't say no."

"Yes, I'm going."

"Good. Pick me up at ten, then."

He hung up, leaving Jessica annoyed. But after a second, her annoyance was replaced by relief. Now she had the perfect excuse to leave Guillermo's show early. Even if he *begged* her to stay, and to forgive him, and to take him back.

# 30

She'd decided not to go with the sunglasses. That would have looked ridiculous, because it was seven o'clock in the evening, and the exhibit was indoors.

Instead, she was wearing a short black skirt, a tank made of fuchsia sequins, and silver sandals. *Not* because she was going to see Guillermo, but because she was going out with Toby after the exhibit. That was how she'd explained it to herself as she'd flat-ironed her hair and then picked out silver drop earrings and bangles. At the last minute, she'd put a black suit jacket over the whole outfit. That would be disguise enough.

As she headed to the door, Ricky jumped down from her bed and ran toward her for some affection. He wound himself around her legs one, two, three times, almost making her fall. "Quit it, Ricky!" she told him. "I'll come back and play with you later tonight."

The Centro looked great, she had to admit as she pulled into its newly asphalted drive. Since she'd quit working there three years ago, their neighborhood had gone from shotgun shacks to expensive bungalows, and the Centro had gotten enough funding to totally renovate their building. The whole thing was done up in a classy twenties Spanish stucco style. The only thing ruining it was the cheesy murals painted all over the sides and back. She recognized the artist—Robert

Fernandez, her ex-boyfriend from her days as the Centro's curator.

She got to see his whole masterpiece as she drove around the building trying to find parking. All three murals were full of skeletons, corn plants, fire, struggling brown youths climbing mountains in trousers, and wife beaters. It was totally depressing and, worse, unoriginal. His art, now that she thought about it, was full of omens that she never should've hooked up with him in the first place.

She finally squeezed into a space next to a double-parked Mercedes, rolling her eyes at rich people's driving habits.

As she made her way through the parking lot, Jessica adjusted her silver faux python bag on her shoulder and thought, for the tenth time since leaving her apartment, of how glad she was to be out of this scene now. No more midnight phone calls for her. No more surprise paint blobs showing up on her clothes after waking up next to another starving artist. She was past all that now. She was on her way to becoming an executive, who spent time with other executives, trading business tips at trendy restaurants. She was dating Jonathan and no one else.

She was about to see Guillermo for the last time. Hopefully, this show would give her something decent to remember him by. Plus, it'd be satisfying to see him finally taking her advice and trying to get exposure for his art, even if she wouldn't be there to see him reap the rewards.

The first thing she noticed when she walked into the lobby was local anchorwoman Yolanda Olivarez. She was standing in front of the cheese trays with a glass of white wine in her hand, talking to two other well-dressed people Jessica didn't recognize. Yolanda looked just as pretty in person as she did on TV but was way shorter than Jessica had expected. Maybe they sat her on phone books for the news, Jessica thought.

The second thing she noticed was that the opening was way more crowded than she'd expected. Sure, there'd been a lot of cars in the parking lot, but she'd just sort of assumed they were for one of the beer joints down the street. Instead, they were all here, inside, crammed elbow to elbow in the gallery halls. Never when she'd worked for the Centro had they hosted an event with this many people. And they were all well dressed, too. Not here just for the free wine and cheese, obviously. Had the Centro hired a new curator? Or an actual publicity person? If so, did they make that person mop floors, as they'd made her do?

The third thing she noticed, and the most surprising of all, was that people were looking at her. And whispering. Pointing, even. Surreptitiously, she glanced down at herself. Had she spilled something on her clothes? Was her pedicure chipped?

"Jessica!"

She turned and saw the Centro's executive director, Felix Montenegro, standing beside her. He clasped Jessica's hand with a warm, completely uncharacteristic smile. Already, this was more attention than he'd ever shown her when she'd worked for him.

"Jessica, I'm so glad you could make it. How long has it been since we've seen you? You should stop by more often, for our other events."

Things were getting weird. Jessica wondered if she were still asleep, having a dream.

"So, tell me," Felix went on. "How do you like what we've

put together here? A small reception, but nice, isn't it? We're already talking about having another event in the fall. But a bigger one. A nicer one. And just for Guillermo this time. None of this other crap...." He waved his hand around, indicating the paintings in the front room, none of which Jessica had even seen yet. "This time it'll be a one-man show. That is, if Guillermo wants to do one. What do you think?"

"I...I don't know. You'll have to ask him that," she said. She wondered what Guillermo had told Felix about her. He must have said that he wanted Jessica to manage his career, after all this time. Or that they had the kind of relationship in which her opinion really mattered. She wished she could find out without having to ask Guillermo himself.

After listening to Felix suck up to her for a few more minutes, Jessica extricated herself from his clutches and escaped into the crowd. The nearest open space was in front of a painting by someone else — someone known simply as Claudia Z, according to the plaque. It was a watercolor of a fairy under a rainbow. A Latina fairy. Actually, now that Jessica was looking at it more closely, it seemed to be done in felt-tip markers. She leaned closer to make sure. Claudia Z, she saw, was asking two hundred and fifty dollars for this piece, which was the size of a piece of notebook paper. She snorted. It wasn't worth two dollars and fifty cents, in her opinion.

Behind her, two women were having a semiwhispered conversation. They were so close, Jessica couldn't help but eavesdrop.

"Girl, I don't care if his paintings are good or not, because that man is *fine*. He can paint me anytime, you know what I'm saying?"

Jessica froze, her ears straining to pick up every word. Were they talking about Guillermo? The other woman spoke.

"So where's this girlfriend of his? Or is she his wife? Hope not. You'd think she'd want to be here, though."

Girlfriend? *Wife?* That was it. It was time to find Guillermo and find out what he'd been saying about her, before he said anything worse. Jessica turned abruptly toward the main room, where he had to be, since his name was listed first on the invitation. When she faced the two women, they became silent. And they stared.

"Um...," said one.

"It's...," said the other.

Jessica pushed between them and forced her way through the crowd to where Guillermo had to be, and where he was most likely doing something that would make her more annoyed with him than ever before.

# 31

The first painting she passed in the main room was his red sun over the mountains. A semicircle of admirers stood around it, staring and whispering. Jessica glanced at the plaque to see what he'd ended up calling it.

The title was simply "Home."

The price: five hundred dollars.

Below the price was a sticky note. It said, SOLD.

Jessica gasped in surprise. A man in a suit turned and looked at her, then turned to the woman next to him and whispered loudly, "There she is!" She hurried on.

The next painting was, somehow, his mermaid. The one he said he'd sold to his friend Carlos. Its title was "Mermaid," and the card explained that it was "On loan from the private collection of Mr. Carlos Iguirre." An even bigger semicircle of admirers surrounded that one, and as Jessica passed through it, she elicited more whispers.

As she pushed deeper into the crowd, she overheard more snatches of conversation:

"This guy has some serious talent. I don't know what he's doing here. He should be at one of the real galleries downtown."

She pushed to the far corner and the thickest part of the crowd, knowing—sensing—that Guillermo was there. On the way, she passed his garlic-and-mango still life, which had sold for four hundred and fifty dollars. An abstract painting of a face — it looked like the one she'd seen at his house — had sold for five hundred and fifty. And a painting she'd never seen, of a snake and an apple, had gone for seven hundred and fifty dollars.

"This is the best time to invest, before he gets too big. But everything's sold out already!"

Jessica kept going, pushing through the ever thickening crowd. She averted her eyes from the nude of the older woman — the one that had started all the trouble. It wasn't for sale. It was on loan from Mrs. J. T. Bennett.

"I heard Yolanda Olivarez say she wants to put him on their morning show."

The whispering, nudging, and pointing got more and more obvious around her as she broke through the circle surrounding him. In fact, everyone cleared a space for her, so that she was finally standing there face-to-face with the man himself.

He had never looked more handsome. He was wearing black pants and a blue silk shirt that perfectly set off his black hair and dark skin. This was her first time seeing him clean-shaven. It made him look younger. And... more vulnerable. She noticed his very favorite boots on his feet, the black ones she'd never seen him wear.

He was looking at her. Just the way he always did, with the calmest expression on his face.

In front of all these people, in the middle of everything, she had a sudden, strong desire to cross the space between them and kiss him. She could smell him, it seemed like. She wanted to run her hands over that shirt and over his now smooth face and kiss him until she couldn't see straight.

By turning his glance from hers, he broke the spell. She followed his eyes, over to the right, on the wall.

"Oh, my God," she whispered.

The painting on the wall was of a woman, lying in a window of dappled sunlight, her eyes closed. Her body was curled around cushions, and a sheer maroon cloth was curled around her body. It covered just enough to keep it from being a nude but left plenty exposed. Her exposed parts were big and round but somehow smooth and beautiful at the same time. The woman's brown and gold hair swirled around the pillow. Her pink lips were curved into the tiniest hint of a smile.

The title of the painting was "Jessica Sleeping."

Half the crowd by now had recognized her from the painting. Now that it was obvious that she'd never seen it before, they whispered excitedly. A man who hadn't yet seen her standing there was in the middle of a persuasive speech, apparently.

"Come on, Guillermo. I'll give you a thousand for it, then. You can paint another one!"

Guillermo's eyes were back on Jessica's, and he didn't look away again as he told the man, "I'm sorry. It's not for sale."

Then he stepped forward and took Jessica's hand, causing the would-be customer to notice her at last and say, "Oh-h-h…"

The crowd parted again, as if under Guillermo's spell, as he led Jessica through the gallery and out the emergency door.

# 32

**C**orazón," he said. "I knew you would come."

They'd stopped under the fire escape stairs, behind the building, under a mural of flames. The next thing she knew, Jessica was in his arms and they were devouring each other, making out as if he were headed off to war.

And it felt good.

There was no guilt in Jessica's mind at all as she let him kiss her mouth, her face, her neck.

"I've missed you so much," he murmured against her skin. "I was scared you were so mad, you would never come back."

She leaned back to look at him after he said these words, which melted into her like hot brownies into ice cream. His eyes were even hotter than that as he looked down at her and ran his fingers through the ends of her hair. She went back to kissing him.

It felt so good to be back in Guillermo's arms. Better than she'd imagined it, every night since the last time she'd seen him. She had to admit it to herself—she hadn't been able to stop thinking about him, and this was why.

What other man could make her feel the way he did? When he kissed her and her eyes were closed, it was as if she were spinning. Dancing.

In fact, she felt dizzy now. She pulled away to catch her

breath and to talk. She had a million questions she needed the answers to.

"Guillermo, how long have you been planning this?"

"The show? Remember, they called me three weeks ago? It's funny how many people came, no? Most of them are friends of the Bennett lady, I think. And some other people whose houses I painted."

That wasn't what she'd meant to ask him. But he continued, "Did you see, I sold all the paintings. Now I can pay my bills, get my truck fixed... And, also, I can take us out for a nice dinner, like I always wanted. Wherever you want to go." He brushed her hair away from her cheek with his fingertips. "Because it was you who made me do this. You wouldn't stop nagging me."

She decided now was the time to interrupt, before he went further with that thought and ruined the moment.

"Guillermo, I meant how long have you been planning to surprise me with that painting, here tonight? It's so beautiful. I almost cried when I saw it."

"You liked it, huh? I knew you would." He smiled and gave her a little kiss. "I didn't decide to do it until a few days ago."

"Really?"

He must have been planning to show it to her when they were alone one night. But then, when she'd stopped speaking to him...

"That's right," he said. "I knew you would come to my show, but since you didn't call, I thought you might still be mad when you got here. So I did the painting so you'd forget about whatever made you mad. It took me two days. I just finished it last night. And it worked, like I knew it would, because look: Here you are, kissing me."

His smile was proud, as if he hadn't just said the exact wrong thing.

As if he hadn't just *completely* ruined the moment.

As if he hadn't just forced her to wonder, *again*, what sickness made her keep coming back to him.

"Chiquitita...," he said as she pulled away, all the way this time.

As quickly as she'd found herself kissing him, she now felt an incredible urge to reach up and slap his face. Instead, she took more steps backward, to keep that from happening.

"What's wrong?" he said. "Did I paint you too sexy?"

Shaking her head in disgust, with him and with herself, she turned and ran under the fiery, sad murals all the way to her car.

Finally, she realized as she drove home with angry tears in her eyes, she'd gotten her sign. There was no longer any question in her mind as to which path she should take.

So, tell me everything. Michelangelo and Christine told me they saw you and Richie Rich at the House. Details, please."

It took Jessica a second to figure out what Toby was talking about. The thing with Guillermo had freaked her out so much, it was as if it had used up all her virtual memory and she had to reboot in order to process the Jonathan thing again. She took a drink of her frozen cosmopolitan to clear her head. She had remained quiet during the ride to the bar, but now she would have to come clean before Toby had a fit.

"There's not that much to tell. Remember, he's that friend of my brother-in-law's. We met a few weeks ago. We've gone out a few times...and so far, that's it."

"Oh no, that is *not* it, girl," said Toby. "Tell me *everything*. How is he?"

"I don't know yet. If you want to find out, you'll have to do him yourself." She took another sip of her drink and faced the stage, where drag queens were lined up in skirted swimsuits. The lights were so bright, they were making her eyes water.

"So, I take it you don't like this new guy too much?" said Toby.

"It's not that. I do like him. He's really nice...." Jessica couldn't figure out what it was. Guillermo's stupid face kept interrupting her thoughts. "We're just...taking it slow."

"Uh, hello! You didn't take it so slow when you were getting it from the Artist Barely Known as Guillermo," Toby interjected.

Jessica rolled her eyes as she felt her cheeks get hot. "Please. Don't remind me, okay?"

She turned away from his piercing eyes to watch the crowd for a while. But then Toby let out a quiet little scream and, alarmed, she spun on her bar stool to see what was wrong. He had one hand over his mouth and used the other to point at Jessica accusingly, as if they were in kindergarten and he'd caught her playing Doctor during naptime.

"Oh, no!" he squealed. "I know! You just got it from Guillermo, didn't you? I see it! I saw the look on your face! That's right, baby. Madame Hortensia ain't got nothing on me!" Toby crowed triumphantly. "Now spill it."

She blushed hard this time, telling him all he needed to know about what had happened at the art opening.

"Oh, my gosh!" said Toby. "That's so romantic. And all scandalous and stuff!"

Jessica sighed for what felt like the hundredth time that night. "No, it isn't, because he ruined it at the end. He messed everything up." For a second, it almost felt as though her eyes were about to mist up. "I was so stupid, Toby. What did I ever see in him? And now..." She decided to come clean all the way. "And now, I'm thinking I'm not supposed to have sex with Jonathan after all, because things keep going wrong with that."

Toby shook his head. "Well, I'm not getting what the big deal is," he said. "Obviously, Guillermo's just a straight-up dog." Jessica looked at him reproachfully. Unabashed, he went on. "But he's a *fine* dog. So, just use him for sex, and keep letting Mr. Goody Two-Shoes buy you dinner."

Jessica rolled her eyes. "I'm not *you*, Toby." She took a sip of her drink. "No, it's over between Guillermo and me." And, she decided, she was still going to see Jonathan. Next time she'd have her own condoms, and if it wasn't meant to be, something else would tell her.

Colored lights rained down as the club's MC announced the winner of the drag queen crown. For the second year in a row, Lady Chantay Devonique won. She took the stage and lip-synched to Céline Dion's "My Heart Will Go On" in a rhinestone bodysuit, six-inch Lucite platforms, and a feathered cape.

"Oh, good Lord," said Toby. By then, they'd had another round of frozen cosmos while commiserating over Guillermo's doggery and the loss of Toby's latest Guatemalan boyfriend to the INS. The queen and all runners-up promenaded off the stage, and the spotlights were replaced by disco lights. The DJ took Tropico back to its usual state, filling the auditorium-size club with the very best mix of salsa and merengue.

"Let's dance!" Toby said, slamming down his glass and pulling Jessica toward the floor, where couples were already starting the gigantic clockwise swirl of rhythm. "Here—spin me around," Toby said. "You're the only one who knows how to do it right."

He was obviously determined to have a good time. Jessica, taller than him by an inch, took his hand and spun him this way and that, just as they'd practiced so many times with Marisol when they were kids.

All around them, big, burly men in cowboy hats and boots held each other close. Young Chicanos in the latest fashions spun and shimmied on tabletops. Here and there, women led each other around the floor.

"Oh-oh-oh, hay...Hay que llorar...," she and Toby sang, along with everyone else in the club.

You have to cry, the song said. Everyone there knew it was true, and everyone danced to ease the pain.

# 34

This time, Jessica woke up with the proverbial splitting head-ache and ended up getting to Bella Cucina twenty minutes late. She parked, smoothed her skirt, and wiped the last of the sleep out of her eyes before passing under the vine-draped arch to the hostess's podium. Their parents were even later than she was, apparently, even though Papi was the guest of honor. Sabrina and David were the only ones at the table.

"You're late," Sabrina pointed out.

"Hi, Jessica," David said cheerfully.

She greeted her brother-in-law, then leaned forward to whisper to her sister, "Sabrina, listen. About the other day. I'm really sorry I—"

Sabrina interrupted her. "I don't want to hear it. We're here to have a nice lunch for Papi."

Taken aback, Jessica sat back in her chair, at her corner of the table. She glanced at David to check his reaction. He was fiddling with his napkin and didn't seem to have noticed their exchange. Jessica decided to pretend it hadn't happened. She would let Sabrina hold her grudge for now and worry about reconciliation later, when her head hurt less.

"Where are Mami and Papi?" she asked.

"They're on the way," said Sabrina. "Mami said to order them both lasagna."

When the waitress had taken their order to the kitchen, Sabrina leaned over and said in what was supposed to be a quiet voice, "I'm worried about Mami."

Jessica glanced at David again, wishing they didn't have to discuss all their family issues in front of him. "Why? What happened?"

"Nothing. It's just that—"

"Hey, hey, hey," their father called out from behind the hostess leading him to their table. "Here's my two favorite daughters!"

They both stood to kiss him on the cheek and wish him a happy Father's Day.

"And my favorite son-in-law, too," Papi said to David as he shook his hand. "So far," he added with a wink at Jessica.

Sabrina rolled her eyes, and so did their mother, who had silently taken a seat while Papi was busy greeting everyone. The waitress walked up and Papi asked her for a bottle of her finest champagne. Mami and Sabrina immediately negated his order. Unembarrassed, Papi winked at the waitress and stage-whispered, "You come back and see me later, okay?" Although she was no more than Jessica's age, she giggled flirtatiously at Papi and then scampered away under Mami's and Sabrina's twin glares.

Jessica quickly introduced a topic of discussion. "So, Papi, how's your work been?"

"Oh, m'ija. You know I hate to talk about work. Tell me what you've been doing, baby girl. Your mother says you're dating some bolillo now."

Jessica winced, caught between Sabrina's renewed glare and David's good-natured smile.

"She's seeing one of David's friends, Daddy," her sister explained. "He's very nice—a vice president at David's company."

"Oh, a big shot," said her father. "So, dirty mexicanos like your papi aren't good enough for you anymore, huh? Hey, maybe David has a friend for your mother, too."

Jessica winced again. Papi was kidding, obviously, but it was so disrespectful to say that while David was sitting right there. He couldn't help that he wasn't Mexican.

She peeked over at him. At least he was smiling—probably pretending it didn't bother him. Or maybe it really didn't bother him. He must have been used to Papi's ways by now. Sabrina, on the other hand, obviously did get the joke and didn't find it funny at all. She looked far from amused.

Jessica changed the subject. "So, Papi, guess what we got you for Father's Day."

He smiled broadly. "I don't know, but I hope it's a bottle of tequila."

Mami shook her head resignedly and looked around at the restaurant decor as if Papi were just a spoiled child to be ignored.

Okay. The third time had to be the charm. Jessica changed the topic one last time. "So, Papi, are you ready for the barbecue tonight?"

"If anybody had asked me," said Papi, "we wouldn't be having one. I don't need to sit around with a bunch of my in-laws, being bored. I'd rather take a nap, then have your mother wake me up after she's cooked some pork chops."

No one said anything.

"And a cake," he added.

Mami looked out the window as if she were pretending to be someplace else.

"Chocolate cake," her father clarified. His smile *was* like a child's as he looked over at Mami, as if expecting her to give in and smile at any moment.

Jessica loved her father very much, and she always found his little jokes hilarious. Or had, until now. Now, she was imagining how they must have sounded to her mother. Insensitive, maybe? Crass?

She thought of Guillermo, always saying the wrong thing at the crucial moment. Until now, his good looks and charm had made up for it. Obviously, Jessica thought as she studied her mother's distant attitude, Mami had a much higher tolerance level for that sort of thing, considering that she'd been married to Papi for so long, but it looked as though she'd finally reached her limit.

After lunch, they all drove to the house and stood in the yard to watch David unload the lawn mower from his SUV.

"Surprise!" Sabrina sang out.

A polite smile was frozen to Papi's face. "Wow. That's real nice. I bet that cost a lot of money, huh?"

"Now you don't have to use that old push mower anymore, Papi," Sabrina explained. "Now you can mow the lawn with this new one, every weekend."

"Thank you, baby." Papi said somewhat mechanically. He gave her a kiss on the cheek, then turned to Jessica with a gleam of anticipation in his eye. "What about you, Jessi? What'd *you* get me?"

"Uh...the lawn mower is from all of us, Papi."

"Oh. Well, thank you, girls. It's very nice."

He reached over and hugged them both at once and then shook David's hand, too. It was obvious, to Jessica, at least, that he was hiding his disappointment. He was trying, finally, to behave appropriately, and for some reason, that broke her heart. Despite her annoyance with her father for ruining their lunch, Jessica wished that she'd woken up early and bought him something good after all.

After Sabrina and David left, Jessica went inside to help her mother get ready for the barbecue. Papi sat on the couch the whole time, criticizing the people on TV.

"Viejo, why don't you go outside and try your new lawn mower?" Mami called to him as she peeled potatoes.

"Because this is supposed to be my day to celebrate, not to do extra work," he called back.

Mami rolled her eyes and muttered, "What do you think *I'm* doing?"

Jessica looked down at the pickles she was chopping. The last thing she needed was Mami and Papi starting more drama. Her head was pounding, and she wished like crazy that she'd made some excuse to miss the barbecue.

"You call that Miss America? Girl, you better get in the kitchen and eat something!" her father exclaimed. Mami chopped a potato in half with a loud *thwack*.

"Papi, why don't you go tune your guitar so you can play it tonight?" Jessica called to him. "I haven't heard you play in a long time."

Long ago, before Jessica was born, her father had played in a mariachi band. That was how he and Mami had met, in fact.

Back then, their names had been Alejandro and Maria. He'd first seen her when he and his group had played at her cousin's wedding one Saturday night. Afterward, Alejandro had followed Maria home and serenaded her under her bedroom window. Although it sounded a little like stalking now, Jessica knew that in the old days, that sort of thing was considered romantic. By the time her parents were married and Sabrina came along, Papi had given up his mariachi gigs and started working full-time at the bottling plant. And now, so many years later, he was a supervisor there. He still kept a guitar, but he played it only once in a while. That had always been Jessica's favorite part of their family parties—when her father sang those old romantic songs, like someone out of a movie.

"I'm not going to play tonight," Papi called from the couch. "Your mother doesn't like it. She says it's embarrassing."

"It's not your playing that embarrasses me," Mami retorted. "It's the way you're always drunk when you do it."

"Fine…" Papi's voice got louder. "Maybe I'll sell my guitar, then, and use the money to buy something you'll like. Like a new vacuum cleaner."

"Why not hire me a maid instead?" Mami called back just as loudly. "She can clean up all the mess you make."

Jessica pushed all the vegetables she'd chopped into a bowl, all the while wondering if she should get involved. Obviously, her attempts to distract them weren't working.

Her father had come into the doorway by then. "Maybe I will hire a maid," he said to Mami. "Maybe she'd appreciate me more than you."

Jessica was frightened of the look in his eyes. It was as if he were goading Mami, daring her to argue back.

She did more than just that. She slammed the potato and knife she'd been holding into the sink, causing potato skins to fly into the air. She turned to face Papi full on and practically yelled in his face:

"What is there to appreciate? All you do is sit on your ass, watching TV and drinking beer. You don't appreciate *me*. I work all day, then come home and clean up after *you*. Cook your dinner! Do your laundry! And you know what?"

She took a kitchen towel from the counter, wiped her hands with it, and threw it on the floor. "I'm sick of it." Then she untied the apron she was wearing and threw it to the floor, too.

"Mami," said Jessica. But her mother ignored her. She pushed past Papi, who had been standing in the doorway with his arms crossed. Jessica followed her into the living room in time to see her disappear through the bedroom door. Jessica turned to her father, but he also ignored her and watched the bedroom door instead.

Mami came out with her purse and her keys.

"There you go," Papi called in a mocking voice. "Go ahead. Throw your little tantrum! Why don't you go to the mall and spend all the rest of my money? That always makes you feel better."

Mami fixed him with an icy glare. "Why don't you go to hell? I'm not going to the mall. And I'm not coming back, either, so you're going to have to cook your own damn dinner."

And with that she went out the front door, slamming it hard behind her.

Jessica stood absolutely still. Her mouth hung open in complete shock.

Her father ran to the door and opened it. Already, Mami was in her car, starting the engine. "Again!" he yelled. "You mean, cook my own dinner again!"

Mami's car made a loud noise as it peeled out onto the road. Papi stood and watched it disappear.

"Papi," said Jessica. She didn't know what she was going to say, but she had to say something.

He turned to her and spoke before she could. "Here comes your mother's family, m'ija. Tell them we're not having the party anymore. I'll be in the garage."

He went out the door, opening it wide enough for Jessica to see a car full of relatives pull up.

After she'd sent everyone home with excuses and foil-wrapped plates of brisket, Jessica had cleaned up her mother's kitchen and then gone home without another word to her father. She was angry with him for the first time in a very long while. She couldn't believe the inconsiderate things he'd said to her mother. She couldn't believe he'd left her to deal with the barbecue guests like that.

Then again, she thought as she drove home, she couldn't believe her mother's behavior, either. Papi had been the same way throughout their marriage. Why did it suddenly bother her now?

Sabrina, Jessica thought. It was Sabrina. Ever since she'd married David and moved out to that big house in Sugarland, their mother had slowly become more and more dissatisfied with Papi and his ways.

The minute she got back to her apartment, Jessica called her sister.

"Hello?"

"Sabrina. Is Mami there with you?" Jessica's voice came out accusing, but she didn't care.

"No. Why?"

"Because she got mad at Papi and left before the barbecue. She said she wasn't coming back."

"Oh, God," her sister said. "Did she say she was coming over here?"

"No. But she must be. That's where she went last time, to your house."

"Well, she's not here. But David's parents will be here any minute now. Dang it. Why won't Mami get a cell phone?"

For some reason, hearing the alarm in Sabrina's voice made Jessica feel better—maybe because now she wasn't alone in her concern. "Well, where else would she have gone? Papi said something about the mall."

"I don't know. I don't think so. With Mami, who knows? Where does she ever go besides work and the grocery store? And my house?"

The two sisters sat in silent worry, connected by blood and a telephone signal.

"I didn't realize it'd gotten so bad between them," Jessica said then.

Sabrina sighed. "Mami didn't want you to know. She didn't want you to worry."

"Oh, but it's okay for *you* to worry? What's up with that?"

Sabrina sighed again. "I don't know. You'll have to ask her. Listen, I'll call you if I hear anything, and you do the same, okay? In the meantime, why don't you try to talk to Papi? Make him apologize so they can get over this."

Jessica's thumbnail had gone to her mouth, and she chewed it very lightly, not wanting to give in to her worries. "Do you think that'll help? I mean, it kind of seems like they're past that point, doesn't it? The way they were yelling at each other today...Sabrina, it sounds pretty bad." Even though she resented her older sister knowing more about the situation than she did, Jessica found that she wanted Sabrina to reassure her.

"I don't know, Jessi. We'll just have to see, I guess."

After renewed promises to call each other if they heard anything, the sisters hung up.

Jessica spent the rest of the evening lying on her couch, watching a bunch of teenage dramas on TV. She called her father more than once, but he didn't answer. Guillermo called and hung up on her voice mail twice.

The third time, he didn't hang up. But it wasn't Guillermo, either. It was Jonathan. By the time Jessica realized this, the call had already rolled to voice mail. She waited for him to finish, then played back his message. He said he'd had a good time Friday night, and he wanted to know if she was free the following weekend, because he had a little surprise.

Jessica decided to call him back tomorrow. Right now, she wasn't in the mood to talk to anyone. Her parents' fight had really brought her down. It was coloring the way she felt about everything.

More than ever she felt that the path of her life was already laid out for her but clouded over so she couldn't see where it went. If she'd been a character in a movie, or in one of the novels on her bookshelf, Jessica would start out as an assistant, sure, but then something magical would happen. She'd get discovered at a club and become one of Amber Chavez's backup dancers. Or else she'd find out she was a long-lost princess of an island no one had ever heard of before.

But that wasn't the way real life worked. Her choice of plotlines was pretty limited. She could work at McCormick for the rest of her life, like her mother at Hawthorne Elementary, or she could marry someone with money and quit her job, like Sabrina. Or she could marry someone like Guillermo and struggle along, hoping her kids would do better in life than she had. Like her mother? she wondered suddenly. Maybe her mother felt that way about her marriage to Papi.

She stopped herself there. She didn't want to think about her parents in that way.

The truth was, Jessica knew, that she didn't *have* to do any of those things. She could always strike out on her own and try to get her web design business going full-time. She might meet someone completely new, sometime in the future, who ended up being perfect for her in every way.

But those ideas scared her. She had to admit to herself that she was afraid to try something new.

All the fortune-telling and magic soap she bought wouldn't change that. But she wished, at least, that it could tell her which choices would be the right ones—the ones that would make her happy.

She didn't want to end up like Sabrina, spending her days decorating and selling kitchenware to her friends. And she didn't want to end up like Mami, screaming at her husband and then running away from home and making her daughters sick with worry. Maybe that was part of why it bothered her so much when they tried to tell her what to do. It wasn't only that their "advice" made her feel childish; maybe it was also that if Jessica was completely honest, she didn't respect the choices they'd made in their own lives.

After Jessica had watched *Manhattan High* and *Love Search: San Antonio*, Guillermo called again. This time, he left a voice mail. "Chiquitita. Come on. Call me back, corazón."

Right as she was carrying Ricky to the bedroom, the phone rang again. It was Sabrina, finally.

"Sabrina, what happened?" she said into the phone a little breathlessly.

But it wasn't her sister. It was Mami, calling from Sabrina's house. "M'ija, it's me. I'm just calling to let you know I'm okay."

"Mami. What happened? Where did you go?"

"Nowhere. I'm spending the night at Sabrina's tonight. If you talk to your father, please let him know. Also, I'm sorry I left you there to do the barbecue by yourself."

Her mother's calm tone was completely exasperating. Jessica tried to keep her voice patient. "It was fine. I told everybody you got sick and went to take a nap. But, Mami, why did you leave like that? When are you going back home? You and Papi can't keep fighting like this. You have to go home and work this out."

Her mother was silent for a long time. Every second of her silence gave Jessica more and more reason to be afraid. Then, finally, Mami said, "I don't know yet, m'ija. I have to think things over."

Before Jessica could say anything else, her mother said,

"Listen, I have to go now. But I'll call you back tomorrow, okay? If you talk to your father, tell him I'm okay, but don't tell him anything else."

Jessica agreed unhappily, and her mother hung up the phone.

# 35

Monday morning, Jessica sat at her desk typing up insurance certificates, trying her best to put her family's troubles out of her mind. But they wouldn't let her.

First, Papi called. On her cell. Right as Ted was walking by. He raised an eyebrow at the ringing coming from her purse but didn't say anything, luckily.

"Hello?"

"Jessi, I need you to call your mother and tell her you need her to come home. Did you know she never came home last night?" His voice rose to a bellow.

"Shh...I know." Jessica felt the need to quiet Papi down, as if her bosses might overhear him. "Why don't you just call her yourself? You know she's at Sabrina's house."

"Because I don't want to bring Sabrina and David into it. This is between your mother and me."

Why, then, Jessica wondered, was Papi bringing *her* into it? "Papi, you really need to call Mami yourself. You need to apologize."

"For what?" Her father's voice became loud again. "For not jumping up and mowing the lawn every time she tells me, like I'm her slave? *She* needs to apologize to *me*."

"Papi..." Jessica tried to think of something soothing to say, then realized that soothing her father's ego wasn't going to get him to do what needed to be done. "I know you hate mowing the lawn, but did you ever think that maybe Mami feels like a slave when she has to cook dinner for you guys every night? When's the last time you cooked?" Her father snorted derisively, so Jessica amended her question. "When's the last time you took her out to eat, then?"

"She never wants to go!" he said. "I've asked her a hundred times to go to Rudy's with me on catfish night, and she always says she has to clean the house instead!"

Jessica was about to suggest that maybe her mother would like something a little nicer than Rudy's fried catfish, but just then Ted came by for the second time with a file in his hand. He stopped near Jessica's desk and cleared his throat.

"Look, Papi, I have to go now. I'll call you later, okay? But please think about what I said." In a whisper, Jessica added, "And call Mami!" Then she hung up and gave Ted her full attention while he gave her instructions on the file.

The moment he stepped away, her cell rang again. This time it was her mother. Jessica sighed in quiet exasperation. She saw Rochelle and Olga giving her curious looks. She bent down toward her desk for relative privacy and answered the phone.

"Mami. Did Papi call you?"

"No. Why, did he say he would?"

"Well, no, but—"

"Jessica," her mother interrupted, "you and I need to talk. Can we have lunch tomorrow?"

"Uh...yeah, sure." Jessica really was afraid now. Why was her mother asking to have lunch with her, as if she were planning a business meeting? She almost didn't want to find out. She almost told her mother no.

But instead they made plans to meet at Joe's Mexican Restaurant the next day at noon.

"I know you're at work, so I won't keep you," her mother said in the same emotionless voice she'd been using since the night before.

Jessica hung up with her and went back to work unhappily, trying her hardest not to worry about what her mother might say the next day.

Instead she worried about her promotion all morning long. By the time she came back to the office from lunch at Shoe Warehouse, Jessica was ready to march into Mr. Cochran's office and *demand* her promotion right then and there. Or at least she was ready to demand it if he ever showed up. Olga was away from her desk, and Rochelle ran off to the ladies' room the moment Jessica sat down. To distract herself, she worked like a maniac on her files. As the afternoon went on, she felt the anxiety creeping back.

What if she asked Mr. Cochran for a promotion and he said no?

What if her father never called her mother to apologize?

What if her mother wanted a divorce?

Fred rushed into the office at two, hysterical over a renewal he'd let slip. Jessica calmed him down and immediately set to work, scanning and e-mailing applications to the underwriters she knew would give good last minute quotes. She was right in the middle of all that when Mr. Cochran strolled in, at three, and shut himself up in his office. He still hadn't opened his door when it was time to go home.

Jessica turned off her computer and picked up her stuff to leave. At least she'd saved Fred's account. It was a good opportunity to remind them of how valuable she was around here.

As she left work, a light summer thunderstorm started, echoing her mood. She turned on her windshield wipers and drove straight to Madame Hortensia's.

The old woman was standing on the covered porch, almost as if she'd foreseen Jessica coming. Lightning struck as Madame Hortensia led Jessica inside to the little velvet table.

"Cards or palm, m'ija? Or did you like the runes last time?"

"No, not the runes. And not the palm...." Jessica didn't think the lines on her hand could have changed very much in the last few weeks. Should she have Madame Hortensia do the cards again? Everyone on them had the same color hair.

"How about something new? Tea leaves? Or the I Ching? Or the numbers?"

"The numbers? What's that?"

"It's a new one I just learned. You combine all the important numbers of your life to make a master number that tells you everything you need to hear," Madame Hortensia said.

"Okay. Do I get a discount on that one, too?"

"Sure. Eighteen dollars."

Jessica handed over the money and waited impatiently for Madame Hortensia to remove a pencil and a notepad from her mystical box. She'd driven over right after work to beat out any housewives needing their own fortunes read. She needed to find out what was supposed to happen before she did anything else.

"Okay," said Madame Hortensia. "What year were you born?"

Jessica told her, and the old woman wrote down the number. "Tan jovencita. That makes you...twenty-six, no?"

Don't remind me, Jessica thought.

"Now, what is your birthday?"

"April sixteenth." Jessica saw her write down "516." "Um, Madame Hortensia, April is fourth."

"Mande?"

"April is the fourth month of the year. It's four, not five."

The old woman fixed her with the same sort of look Mami used to give her for having a smart mouth. "I'm not using the number of the month. I'm using the number of the House under which you were born."

"Oh. I'm sorry." Jessica blushed and decided to leave the fortune-telling to the professional from here on out.

"What time were you born?"

"I don't know. I think it was late at night."

The old woman looked at her impatiently again. "Before midnight or after?"

"Let's say before," Jessica said quickly.

"Ándale." Madame Hortensia wrote "1130" under the other numbers and a "2" under that. What was the 2 for? Jessica wondered. For p.m., maybe?

"Okay. Now, what is your favorite number?"

That one was easy. "Six." She'd always liked its swirly shape.

Madame Hortensia wrote all the numbers in the column and started to add them up. "One...nineteen," Jessica heard her whisper. "Carry the...four...chinelas..." She erased a sum and added again. She wrote a few more digits, then counted on her fingers and finally wrote a single number—a 3.

"Okay. Esperame un momentito, m'ija. I'll be right back." Painstakingly, she got up and hobbled to what must have been her bedroom.

Poor Madame Hortensia. Jessica hoped she wasn't interrupting the old lady's medicine schedule or anything like that.

Much to Jessica's surprise, however, she came back into the living room carrying a laptop.

"Madame Hortensia! You have a computer!"

"Of course I do, m'ija."

"But... why?"

"Well, I have a business to run here. I sell my soaps on eBay. Also, I have clients in other cities, and I do readings for them over e-mail."

Jessica felt silly for underestimating her. Madame Hortensia opened her laptop on the table, typed into it rapidly for a moment, then peered at the screen.

"Hmm." She went back to her piece of paper and studied it intently. She took her pencil and erased the 5 in 516. She changed it to a 4, then recalculated everything. She changed the final 3 to an 8, then consulted her monitor again.

"Ándale—here we go."

By then, Jessica was dying of impatience.

"Okay. As far as your health goes—"

"Madame Hortensia, please, can we skip the health?"

"Oh, okay. Next is your lucky numbers, then. You want to write these down, m'ija?"

"No. Madame Hortensia, can we please skip the lucky numbers, too?"

The old woman looked up at Jessica's face. "M'ija, why don't you just tell me what it is you want to know?"

What Jessica really wanted to know was whether or not her parents were on the way to divorce. But the last time she'd been here, the old woman had told her to let her parents work out their own issues. So Jessica decided not to ask and moved on to the next most pressing problem in her mind. "I want to know if I'm going to get promoted."

The answer to that one came to the fortune-teller immediately. "Well, of course. Why not? You're a smart girl. You're good with numbers. Eventually, your boss will see this and promote you."

"I meant, will I get the promotion that's available right now? I haven't been able to talk to my boss, and I need to know what he's going to say before I buy any more new work clothes."

Madame Hortensia sighed and closed her laptop. She leaned over it and gestured for Jessica's hand. "Dámelo...déjame ver."

She studied Jessica's palm for a few moments, tracing the lines with her index finger. Then she said, "He will say...what he's meant to say. *If* this job is right for you, then he'll say yes."

What? What did that mean? Jessica looked down at the line Madame Hortensia had left off at. Was there a mole or a wrinkle or something that would mean plain yes or no?

"M'ija, what I'm telling you is that you will do what you're meant to do. If it's the right job you're asking for, then yes, you'll get it. If it's not, then you will look for something else. But you will end up with the right job."

Jessica sighed. "Okay, then, what about the guy?"

"Which guy?"

"The blond one—the bolillo. The one you said I have to

give a chance to. I think I got my sign, so I'm not going to see the mexicano anymore. But is the bolillo the man I'm supposed to end up with? Is he...the man I'm going to be with for the rest of my life?"

Madame Hortensia examined Jessica's hand again. "The answer's the same. If he's the man you're meant to be with, then you'll be with him. But if he's not, then you will look for the real one." She pushed the hand back gently.

For the first time, Jessica began to think that maybe this woman didn't know any more about the future than anyone else.

The cards, the runes, the lines on her hand...none of it really meant anything, did it? She'd already wasted enough money on coming here, and nothing the fortune-teller said really told her what she was supposed to do. Why did she keep coming back, then? She wished she knew. If Madame Hortensia didn't really know what was going to happen, then no one did, and Jessica was destined to mess everything up, just like before, when she'd tried to have a real art career at the Centro and date a real artist. And both those things had turned out to be fake, proving she didn't know how to make the right choices on her own.

The old woman sat studying Jessica's sad face for a while and then sighed. She put one hand on her card box and one hand on the crystal ball next to it and pushed them both aside, to the edge of the table, so that there was nothing between her and her client anymore.

Then she leaned over and put her wrinkled, callused but soft hand on top of Jessica's. "M'ija, do you know why people come to see me?"

"So you can tell them what to do?"

"No. So that I can give them *permission* to do what they want."

She smiled gently at Jessica's confused expression, then went on.

"Married women come here and ask me if their husbands are cheating. In five minutes, I can tell if they want me to say, 'This card means you will leave him,' or if they'd rather hear, 'This card means you will work it out and stay together.' Pregnant women come here to ask about their babies. They need the cards to say, 'You are doing all the right things. You will be a good mother.' Women come here over and over to hear the cards say the same things. 'Yes, you are right to be angry, or sad, or confused. Keep on doing what you're doing. You're doing the right thing.'"

Jessica's mouth fell open as she listened to the older woman's words. Once again, someone was shocking her with the real, honest truth. Why was Madame Hortensia giving away her secrets like this? Didn't she know that she'd be missing out on money?

"M'ija, you're a smart, pretty girl. You have a good job, plenty of men are interested in you, and you have a family that loves you."

Jessica interrupted. "I know. But —"

"Even though your parents are having problems," the old woman added as if she really were psychic, "they love you, and they will always love you, even if they end up breaking up. So don't worry."

"But," Jessica said again.

"No, m'ija. That's it. Houston, we have no problemas. Verdad?"

Jessica had to nod reluctantly at that.

Madame Hortensia smiled kindly and went on. "You keep asking me what's going to happen to you, but I can't tell you what you want to hear any more than your mother or sister can because you yourself don't know what you want. And I'm running out of lucky charms to sell you."

Jessica thought that over. It was true. All the questions Madame Hortensia had been asking had been her attempts to discover what Jessica wanted to hear. And it was true—Jessica didn't even know herself.

"But something I can tell you for certain," said Madame Hortensia, "is that everything's going to be okay for you. Because as soon as you decide what you want, you're the kind of young woman who will find the way to get it. That, I can see without any cards or magic numbers."

She got up and hobbled around the table. With a hand on Jessica's shoulder, she steered her to the door.

"But...," said Jessica as the woman prodded her through the doorway. "But—"

"Enough, m'ija. I have customers waiting. And you...you have your fortune to make."

# 36

Jessica strutted into the office wearing a silver suit with a pink silk shirt and oxblood stilettos. Today she was going to get what she asked for. She didn't care if she had to camp out in Mr. Cochran's office to do it.

"Jessica, do you want these last few SpeedSlim bars?" Olga asked.

"No thanks. Do you know when Mr. Cochran's coming in?"

"It should be any minute now."

Jessica took her seat, rotating her chair so that it pointed to his door.

"You sure are getting your desk clean over there, Olga," said Rochelle. Jessica looked over. It was true. Olga was throwing away old papers and putting all her Beanie Babies in neat little stacks.

The door to their department's section opened. It was Mr. Cochran. Jessica stood up. So did Olga.

"Mr. Cochran, can I speak to you for a minute?"

"Sure, Olga. Come in."

She closed the door behind her. Jessica fell back into her chair, supremely annoyed. What did Olga want? A bigger monitor so she could see her solitaire games better?

Immediately, she was ashamed of herself for thinking such

a catty thing. She turned to Rochelle, who was sitting there serene as ever, reading an online article about reversing the effects of menopause.

"Rochelle, can I ask you something?"

"Mm-hmm. What do you need, sugar?"

"We haven't talked in a while. I was wondering..." How should she put it? "Do you still *not* want a promotion?"

Rochelle laughed. "Girl, are you still thinking about that? No, I sure don't. I have enough on my plate already as it is."

Mr. Cochran's door opened. Olga walked out stiffly, with Mr. Cochran right behind her.

"Don't worry about shutting down your computer, Olga. The ladies will take care of that for you. Just take your... your purse, there. And your umbrella. And your tennis shoes, that's fine. We'll take care of the rest and have it couriered over to you."

Jessica and Rochelle stared as Olga grabbed her personal belongings. "All right, Mr. Cochran. Thank you. Have a good one." She turned and walked to the door. At the last minute, as if it were an afterthought, she turned and waved at her co-workers of three years. "Bye, Rochelle, Jessica. Y'all have a good one." And then she was gone.

Mr. Cochran had left the office right behind Olga, and he still hadn't come back half an hour later. While they waited, Jessica and Rochelle didn't get any work done at all.

"It was probably all the online bingo she was playing," Jessica whispered.

"No," Rochelle whispered back. "He wouldn't have even noticed that."

"Maybe Tech Support noticed it and told him." Jessica said it but couldn't believe it would've happened without Xavier giving her a heads-up.

"No, I don't think so. I just can't see that making a difference to him one way or another, as long as she was sitting there when he needed her."

"Maybe she asked for a raise." Jessica hated even saying that aloud. If Mr. Cochran would fire Olga for asking for more money...

"Uh-uh," said Rochelle. "She just got her two-year raise in May."

"Well, then what? Why else would he let her go? Unless she quit. She did ask to see *him*. And now that I think about it, she didn't look too upset."

"Why would she quit, though? That'd be stupid." Rochelle frowned in concentration. "Maybe she was having an affair with someone at McCormick, and Mr. Cochran found out about it."

"Who, Olga? No way!"

By lunchtime, they still hadn't found out what had happened. But Jessica couldn't worry about that anymore. She had to meet her mother for lunch and try to convince her to go back home.

# 37

Jessica hurried out of the building and drove to Joe's Mexican Restaurant, a dumpy little place near Mami's work. She found parking, then went inside and saw that it hadn't changed at all since the last time she'd been there several years ago. At the door, the hostess was still stationed behind a glass case of dusty Mexican candies. On the back wall, there was still a jukebox playing Tejano favorites. On the side walls, there were still Christmas decorations from the 1970s, along with various depictions of the Virgen de Guadalupe. It was as though Jessica had gone through a time machine back to her childhood.

Mami was there waiting for her, at a quiet booth in the corner. Jessica took a salsa-stained menu from the hostess, then went to join her mother. She stood up to receive Jessica's hug, then they both sat down. Before Jessica could say anything, the ancient waitress ambled over.

Mami took her time ordering, asking about all the ingredients in the tacos and if the tortillas were fresh. By the time the waitress had gone away, Jessica was impatient to discuss what they needed to discuss.

"How's your work?" her mother said.

"Fine." Jessica left it at that. There was no use getting into all the details of what was really going on with the new broker position. Her mother, like Rochelle, would only wonder why Jessica wasn't happy being a secretary for the rest of her life. Plus, she had only about forty-five minutes left in her lunch hour. Best to cut to the chase.

"Mami, what's going on? Have you talked to Papi yet? When are you going back home?"

Her mother raised an eyebrow. She wasn't ready to discuss any of that yet, apparently, because she acted as if Jessica hadn't said it. "The reason I asked you to lunch was to talk about you, m'ija."

Although Jessica was frustrated by her mother's avoidance of the issue, she had to take the bait. "About me? What about me?"

"M'ijita, I know I can't tell you what to do. But I want you to stop seeing this painter."

Jessica's mind raced. Did her mother mean Guillermo? Of course she did. But how did she know? Jessica had never told Sabrina, so it couldn't have been... Oh, damn, Jessica suddenly thought. Loudmouth Toby and his nosy, tattletale mother.

"I don't know who you mean, Mami," she said. "If Mrs. Jimenez is telling you stories about—"

"Jessica, please. That's enough."

"Enchiladas verdes?" said the waitress, setting the plate in front of her mother and a plate of chicken tacos in front of Jessica.

When she was gone, Mami fixed Jessica with her most serious eyes. "Your father and I have done the best we could for you. We both worked hard in order to buy you nice clothes and then send you to college. And now you've had a good long time to run around with your friends and live in your own apartment."

How, Jessica wondered, had the conversation turned into this? She was there to find out what was happening between her parents. And instead, her mother was sitting here giving her a guilt trip over a man who wasn't even in her life anymore.

"It's time," Mami continued, "for you to start thinking about the rest of your life. About how you're going to live."

What was she talking about? Jessica already had a job, an apartment, and a car. How did this relate to whatever Mrs. Jimenez must have told her about Guillermo?

"You have to think about who's going to take care of you," her mother said.

"I'm already taking care of myself."

"Jessica, please. Let me finish." But instead of finishing, Mami sipped her coffee and looked at the gold and silver tinsel garland draped above their heads.

Jessica took the opportunity to eat some of her chicken taco. Joe's didn't serve quesadillas. And they didn't give her guacamole or sour cream. As she chewed the boiled chicken in its beans, tortilla, and meager amount of cheese, Jessica felt like a child again. Back in the first house they'd had, near the rice plants, when she was very young. Before Papi had gotten promoted at the bottling plant and they'd moved to the house in the Heights.

When her mother had collected sufficient thoughts, she said, "M'ija, pretty soon you're going to get married. You need to make the right choice."

"By marrying someone rich. Is that what you mean?"

"No, m'ijita. By marrying someone *good*."

"Like Sabrina did, you mean?" Jessica tried to contain herself, but the anger and frustration were starting to leak into her voice.

"Yes. Like that."

Jessica sighed. She was about to do something she never did: talk back to her mother. But it was time for her to stand up for herself. "Mami, I'm not Sabrina. What's right for her may not be what's right for me. I'm doing fine. I have a good job. I have a nice place to live. I have enough money to buy whatever I want. Almost."

For the first time, her mother's emotionless shell cracked. Looking sad and worried, Mami said, "But are you happy, Jessica? That's what I worry about, m'ijita. I don't want you to be miserable, because then you'll end up marrying the first man who asks you, whether he can take care of you or not...." Her voice trailed off. "I just don't want you to end up like I did."

She stopped talking again and took a long sip of coffee. Then she stared out the window at the cars going by. It didn't look as though she were going to say any more.

"Mami...," said Jessica. All her anger had stopped and was now trying to go backward, getting clogged up in her throat. For the first time, she was starting to see that maybe Mami's issues weren't with *her*.

"Mami, are you that unhappy with Papi now? Are you thinking of getting..." She didn't want to say "divorced." She let her voice trail off.

Her mother turned and looked her directly in the face. Oh no, Jessica thought. It was true, then.

Mami laughed. But not as if it were funny. She laughed as if it were sad, the way the singers always did in ranchera songs. "I don't know what I'm going to do. But you're right. I'm not happy, and I'm starting to see that I made the wrong choice."

For some reason, Jessica suddenly had a vision of the Virgin Mary on her mother's porch rocking back and forth. She couldn't believe what she was hearing.

"Mami, how can you say that? You didn't make the wrong choice! You and Papi go together. He's the funny one, and you're the serious one. Of course you love him...he needs you. He needs you to make him..."

Make him what? Jessica didn't know the ending to that sentence. She was surprised to see her mother wipe her eyes. Mami never cried.

"I know he needs me," she said quietly. "But I'm tired. Who do I need? No one. I'm the one who's always doing the right thing—going to work, taking care of the house, worrying about you and your sister. And then, on top of that, I'm supposed to worry about your father, too? Why can't he do the right things on his own, without me nagging him all the time?"

Jessica heard her own question about Guillermo in her mother's words. Suddenly, her choices and her mother's didn't seem so different at all.

Mami continued to stare out the window and talk, almost as if she were talking to herself. "You know, when I met your father, I thought he was so romantic. He was always playing me songs on his guitar. Always wanting to drop everything and run off to the country with me. And the way he talked to my parents... They didn't like him, but he didn't care. And I didn't care. And he was so handsome...." She sighed.

Jessica listened intently, imagining her mother as clearly as if she were a character in a movie. She could imagine Mami as a young woman, just as serious and hardworking as ever. Of course she would be drawn to a man like Papi—a good-looking, free-spirited musician who seemed custom-built to take her mind off her troubles.

Her mother continued, "Back then I was young and stupid. I thought those things were enough for a good marriage, as long as I was the serious one and kept your father in line. And I was so proud to be the one who finally made your father settle down, Jessica. A lot of other girls were after him, in those days." She smiled wistfully at the memory. "But now, after thirty years of that, I'm tired of keeping your father in line. And I realize now that he's never going to change. I wish I had listened to my mother and married someone...someone different."

Suddenly Jessica had to wipe her own eyes. Hearing her mother say these things made her feel again like a child, small and afraid. "But, Mami, you still love Papi, don't you?"

Her mother didn't answer immediately.

"Don't you?" Jessica pressed.

"Yes. I love him. But sometimes that just isn't enough."

Jessica didn't know what to say. She didn't know how she could make things right. She needed someone's help. Suddenly, she had an idea.

"Mami, listen. I know someone who can help. Let me take you to see Madame Hortensia."

Her mother snorted, then wiped her nose on her napkin.

"That old fortune-teller in the purple house? Now you're just being silly, Jessica. This isn't something that can be fixed with a crystal ball."

"No, I promise you, Madame Hortensia is different. Please, let me take you. Please, Mami, just try it."

# 38

In the end, her mother agreed to go—probably only because Jessica had practically begged her. After work, then, Jessica found herself sitting in her car outside the little purple house, with the engine running so that her air conditioner could battle the summer heat. Mami had been inside Madame Hortensia's house for an hour, and Jessica was resisting the urge to bite her nails when her cell rang. It was Sabrina.

"Hello."

"Jessica, is Mami with you?" Sabrina sounded concerned and not a little frustrated.

"Yes. Listen, did she tell you she wanted to divorce Papi?"

There was a pause. "Well, no," Sabrina finally said. "Not in so many words, but—"

Jessica didn't wait to hear the rest. "Babosa, why didn't you tell me? I had no idea it was this bad between them."

Sabrina sighed. "I *couldn't* tell you. Mami wouldn't let me."

Of course she wouldn't, Jessica thought. Once again, her mother and sister had been making important decisions on their own—decisions that affected the rest of the family. And once again, Jessica couldn't help but be annoyed with her sister.

"You should have told me anyway," she fired back at Sabrina. "Then things wouldn't have gone this far."

"Jessica," Sabrina said in her most annoying older sister voice, "I know what you're thinking, but it's not like that. I wasn't trying to keep it secret from you. Mami really didn't want anyone else to know about this—especially you. She didn't want you to worry. And, well, she knows how close you are to Papi..."

At that point, Mami came out of Madame Hortensia's house.

"I've got to go," Jessica hissed into the phone. "We'll talk about this later." She hung up as her mother got into the car. As usual, Mami's face gave no clues. As she pulled away, Jessica glanced at the Virgin Mary. But the figurine remained still.

"So? How was it?" she finally asked.

"Okay," said her mother. "That old lady can't really tell the future, you know."

"I know. But did she help you?"

"I don't know yet," said Mami. "We'll see."

Jessica put the car in drive and pulled away from the curb. "So," she said hesitantly, hopefully. "Do you want me to drive you back to the house now so you can talk to Papi?"

"No." Her mother's voice was quiet but resolute. "Just drive me back to the school so I can pick up my car."

"Where are you going?" Jessica couldn't resist asking. "Back to Sabrina's?"

"Maybe." Her mother looked out the window for a while in silence. "Or maybe I'll go somewhere else. I think I need to be alone for a while."

Jessica didn't know what else to say. This was new to her—questioning her mother as though she were a teenager.

If Mami didn't want to go home, there was nothing Jessica could do about it. She took the turn that led to Hawthorne Elementary and Mami's car.

In the deserted school parking lot, Jessica parked next to her mother's car. Behind them, teenage boys played at the basketball court. The first streetlights were beginning to come on.

Mami turned to her. "Thank you for taking me there, m'ija. I appreciate you trying to help."

Jessica smiled weakly. Again, she felt as if she might burst into tears at any moment. Surprisingly, her mother leaned over the gearshift and hugged her. Then, a tear did escape Jessica's eye. She wiped it away quickly before her mother could see.

"M'ija, I'm sorry. I know this is hard for you. But I want you to try not to worry, okay?"

"Okay." Jessica refrained from saying anything else. She didn't want to get any more choked up than she already was.

Her mother smiled. "I just need some time to myself, baby. A little break, so I can think things over. Do you understand?"

Even though Jessica was afraid her parents might divorce, and that fear was breaking her heart, at the same time she completely understood her mother's need to take a break for a while. In a way, suddenly, she even felt glad for her mother. She could see that it might be the best thing for Mami to step back and think for a while before she made her next decision. To meditate on it, as Madame Hortensia had said.

She nodded at her mother. "Do what you have to do, Mami. But I want you to call me if you need me. Or if anything happens. Okay? I'm old enough to hear the truth. You don't have to tell Sabrina only."

Her mother laughed, then hugged her again. "Okay, m'ija. You're right. I will."

They said good-bye, and Jessica watched her mother get into her car. Then she followed her out of the lot long enough to see that she wasn't going toward her own house.

Then Jessica turned toward her parents' house.

It was time to have a serious talk with her father.

She knocked at her parents' front door and heard her father call out, "It's unlocked." When she came in, he was standing in the kitchen, glaring at the microwave.

"Jessi. Hi, m'ija. I'm glad you're here. Come help me with this stupid pot pie, would you?"

Jessica hurried over and removed the foil-plated chicken pot pie from the microwave right as it emitted its first spark. "Papi, you can't put foil in the microwave. You'll blow up the house." She turned on the oven. "Here. You'll have to wait for it to heat up." As she spoke, she glanced around and noticed that the kitchen, having gone two days without her mother's care, already looked like a disaster area.

Her father was sulking. "It's a good thing you came over, then. I can just see it—the whole house blows up, and your mother doesn't even care."

He took a beer from the refrigerator and walked into the living room. Jessica followed him and sat next to him on the couch.

"I'm sure she would care, Papi. But is that what you're going to do? Let the house blow up? Or fall apart?" She looked pointedly at the empty cans, wadded-up napkins, and various fast-food wrappers littering the coffee table.

Her father shrugged irritably. "Maybe. Have you talked to her? I know she went to work today, because I called them and asked. But did she tell you when she's coming back?"

"Papi, I'm scared she's *not* coming back."

He sighed heavily. "What does she want? Flowers? A present? Maybe I should go to Sears and get her one of those diamond necklaces. I can put it on the credit card." He wrinkled his nose, as if the thought of all this trouble were annoying to him. "Last time I just got her flowers, and she was okay with it."

Jessica shook her head in exasperation. Now she saw that these problems with her parents had gone on way too long. And it was mostly her father's fault. She totally saw her mother's point of view. And now here was her opportunity to convey that to her father.

"Papi," she said sternly, "do you want Mami to come back?"

"Of course I do. I'm hungry for real food," he said peevishly.

Jessica made her voice more stern and louder. "Papi! Do you want Mami to stay married to you? Or do you want a divorce?"

He looked surprised for a second, then quickly recovered. He took a casual sip of beer. Then, smiling at her as if she were a child, he said, "That's not going to happen, m'ija. Don't worry. Your mother will come back soon."

"No, she won't, Papi. Not unless you make some big changes. That's what she told me. I talked to her today."

He lost all his casual attitude then. He set down his beer and turned to face Jessica. His face, worn but still handsome, showed equal parts shock, concern, and complete confusion. Jessica would have laughed if the situation hadn't been so serious.

"What'd she say?" he asked. "She told you she wants a divorce?" His voice was completely stricken. "I didn't think she was *that* mad."

Jessica took his hand and patted it. "Papi, she's been mad for a while, about a whole lot of things."

"Like what?" He sounded genuinely puzzled.

"She's tired of working and then coming home and cleaning the house all the time, while you sit around and goof off. She's tired of you drinking and talking about other women, and never taking *her* anywhere. It makes her feel like you don't appreciate what she does. Maybe even like you don't really love her."

"Hijole!" her father said. "M'ija, I keep telling your mom she doesn't have to clean the house so much. All I want is for her to cook me dinner! And I've already told her to quit her job, if she wants, since it's making her so miserable. And the talking about other women—Jessi, you know I'm just playing when I do that. I just say that stuff to see if your mother will get jealous. Well, I guess she does get jealous...but she should know I'm just playing around. She should know that I still love her! Hijo de su madre!"

Her father said that only when he was really upset. Jessica knew that Papi loved Mami. She'd always known that. But hearing his words now, she could totally see how her mother might have doubts. He went on.

"If I didn't love her, would I go to that stupid job every day, when I could be doing something fun instead? No, I do that for *her*. How can she say I don't appreciate her? *She* doesn't appreciate *me*. Sometimes I think she wishes I was somebody else—some big shot like her boss."

And just like that, Jessica saw her father's point of view again. Although he didn't talk about it often, she knew that he'd had to totally work his butt off since coming to America as a teenager. He'd worked all the way up from janitor to one of the supervisors at his company. Yet there were men his age everywhere who were doing better—making more money—than he was. Like Mami's bosses. Or Jessica's bosses. Or even Papi's own son-in-law.

Looking at his face, now filled with pain and shame at admitting his true feelings, Jessica could understand how painful it was for her father, imagining that he simply wasn't good enough for Mami.

"She doesn't wish you were somebody else," Jessica told him. "Papi, she loved you before, when you were just a mariachi singer. She loved you when you were a janitor. Why wouldn't she love you now?"

"I don't know," he said. "She's older now. Maybe she sees it differently now. Hell, look at how she's so happy about your sister marrying a guy with money. Look how she's always pushing you to do the same thing!"

Her father had a point, Jessica thought. His words even echoed Mami's own. She needed time to think of something she could say in response. Something that would comfort her father. She got up and went to the kitchen. After putting his pot pie in the oven, setting the kitchen timer, and walking slowly back to the living room, she had it.

"She isn't happy about David because he has money," she said.

"She isn't?" Her father raised an eyebrow skeptically, daring her to deny it.

"No." As Jessica thought it over, she realized that what she was about to say was the absolute truth. "Mami likes David because he treats Sabrina like gold. The way he talks to her, the way he does things with her... Even if he had a crappy job and Sabrina was working, too, he'd still treat her the same way. He loves her and he does everything he can to show it."

Her father muttered something then. She didn't catch it, but she knew it contained the word *whipped*.

"He isn't whipped, Papi," she said. "He just loves Sabrina and doesn't have a problem showing it."

That was the *real* problem. Her father loved Mami, but he had a problem showing it. He was too macho. Or too spoiled. Exactly like Guillermo. Jessica saw it clear as crystal now. Her father was just like Guillermo. She'd fallen for a guy just like her father. It was classic. And pathetic, now that she saw it clearly. She smiled wryly to herself.

Her father made an impatient noise. "Okay, fine. He's not whipped. So, what am I supposed to do now? Let your mother whip me, too?"

Jessica became impatient. "No, Papi. Stop it. You're just being silly now." The look on his face told her he was surprised and didn't know if he should take that kind of talk from his daughter or not. But she went on. "What did you do back when you guys were still dating? You must have done *something* to make her want to marry you."

Her father thought for a little while. "I guess we went dancing. She used to like that. I don't know. We used to... Well, you don't want to hear about that...."

Jessica shook her head to keep from imagining whatever he'd been about to say. "Okay, fine. Don't tell me. But whatever it was—whatever you did to win her over in the first place, you need to do again. You need to win her back now."

Her father didn't say anything. He looked down at the space near his hands, lost in thought.

"And you need to *keep* doing it, so you don't lose her again," Jessica added. "And you need to clean up this mess, and help Mami keep it clean." The kitchen timer went off, snapping her father out of his reverie.

Jessica stood up. She'd done enough. Her father could handle it from here. "I'm leaving, Papi."

"Okay." He stood up, too. "M'ija...thank you. Tell your mother I'm—"

"No, Papi," she said firmly. "*You* tell her. You call her tonight, at Sabrina's."

He nodded his head slowly, as if the concept of communication in a relationship were just beginning to dawn on him. "No, you're right. I'll tell her. I'll call her."

When Jessica left, he was taking the pie out of the oven. "Ai, chingado!" she heard him say. He'd probably burned his hand.

She didn't turn back. Her father would learn not to touch a hot chicken pot pie without a pot holder, she told herself. And he'd learn not to let a good woman go, either.

# 39

Jessica walked into work the next morning feeling as though she'd aged several years. Between dealing with her mother's unhappiness and recognizing her father's denial of it, she was emotionally wrung out. She'd called Sabrina at ten p.m. and got voice mail. Eventually, she'd decided her parents' situation was out of her hands. It was time to get back to her own life.

So she'd put on a suit again and dragged herself into work.

As she walked past Mr. Cochran's office to her desk, Jessica couldn't help overhearing part of her boss's phone conversation.

"What's the name of that assistant on forty-one?... The blonde, yeah. Sarah? Susan?"

Jessica put her bag on her desk as quietly as she could, her ears on hyperalert. She knew that Mr. Cochran meant Susan Wright, in Sales. She looked over at Rochelle and saw that she was listening to their boss, too.

He went on: "Didn't Dwight say she was looking to transfer to another department? Maybe I can bring her in to replace Olga." There was a pause, then Mr. Cochran laughed and said, "Exactly. Probably should have gone with someone like that to begin with."

Jessica stifled a gasp. "Someone like that"? What did that mean?

The moment Mr. Cochran left the office, Jessica turned to Rochelle. "Did you hear what he said?" she demanded. "That he should have hired someone like Susan Wright in the first place? What do you think he meant—that he should've hired someone white?"

Rochelle looked surprised and shook her head. "No. You think? No, I'm sure he meant something else."

But Jessica wasn't so sure by then. The more she thought of it, in fact, the more she became sure that was exactly what Mr. Cochran had meant. She didn't want to think it, but the evidence was all around her. He and all the other brokers were white, weren't they? While Jessica, Rochelle, and Olga weren't.

In fact, she didn't know why she hadn't realized it before. *None* of the brokers at McCormick were people of color. Except, she amended, for Troy Williams upstairs. And Brad Wu. And Joe Vargas. But still, she told herself. That was almost none, considering that McCormick employed over two hundred people.

Jessica looked over at Rochelle and noticed that she'd gone back to surfing the web, complacent as ever. But Jessica couldn't be that calm. Her nerves had already been on edge when she'd come through the door. And now she was starting to suspect that Mr. Cochran might never promote her, no matter how hard she worked or how much she deserved it.

*Calm down,* she told herself. *You're overreacting.*

What she needed, she realized, was some good advice. Then she smiled to herself. A week ago, that thought would've been followed by a visit to Madame Hortensia. This time, however, she meant real advice. She pulled her cell out of her purse and found Jonathan's number, then dialed it from her office phone.

No answer. His voice mail came on, and she said, "Hey. Just me. Don't worry—I'll call you back later."

Then she remembered whom she would have called before she'd met Jonathan. Her *other* Madame Hortensia. She stood up. "Rochelle, I'll be right back."

She walked down the hall to the door that led to IT. She went in and waved to Ling, who smiled, then let herself into Xavier's office.

"Xavier." She saw then that he was on the phone. "Oops! Sorry!" she whispered.

He cupped his hand over the phone and motioned for her to sit and wait. She did.

"Right.... Right," he said. "Okay, I'll see you at lunch tomorrow, then.... All right. Bye."

Jessica looked down at his phone screen. She couldn't help but notice the name on it—C. Ortiz. He was talking to Cynthia again.

Xavier hung up and began typing on one of his computers, his face only half-turned in Jessica's direction. He looked...not annoyed, exactly, but busy. She wondered if maybe she should come back later. But she couldn't go back yet. She needed to talk to *someone*.

"What's going on?" he finally said.

"I'm completely freaking out here. I'm scared Mr. Cochran isn't really considering me for the broker job after all."

He stopped typing and gave her his full attention. "Why do you say that?"

As calmly and quickly as she could, Jessica summarized

everything that'd been happening lately, up until the conversation she'd just overheard Mr. Cochran having. "And now that I'm thinking about it," she ended, "there are hardly any nonwhite brokers here."

"There's Joe Vargas," Xavier pointed out. "And Brad Wu, and Troy Williams."

"Right," said Jessica. "One Latino, one Asian, and one black guy. Just enough for the company to _claim_ diversity. But that doesn't mean anything. And none of them are women, either."

"There's Cathy Baumgardner, and Carol Simon. Glenda What's-her-name...Linda Corelli," Xavier said. Then he stopped, seeing the look on Jessica's face.

"I know," she said. "I'm just..." She was just nervous, she realized. About the job, about her parents, about everything all of a sudden.

"Look," Xavier said. "He's _not_ going to _not_ hire you because you're Latina, or because you're a woman, or anything like that. If everyone else who applies is less qualified than you, and he hires a white guy anyway, then you can sue the company. And he knows that. You know how paranoid everybody is about lawsuits around here. He's not going to be that stupid."

Jessica thought that over. It was true. Mr. Cochran _was_ completely paranoid about lawsuits. But... "What if someone more experienced _does_ apply for the job?"

Xavier shrugged, but not unsympathetically. "Did you remind him that you've been gaining experience ever since you got here?"

"Yes. I mean, I tried."

"Well, that's all you can do. Sometimes it takes a while, you know? Sometimes you have to put in a real effort to show them you're ready to move up, you know? Look at me. You know how many times I got passed up for promotion before I moved from full-time support to part-time programming?"

"How many?" she asked.

"Three. And even then, I had to do a lot of programming for them in my spare time before they even gave me the pay raise."

Jessica frowned. "That sucks. It shouldn't be that way."

"I know," said Xavier. "But it is that way. Unless you're the boss's nephew or something like that." He smiled, and she smiled back. They both knew how that went — several of the boss's nephews were working in other departments at McCormick.

"Well, don't give up," Xavier said. "Maybe you should try to talk to Mr. Cochran about it again. This time take him a list of things you've done to save or make money for your department. Show him what he has to gain by promoting you."

"That's a good idea," Jessica said. Although she was already trying to compose that list mentally and realized there wasn't much she could put on it. She laughed. "Then again, maybe I should just forget it. I already work hard enough as it is. Maybe I should try again to get a job doing web design somewhere else." She was half kidding but wanted to see what he'd say.

"You should do both. Try to get the promotion here, and apply for other jobs at the same time. Always keep your options open."

Jessica and Xavier sat there for a little while, reflecting.

She was glad she'd talked to him. His advice was just as good as Jonathan's would have been, she was sure.

When Xavier glanced down at his phone, Jessica remembered he'd been talking to Cynthia and assumed he wanted to get back to her. "Well, I know you're busy," she said. "I'd better let you go. I didn't mean to interrupt—"

"No, it's fine. I'm glad you came over. I haven't seen you in a while."

She felt the need to say more. "Thanks for listening, Xavier. Even though everything about my career is totally screwed up now, talking to you made me feel better."

He shook his head. "That's because you know that *I* know that you're just having one of your dramatic moments. Your career isn't totally screwed up. Either Mr. Cochran will come to his senses, or else you'll find a better job somewhere else. You'll be fine."

She had to laugh at herself. She *was* being dramatic. It all sounded so easy, the way Xavier described it. But she couldn't help getting the last word. "You'd better hope I *don't* find a better job, because then who would you whine to at lunch?"

Xavier pretended to throw a pencil at her. "Get out of here."

Jessica scampered away in a much better mood.

# 40

Xavier's pep talk had gotten Jessica through the rest of Wednesday afternoon. But when Thursday morning rolled around, she lay in bed, awake since four a.m., and seriously considered calling in sick. The thought of going back to her desk and doing her work with a smile, without hope of being appreciated for it, almost made her sick for real.

*Don't be a baby,* she told herself as she sat up to turn off the alarm clock. Now wasn't the time to fall apart.

Later, in her car, as she circled the skyscrapers that surrounded McCormick, Jessica thought again of the conversation she'd had with Xavier. Maybe she didn't really want this broker job enough.

Sure, she liked wearing nice suits, and she'd love to make more money, but the golf thing and *The Wall Street Journal*... the butt kissing on the clients and the big bosses... that wasn't exactly how she'd envisioned her career. Really, now that she was thinking about it, had she ever even imagined being in insurance this long? She'd started working there only to get away from the Centro and all the bad choices she'd made there. It had seemed, when she got the McCormick job, like a good omen at the time. As though she'd changed her life for the better and put herself on a path to success.

What did she really want? Well, to be appreciated, for one thing. There was no use working hard if no one was going to notice. Or, worse, if everyone else was just going to take credit for your work.

Also: She knew work wasn't supposed to be *fun*, but did that mean it had to be boring *all* the time? Insurance, she had learned over the last three years, was exactly as boring as everyone imagined it was.

Obviously she needed to leave McCormick, and not for another insurance job, either. But where would she go? With her level of experience, she could probably be an assistant at another kind of company. But what if all the corporations ended up offering the same thing? The chance to work hard, with no chance for advancement.

She *could* be an assistant at a nonprofit — if she wanted to be poor.

None of the galleries or museums in town wanted someone with an art history degree. No, they wanted either MFAs or socialite volunteers. Her job as "curator" at the Centro had been a complete fluke, she'd realized since leaving it.

For a while now, she'd been fantasizing about starting her own multimedia minifirm. She could design web sites, business cards, brochures, safety posters — anything. But that was a long way off. She didn't yet have enough clients to make it more than a hobby. Certainly not enough to quit her job. Unless, of course, she wanted to move back in with Mami and Papi.

She wound through the parking garage on mental autopilot. Like a mouse in a well-known maze, she scurried through all the elevators and security checkpoints that led to her office. When she reached her desk, she still hadn't figured out what to do.

But she *would* think of something, and soon. She'd start combing through the job sites on her lunch break.

"Did Lois tell you what she heard about Olga?"

"No. What?" Jessica had just sat down and turned on her computer.

Rochelle rolled her chair closer to Jessica's. "Remember that trip she took to the casinos a while back?"

"Yeah?"

"Well, maybe she won a bunch of money. Enough to quit her job."

"What? That doesn't make sense," said Jessica. "Didn't she go with Shelley from Accounting? If she'd won that much, Shelley would have told the whole building the moment they got back."

"Well, that's true. That's a good point." Rochelle concentrated for a moment. "Maybe she finally sold enough of those SpeedSlim things to win the big prize. Maybe she's in Aruba right now."

Mr. Cochran walked in, and Rochelle rolled back to her desk. Jessica stayed very casual as she turned to her own computer and pretended to be busy. He didn't say anything to either of them, which he'd been doing more and more lately. These days, he went into his office without a word and closed the door behind him. It occurred to Jessica that even if she did get her promotion, things wouldn't change much. She would still be in an environment where people showed up, did their work, and went home. Was it too much to ask that

Mr. Cochran show a little appreciation? Or that they all work more as a team? What this place was missing, she suddenly realized, was a sense of community.

It was almost lunchtime. Jessica wondered if she should call Xavier and ask him to have lunch. They'd gotten off schedule with their weekly lunches, both of them busy with their own drama. Jessica remembered the phone conversation she'd walked in on the day before. If she'd heard correctly, he was having lunch with Cynthia today. She sighed. Maybe it'd be best if she didn't count on regular lunches with him anymore.

Jessica supposed she had to be happy for her friend. Xavier had never really said why they'd broken up—he wasn't the type to kiss and tell, and Jessica had never had reason to believe that Xavier found any fault with Cynthia. From her outsider's perspective, though, Jessica had always thought that Cynthia pushed Xavier around too much.

At least, that's what she'd thought *then*. Now...now that she'd been going out with Jonathan and *not* wasting time with Guillermo, and especially since her conversation with her father, she finally saw that a guy could be nice and do things for a girl selflessly, without being a pushover. Now that she rethought the whole thing, Xavier had probably *wanted* to take Cynthia to the church suppers and the petting zoo and all those other places, because he was a good guy, and he was happy spending time with her. And seeing how cute she was, who could blame him? Although, then again, she did have to wonder how much a girl who loved teddy bears would be willing to put out.

It was too bad Jessica hadn't met Xavier first, before Cynthia, she mused. She would have been a better match for him, and if they'd been dating all along, they both could have avoided a lot of personal drama. She tried to imagine it: herself, wanting to go out and party all the time, and Xavier in his serious professor shirts and glasses, wanting to stay home and talk about programming. She would try to get him to make out in the stairway, the way she had with her ex back at the Centro, but Xavier would be too worried about his boss and the work on his desk. She stifled a giggle. It was probably for the best that Cynthia had found him first.

Rochelle's voice cut through Jessica's thoughts.

"Uh-huh... uh-huh... Well, I can't say I blame you, girl.... Uh-huh... Okay. Okay, I'll tell her.... All right. Have a good one, then, Olga. Keep in touch, you hear?"

Rochelle hung up and turned her chair to Jessica's, shaking her head in amazement all the while. "You were right, Jessica. Olga sure did quit."

"What? I can't believe it. Did she get a job at another brokerage?" If so, Jessica would have to get her new number. Maybe, if she got desperate, she could ask Olga to hook her up.

"Nope," said Rochelle.

"Did she quit so she could sell SpeedSlim full-time, then?" Had Jessica been missing out on an entrepreneurial opportunity?

"Nope."

"Did she win big at the casino, then?" Maybe, Jessica thought frantically, she should at least start playing bingo online....

"Nope. None of that. She didn't have anywhere else to go to at all. Just a little money put away in savings."

Jessica was completely puzzled. Had Olga gone crazy?

"She said," Rochelle explained, "that she left because of *you.*"

"Me?"

"Looking at you, sitting here doing your work all the time, had got her to thinking. She was about your age when she started here, you remember."

"It got her to thinking about *what?*" Jessica was almost afraid to hear the answer.

"That she'd been here long enough, and she didn't want to sit over there at that desk for the rest of her life."

Jessica shuddered. It was as if, with that one remark, Rochelle had sentenced her to a life in prison.

"I'll be right back," Rochelle said. She got up and practically ran down the hall — probably to spread the gossip, Jessica knew.

Normally, Jessica might do the same — call Tiffany on forty-two to tell her what had happened. But she couldn't talk to anyone now. She was too disturbed. Olga had been Jessica's age when she'd started at McCormick. She'd been here that long, and she was a secretary. And now, after all these years, she was finally tired of it.

Like a scene from a sad movie, Jessica saw a vision of herself at this desk, with a calendar above her head, its pages blowing off one by one. Always doing the same things, every day. Joking with her co-workers about a rich man coming to take her away.

Jessica shuddered again.

That was it. She had decided. She wasn't going to wait around for Mr. Cochran to change her life anymore.

## 41

That night, Jessica multitasked. On the couch, while holding her laptop on her lap, she ate a PowerBar with her right hand, petted Ricky with her left, and carried on a conversation with Marisol on her cell's headphone.

"So Esmeralda hasn't found any more money for the site?"

"Yeah. She's going to e-mail you about it when we get rid of our computer's virus. She can't pay you for any more work until we get another grant. But she does love what you did so far, and so does everybody else, so they're going to try really hard to find the money."

"And in the meantime, don't quit my day job, right?" said Jessica. "Mari, I have seriously got to get the hell out of that place."

"I'm sorry. Hey, I'll ask around. Maybe someone here knows about an opening."

"Thanks." Jessica had just finished another long, eye-searing job search, and she wasn't really in the mood to talk about it anymore. Marisol probably heard it in her voice, because she promptly changed the subject.

"Hey, so how're things going between your parents?"

Jessica frowned. "I don't know yet. I talked to Sabrina earlier, and she said they had lunch today. But then Mami went back to Sabrina's after work, and she wouldn't say anything about it."

"Do you think they're going to work it out?"

"I don't know. Honestly, Marisol? I'm trying really hard not to think about it at all." Jessica crumpled up her Power-Bar wrapper and set it on the table.

Her friend clucked sympathetically, then changed the subject again. "Hey, so what are you going to do about the painting? Did Guillermo sell it?"

"I don't think so. But he never said he was going to give it to me, either. Not that I'd take it *now*, now that I know he just slapped it together real fast so I wouldn't be mad."

"Did it look like he slapped it together, though? I thought you said it looked really good."

Jessica sighed. "It did. It was beautiful."

"Well, maybe he didn't mean it as bad as it came out. I'm sure he worked hard on it, even if it was last minute."

Ricky rubbed his little face against her hand, and Jessica stroked him thoughtfully. "It doesn't matter. I've finally learned my lesson. You know why he painted that picture of me, really? Because he realized how much he needs me. He just needs someone to help him organize his life now that he's finally making money. But that someone's not going to be me. He had his chance to prove himself to me, and he blew it. I've moved on."

"Yeah, speaking of...," said Marisol. "What's up with you and Jonathan? Are you going out this weekend?"

"Yep. Tomorrow night."

"What is this, the fourth date now? Have you let him get to third base yet?"

Marisol's voice was teasing. But at the same time, it made Jessica not want to say anything about the last date and her thwarted attempt to consummate their relationship. She didn't think that Marisol would understand. Maybe she would say that Jessica *had* moved too quickly. And Jessica didn't want to hear that. She already felt embarrassed enough about the whole thing as it was. She shifted the focus of the conversation.

"Actually, he said he had a big surprise for me tomorrow night. I'm trying to figure out what it could be."

"Maybe he'll take you for a picnic in the park, and then he'll tell you to look up, and there'll be one of those skywriter planes asking you to marry him." Marisol laughed at her own joke, and Jessica had to join her.

"Yeah, sure."

Marisol dropped her teasing tone for a moment. "So you really like this guy, huh?"

"Yeah, I have to admit that he's growing on me."

"Like a fungus?" said Marisol, cracking herself up again.

"Exactly."

After they got off the phone, Jessica went back to her task, furiously searching through all the job sites, corporate web pages, and online classifieds she could find. She'd already sent e-mails to all her noninsurance friends, discreetly asking for leads.

Maybe, she thought, she could ask Jonathan for help. He could probably get her a job at Halronburco just by snapping his fingers. But that would be a last resort. Ever since all the mess she'd gone through with Robert at the Centro, she'd made it a rule not to date co-workers. If she did get a job at Halronburco, she'd have to work in a department far from Jonathan's.

Thinking about this tickled something in the back of her mind. She felt she was forgetting something.

She ran through a mental list: job search, the Centro, Halronburco, and then Sabrina. Sabrina had worked at Halronburco, too, before she'd married David and decided to cash in on a life of leisure. Jessica smiled as she realized that her sister probably still had contacts there. She would have to ask. In fact, she'd ask David himself for help.

For the third or fourth time since her job search had started, she thought of Guillermo and his booming art career. It was too bad she wasn't planning to see him anymore. Now that it was over between them, the opportunity she'd been fantasizing about all along had finally presented itself. She could have been Guillermo's manager, handling all his exhibits and sales, for a small percentage of the profits, which would undoubtedly get bigger and bigger.

But that really *would* be dating a co-worker, wouldn't it? Not that it'd been quite the same thing back when she'd first thought of the idea. Back when they were still together, she would've been perfectly willing to do it for free. As Xavier had said—she would have been Guillermo's consultant for payment in rice and beans.

# 42

Friday, Jessica woke up with the sun in her eyes and then realized that she'd never set her alarm. It was eleven a.m. She called Rochelle to say that she'd be in late. Then, right before Rochelle answered, Jessica decided she might as well just say she was sick and stay home. Fortunately, Rochelle said everything was under control and she'd see Jessica on Monday.

Jessica hung up the phone with a relieved sigh. Obviously, she realized, she'd needed the rest. She'd been through so much stress over the past couple of weeks. Now that she'd called in sick, she had nothing to worry about. Only something to look forward to—her date tonight with Jonathan. She stretched languorously. Ricky woke up and did the same beside her. Then she popped out of bed. After her shower, she decided, she'd go shopping and find something awesome to wear tonight.

She got up and lifted Ricky from her bed. He mewed as she kissed him and gave him a good-morning hug. Tonight, Jessica decided, she wasn't going to worry about anything at all. She would let things happen the way they were meant to happen, and she'd sit back and enjoy it.

"Wow!" said Jonathan as she opened her apartment door to him several hours later. "You look even better than the last time I saw you. I didn't think that'd be possible."

Jessica laughed, then stood on tiptoes to kiss him. She knew the little Japanese floral print dress was perfect the moment she'd seen it in the window. And the pink brocade wedges she'd found went with it perfectly.

Jonathan drove her to a tiny Italian restaurant that Jessica had never noticed before, even though it was downtown and just a couple of blocks from her work. It was one of those places where all the tables were for two, and all were decorated with candles and flowers. It was very romantic.

"The salmon here is really good," he said. "But order whatever you want. It's all good."

She ordered the tortellini, and he ordered the salmon, plus calamari, plus a bottle of Shiraz. "It's still my turn to pick up the tab," she reminded him. "You keep tricking me out of it."

"Since I picked the restaurant, this is my treat. Next time you pick," he replied mischievously.

They made small talk about his upcoming business trips and his neighborhood renovation efforts. He kept asking about her work, but it wasn't until after her first glass of wine that Jessica relaxed enough to tell him all the drama. She went over it as briefly as she could, feeling embarrassed that she hadn't been able to snatch up the broker job as easily as he'd said she would.

"Wow. That's pretty rough." He passed her the calamari as though it were a consolation prize.

She shrugged. "I've started looking for a new job. It's not worth wasting my time there anymore."

"What are you looking for? Web design?"

She sighed and dipped a squid ring into the horseradish sauce, then described her job-hunting woes. When she was done, Jonathan poured each of them more wine. "Well, let me look around Halronburco and see if there's anything you might be interested in."

"I was thinking of asking you that, actually. But then I went ahead and checked out their job site. The only listings are for price analysts and IP analysts, and I don't even know what those are."

His smile widened. "Let me ask around. I might be able to find something that's not on the job site yet."

She caught his eye and finally realized what he meant. He was an important person at Halronburco. He could probably just *invent* a job for her. She bit into tiny, spicy tentacles and took another sip of Shiraz. That hadn't been her plan—to hint that he should *make* his company hire her. But screw it. She reasoned that if he could do it easily, and it made him happy to do it—and it did seem as though it would—then why not let him.

"That was seriously the best Italian food I've ever had."

It was no exaggeration. Jessica didn't play around when it came to food. She and Jonathan walked slowly down the street to his car. Behind them, the skyscrapers shone sunset gold.

"I'm glad you liked it. We'll have to go back again."

She nodded. They would go back again, probably. She could imagine it clearly. It would be one of their favorite places as a couple. "So, where to now?"

"It's a surprise, remember?" he said.

"Give me a hint." It had been in the back of her mind all week, but she'd been completely unable to guess.

"I can't. But I promise you'll love it."

They got into his car and rode a couple of miles to the warehouses on the edge of downtown.

"Are we going to a rave?" Jessica asked.

"No."

"An art opening?"

"Nope."

They stopped next to one of the warehouses right on the edge of everything, where it got dark fast. There were only a few other cars there, and no one was on the sidewalk. Jessica couldn't decide whether to be excited or apprehensive.

"What is this place?"

"Don't worry. It's totally safe." He pointed to the corner, where a security guard stood scanning the street. Then he pointed to the shadiest corner of the parking lot, where another guard sat on a stool watching them.

Jonathan opened her door and helped her onto the crumbling curb, then said, "Just a second. I forgot something."

Jessica stood on the sidewalk and watched him run back to the car to take something out of the trunk. As he ran back to her, she saw him tuck a small gift-wrapped box under his arm. Since he was obviously trying to keep it hidden, she pretended she hadn't noticed. But inside she was dying to find out what it was.

The box was too large for a ring, so she wasn't worried about him pulling a surprise proposal, as Marisol had joked. It was about the right size for a necklace, though. Jessica wasn't sure what to think about this. No guy had ever bought her a necklace before. Unless she counted Tony Garcia, who'd given her an Avon unicorn pendant in the fifth grade. And even then, that had been after she'd made out with him behind the monkey bars.

Jessica had to wonder, then, why Jonathan was getting so serious already. They hadn't even done it yet.

They stood at the wide, black metal door. Instead of knocking, Jonathan checked his watch. By then, it was around nine. A man in a white shirt and thin black tie opened the door just a crack, recognized Jonathan, then opened it all the way.

"Hey, man," he said. They gave each other a handshake with mutual arm slapping.

"Jessica, this is my buddy Dean. And this is his place."

Dean led them over the threshold into the warehouse, which was only dimly lit. But once Jessica stepped into the huge room and saw everything in it, she knew exactly what it was.

"Oh, my God," she shrieked quietly. "This is so, so *awesome!*"

It was a roller rink.

It was the coolest roller rink she'd ever seen — like something straight out of her childhood, but completely redone to look shiny and new. On one side of the warehouse, old-school arcade games took up a whole wall. Opposite that was a snack bar, with chrome-accented tables, bar stools upholstered in glittery vinyl, and neon-framed pictures of hot dogs and fountain drinks. In the middle, taking up most of the warehouse, was the rink itself, impossibly huge. It called out to her with its glossy wooden surface that reflected the disco lights.

"Surprise." Colored circles flashed across Jonathan's smile.

She smiled back at him, probably like a crazy person, too ecstatically shocked to say anything.

"Okay, man," said Dean. "I'll be back at eleven. The games

should all be up and running, except Ms. Pac-Man. We're still working on that one. Oh, and there's no food in the snack bar yet, except some ice cream in the freezer. And the water's on, so you can use the sinks and the restrooms and whatever. You guys have fun. Try everything out and let me know what you think." He slapped Jonathan on the arm again. "Nice meeting you," he added to Jessica. Then he was gone, and they had the whole place to themselves.

Jessica was still in a daze and couldn't do anything but stare all around at the pretty colors.

"I hope you know how to skate," said Jonathan. "Otherwise, we'll have to play Asteroids for two hours."

"I know how to skate. At least, I hope I still can. It's been a while." She looked over and noticed that the counter they were standing against hid a bank of in-line and old-fashioned roller skates in all sizes. "Oh, but . . ." She looked down at her sandals. She wasn't even wearing hose. Disappointment settled over her like a smoggy cloud. There was no way she could skate in bare feet. Not only was it gross and unsanitary—it would give her blisters. She knew that from experience.

"I brought you a gift."

Jonathan pulled the little present from behind his back. Jessica forgot about her feet and tried to compose her face in the right kind of expression—not too nervous, but not too expectant, either. He grinned like a maniac while she slowly untied the string and pulled the paper off the black velvet box. She held her breath as she pulled open the lid.

It was a pair of socks.

Jessica laughed. Now, all the tension she'd been working herself into was gone. "Thank you," she said, reaching to hug him. He hugged her back, and they shared a quick kiss. She could tell he wanted to do more, but instead he pulled back and led her to the skates.

The place was complete magic. It brought back every happy memory Jessica had of going skating with Marisol and Toby back in middle school. The first time she ever skated, the first time she kissed a high school boy. The first time she wore eyeliner and the *last* time she wore leg warmers.

Not only was the jukebox stocked with every single good song from the eighties, but when they loaded it up and pressed play, it activated a giant videoscreen on the wall above the rink. Jessica squealed in delight as Duran Duran lit up the floor, all hungry like the wolf.

"So your friend Dean owns this place? He's going to make a fortune."

"Well, I'm glad to hear you think so. He's one of the owners, and also the manager. He's been doing most of it himself—all the design and renovations. I think tonight's the first time in weeks he's left the place for more than an hour."

"It's so nice of him to let us use it. He must have owed you a big favor."

Jonathan shrugged. "Not really. We're doing him the favor. We are helping out by testing everything."

Jessica raised her eyebrow, sensing there was more to it than that.

"And I've been meaning to come check it out anyway, since I'm part owner, too."

She laughed and shook her head at his modesty. He was full of surprises.

"Come on. Let's get our skates on."

At first, as they hobbled across the carpet to the rink, Jessica worried that she really had forgotten how to skate. But once they touched the shiny floor, she remembered, just like that. Just like riding a bike. Except that she was ten years older and ten or more pounds heavier. She glided across the floor, all the way to the end, then tried to take a sharp turn and nearly ate it at the carpeted rail.

"Are you all right?" Jonathan skated over to make sure.

"I'm fine. Oh, look!"

Cyndi Lauper had just come on the videoscreen, dancing around in her combat boots and multicolored waffle-iron hair.

"I used to love this video," Jessica said. "I wanted to do my hair just like that, but my mom wouldn't let me."

"Really? I got my hair cut and bleached like the lead singer of Scritti Politti. My dad almost had a heart attack."

They skated around, watching the videos and reminiscing. And it was nice to have the whole place to themselves. They could talk and laugh across the entire rink. Whenever a new song came on, one of them would play the part of the rink announcer and call out instructions.

"Reverse skate! Please turn around and skate in the other direction now!" Jessica called. They laughed and continued looping in all directions.

"All skaters line up for the race!" Jonathan called. Jessica let him catch up to her, then called go and peeled out before he was ready, cheating him out of the head start. He laughed and sped up, overtaking her and winning. She slowed to a halt and booed him as he pretended to accept accolades from the crowd.

"Hokey Pokey! All skaters line up to dance the Hokey Pokey!" she cried.

But he shook his head. "Couples skate! Ladies' choice!"

There was only one man to pick, so she picked him, and they skated around slowly with their hands shyly clasped. Her laughs had subsided to giggles now as the parade of new wavers and hip-hoppers serenaded them from the screen.

Eventually, Jessica's ankles began to wobble, so they rolled over to the snack bar to rest on one of the benches. Jonathan went to the freezer and brought them each a tiny cup of ice cream and a tiny wooden paddle for a spoon, just like the ones she remembered.

Annie Lennox sang in the background. Jonathan leaned over to wipe ice cream from her chin. Then he leaned over a little farther to kiss her. Setting down her little wooden spoon, she kissed him back.

# 43

Before she knew it, Dean was back to lock up and it was time for them to go.

"Want to go to my place?" he asked quietly, as if he were unsure of her answer. Still, after all this time...

"Yes," she said. "Oh, but..." She remembered the condoms. They were back at her apartment. "I need to get some things from my place first. Can we stop by there? It won't take long."

"Of course," he said.

In the car, on the way to her apartment, she knew neither of them could hear what the other was saying. She wasn't saying much anyway, just random comments about the scenery or the songs on the radio. The air between them was filled with a sort of humming, like the sound of dragonflies. It was the hum of expectation.

When they finally got to her apartment complex, when he led her to the foot of the stairs, all the expectation crashed to a screeching halt. Someone else was already upstairs, at her door.

She studied the man's silhouette. It was Papi. He was there with his toolbox and something big and flat leaning against the rail next to him.

No, she realized as they got closer, it wasn't her father.

It was Guillermo. He was up there with the painting. Waiting.

Jessica felt a sudden, violent urge to throw up.

Jonathan hadn't yet noticed Guillermo when he launched into, "I had a really good time tonight. Thanks for helping me test out the place." Then he noticed. "Who's that?"

"It's... it's... um..."

No answer came to mind. She had no idea what to say. Just as she didn't know what she would say when they got to the top and Guillermo asked who Jonathan was. And here they were, going up the stairs to that moment, rising up just like the bile in her throat.

What in the world was she going to do?

Guillermo watched them steadily, his expression unreadable. It looked as if he'd been waiting there a while. He stood against the railing, his arms and legs crossed.

She cringed inside herself, trying to keep a completely normal face on the outside. This was going to be, she already knew, the most awkward thing that had ever happened in her life. If she survived it, they'd put it in *The Guinness Book of World Records*. If she didn't survive it, her tombstone would read, "Jessica Luna, beloved daughter and almost girlfriend. Died of awkwardness."

After what felt like a million years, each one filled with Jessica trying desperately to think of what to say or do, she and Jonathan reached the top of the stairs. Guillermo's eyes were like bullets. He said nothing.

Maybe if I faint, Jessica thought. If she could make herself pass out right there and now, that would solve everything. She could feel the faintness starting up. She started to close her eyes.

"Wow," said Jonathan. "Look at that painting. Is that you?"

Jessica looked down at the painting, then up at Jonathan, then over at Guillermo, who was looking at Jonathan and still saying nothing.

"Yes. That's me. I mean, it's a picture of me. It's supposed to be, yes."

"It's beautiful. Did you do it?" He was asking Jessica, for some reason. As if she would paint herself in that way.

"No," she said.

Still, Guillermo said nothing. And Jonathan hadn't appeared to notice.

"Who, then? A friend of yours?"

Jessica looked over to Guillermo again. Weirdly, a very slight smile was starting at the corner of his mouth.

"I did it," he said softly.

Jonathan turned around and looked at Guillermo for the first time. "Sorry?"

"I painted it. Over many months, while she was sleeping at my house," Guillermo said. Jessica rolled her eyes upward but couldn't faint. Maybe she could take a step backward and fall off the balcony.

Guillermo had spoken loudly and clearly this time, but Jonathan made a face as if he hadn't heard. Maybe, Jessica realized, he hadn't understood because of Guillermo's strong north Mexican accent. She fervently hoped that was the case and decided to interrupt and get Guillermo out of there before he said anything else.

Jonathan obviously *hadn't* understood, because instead of acknowledging Guillermo's statement, he turned to Jessica and asked politely, "Is this your maintenance man?"

A loud, loud silence filled the air then. Jessica blinked once, then again. Over Jonathan's shoulder, she saw Guillermo's face. Finally, he looked angry.

"I'm her boyfriend. Who the hell are you?"

Jonathan turned slowly to look at Guillermo, then back to Jessica. "Your *boyfriend*? Is that what he said?"

"That's right. Who are you?" Guillermo looked so angry now, Jessica became afraid. His hands had balled into fists at his sides.

Jonathan laughed, looking from Guillermo to Jessica and back again. "*I'm* her boyfriend. I'm the one *with* her, see?"

Jessica put out her hand, as if to physically keep Jonathan from saying anything else. "Jonathan, stop. Please." She turned to Guillermo. She had to get him out of there. "Guillermo, you need to leave."

"Why?" said Guillermo. "Is he your boyfriend, too? Do you want to be alone with him?" Jessica didn't immediately answer, and Guillermo continued. "At least tell him, then, that you're seeing me, too. So everybody knows what's going on, corazón."

Both men looked at her expectantly.

"Guillermo, you aren't my boyfriend anymore. I'm not seeing you anymore. So, I want you to leave. Now."

Jonathan's face was incredulous, as if he couldn't believe what he was hearing. "Wait — you were dating your *maintenance man?*"

His tone was so shocked — almost disgusted. Now it was Jessica's turn to look incredulous. After everything that had just happened, that's what Jonathan had to say?

Guillermo smirked bitterly. "That's right, mister. And she

loved it. Right, chiquitita?" He picked up his toolbox and, leaving the painting, shoved past them and down the stairs.

As Jessica watched him go, the familiar heat filled her face and burned her eyes. She was torn between embarrassment and anger. She felt Jonathan's stare and knew they'd have to talk this out, but at the moment, she didn't think she could open her mouth again without screaming. Guillermo was such a jerk, showing up like that and acting as if she were his property — claiming her as his girlfriend, after everything he'd put her through.

"I guess . . . ," said Jonathan. "I guess we never said we were dating exclusively, did we?" He sounded shell-shocked.

Jessica turned to him. "Are you surprised that I was seeing someone else, or just surprised that he looked like a maintenance man?" Her voice was like steel.

"Both," he said. Then, immediately, he amended this with, "I mean — you can date whoever you want. I'm not saying that. I'm just . . . surprised. Because . . . I didn't know. But I never asked, so . . ."

Jessica nodded curtly. "Right. Well, I'm sorry I never told you I was seeing someone else. Like I said, that relationship is over. But, just so you know, Guillermo's not a maintenance man. But even if he was, I don't see why that should be a concern of yours." She didn't know why she felt compelled to say this. Guillermo was a jerk, and he deserved what he'd gotten just now. But still, she felt the need to point out Jonathan's inappropriate attitude.

"It's not," said Jonathan. "You can date whoever you want, I know that. Jessica, don't think . . . I'm not trying to . . . I was just surprised, that's all."

"Because he looked poor? Because he was a Mexican, maybe?" Jessica asked loudly. She knew she sounded irrational now, but she couldn't stop herself. She had to say this, to confirm whether her worst fears were true.

"No!" he said. "Not because he was Mexican! I'm not like that. I'm just saying... I never would have pictured you with someone like that."

*Someone like that...* Jessica felt the hot tears fill her eyes. "Jonathan, I need to be alone now. Would you please go home?"

Before he could say anything else, she went into her apartment and closed the door, just as she felt the first tear run down her cheek.

# 44

The next morning, Jessica lay in bed, recovering and recounting the events of the night.

"Oh, my God," said Marisol through the phone. "I can't believe you went through that."

"I know! Right? It's like, in one night, I lost two men, just like that." Jessica shifted Ricky from her pillow to the top of the comforter and switched the phone to her other ear.

"Wait. Wait a minute. What do you mean, you lost two men? Are you saying you're going to dump Jonathan over this?"

"Well, yeah," said Jessica. "I think I have to." Once again, she felt her eyes misting up. She'd spent half the night before crying already—after she'd gone outside and gotten Guillermo's painting from her balcony, of course. "I mean, it was so horrible, the way he said it. A *maintenance man*! Like it was so gross to him, you know? And, I just didn't think he was like that, but apparently he is." She reached over to the roll of toilet paper on the nightstand, tore off a piece of it, and used it to dab her nose. "God—why did stupid Guillermo have to be there in the first place?"

Marisol made a sympathetic noise. "To bring you the painting, I guess. I can't believe he said all that stuff, about you being his girlfriend and loving it."

"Oh, I know," Jessica said. "It's like, he has six months to tell me how he feels about me, but he doesn't say a damn thing until now—when he's feeling threatened by some other man. And then he says it like *that*." She thought again of how he'd behaved last night. "It was so gross, the way he was suddenly Mr. Possessive and sexist and everything. I swear, he said more to Jonathan about our relationship than he's ever said to me in his life."

"Well, at least all that's over now, right?" Marisol said. "Good riddance, right?"

"Yeah, you're right."

"So, are you going to call Jonathan? Tell him why you're upset?"

"No. I think he gets it already." Jessica pulled the covers up to her neck. She wished that she could just go back to sleep instead of having to think about that. Or else go back in a time machine and avoid last night's situation altogether. She petted Ricky and just held the phone to her ear, letting her friend's presence comfort her from the other end of the line. "Why," she finally said, "did Jonathan have to turn out to be the typical rich white guy?"

"What do you mean?" Marisol sounded exasperated. "Jessica, come on. What does his being white have to do with this?"

"I'm not saying it's because he's white. It's...everything. He's a white guy who grew up having everything handed to him, and he just sees the world in a way that I don't see it. No, he's not racist, but he did see Guillermo and assume he had to be a maintenance man—"

"But," Marisol interrupted, "didn't you say Guillermo had

his toolbox, and he was wearing his painting clothes? Why wouldn't Jonathan think that?"

"It's not even that," Jessica countered. "It's the attitude — his total shock that I would date someone like Guillermo. 'Someone like *that*,' as he put it. Marisol, what if it had been my dad standing there, wearing his coveralls? And Jonathan had said, 'Oh, I never pictured your dad like *that*'?"

"Well, you would tell him that was your dad, and if he didn't like it, you'd dump him. But do you really think he'd be that way about your father, or anyone in your family?"

"Not intentionally," said Jessica. "But that's the problem, see? He said that stuff about Guillermo without even thinking about it. Because that's the way he thinks. Sure, he'd probably eventually accept the fact that my ex-boyfriend is blue-collar, or that my dad is.... But I shouldn't have to *explain* it to him, and to *ask* him to accept it. And to wait for him to get over the surprise. I just don't want to deal with that. You know?"

"No, I see what you're saying." Marisol sighed.

Jessica sighed in turn. It was good to be understood. Too bad that understanding had to come at the expense of losing what had seemed like a really good boyfriend. "I knew I shouldn't have tried to go out with someone like him."

Marisol didn't say anything. Jessica replayed her last comment in her mind. *Someone like him.*

"I mean...not someone like him, as in someone white," she amended. "I just meant...you know."

"Yeah, I know. It's not because he's white. It's just because he didn't know any better."

"Right," said Jessica. "You're exactly right. It was just him."

"Listen, try not to take it so hard, chica," Marisol said in a halfhearted attempt to lighten the mood. "This was a good learning experience for you. You tried something new, and it didn't work out. But now you can move on and try more new things."

Jessica laughed. "Like restaurants, you mean? I tried a Thai restaurant, and the curry gave me food poisoning, but at least now I can eat other kinds of Thai food?"

Marisol laughed, too. "Yeah, something like that."

After they'd hung up, Jessica thought over everything again. She did need to call Jonathan and talk this out. It was only fair. And she would call him, but not right this minute.

Instead, she settled back among her pillows, pulled her kitten to her chest, and let a few more tears flow. Making these kinds of decisions was emotionally exhausting, she thought. But she would get better at it. She had to.

# 45

Later, when she finally got out of bed, Jessica had a head-ache. She fed Ricky and cleaned his litter box, then turned on her computer out of force of habit, even though she didn't really have anything to work on. In her mailbox, she had one forwarded prayer from her mom, and another forwarded e-mail about sisters, and a question from Xavier about ALMA's site, presumably because he wanted to plan the database cod-ing she'd asked him to do. She replied with the answer to his question but told him not to worry about it anymore, since their funding had dried up for the moment.

While she served herself a bowl of cereal for breakfast and lunch, last night's fiasco replayed itself in her mind. Guilt-ily, she looked over at Guillermo's painting, which she had turned against the wall, in the corner by the TV, in hopes that seeing it *wouldn't* make her feel guilty.

She was going to have to call him, too, she realized. Not because she owed him any explanation regarding Jonathan, but because she owed him an apology. Whether or not he had any right to wait at her door like a stalker, he did have the right to take credit for his art and to be treated with as much respect as everyone else. She should've said who he was right from the beginning.

Why hadn't she? Obviously, she hadn't wanted Jonathan

to know she'd been seeing someone else. But she and Jonathan weren't serious yet, so there really was no reason to hide another relationship—especially one coming to an end. Jessica thought this over and came up with a troubling answer she couldn't shake. Could it have been that she herself had issues with dating "someone like" Guillermo? Had she been ashamed to admit to Jonathan that she was?

Her phone rang. It was Sabrina. Jessica took a deep breath and prepared for possible bad news about her parents.

"Hi, Sabrina."

"Okay, so I forgive you for what you said the other day at the restaurant, Jessi, *if* you tell me everything that's going on with you and Jonathan." Her voice was completely glib. "Did you two go out last night? Where'd he take you?"

Jessica couldn't believe it. Here she was, all ready to have a big, sisterly heart-to-heart about their family's problems, and all Sabrina cared about was meddling in her love life again. And this was the exact wrong moment for it. Jessica was *not* in the mood. She got up to dump her cereal in the sink. "Yes, we went out. And no, we probably aren't going out anymore, so you can stop asking, okay?"

"What? Why? What happened?" From Sabrina's tone, it was unclear whether she was concerned for her sister or upset that her matchmaking plans had gone astray.

"I don't want to talk about it."

"Come on. Tell me. Did he *do* something, or did he just wear a shirt you didn't like?"

Jessica rolled her eyes. "It doesn't matter. The point is, I'm not going to end up marrying this guy, and the sooner you realize that and get over it, the better."

"Man," said Sabrina. "What's up your butt?"

Sabrina's remark made Jessica even more upset. "You know what's up my butt?" she told her sister. "You and Mami. I'm sick of you two bugging me about this guy — about any guy — all the time. You don't even know if he's right for me, but you want me to hurry up and marry him just because he has money. And now you have Mami saying the same thing, when for all she knows he's an ax murderer. You know what? I can make my own decisions! And I'm tired of you two whispering together all the time about me and Papi — how I'm not dating anyone good enough and how Papi's not good enough for Mami anymore."

"What? What are you talking about?"

Jessica went on, getting louder by the minute. "Maybe I don't want to marry some rich white guy who'll make me into a white suburban housewife who forgets her own people. If that's what you and Mami want so bad, hook *her* up with Jonathan, and then they can live happily ever after and make Papi mow their lawn!"

Jessica finally stopped yelling and took a deep breath. It felt good to get all that off her chest.

Sabrina was silent for so long that Jessica wondered if she'd hung up. When she did speak, she didn't yell, as Jessica had expected. Instead, her voice was a block of ice.

"You are so spoiled, Jessica. You're a spoiled little brat, and you don't know what you're talking about. Just because you went to college, you think you know everything. But you *don't*. First of all, I'm not telling Mami that Papi's not good enough for her. Mami's been telling *me* that she's tired of being the only one being responsible all the time. And you know it's true. You don't want to see it because you're Daddy's little girl, but I don't blame Mami for being tired of it. I love Papi, but he doesn't appreciate her at all."

Jessica's momentary bravado began to fade.

"Second of all," Sabrina continued, her voice gaining speed and pitch, "you're sitting here saying Mami doesn't even know Jonathan. Well, you don't even know David, and he's been your brother-in-law for two years now. If you don't want to go out with his friends, fine, but don't make it like I'm trying to turn you white, and don't make it like David's forcing me to stay home. You don't even know what you're talking about."

Jessica couldn't say anything and was in fact swallowing tears at this point. Deep down, she knew what Sabrina was saying was true, and she felt a twinge of guilt at having taken a shot at David like that.

"You know what?" Sabrina's voice got even louder. "I wasn't going to tell you this, because I didn't want you to worry, but now it's time for you to hear the *truth*. You know why I quit my job? *Not* because David told me to. No, I quit because David and I have been trying to have a baby, but I haven't been able to get pregnant. And *my doctor* told me to quit my job, because it was too much stress. And I felt *bad* about it, because I didn't want to be lazy while David worked. But you know what David said? He said he wanted me to be happy and for us to have a healthy baby, and that he'd be *glad* to work until I was ready to go back again. So you don't know *anything*. David treats me like a queen, and all you can see is that he's not like Papi, so you don't like him!"

"Sabrina, I—"

"No! Here's my last thing. Mami and I *don't* sit around talking about how your boyfriends aren't good enough, or whatever it is that you're thinking. Mami tells me all the time that she's *worried* about you, because all you do is run around partying and spending money, and you *still* don't seem happy. She's worried to death that this guy you're seeing—Mrs. Jimenez's cousin's son or whatever—is going to hurt you just like that other artist loser did. And, yes, Mami's old-fashioned and thinks you need to get married to be happy. And, okay, fine, I admit that I *did* hope you would get married, too, so we could have our kids together. But forget it. Now I see what a waste of time it was for us to care about you."

"I—"

"Because we do care about you, Jessica. And if you can't see that, then I don't know what to tell you. Except that you're selfish, and you're spoiled, and I'm sick of it."

"Sabrina…"

But Sabrina had said her piece, had gotten the last word, and had hung up the phone.

# 46

This time Jessica had held Ricky and cried until she'd fallen back to sleep. In her dream, her mother complained about the web site she'd made for the family, and Guillermo painted her picture with roller skates.

When she woke up again, it was almost five. Feeling dizzy from too much sleep and too much emotion, she got out of bed and fortified herself with a can of cream of chicken soup.

She needed to get out of this apartment, Jessica realized. Otherwise she'd lie around moping for the rest of the day. She went back to her computer to check the local movie listings. Going to the movies alone sucked, but it was better than sitting around here applying for more crappy jobs. Maybe she'd call and see if Marisol felt like driving in from the suburbs, she thought.

The knock on the door startled her and woke Ricky, who'd gone back for extra napping on the couch.

It was Guillermo. He was holding a hammer.

Oh God, she thought. Had he come to kill her in a jealous rage?

"Hola, chiquitita. I came to help you hang your painting."

She noticed, then, the small toolbox in his other hand. But still ... that was no reason to trust him. "Guillermo, what are you doing here?"

"I told you. I came to hang the painting for you."

She turned and looked at it, standing there facing the corner. It *did* need to be hung, but not by Guillermo.

Then again, she didn't own a hammer herself.

While she was wondering what she was supposed to say, he slipped through the doorway, brushing close enough to make the ends of her hair crackle.

This was definitely a bad idea.

"So, where do you want it? How about right here?" He indicated the space above the couch.

Jessica didn't say anything. She couldn't believe that he was there, acting as if none of last night had happened.

He took off his shoes and stepped up onto her couch, and before she knew it, he had punched a nail into the wall. Then he brushed by her again to pick up the painting, went back to the couch, and hung it.

"Is it straight?" he said.

"Yes." She couldn't say anything else.

He stepped off the couch, dusted off his hands, and slipped his shoes back on. "Ándale. There you go."

"Uh . . . thank you."

"All right. Good-bye, then."

He made as if to leave. Jessica was spellbound. That was it? He'd come and hung up the painting, and now he was leaving?

"Hey . . ." Before she could say anything else, Ricky came out from under the desk, where he'd been observing unseen, and sat in Guillermo's path.

"Is this the one I gave you? Man, he's big." Guillermo reached down to pet the kitten. "And fat. His brothers and sisters are skinny from running all day. What are you feeding this guy?"

This comment snapped Jessica out of her stupor. She snatched Ricky up off the floor, out of Guillermo's grasp.

"He's not fat! Don't come over here and call my kitten fat. In fact, don't come over here at all. Who do you think you are, showing up all the time without even calling?"

Guillermo faced her with a smile. "Are you mad about right now, or mad about last night?"

"Both," she said. Then, "Neither. Why should I be mad? *I've* moved on. *You're* the one who's mad."

"I'm not mad, chiquitita."

He took a step closer, still with that crazy-making smile.

"Yes, you are," she said. "I was out with another man. Didn't you see that?"

"I saw it. But I'm not worried about him." He took another step closer. Jessica took a step back but hit the kitchen counter. "You may have gone out with that man last night, but you don't care about him. I saw it in your face."

"No, you didn't. I do care about him. Very much. So that's it. I don't want you anymore. You can go now."

She shrank back as close to the counter as she could, holding Enrique Salvaje in front of her like a small, furry shield.

Guillermo took another step forward and reached out to touch her cheek. *Oh no . . .*

"No, querida. You don't want that guy at all. Because if you do, why isn't he here right now? Why am I here instead?"

He took the kitten from her hands and dropped him gently to the floor. The air all around had turned blurry, like the air right above a hot sidewalk. In superslow motion, he closed the space between them with a kiss.

Just like last time — just like always — she felt herself melt. Her arms betrayed her by wrapping around his neck.

This is what it feels like, she thought, when the devil possesses your soul.

After what felt like a hundred years, each year of which she spent burning in hell and not minding one bit, they pulled apart.

"Corazón," he whispered, "I've been missing you."

She didn't want to say it aloud, but, as always, she had to admit to herself that she'd missed him, too.

"You're not going to see that bolillo anymore, are you?" he asked.

She shook her head no. There was no use lying about it now.

"Good. Because if you're going to see other men, this isn't going to work out between the two of us."

He smiled, still, as he said this, as if he were talking to a child. Slowly, his words sank into her brain. Slowly, something around her chest broke, like a wrestler's grip on a stronger opponent. Then she returned his smile.

"What isn't going to work out? You calling me whenever you feel like having sex?"

Confusion flickered over his handsome face. "No...I mean, yes. Yes, I can't do that anymore, if you're going to..." His voice trailed off.

She took a deep breath. It was time, once again, to stand up for herself.

"Well, I'm not going to see him anymore. But this thing between the two of us, with you showing up when you want sex, or whatever else? And you neglecting me until I get mad enough to leave? And then being nice only long enough for me to come back? That's not going to happen anymore, either. I'm tired of it, Guillermo. I'm through."

Now his face was totally eclipsed by confusion. It was as if he genuinely couldn't understand. Maybe this had never happened to him before. She had a sense of déjà vu. No — double déjà vu.

"Chiquitita, please." He took her hand in both of his and squeezed it softly, then pressed it to his chest. "Please, Jessica ... I know that the way I sometimes treated you was not very nice. But please understand — escúchame, corazón — I'm not used to having a woman telling me what to do, and where to be. I'm used to being on my own — being free. But you're the first woman..." He paused, searching for the words.

She held her breath. Was he going to tell her that she was the first woman who made him want to change his ways? Because he was in love with her? Jessica's heart had already been beating fast from the adrenaline of telling him off. Now it felt like a big red hummingbird in her chest.

"You're the first woman," he went on. "I love ... I love the way you make me feel, when you call me and want to be with me. When you listen to my stories and laugh. When I come over in the middle of the night and you don't throw things at me," he said, lifting her fingers to his mouth to kiss them reverently. "You're the first woman who made me feel like I wasn't just some ... some dirty Mexican. And I don't want to lose that feeling, chiquitita."

He sounded like someone in a movie.

A bad movie, on the Movie Network for Women, about

women who never learned. Jessica pulled her hand out of his and broke away to face him full on.

"Well, you know what you made me feel like, Guillermo? Every time I wanted to be with you and laugh at your stories, and you didn't call me back? And all the times you disappeared for weeks, and then walked right back into my life like nothing had happened? It made me feel stupid. Like you didn't care. Like you thought *I* was some dirty Mexican."

She felt those words pump out of her from deep inside herself, where everything was secret and true.

He just looked at her, mouth hanging open.

She continued telling the truth. "And I don't want to feel like that anymore."

He said nothing as she led him to the door and closed it behind him.

When he was completely gone, she threw herself on the couch. Her eyes began to mist up a little, for the third time that day. But for some reason, the sob that came out felt more like a laugh.

The next day, Sunday, Jessica woke up early. In the bathroom, she looked at her reflection. Her eyes were only a little puffy from all the crying the day before.

Back in her bedroom, she took her phone off the charger and was about to turn it on, then thought better of it. At that point, there was no one she was in the mood to talk to. She needed a break from everything and everyone in her life.

Her kitten woke up with a little yawn and watched as she changed out of her sleep shirt, then searched the room, filling a bag with various things. Within a few minutes, she was kissing him good-bye.

And then she drove to the beach.

People said that the Texas Gulf Coast was nasty and that Galveston Island was the nastiest part of it—a floating ghetto. A giant sewer. The big toilet of the Atlantic Ocean. But it was the only beach Jessica had ever known. Sure, the water was green and gray instead of postcard blue. Sure, there was seaweed wadded up everywhere. There were little kids in diapers and out of them, jumping and screaming in the water. But at the same time, the sun was shining, the seagulls were calling, and the salty, warm wind blew through her hair as she lay under an umbrella on the sand.

She'd felt a little weird, driving there by herself. But once she got there, she was glad she'd gone. The smell of the beach was always the same. It reminded Jessica of her childhood, when she'd been happy and hopeful and full of dreams for her future.

After sitting by herself on the shore for a while, she came up with an idea.

She looked out over the waves. *If I'm supposed to go through with this idea, give me a sign.*

But then, instead of waiting, she closed her eyes. She already knew she would go through with it either way. She'd left behind the signs, fortune-telling, and allowing anything or anyone else to tell her how to run her life.

Now, she trusted herself. She might not always make the best choices, she thought, but it was okay. If everyone else in her life could manage on their own, then she could, too.

# 47

This is Floyd Harrelson, our go-to for actuarial analysis. And this is Shelley. Shelley makes the best coffee on the fortieth floor."

Jessica couldn't hear Shelley's reply, but she heard the giggling. All the older women here thought Brad was cute for some reason.

"And here's our department," she heard Brad say to whomever he was showing around. Maybe another candidate for the broker job. Jessica's phone rang. Outside line.

"Jessica Luna."

"Jessica? This is Esmeralda Vargas." The director of ALMA, returning her call.

"Mrs. Vargas. Hello." Jessica hunched down behind her file stacks for some relative privacy. Luckily, Brad was talking steadily and someone was making a racket in the file room, so no one would hear the details of her conversation. "I was wondering if you have time to meet with me this evening. Or for lunch, maybe. I have an idea I'd like to pitch to you, regarding the web site."

"And this is Jessica," interrupted Brad, right above her head. "Oh, she's on the phone." He was leading around a big corn-fed-looking guy in a white shirt and striped tie. A young guy, no older than Brad himself.

"Let me look at my calendar," said Mrs. Vargas, on the phone. "I can't meet with you tonight. What about tomorrow?"

Jessica checked her own calendar. "That's fine. That'd be great, Mrs. Vargas." She felt eyes on her. She turned and saw that Brad and the other guy were standing there, waiting for her to get off the phone. "All right, well, I'll meet you tomorrow, then, at your office. Good-bye."

She turned around to face Brad with a cold, fake-polite smile. It was really annoying, the way they treated her like an animal at the zoo sometimes. She had no privacy at all. It wasn't as though *she* ever stood in *their* doorways, staring at them until *they* got off the phone.

"Ryan, this is Jessica Luna. She's one of our best and brightest—you definitely want to get on her good side so she'll help you out. Jessica, this is Ryan Ercher, our new broker."

*New broker?*

"Hi, Jessica. Pleased to meet you," Ryan Ercher said, extending his hand. Jessica just stared at it and then back at him.

"Ryan's an old school friend of mine," Brad said. He didn't notice that Jessica hadn't shaken his school friend's hand. "You're going to love him. Come on, Ry. Let's go see your new office."

*New office?*

Brad led Ryan to the file room. But it wasn't the file room anymore. Jessica saw now that the mailroom guys were carrying the files out in boxes and hauling in a desk and computer. She turned to Rochelle, who was taking the opportunity to check the lottery numbers online.

"Rochelle, what's going on?"

"They're cleaning out the file room for the new broker."

"I know. I can see that. But I thought they weren't hiring anybody yet."

"Oh, girl, you knew. Mr. Cochran and them have been talking about it for weeks."

Jessica tensed, waiting for the shock to hit her.

Then, nothing. No shock at all. Of course Mr. Cochran had gone ahead and hired someone else. What had she expected?

And it didn't hurt at all. Instead, Jessica felt an immense sense of relief. Now she wouldn't have to worry about playing golf. Now she wouldn't have to suck up to the top brass all the time, like all the other brokers. Now she knew that she'd never wanted that promotion after all.

She laughed, then stood up. There was one more thing she didn't want.

"Jessica? You okay, girl?" Rochelle asked as Jessica crossed the room silently, making straight for Mr. Cochran's office.

"Jessica. Good morning. I, uh, I'm sure that by now you've met Ryan," Mr. Cochran started, rattling his paper and letting it fall to his desk. "I just want you to know that—"

"Mr. Cochran," said Jessica, "I quit."

"—I did consider your interest— What's that?" he asked.

"I quit," she said again, louder. Because it felt good. She felt a smile starting on her face and held it back for the sake of professionalism.

Mr. Cochran's eyes went wider than she'd ever seen them. "Now, Jessica, hold on just one minute here. Let's not be hasty." Quicker than she'd ever seen him move, he jumped up and closed his office door behind her, then motioned for her to take a seat. But she didn't. She remained standing, the serene smile returning irresistibly to her face. Jessica felt as if she were floating up into the ether or, at least, out of this dusty office building.

"I understand that you're upset," Mr. Cochran said. "But I think you're taking things way too personally. You're a good employee, Jessica, and I've been meaning to show you McCormick's appreciation in the form of a raise. I just haven't had the chance—"

Jessica shook her head, still smiling as beatifically as a saint. Now that this moment had come—a moment she'd fantasized about more than once—she found that there was no need for anger or passionate declarations. "Mr. Cochran, I'm not upset at all. I just don't want to work in insurance anymore. And now you have Ryan, who's more qualified than I am, so I can leave with a clear conscience, and you guys won't be stuck trying to find someone to replace me. So, I'll just let myself out. Thanks, Mr. Cochran, for everything you've done."

With that, she turned and let herself out of his office, leaving him stunned in her wake.

"Did you tell him something?" Rochelle whispered as Jessica made her way back to their desks.

"Oh yeah. I told him something." Jessica sat and, systematically, deleted every bit of her own personality from her computer's hard drive. After that, she would put her personal items into the tote bag she kept in her bottom drawer. After that, she would neatly stack her unfinished work and then leave.

As she cleared her space bit by bit, Jessica hummed. The floating sensation was filling her. It was as if she were tipsy on the dance floor, spinning under the lights. Or driving fast down an empty road to an exciting destination.

She knew she should have been worried, because she'd just done what you weren't ever supposed to do. She'd quit her job without another job to go to, and her future was completely uncertain.

Despite all that, Jessica felt good. For the first time in a long, long while, she felt in control of her life.

# 48

Jessica's newfound sense of power carried her out to the parking garage and into her trusty Accord, where she deposited her little tote bag of office supplies and sugarless gum. Then she took the wheel. Where should I go? she asked herself. The answer was, anywhere she wanted.

She wanted to go to the park — the one next to the zoo, where there were squirrels and ducks to watch. So she drove there, as exhilarated as a kid skipping school. But better, because there was nothing to feel guilty about in this case. She'd just gotten rid of a dead-end job and a boss who didn't appreciate or respect her. It was a landmark day. "Today," she told herself as she pulled into the nearly empty zoo parking lot, "is the first day of the rest of my life."

Her jobless life, that was. But Jessica refused to worry about that just yet. She got out of her car and walked through the picnic tables and giant trees, across acorn- and pine-needle-strewn grass, to a shady park bench. The job thing was a technicality, and it didn't even scare her. What was there to be afraid of? Worst-case scenario, she told herself, she'd go to a temp agency and hire herself out as a personal assistant again. No, she amended to herself. *Worst*-case scenario would be getting a retail job. Or a waitressing job.

"No," she said softly to the first squirrel that ran up, hoping for food. The absolute worst-case scenario would be moving back in with her parents.

With that many scenarios to go through before total disaster, Jessica really had nothing to worry about. It wasn't as if she were in danger of starving to death. She knocked on wood at that thought, then smiled at the squirrel and reached down with a coaxing hand. He stared at her quizzically for a moment before sauntering off.

She found, suddenly, the headiness of taking control—of taking action—was addictive. Already, the high of leaving her job was fading and she was ready to take on something else. She was on a roll—a self-help role.

Jessica tucked her legs onto the bench and pulled her cell phone from her purse. It was time to set something else straight. She flipped open the phone but paused before dialing. Whom should she call first?

She needed to call Jonathan. It had been eating at her mind all morning. What would she say, though?

Jessica was so still as she sat there thinking, several more curious squirrels scampered right up to her bench and she didn't even notice. There was something else eating at her mind. Something she'd said to Marisol.

*Someone like that.* She had said that she never should have tried dating someone like Jonathan. Just as he'd never imagined her dating "someone like that," meaning Guillermo.

How could she be angry at Jonathan for thinking of Guillermo that way, when she'd been thinking of Jonathan that way all along?

Had she ever really given him a fair chance? Jessica had to ask herself. Or had she lumped him in with Sabrina's other friends right from the beginning?

And what about Sabrina's other friends? How fair was it to think of them as one solid entity — a big white, middle-class, multiheaded monster?

It was an uncomfortable train of thought, but Jessica forced herself to follow it. She'd thought she had a good reason to dislike Sabrina's friends. She'd blamed them for making Sabrina go suburban, for making her leave the family behind. But that wasn't the case, was it? If Jessica was being honest with herself, she knew better than anyone how hard it was to keep Sabrina from getting her way. If her stubborn sister had really wanted to stay near the family, David would have let her. He wouldn't have been able to say no.

And he hadn't said no, because he loved her. Just as he never batted an eye at their father's borderline-racist jokes. And now that Jessica thought about it, Sabrina probably wouldn't tolerate her husband or her friends being racist, even if she did have to put up with it from Papi.

So why hadn't Jessica given Sabrina's friends — or her husband, for that matter — more of a chance?

Because she herself had been too quick to judge. She'd assumed that anyone who lived in the suburbs and cared more about property taxes than fashion must be a loser, not worth her time. And she'd assumed that because Jonathan liked trendy music and trendy restaurants, he might be the exception to the rule.

Most painful of all, she'd assumed that she and Sabrina would be alike forever — that they'd always want the same things out of life. And when that changed, that someone was to blame. A white someone. Just like the white someones her father had been blaming his problems on for years.

And she'd been wrong. About everything.

She needed to call Jonathan. He wasn't right for her, she knew now, but she needed to give them both the opportunity for closure. But first, she needed to adjust her attitude as far as people like Jonathan—or anyone different from her—were concerned.

She would start by making amends with her sister. Jessica dialed Sabrina's number.

"Hello?" said her mother on the other end of the line.

"Mami. You're still staying at Sabrina's?" Jessica sighed. In the midst of her own personal drama, she'd almost forgotten that her mother wasn't sleeping at home anymore.

"No," said Mami. "I'm here right now to help Sabrina a little, but I went home on Saturday."

"Help Sabrina do what? Mami, why aren't you at work? Is Sabrina okay?" Jessica felt fear grip her like an icy fist. Her mother never took the day off. And Sabrina had been having health problems. This could only mean . . .

"She's fine, m'ija. Don't worry. I just came over to help her put the guest bedroom back the way it was, and to look at some clothes she wanted me to see. And then I'm going back home, because I'm on vacation."

"What?" Jessica couldn't have been more surprised if her mother had said she was on a reality show.

"That's right. I took the whole week off." Her mother sounded proud, like a child presenting a macaroni collage.

"What are you going to do?" Jessica asked. "What about Papi? Are you going somewhere together?"

"Your father had to go in today, but he's taking off the rest of the week. We had a talk about some things. I don't know what we're doing yet. We might go somewhere, or we might just stay home."

"Mami..." Jessica felt shy about delving into her mother's personal business. Especially when Mami sounded so confident and like her usual self. "How are things going, then? Are you two okay?"

"We're okay. We will be. I don't know yet what's going to happen, but whatever it is, it'll be for the best, m'ija. You have to understand that." Before Jessica could say anything else, Mami said, "Were you calling for your sister?"

"Yes, but—"

"She's in the garage right now. I'd better go help her. But I'll tell her you called, and she'll call you back, okay?"

The phone call was over, and Jessica had to be content with the way things were between her parents. She could control her own life, but not anyone else's.

# 49

The next day, as she drove to ALMA, Jessica felt the same empowerment high from the day before. She wouldn't be able to predict the outcome of this meeting, of course, but at least she was *doing* something. She was trying to make a change in her life, instead of just waiting around for something to happen.

"Come in, come in," said Mrs. Vargas, who'd arrived fifteen minutes late for their meeting. Jessica had spent the time cooling her heels in the lobby, examining the latest student art exhibit and talking with a few of the artists themselves.

"So, Jessica, what's on your mind?"

"Mrs. Vargas, I understand that you recently lost an instructor."

"Yes, that's right. We're still looking for a replacement so we don't lose the grant money that was funding his residency. Do you know anyone who plays accordion?"

"No. But, actually, I have an idea for how you can replace him. I don't know the terms of your grant, but I was wondering if it would fund a different kind of arts teacher. A digital art teacher. I was thinking that you could hire me. I could teach web design and digital art editing to the older students and adults. Or to the other arts teachers."

Esmeralda was still listening. Jessica hurried to fill the

silence with something that made sense. "That way, I could also keep working on the ALMA site, as a member of the staff. And we could incorporate the idea we talked about — the kids having their own web pages — into the classes, so that they could actually make the pages themselves. Or . . . ," She had run out of things to say. "Or, whatever you see fit."

Esmeralda looked out the small bit of window visible through all the artwork, photos, and awards crowding her office. She was obviously considering the idea, but Jessica had no way of knowing whether she liked it or not. Her face, as always, was as impassive as a portrait's. Finally, she turned to face Jessica again.

"That's a good idea. But, really, the community needs basic computer skills more than they need to learn how to do web sites. They need job skills."

Jessica knew just how to solve that. "I can teach basic computer skills. I could teach word processing, spreadsheets, presentation skills — everything. I could do all that, plus the web design, and we could call it computer arts."

"That's an even better idea. But where would we get the computers to do it? I could probably put your salary on the program budget, but the students can't learn by looking over your shoulder at your laptop." Esmeralda smiled, inviting Jessica to come up with an answer to that.

And she did. "I can get a corporate donation for them. I'm sure McCormick . . ." Well, not McCormick, actually. They probably wouldn't want to donate anything now that Jessica had quit her job. She had to think fast. "Halronburco. Have they ever contributed anything to ALMA?"

Esmeralda smiled and shook her head.

"Well, I have a contact...I have two contacts there, in pretty high positions. I'm sure I could get them to donate the computers, as long as they could put their logo on one of ALMA's brochures."

Esmeralda narrowed her eyes and looked out her window again.

Jessica waited. Really, it *was* a good idea, if she could make it work. Wasn't it?

"It is a good idea, Jessica. Let me think about it for a while and talk to my staff."

# 50

Two down, two to go, Jessica thought as she drove away from ALMA. Three down, if she counted the way she'd dispatched Guillermo. Now all she had to do was clear the air with Sabrina and talk to Jonathan. And she didn't know which would be more difficult. She sighed to herself and drove toward the zoo park again. She liked being there, she'd found. Being outside, away from her computer and TV, helped her think more clearly. It was only six-thirty, so there was plenty of June daylight left, but not so much heat anymore.

Back at the same park bench as before, with only the squirrels to eavesdrop, she dialed Jonathan's cell number.

"Hello?"

"Jonathan. It's me. Hi."

"Jessica." He sounded relieved. "I'm glad you called. I wanted to call you myself, but I thought... Well, I thought I'd wait until you wanted to talk to me."

"Thanks," said Jessica. She had wondered, a little, why he hadn't called. He and Guillermo really were polar opposites, she saw now. Whereas Guillermo was emotional to the point of stalkerhood, Jonathan was as proper and polite as a distant moon. And it had turned out that neither of those qualities was to her taste.

"Listen, I talked to Sabrina," he said. "I hope you don't

mind, but I called her, and she explained what was going on."

"Did she?" Jessica was immediately annoyed. What had Sabrina said? Had she told Jonathan that Jessica had been apprehensive about dating him all along? That she was racist? "What did she say?"

"She told me that you'd been dating Guillermo for a while, but that you'd kept it quiet because you didn't want your family interfering with your personal life. And she told me that you only went out with me because she'd pressured you into it. And, Jessica, I just want to say that, as embarrassing as that was for me to hear, I understand, and I apologize for my part of it. I see now that I rushed you into something that—"

"Wait, wait. Jonathan, stop." Jessica shook her head, as if he could see her. As if that would erase all the suspicions she'd just entertained about her own sister. "What she told you was wrong. I mean, it is *partially* right, but that has nothing to do with you and me or why I agreed to go out with you. The thing with Guillermo wasn't serious, and I really was interested in you. I wouldn't have gone out with you if I weren't."

He sighed audibly into the phone. "Well, that's a relief, at any rate."

A squirrel dug into pine needles under the next park bench. A shiny black grackle landed on top of it and looked at Jessica with a yellow eye. She took a deep breath and readied herself to tell the truth.

"What she didn't tell you, Jonathan, is that I've had issues with dating you all along. Nothing to do with you, but my own issues."

He waited. Said nothing.

"See, I never gave you a fair chance. I realize that now. Instead of taking time to find out who you are, I've been too busy worrying about *what* you are."

"What do you mean?"

"You're white, you grew up middle-class, and you wear a suit to work every day. And, I'm really sorry—I know this makes me shallow...and worse...but I've never dated a guy like you, and I had a lot of...preconceived notions about you. And I let those get in the way."

He laughed, not happily, but as if he were surprised. "What kind of preconceived notions? Jessica, I'm honestly one of the most liberal white guys you could meet."

She chuckled, too. It eased the tension. "I don't know. Maybe I thought you were only dating me because I looked similar enough to your friends. Maybe I was worried that I'd never be able to introduce you to some of my friends." She couldn't help adding wryly, "Who look like struggling painters. Or maintenance men. Or bottling plant foremen, like my dad."

"Oh God. Jessica, I really am sorry for that. You have to believe me—if I'd had any idea that guy had been someone you were dating... Well, I guess I would've been uncomfortable on a whole other level, then, wouldn't I?" He gave another awkward laugh. "But I hope you aren't judging me based on that one incident. I hope you know that I have the utmost respect for you and that would automatically carry over to anyone you care about."

"I know," she said.

She decided not to bring up his comment about her dating

"someone like that." It was pointless by now. He'd said it without thinking and probably didn't even remember it anymore. And she did believe that he had the best intentions—that he would never *consciously* judge someone by their race or class. It was time to get back to the point.

"The thing is, Jonathan, that night made me realize how much baggage I was bringing into our relationship. And I was so busy struggling with that baggage, I couldn't judge what was happening on its own merits. Honestly, I suspect that you and I aren't an ideal match. But whether we are or not, I need to let you go. I need to deal with my culture issues and let you find someone who doesn't have any to work out."

After the last word, she expelled her breath slowly. Although her head felt as if it were buzzing, it felt good to get the truth out, she thought. Even when the truth was not so pretty.

Jonathan was quiet for a moment, then let out a slow sigh. "Okay. I understand."

She felt a flash of pity for him, but at the same time, she felt relief for them both.

There were a few stock phrases after that, in which they assured each other there were no hard feelings and they could still be friends.

And then it was over. Jessica drove home.

## 51

While she'd been talking to Jonathan, someone else had called. Back at her apartment, she set her phone on the kitchen counter and called her voice mail, putting it on speaker so she could listen while she filled Ricky's bowl with kitten chow.

"Jessica, this is Felix Montenegro." She wondered if he was calling because he wanted her to give Guillermo's painting back, so he could sell it and get a commission.

"I don't know what you said to Guillermo," he continued, "but you and I need to talk. He came by to pick up his money and told my assistant that he was leaving town. I thought you and I had an understanding, Jessica. Have you booked Guillermo for shows with another gallery? Call me back. Please."

Jessica deleted the message. That was it, then. She was no longer seeing Jonathan, and Guillermo was gone. He'd gone back home to Monterrey, maybe. Or to Washington State, to pick cherries.

Now she really did have Ricky and no one else. Not that she'd been planning to go out with either man again. But still...

Ricky rubbed against her ankle, as if to prove his loyalty. She reached down and stroked him idly.

Madame Hortensia had told her to figure out what she

wanted. And Jessica had done that, as far as her job was concerned. But what about the rest of her life? What about, as Madame Hortensia would say, what was coming for her in love? It was one thing to know what you wanted in a man and another thing to make that man appear.

If she could meet a guy as nice and successful as Jonathan and, at the same time, as hot and exciting as Guillermo . . . *that* would be the perfect boyfriend.

No, wait—even better . . . someone like that, who also made her laugh. And, also, who appreciated her for who she was and not just because she supported his career or looked like Amber Chavez.

But you couldn't just sit around waiting for the perfect man to show up, could you? Maybe she should take one of those Leisure Learning courses after work, so she could meet a man who shared her interests. Maybe she could pick up some programming skills at the same time.

Or maybe, she reminded herself, she needed to take some time to iron out her issues—to do a little mental housecleaning—before she jumped back into the romance saddle again.

Yes, that was probably the answer, she told herself with a sigh. She picked up the phone again and carried it to the sofa, where she flopped down and dialed Sabrina's number.

No answer. Jessica hung up before the answering machine beeped. Sabrina would call her back, probably. This was last on her list—setting things straight with her sister. She wasn't going to forget about it, to just let it go or wait for some sign.

But for now she'd done enough straightening, hadn't she? Jessica lay back against her throw pillows and turned on the TV.

# 52

Three days later—three days that had been a blur of job searches and soul searches—Jessica was sitting on her sofa again. She'd just seen Esmeralda Vargas on Tuesday, and now it was Friday—too soon to call and demand a response to her proposal, no matter how badly she wanted one. So, instead, she'd been e-mailing all her friends, looking for job leads and telling them how she'd quit her job. Xavier in particular had wanted all the details, as gossip had been flying around McCormick a mile a minute.

And now she was talking to Marisol on the phone. Marisol had called on her lunch break, which meant something important must have happened. Jessica switched the phone from one ear to the other and airlifted Ricky from the floor to her lap. "Tell me if Esmeralda said anything about giving me the job."

"Well, I'm not supposed to say yet—"

"Oh, my gosh! She's going to give it to me, isn't she?"

"Well, it isn't one hundred percent for sure yet. And you *can't* tell her you heard it from me."

Jessica squealed with joy.

"The only thing she's waiting on is approval from the board," said Marisol. "But I can't see why they wouldn't approve it. We only had the one accordion student anyway.

Plus, they've been talking about sponsoring computer skills classes for the community for a while now, so this would totally kill all the birds with one stone."

"When is she going to ask them?"

"Monday night, at the board meeting."

"Marisol, you have *got* to call everyone you're friends with on the board and convince them to let her hire me."

Jessica's mind went into work mode overdrive. The principal of Hawthorne was on the board. He knew and liked Jessica. And what about Mr. Santiago? Wasn't he Mrs. Jimenez's cousin? Did Jessica have time to make copies of her portfolio for Mrs. Vargas to pass out at the meeting?

"The only thing about it," said Marisol, "is the pay. It's not that great.... Jessica?... Jessica, are you still there?"

"Yeah, I'm here. The pay's not great. I get you. That's okay."

"No, seriously. It's only twenty dollars an hour."

"Twenty an hour? Dude—that's a dollar more than I make at McCormick."

"Yeah, but you're not going to be doing eight-hour days at ALMA." Marisol sounded hesitant, as if she were worried she'd make Jessica change her mind.

"Well, that'll give me more time to work freelance, then," said Jessica. "Seriously, Marisol. I am *so* ready to work again."

"Jessica, seriously for real...you remember how nonprofit is. You know it won't *just* be teaching. Esmeralda wants you to do this so you can update our web site at the same time. Also, she'll have you doing everything else, from taking pictures at all the events, to making the brochures, to driving the bus—"

"I'm ready. How soon will I start? Is tomorrow good?"

"Well, I'm sure Esmeralda will take you as soon as she can get you," said Marisol. "You know how she is."

Jessica laughed. She felt as if a big, ugly weight had been lifted from her shoulders and flung out the window.

After making lunch plans and hanging up with Marisol, she called Toby and told him the good news.

"Hey. I got the ALMA job! Let's go out and celebrate."

"Sorry, Jessi, I can't." He sighed. "I promised Mami I'd stay home tonight. We're doing each other's highlights. Let's go out tomorrow, though, okay? We need to party our asses off, and drink to you breaking out of that hellhole."

After hanging up with Toby, Jessica considered calling her own parents. But, no...she didn't want to interrupt their time off from work. Lord knew it was a break they both sorely needed. And she hadn't even told them that she'd quit her job, because she'd known it would freak them out. Better to wait and call them *after* she'd started the ALMA job, she decided. That way, they wouldn't even have the chance to worry.

She thought of calling Sabrina but immediately nixed that plan, a little guiltily. She hadn't talked to her sister at all since their blowout on the phone. She'd called three days before, and Sabrina had never called back. True, Jessica hadn't left her any message. But Sabrina had caller ID, so she would have known and would have called back if she'd wanted to. That was enough to make Jessica suspect that her sister simply didn't want to speak to her.

Or maybe, she told herself, Sabrina was just busy. She was trying to have a baby, wasn't she? Maybe, Jessica thought wryly, Sabrina actually had more important things to do than hold a sisterly grudge.

She *would* call Sabrina, she told herself, but not now. Later, after she'd unwound a little. Didn't she deserve some time to relax after all she'd been through?

The phone was warm in Jessica's hand. She looked at its bright face and felt a little pitiful about not having anyone else to call. If she were still seeing Guillermo or Jonathan, she could have called one of them. But she wasn't.

She could always call Madame Hortensia. . . .

No. That would be a pretty desperate move.

Jessica set down her phone and went over to the desk, where her laptop sat up and running. At seventy-five words a minute, she tapped out an e-mail:

hey. guess what. I got the job.

Then she waited, feeling a little silly. She probably should have just called Xavier's office. But for some reason, she didn't feel that would be appropriate anymore. Things had changed, in her mind, now that he and Cynthia were an item again. It was one thing for a guy to get e-mails from his female friend. It was a whole other thing for her to be calling him up on a Friday afternoon.

After a few minutes, Xavier wrote her back:

Congrats. Let me buy you a drink?

She smiled, then immediately frowned.

Can you?

He responded:

Don't worry. For once, I have a Friday evening to myself.

It was settled, then. If he was free, she was free. Jessica's smile returned to her face. It'd be good to see her friend again. She'd missed him.

# 53

They'd agreed to meet at Zona Azul, a downtown bar a block away from McCormick. Jessica circled the skyscrapers for a while, then ended up finding a space right outside McCormick's parking garage. I should have kept my parking pass, she thought. It would have come in handy. Sighing, she parked under a shadeless little birch tree, then turned off her stereo and mentally prepared herself to walk through the sweltering rush-hour heat.

But first, she thought as she checked herself in the rearview mirror, it was time to make another change. She reached up and carefully pulled the Virgin Mary off the mirror by its elastic string. Then, giving it a little good-bye squeeze, she opened the glove compartment and put it away for the last time.

Tiny white Christmas lights shone over the mirrored bar, which reflected the candles in red jars that decorated the tables behind her. A postcard lying on the bar next to her drink proclaimed that it was Salsa Night. Jessica stirred her Cape Cod and sighed. Strangely, despite all the good things that had recently happened, she felt . . . not unhappy, exactly, but less exhilarated than she would have expected. It was almost as if she were emotionally spent after all the drama that had gone down in the past month.

Well, she told herself, it's time to relax now. Time to unwind. Really, it was a good thing that Toby had been too busy to come out tonight, she decided. Xavier was the better choice, because he was the least dramatic person she knew.

The bar was inhabited mostly by couples. Some of them were going out to dance to the jazzy stuff that was playing through the speakers, while workers set up the corner stage for a band. Jessica watched idly. How long had it been since she'd danced?

"Jess," she heard Xavier say.

"Hey! How'd you sneak up on me like that?" Turning to face him, Jessica almost didn't recognize him. He'd taken off his glasses and tie. Without them, he looked nothing like the nerdy guy she was used to. In fact, just as she'd always suspected, the loss of his unfashionable accessories left him looking pretty good. He pulled up the stool beside her and sat.

"You should hear how everyone's been talking since you left. You're practically a hero," he said. "I heard a rumor that Personnel is scared now. They're worried you'll inspire every other woman in the company to quit."

Jessica snorted. "Funny."

The bartender came over and took Xavier's order for a Negra Modelo and another Cape Cod for her.

"What did Cynthia say?" Jessica couldn't help asking. She wondered if Xavier even talked to Cynthia about her.

"What do you mean? I don't talk to her much anymore," he said.

"Xavier. Come on. Don't play dumb. Listen, you can tell me the truth. I promise not to make fun of you for going back to her, okay? I'm through judging people for dumb reasons. I've turned over a whole new leaf."

Xavier looked at her quizzically for a moment, then laughed. "Jess, you're such a drama queen. I told you, I'm not seeing Cynthia. Why, do you *want* me to get back with her?"

Jessica felt a sheepish expression cover her face. "Well, *no.* She's totally wrong for you."

"I know. I told *you* that, remember?"

"Yes. But then I overheard you making plans to have lunch with her. And I saw her name on your caller ID. And, well, you've been too busy to have lunch with me lately, so I just assumed..."

"I did see her at lunch, but it was with a whole bunch of other people. McCormick made me host a training luncheon for some of the assistants upstairs who need extra help. You can't tell anyone I told you this, but if Cynthia and the others can't learn the company applications by the end of the year, McCormick's going to let them go."

"Really?" Jessica's eyes went wide.

"Yeah. And Cynthia knows that, so she's been freaking out. She keeps calling me to help her so she'll pass the test."

"No *way.*"

"Yes way." Xavier's face turned serious suddenly, the way it always did after he'd told her something he shouldn't have. "I wasn't going to tell you all that, because it's confidential, but if you're going to accuse me of *dating* Cynthia again..."

Jessica thought it all over. Really, it was kind of funny, now that she knew what was going on. She hadn't realized Cynthia was so...well, dumb.

He smiled. "Come on. Let's quit talking about the poor girl. Her ears are probably burning."

The band took the stage and began tuning their instruments. When the bass player hit his first note, Jessica felt a little shiver run down her back. "It's Salsa Night," she informed Xavier.

"Yeah, it looks like it. You want to dance?"

Jessica laughed out of pure surprise. "Um...yeah. I do, actually."

They went out onto the floor. Jessica was prepared to dance next to him while he sidestepped back and forth, like half the other guys on the floor. Instead, he took her in his arms. Because it was their first time together, their steps were small and experimental.

"Do you want me to lead?" he said.

"Sure."

"Okay, well, let me do it, then."

He was a good dancer. She should have known that, because he'd told her about the constant weddings and quinceañeras his mother and sister dragged him to, where he was expected to dance with every woman in the room. But she hadn't been able to imagine it—Xavier, her computer-programming friend, dancing as well as this.

He spun her round and round the floor, and she couldn't stop laughing. It had been a long time since she'd really danced like this. They went through three songs like nothing, until the fourth made her blood rush and her heart beat fast.

"You want to sit at one of the tables?" he said.

They did, and the waitress came to take their order for another round. This time Jessica asked for water.

"If I had known you danced that well," she said, "I would've made you come out with me a long time ago."

"Really?" he said.

"Heck, yeah."

Over their drinks, they talked about Jessica's new job and the possibility of Xavier getting his department to donate computers to ALMA. Then they ordered a plate of nachos to share and talked about everything else. It was just like their weekly lunches at McCormick, thought Jessica. But better, because they had more time now, and especially because she wasn't working at McCormick anymore. She sighed happily.

"You know what?" she told him. "I'm going to miss having lunch with you."

"Oh, yeah?" he said.

"Yeah. You know—making fun of everybody the way we did. Complaining about stuff. You were my best friend at work, you know that?"

"Well, it's not like ALMA's far away. They'll let you have lunch, right? We can still meet at Taqueria Aztlán, like always."

He made it sound easy. Because it was easy, now that she thought about it. She smiled. "Awesome. Now I don't have any reason to miss McCorporate at all."

He asked her to dance again, and she couldn't resist. They danced two, three, four, five songs, and then the band stopped playing.

Everyone on the floor looked at the stage askance. It was only nine o'clock.

"Sorry, everybody," said the singer. "Poetry open mike is coming up next."

Xavier turned to Jessica. "I guess that's our cue to leave."

\*          \*          \*

It was a short walk to her car, and he'd left his in the garage, right next to her spot.

"That was fun," she said as they neared the corner, where the streetlight was just coming to life.

"It was," he said. "We should do this again. Soon."

"Yeah?" They arrived at her car, and Jessica turned to lean against her door and face him. She thought she understood what he was saying, but she wanted to hear him say it. "Do what?"

He took a step closer to her and looked into her eyes. "Go out. Together. At night."

"You mean, as in dating?"

He laughed. "Yeah. As in dating. We don't work together anymore. I'm not seeing Cynthia, and you're through with What's-his-name and the other guy. So, why not?"

Jessica felt a sense of surreality wash over her. Why not? Everything he said was true, so why not indeed?

Because, she reminded herself, after everything that had recently happened, she wasn't going out with anyone. She had issues to iron out first. She'd already decided.

"I'm not way off here, am I?" Xavier asked. "I mean, are you interested at all, or am I just doing some seriously wishful thinking?"

She laughed. "No, you're not. I'm definitely interested."

His smile melted away as he leaned down and kissed her. She let him, and it was nice. It was better than nice. He was as good a kisser as he was a dancer.

When he let her go, she decided she had to set him straight quick, instead of leading him on.

"Xavier, I am interested...I like you a lot, but...I can't do this right now. I've gone through so many crazy things in the last month, and I need time to deal with it all. There's no way I could start seeing someone right now. It wouldn't be fair to you."

He nodded seriously, as if she were a program that just wouldn't calculate. "Okay. I get you. You can't blame me for asking, though, can you?"

Jessica bit her lip. All of a sudden, she wished she *had* led him on a little bit, because she would've liked to kiss him once more.

Why, she asked herself, was being in control of her life suddenly such a pain in the ass?

Because, the answer came to her, as if from above: She wasn't doing what she really wanted to do. Was she?

Before he could say anything else, Jessica leaned forward and kissed him back. She was a good kisser, too, and wanted him to know it.

He pulled away and looked at her in surprise.

She laughed. "That's to tide you over until I'm done dealing with everything. Because when I am, I'm going to take you up on your offer. Will you wait for me?"

He smiled. "I guess I have to, don't I?"

# 54

"Why do we need to answer the phone? Isn't that for the women only?"

Jessica looked across her classroom and shook her head gently at Mr. Nguyen, one of the seven adults crammed into old-fashioned wood desks for her Tuesday/Thursday office skills class. "We're all going to learn to do everything for ourselves. And until we get our computers, that includes answering phones. Now, where were we?"

"Take a message, or put them in the voice mail," said Mr. Lopez from the front row. Jessica beamed at him and got a shyly proud smile in return.

The rest of the class went smoothly, with everyone listening very seriously to her every word and some taking notes while Jessica went over phone etiquette, alphabetization, and basic office tasks. Although they didn't yet have computers, she already had two more students than the week before, when the class had started.

Although it was still light outside, the clock above the chalkboard showed eight. "Okay, everyone. That's all for tonight. Remember to bring your résumés for next time and we'll start working on those."

One of her students, an older woman who'd asked Jessica to call her Belen, walked up to Jessica's desk with a woman slightly younger than her. "Ms. Luna, this is my sister, Marta," she said.

"Hi, Marta," said Jessica. "I'm glad you came out tonight—"

"Ms. Luna," interrupted Belen, "my sister doesn't speak much English. I wanted to ask you... She doesn't have a résumé. She's only been cleaning offices since she came here."

Jessica felt a small pang in her chest. "Well, that's okay. Those are still jobs, aren't they? Tell her to make a list...." Jessica turned to Marta then and told her, in painfully labored Spanish, to bring a list of her work experiences, including those she'd had before coming here.

Marta smiled and thanked her, then rattled off a long, quick sentence that Jessica couldn't follow. She looked to Belen for help.

"She says thank you for teaching this class. Also, are we going to learn to make blogs?"

Jessica laughed. "Of course. We'll make blogs, web sites, and everything else."

As she made her way to ALMA's lobby, Jessica said good-bye to the students and other instructors who were also there late that Tuesday night. On her way out, she waved to Marisol, who was talking to Esmeralda in her office. She would have plenty of time to talk to Marisol the next day. She was coming back to present the web site's progress to the board and to cover an afternoon art class for Lupe, and she'd probably end up getting asked to do something completely unrelated as well. Even though she'd been working there officially for only four weeks now, it already felt like much longer. Besides working on the web site and starting up her classes, she'd already chaperoned several field trips, repaired the fax machine, redesigned two brochures, and helped some of the older students with their college essays. Every day at ALMA was turning out to be an adventure.

As she walked out to her car, waving to the kids out playing basketball in the fading light, Jessica couldn't help looking back at the building wistfully. Sometimes, after a long day there, she didn't want to leave.

Jessica got into her car and turned the A/C on full blast. As soon as she got all the computers they needed, she decided, she'd go to work on getting ALMA some donated central air.

She turned on her phone. It showed that Sabrina had called. Jessica hesitated for a moment before calling back. She hadn't talked to her sister at all since their argument, more than a month ago now. But she really did want to talk to her, she realized now as she dialed the number.

"Hello?" It was Sabrina's husband, David.

"Hey, David. Is Sabrina home?"

"No, she's out shopping."

Jessica was half-disappointed, half-relieved. She hadn't known what she would have said to Sabrina, anyway.

"Did you get my message?" David continued. "I called about an hour ago, but I guess you were in class."

Jessica frowned. So Sabrina hadn't even called, after all. "I haven't listened to voice mail yet, no."

"Well, I have good news. I talked to Community Relations, and you're getting your computers. They said they can give ALMA thirty-eight desktops, four old laptops with stations, and twelve printers. We lucked out. They're upgrading a whole department and were just going to get rid of all that stuff. The laptops are pretty old, though. And the printers probably need toner."

Jessica hurried to reassure him. "No, no—that's great. That's way more than I was hoping for. Gosh, David—thank you so much."

"No problem. I'm glad to help. They were just going to throw that stuff away. I'm glad to see it getting put to good use, you know? Plus, you know—Halronburco gets to write off the donation, so it makes me look good for suggesting it."

Jessica laughed. She was glad she'd e-mailed David for help. But now that that part of the conversation was over, she didn't know what else to say. Apparently, he didn't, either. Besides the work she'd done for his web site, they'd never really talked much.

"So...how's the Fairlane site holding up?" she asked.

"Good. Really good," he said. "In fact, I'm glad you brought it up. I've been meaning to ask you about doing a site for a friend of mine. If you have time, I mean. You'll meet him at the barbecue next week."

Jessica frowned. "You guys are having a barbecue next week? Sabrina hasn't mentioned it to me. I mean, we haven't...I haven't had a chance to..." She stopped. She wasn't going to talk about their argument with David. That was between her and her sister.

An awkward pause ensued. Then David cleared his throat and said, "Well, *I'm* inviting you. It's next Saturday. I'd really like it if you'd come."

Jessica didn't know what to say. It was weird for David to call up and invite her over, out of nowhere. Oh no, she thought. What if he had talked to Jonathan and was trying to get the two of them back together?

"I don't know. I've been pretty busy," she started to say.

"Jessica," he interrupted, his voice as mild as always and yet, at the same time, very serious. "Listen...I know you and your sister had it out a while back. And I'm not blaming you—believe me, I know how Sabrina can be when she doesn't get her way. But I also know that she misses you a lot, and she'd really like to see you. Even if she's too proud to come out and tell you herself."

Jessica laughed. He really did know her sister. Sabrina could be just like Papi sometimes, refusing to admit when she was wrong. But then again, so could Jessica. In this case, she'd been the one in the wrong, and she was honest enough to admit it to herself. It was time for her to admit it to Sabrina, too.

"Okay. I'll be there."

"Great!" She could hear David's grin in his voice. "Sabrina will be really happy to hear it. Oh, and my parents are driving in, too. They haven't seen you since...when?"

"It's been a long time," Jessica supplied. She had seen them only once since Sabrina's wedding, in fact. Really, it was sweet of him to act like his parents would care. She glanced at the clock on her car's stereo. She'd been planning to stop by the used-book store before going home and see if they had some old keyboarding manuals, so she needed to go ahead and get off the phone. But first she had one thing to make sure of.

"David, Jonathan's not going to be there, is he?"

"Jonathan?" He paused, as if trying to figure out why she'd ask—or maybe he was pretending not to know, to be polite. "No, no. He's out of town on business. I didn't invite him."

"Okay." Jessica felt a tinge of guilt. "How's he doing, anyway?"

"He's fine. He's been really busy with his work and that neighborhood thing he's into." There was another pause. Then he added meaningfully, "Don't worry about him, Jessica. He'll be fine."

She didn't know how much David knew about what had happened, but she was starting to realize that he probably knew more about everything than she'd ever given him credit for.

# 55

Jessica gripped the steering wheel a little firmer than necessary as she headed down the freeway to Sugarland, without even the radio to keep her company. She was nervous about seeing Sabrina. What if she was still angry and hadn't really wanted Jessica there at all?

The backyard was filled with all the usual suspects, plus David's parents, who had shown up with piles of Pyrex containers. Jessica recognized them from their sandy blond hair, the mom's big and the dad's thinning. Plus, they both had David's blue eyes.

"I brought meatballs," David's mother was saying, "because, you know, they're David's favorite."

Sabrina turned away with a secret eye roll, then saw Jessica standing there, waiting. Her look of annoyance was replaced by surprise, then trepidation, then pleasure, all within the space of two seconds.

"Jessica!" she called, practically running over to give Jessica a hug. Sabrina squeezed her so hard, Jessica almost felt the breath leave her lungs. Just before she suffocated from this violent display of affection, David called her name. Sabrina let her go and walked her over to the patio table where he was standing with his parents.

"I'm so glad you made it," he said. "You remember my parents...."

"You're Sabrina's sister," said his mother. "So pretty. Here, give me a hug."

Jessica dutifully hugged her. "Hello, Mrs. Hoffman."

"Here. David, give her a meatball." His mother watched until David picked one up with a toothpick and handed it over. He seemed a little embarrassed about it.

Jessica accepted it graciously and immediately took a bite. "Mm. This is really good," she said, causing David's mother to beam proudly. In the background, David's father had already popped open a beer. Jessica had to laugh. Obviously, David's family wasn't so different from hers after all.

After everyone was settled with meatballs, rice, beans, and dry hamburgers, Sabrina broke away from her friends. "Jessica, come inside for a second. I want to show you what we've done with the bedroom."

Jessica took a deep breath and followed her sister inside and up the stairs. Here it comes, she told herself. The big talk.

But once they made it to the bedroom, Jessica saw that nothing in it had been changed. Everything was still purple flowers and satin. Sabrina jumped and flopped across her king-size bed, then faced her sister with a grin. "Come on!" She patted the comforter, inviting Jessica to lie beside her. Just like when they were kids. It was as if Sabrina were about to break out the Barbies and candy stash. Unsure of what to expect, Jessica gingerly climbed over the oak footboard.

"So tell me," Sabrina squealed, "what's going on with you? We haven't talked in *forever*. I've missed you."

The weirdness had gotten to Jessica. She couldn't act as if

everything were normal for any longer. She rolled up into a kneeling position, trying not to sink into the deep feather-top mattress.

"Sabrina, wait."

"Oh, come on. Don't start with the secrets again. I won't say anything stupid, I promise," Sabrina pleaded, looking starved for gossip. Or for her sister's confidence.

"No, it's not that. Sabrina, we have to talk. About the things we said, last time on the phone."

"Oh, that." Sabrina's eyes were far away for a second, as if she were remembering. Then she sat up and looked at Jessica with a rueful smile. "Listen, I'm sorry about that, muñeca. You were right. I was getting way too deep in your business, and I shouldn't have. Listen, if you don't like Jonathan, that's fine. I totally support you. And if you don't want to tell me what happened, I guess I deserve that. But I hope you aren't going to stop talking to me just because—"

"No." Jessica wasn't going to let her sister run over her with words this time. She was going to say her piece. "Sabrina, listen. I know you were mad, and you had a right to be. Everything you said was true. I have been selfish, and I hadn't given David or your friends a chance. I was just being..." It was hard to say. "I was being a racist jerk. I'm sorry."

Sabrina waved it all away. "It's okay. Don't worry about it."

"No, seriously. Listen," Jessica continued. "Mostly, I'm sorry for what I said about you being lazy and not wanting to work. Sabrina, if I'd had any idea why you were staying home all this time—"

"Shh, shh," said Sabrina. Jessica saw now that her sister's eyes were glistening, that she was trying to hold back tears.

And yet she was still smiling, trying to act as if nothing were wrong. Jessica couldn't hold it anymore. Her own tears welled up, and one escaped down the side of her face.

"Aw," said Sabrina. "Jessica...come here." She reached out and hugged her sister again. And that was it. That was all they needed to start bawling like babies.

"I'm sorry, Sabrina," Jessica sobbed. "I wish I'd known."

"No, I'm sorry," Sabrina said, sniffling. "I should have told you before. Plus, like I said, I shouldn't have been trying so hard to get in your business. I shouldn't have made you go out with Jonathan."

Jessica pulled back and sniffled loudly, then wiped her eyes with the back of her hand. "You didn't. I went out with him because I wanted to. And I'm glad I did. He...it changed my mind about some things."

"What? You mean you're going out with him again?" Sabrina looked surprised as she wiped her own face with the corner of her pillowcase.

"No," Jessica said. "I'm not going out with him again. I'm just saying—being with him made me realize that I need to judge people on their personalities and not on what they look like or what they do for a living. I mean, in the end his personality didn't really work with mine, but that doesn't make it okay for me to hate on people just because they're white or rich or whatever. You know? I mean, you don't know this, but I've secretly been having these mean thoughts about your friends, just because they're different from me. I mean, I thought they were different from you, too, but obviously they aren't. I mean—they're your friends, so I should have respected that, and taken the time to get to know them.

Instead of acting like Papi. So... I'm really sorry, and I'm not going to do that anymore."

Sabrina laughed. "Yeah. Well, actually, it wasn't that big of a secret. I knew you didn't like them, and I figured that was why, but I also thought you'd snap out of it, eventually. But, you know, I can't blame you for thinking that I was trying to set you up with a white guy on purpose. I wasn't. I was just trying to set you up with someone nice. I didn't care if he was purple or green."

Sabrina wiped her face again, then propped the pillows against the ornate headboard. She and Jessica leaned back against them, each lost in her own thoughts for a while. Jessica was glad she'd come to the barbecue. Now that she was here, she realized just how much she'd been missing Sabrina, too.

"Have you talked to Mami?" Sabrina asked after a while.

"No. Not since they went on vacation. Have you?"

"No," Sabrina said.

"Do you think they're going to be okay?"

"I hope so. I think they will, but who knows."

"Mami told me that whatever they ended up doing, it'd be for the best." Jessica hated to say the words aloud but felt she could share that fear with her sister.

"She's probably right," said Sabrina. "Either way, there's nothing we can do now. We just have to let them live their lives."

Jessica sighed. It wasn't a comfort, exactly, but at least she didn't have to worry alone. "So, is all this stress getting to you? What does your doctor say? How've you been feeling?"

"Good. Just a little nauseous, sometimes," Sabrina said idly.

Jessica was confused. "Is that...is that something that happens when you're trying too hard to get pregnant?"

"No, mensa!" Sabrina laughed. "It's what happens when you *are* pregnant." The glint in her eye showed that she'd been waiting to spring the news on Jessica for a while now.

Jessica sat up straight with shock, hitting the back of her head on the wall. "What? You're pregnant?"

"Yes," Sabrina said happily. Serenely, almost. "I'm going to have a baby, Jessica." Her eyes misted up again. Jessica saw now that she was crying with joy. And messed-up hormones, maybe.

She hugged her sister again. "Congratulations." She didn't know what else to say. It was so strange, for Sabrina to be pregnant. Scary, in a way. But exciting, too. "How long have you known?"

"Three weeks. Don't say anything to anybody downstairs," Sabrina said quickly. "Except David, if you want. But no one else knows yet. I wanted to tell you, first."

Jessica smiled, feeling her own tears coming on again. "Thanks." Then the realization hit her fully. "I'm going to be an aunt," she said softly.

Sabrina laughed and they hugged again.

When they went back downstairs, the guests were leaking into the living room, hiding from the heat. Jessica decided to go out and get a drink from the cooler before they were all gone. At the doorway, it occurred to her that the auntlike thing to do would be to offer her pregnant sister a drink, too.

"Sabrina, do you want something from the cooler?"

"No thanks."

Jessica turned to go through the door then and stepped directly into someone else. "Oh, my gosh! Excuse me!"

She untangled herself from the stranger's arms and stood clear on the patio, then saw that the stranger was a man. A good-looking man, with brown skin and black hair.

"Jessica," said David, who was trying not to laugh, "I was looking for you so I could introduce you to my friend, but it looks like you already met him. This is Raj Kumar. He loves the web site you made me, and I told him you'd build a site for his business, so I can get the commission. Raj, this is my sister-in-law, Jessica Luna."

Jessica and Raj shook hands. She mumbled a greeting, and he murmured apologies, but they were drowned out by the message communicated with their eyes. It said: *Hello, mutual attraction.*

# 56

Some days later, the neon hand shone brightly at her as Jessica walked through the doorway of Madame Hortensia's.

"How are you, m'ija?"

"I can't complain."

"How's your new job going?" Madame Hortensia asked as she picked up her box of fortune-telling supplies.

"Really good. They've been keeping me pretty busy."

"And your love life? Any new men in the picture?"

"Oh, there are men in the picture all right." Jessica gave the old woman a sly wink. "I'm weighing my options."

They took their seats, opened Madame Hortensia's laptop, and got down to business.

"So, what did you think?" asked Jessica. "Did you like that font?"

MADAME HORTENSIA, PSYCHIC AND NOTARY PUBLIC, read the title of the web site Jessica had made.

"Yes. The font looks good, m'ija, but I don't like the picture. I meant for it to look mysterious, but instead, it just looks mean. And I have a double chin in it. I think we should take another one."

"Okay. We can definitely fix that," said Jessica. She couldn't resist adding, "As soon as you figure out what you want, I'll work my magic to make sure you get it."

Madame Hortensia laughed. "Ándale, m'ija. There you go."

**Toby-licious!**
**A mix CD for Toby, by J. Lu.**
**10/23/05**

Hey, sweetie. Here's the song list I promised you. Just fold it up and put it in the CD case. Hope you like it — don't blow out your speakers again!

— Jessica

1. **M.I.A. — "Bucky Done Gun"**
   Raj turned me on to this one. The singer, Mya, is from Sri Lanka.

2. **Felix da Housecat — "Watching the Cars Go"**
   Good beat! From Sasha's Involver mix.

3. **Tito Puente — "Que Será Mi China"**
   Off my dad's vinyl collection.... Somebody needs to remix this! You should tell your friend Michelangelo.

4. **Michelle Branch — "Breathe" (The Passengerz Tuff Club)**
   Awesome remix. Nothing like the original.

5. **Gotan Project — "Santa Maria" (Tom Middleton's Cosmos Mix)**
   This reminds me — we should totally take a tango class together.

6. **Bebel Gilberto — "Aganjú" (Latin Project Remix)**
   Very mellow, Brazilian style. You'll never guess who gave me this CD. Xavier!

7. **Sneaker Pimps — "Spin Spin Sugar" (Armands Dark Garage Mix)**
   Here's that one you wanted.

8. **Metle Music — "El Mar"**
   More lounge-y stuff. I must be getting older. ☺

9. **Vanity 6 — "Nasty Girl"**
   I found this on an old cassette and had to download the MP3. Remember our eighth-grade dance? ☺

10. **Blue 6 — "Very Good Friends"**
    Very romantic. Maybe you should play this for your new friend David?

# Acknowledgments

This book took me a long time to situate, so to speak, so I've racked up a lot of people to thank. First: Jenny Bent, who is not only everything a girl could want in an agent, but also cracks me up, talks me down, and keeps me from throwing my writing career off a fifty-story building. Thanks to Jenny and Victoria Horn and everybody at Trident for handling all these pieces of paper so beautifully.

Second: Thanks very, very much to Selina McLemore, who is more than an editor. She's actually a supernatural being who goes inside my brain, sees what I'm trying to say, and makes me say it better. Thanks also to Latoya Smith, Sona Vogel, and the rest of the Grand Central team.

Third on this page but first in chronology: Thanks to everyone who either read this book, read some prototype of this book, or listened to me whine while writing it. That includes Brie McCain, Yvonne Esch, Tiffany Songvilay, Andie Avila, Enrique Gomez, Ashley MacLean, Catherine Poua, and my dad, Enrique Zepeda.

More retroactively still, thanks to Nick Kanellos and Marina Tristán for setting me on this career path.

I'm grateful to Dat Lam, who was my boyfriend when I started this book and my fiancé when I finished it, for his seemingly inexhaustible reserves of support.

Finally, thanks most of all to Jacob, Austin, and Luke for their patience and their tolerance of deadline-time micro-waveable meals, and for inspiring everything good that I manage to do.

# Reading Group Guide

1. At the beginning of her story, Jessica is "dating" Guill-ermo. She hides their relationship from her family and doesn't seem quite comfortable with it herself. Why does Jessica get involved with Guillermo and continue to see him, despite her own misgivings? Is it just the hot sex, or is she getting something else out of it?

2. Jessica talks about feeling more comfortable dating men who grew up the way she did—knowing how it feels to eat beans and rice for dinner or to have the electricity cut off once in a while. Do you think relationships are easier when the people involved have similar backgrounds? Are there challenges to overcome when dating people from different economic classes or different cultures?

3. When Jonathan first shows a romantic interest in Jes-sica, she worries that he is attracted to her only because she is Latina and therefore "exotic." Should that be a concern? Is there anything wrong with being attracted to people of a certain culture? How is that different from preferring blondes or brunettes, or tall men, or men with hairy chests?

4. Jessica's job at McCormick is completely unrelated to the career she'd hoped to have. At the end of the book, she leaves that job for one that pays less but suits her better. Was she foolish to leave McCormick instead of

trying harder for a promotion? Is finding your dream job something that happens only in books or movies?

5. Jessica is very superstitious. She begins to believe in fortune-telling at a low point in her life. Was her superstition a product of her upbringing or an excuse to avoid making tough life decisions? Or both?

6. How does Jessica's relationship with her parents affect her decisions? How does it affect her relationship with her sister, Sabrina?

7. How does Jessica's relationship with Sabrina affect her decisions? How does Jessica feel about the choices Sabrina has made in life? Is she jealous? Disappointed?

8. Madame Hortensia makes money every time Jessica needs help making decisions about her life. Why, then, does the fortune-teller eventually admit that she doesn't have any psychic powers? What do you think about what Madame Hortensia does for a living? Is it dishonest? Is it wrong?

9. In the end, Jessica decides that she and Jonathan don't belong together. Why? Do you think her decision was based on cultural differences, and if so, was it wrong of her to base it on that? What assumptions does she make about Jonathan? Does she end up changing her mind?

10. Did you expect Jessica to end up with Xavier in the end? Were you disappointed when she didn't?

11. How did Jessica change from the beginning of this story to the end? What did she learn? Did you learn anything from her experience, or were her lessons things you already knew? Do you know anyone who might benefit from sharing Jessica's experiences?

# Questions for the Author

1. **What gave you the idea for this book?**

   I was in a friend's office, telling him I couldn't decide what to write next. He had a Magic 8-Ball on his shelf. I took it and asked, "Should I try to write a novel?" It said the answer was unclear. I was annoyed and wished I knew a real psychic who could tell me for certain what to do. Then the idea came to me: What if someone based all her decisions on fortune-telling, signs, and superstition?

2. **Are you Jessica Luna? How similar is your life to hers?**

   I'm not Jessica. There are a *few* similarities. I grew up in Houston, I work in insurance, I've worked for nonprofits, and I'm sometimes superstitious. Like everyone else, I've had doubts about the direction my life is going. But besides that, we're pretty different. I'm older than her. My mom's white, and I grew up with my dad and his family. I have two younger brothers, no sisters. I've been married, and I have three sons. I've been dating the same guy for five years now. Most strikingly, Jessica has way more time to go out drinking and dancing than I do.

3. **Jessica and her friends go to a lot of restaurants and clubs in Houston. Are those places real or fictional?**

They're fictional and yet similar to places I know and love. Come visit Houston. Walk through the Montrose and see it for yourself.

**4. Have you ever met a fortune-teller like Madame Hortensia?**

No. I've been to fortune-tellers who weren't worth the money. I've been to one who told me I'd have three boys and one girl, which was pretty eerie. When I was a teenager, I used to listen to a tarot card hobbyist who worked at my friend's parents' convenience store and gave long, involved readings in Spanish to the same few women, every single day. Also, both my parents used to read tarot cards. But that's it. No one like Madame Hortensia. She's a composite of shrewd women I've met, done up with velvet and a crystal ball.

**5. What was your writing process for this book?**

I started with an outline—a synopsis, actually. As so often happens, I began writing the book according to my outline, and then the story took on a life of its own, and the outline didn't make sense to me anymore. So I abandoned it and just wrote. Then I ended up using a Microsoft Works calendar to map out the timeline and plot events. That was a really valuable tool, and now I use calendars for all my books.

**6. With three kids and a day job, how do you find time to write?**

I always tell people it's easy to find time to write, as long as you never watch TV and never clean your house.

When I'm working on a project, I try to spend an hour or two per day writing, either in the evenings while the kids are doing their homework or early in the mornings before they wake up. Weekend mornings are the most productive time for me.

When I have a deadline, I take my laptop with me to work and write during my lunch hour. I usually spend all my vacation time and holidays writing my brains out. Luckily, my kids are finally at the age where they understand what I'm doing and why, so they give me the time I need, with minimal arguing and video-game noise.

7. **What do you do when you aren't writing, working, or being a mom?**

I hang out with my kids and my boyfriend, mostly. We eat out, shop, go to movies, and walk at parks. We paint pictures and do various crafts. On occasion, I go to clubs with my friends to see DJs play. Sometimes I play video games, badly, and sometimes we do watch TV. My boyfriend likes to cook, and I really like to eat the results.

8. **Who are your favorite authors?**

My taste is all over the place. Jane Austen, Nabokov, Alice Munro, Margaret Atwood, and Sandra Cisneros are the authors I read again and again. I was raised on seventies science fiction, crime thrillers, and Regency romance. I read way more young adult fiction than an adult should and love *Peter Pan* and *Alice's Adventures in Wonderland* to death. New authors I like lately: A. M. Homes and George Saunders.

9. **What advice would you give to someone who wants to write for a living?**

Don't talk about wanting to be a writer. Just write. When you talk about it instead of doing it, you set up expectations that become intimidating when you finally do try to write. When you tell your ideas to people, it takes the creative urgency out of writing them down.

I know people who talked about wanting to be writers for years and years and then finally sat down to write novels and realized that they didn't enjoy the process at all. And I didn't blame them—writing is really hard, boring work. Also, it doesn't pay much, when you break it down to dollars per hour. So if you want to "write for a living," I'd suggest that you find someone willing to support you. People who really want to write usually start out doing it for free, because they can't help themselves.

# Guía de Lector

1. Al pricipio de la novela, Jessica sale con Guillermo. Esconde su relación de su familia, y no parece que ella está cómoda con su relación tampoco. ¿Por qué se compromete Jessica con Guillermo, a pesar de sus presentimientos? ¿Es solo por el sexo caliente, or hay más que Jessica está recibiendo de la relación?

2. Jessica habla de sentirse más cómoda saliendo con hombres que crecieron como ella; los que saben como es cenar arroz y frijoles, y a veces no tener la electricidad. ¿Piensa Usted que las relaciones son más fáciles cuando las personas conprometidos tienen fondos semejantes? ¿Cuáles son los desafíos que se tiene que vencer cuando una persona tiene una relación con alguien de una clase economica diferente o una cultura diferente?

3. Al principio, cuando Jonathan muestra un intrés romantico en Jessica, ella se preocupa que Jonathan está atraido a ella solo porque es Latina, y por eso, "exotica." ¿Debe ser un asunto? ¿Hay algo injusto en estar atraido a las personas de una cultura específica? ¿Comó es different de preferer una rubia o una morena, hombres altos o hombres con pechos peludos?

4. El trabajo de Jessica en McCormick no tiene nada

que ver con la profesión que espera tener. Al fin del libro, deja ese trabajo por uno que paga menos pero le gusta mejor. ¿Fue tonto dejar su trabajo en vez de luchar por un ascenso? ¿Es possible encontrar el trabajo de los sueños, o ocurre ésto solo en los libros y las películas?

5. Jessica es muy supersticiosa. Empieza a creer en las advinas en un momento de depresion. ¿Cree Usted que su superstición es un producto de su crianza, o una disculpa para evitar hacer las decisiones de vida dificiles? ¿O sea posible los dos?

6. La relación de Jessica con sus padres, ¿comó afecta las decisions de Jessica? ¿Y comó afecta la relación con su hermana, Sabrina?

7. La relación de Jessica con Sabrina, ¿comó afecta las decisiones de Jessica? ¿Comó se siente Jessica sobre las eleciones que Sabrina ha escojido en su vida? ¿Está celosa Jessica? ¿Decepcionada?

8. Madame Hortensia gana dinero cada vez que Jessica necesita ayuda hacer una desicisión. ¿Entonces, por qué admite la advina que no es psíquica? ¿Qué piensa Usted de como se gana la vida Madame Hortensia? ¿Es fraudulento? ¿Inmoral?

9. Al final, Jessica decide que ella y Jonathan no deben estar juntos. ¿Por qué? ¿Cree Usted que su decisión está fundada en sus diferencias culturales y, de ser así, es justo basarlo en ésto? ¿Qué supone Jessica sobre Jonathan? ¿Cambia su opinion?

10. ¿Cree Usted que Jessica se queda con Xavier al fin del libro? ¿Está desilucionada cuando ésto no pasa?

11. ¿Comó cambia Jessica desde al principio del cuento hasta al fin? ¿Qué aprendío Jessica? ¿Aprendío Usted algo de la experiencia ed Jessica, o ya sabía todas las lecciones? ¿Conoce Usted a alguien que podría beneficiar en compartir las experiencias de Jessica?

# Una Entrevista con Gwendolyn Zepeda

**1. ¿De dónde vino la idea de este libro?**

Estaba en la oficina de un amigo, deciéndole que no podía decider que más escribir. Tenía un Magic 8-Ball en su estante. La cogí y pregunté, "¿Debo escribir una novela?" Me respondió que la respuesta no estaba clara. Me molestó y deseé que conociera un psíquico quien me pudiera decir que hacer. De repente la idea me chocó: ¿Qué pasaria si una persona quien hiciera todas sus decisiones basadas en la superstición?

**2. ¿Eres Jessica Luna? ¿Comó son semejantes la vida de Jessica con la tuya?**

No soy Jessica Luna. Hay *algunas* semejanzas, pero no muchas. Crecí en Houston, trabajo en seguro, he trabajado por empresas sin fin lucrativo, y a veces soy supersticiosa. Y, como todos, he tenido dudas sobre la dirección de mi vida. Pero, aparte de éso, somos muy diferentes. Soy mayor que Jessica. Mi madre es blanca, y crecí con mi padre y su familia. Tengo dos hermanitos, pero no tengo hermana. Estuve casada y tengo tres hijos. Por cinco años salgo con el mismo hombre. Sobre todo, Jessica tiene mucho más tiempo para ir a bailar y beber que yo.

3. **Jessica y sus amigas van a muchos restaurants y clubs en Houston. ¿Estos son sitios verdaderos o ficticios?**

Son ficticios pero semejantes a lugares que conozco y me gustan. Ven a Houston, pasa por el Montrose y vételo por tí mismo.

4. **¿Has conocido a una adivina como Madame Hortensia?**

No. He visitado algunas adivinas quien no valen el dinero. Y fui a una quien me dijo que tendría tres hijos y una hija. Ésto fue muy espantoso. Cuando joven, escuchaba a una mujer que leia las tarjetas de tarot. Ella trabajaba en la tienda de los padres de mi amiga, y daba lecturas detalladas a las mismas mujeres cada día. Y mis padres leían las tarjetas de tarot también. Pero es todo. Nadie como Madame Hotensia. Ella es una compuesta de mujeres astutas que he conocido, con terciopelo y un globo de cristal.

5. **¿Cómo escribiste este libro? ¿Tienes un proceso especial?**

Empecé con un esbozo, una sinopsis. Como siempre, empecé a escribir el libro según la sinopsis, pero entonces el libro tomó una vida de si misma, y la sinopsis ya no tenía sentido. Pues, la abandoné y escribí libremente. Al fin usé un calendarío de Microsoft Works para proyectar el argumento. Éso fue una herramienta inestimable, y ahorra siempre uso calendarios para todos mis libros.

6. **¿Con tres hijos y un trabajo de tiempo complete, comó encuentras el tiempo para escribir?**

Siempre digo que es fácil encontrar el tiempo para escribir, con tal que nunca mires la television y nunca limpies tu casa. Cuando trabajo en un libro, trato de pasar una o dos horas cada día escribiendo. Ser por las noches, cuando mis hijos hacen sus tareas, o muy temprano por las mañanas, antes de que ellos despierten. Durante el fin de la semana por la manaña es mi tiempo más productivo.

Cuando tengo una línea vedada, llevo mi portátil a mi oficina y escribo durante el almuerzo. Normalmente paso todas mis vacaciones y mis dias de fiesta escribiendo. Afortunadamente, mis hijos estan a la edad de que comprenden lo que hago y por qué. Me dan todo el tiempo que necesito, con pocas peleas y ruido de videojuegos.

**7. ¿Qué haces cuando no estás escribiendo, trabajando, cuidando a los hijos?**

Principalmente paso tiempo con mis hijos y mi novio. Comemos en restaurantes, vamos de compras, vamos al cine y caminamos por el parque. Pintamos pinturas y hacemos arte también. De vez en cuando, voy a los clubs con mis amigos para ver un pinchadiscos. A veces juego (mal) los videojuegos, y a veces, sí, miramos la television. A mi novio le gusta cocinar, y me gusta mucho comer los resultados.

**8. ¿Quiénes son tus escritores favoritos?**

Me gustan muchos escritores diferentes. Jane Austen, Nabokov, Alice Munro, Margaret Atwood, y Sandra Cisneros son los autores quienes leo una y otra vez. Crecí leyendo la ciencia-ficción de los setentas, obras de suspense, y novelas de amor. Ahorra, leo más Ficción de los Jovenes que una adulto debe, y me encanta *Peter Pan* y *Alice's Adventures in Wonderland*. También me gustan A. M. Homes y George Saunders.

9. **¿Qué consejo darías a algien que quiere escribir para ganar la vida?**

No hables de ser escritor. Escribe. Cuando hablas de escribir en vez de hacerlo, se hacen esperanzas que se ponen intimidados cuando, al final, tratas de escribir. Cuando describes tus ideas a otras personas, se quita la urgencia de escribirlos.

Conozco a personas que hablan de escribir por muchos años, pero, cuando empiezan a escribir, se dan cuenta que no les gusta el proceso. Y no los culpo—escribir es muy difícil, y puede ser muy aburrido. También, no paga mucho, cuando se habla de dólares por hora. Si quieres escribir para ganar la vida, sugiero que encuentres a alguien quien pueda mantenerte. Las personas que quieren escribir mucho normalmente al principio lo hacen por gratis, porque no pueden dejar de escribir.

# About the Author

I was born in Houston's inner city in 1971 and managed to live there without air conditioning for eighteen years before escaping to the University of Texas at Austin. Then, right before graduation, I escaped college for the adventure of starting a family.

It was around that time that I turned my casual love of writing into a long-running Web site, gwenworld.com, and gigs at other Web sites such as Television Without Pity. It wasn't until 2000, though, that I worked up the nerve to start reading my work to audiences. Houston's premier Latino literature organization, Nuestra Palabra, gave me my "in real life" start.

In 2004, Arte Público Press published my first book, a short-prose collection called *To the Last Man I Slept with and All the Jerks Just Like Him*. Like most small-press books, it didn't exactly make a big splash. But the reviews were very encouraging, and so I wrote again. In 2008, Arte Público published my first kids' book, *Growing Up with Tamales*. This is my first novel with Grand Central Publishing. I hope you enjoyed it and will look for the next.

I've been profiled and quoted in newspapers and magazines ranging from the *Austin Chronicle* to the *New York Post* to the *Dublin Times*. I've won literary fellowships and even a poetry prize. When I have time, I do readings and seminars at universities. When I'm not working on this writing stuff (or otherwise making a living), I hang out with my three sons, my one boyfriend, and our two cats.

CPSIA information can be obtained at www.ICGtesting.com
Printed in the USA
LVOW08s2200310716

498534LV00001B/39/P